D0018250

The QUEEN *of* BEAUTY

ALSO BY PETRA DURST-BENNING

The Glassblower Trilogy

The Glassblower

The American Lady

The Paradise of Glass

The Century Trilogy

While the World Is Still Asleep

The Champagne Queen

The QUEEN *of* BEAUTY

The Century Trilogy

Petra Durst-Benning

Translated by Edwin Miles

amazon crossing

This is a work of fiction. Names, characters, organizations, places, events, and incidents are either products of the author's imagination or are used fictitiously. Any resemblance to actual persons, living or dead, or actual events is purely coincidental.

Text copyright © 2015 Petra Durst-Benning & Ullstein Buchverlag GmbH
Translation copyright © 2017 Edwin Miles
All rights reserved.

No part of this book may be reproduced, or stored in a retrieval system, or transmitted in any form or by any means, electronic, mechanical, photocopying, recording, or otherwise, without express written permission of the publisher. Previously published as *Bella Clara* by Ullstein Buchverlag GmbH in Germany in 2015. Translated from German by Edwin Miles. First published in English by AmazonCrossing in 2017.

Published by AmazonCrossing, Seattle

www.apub.com

Amazon, the Amazon logo, and AmazonCrossing are trademarks of Amazon.com, Inc., or its affiliates.

ISBN-13: 9781477806128
ISBN-10: 1477806121

Cover design by Shasti O'Leary Soudant

Printed in the United States of America

Become the woman you are.
　　　　　—Hedwig Dohm

Chapter One

Late summer 1906

The August air in the Berlin courtroom was stale and thick. The spectators were packed shoulder to shoulder on the public benches: saleswomen who had left their market stalls in the care of an employee for a few hours sat beside elegant townswomen who waved at the soupy air with lace-trimmed fans. Several respectable-looking men—doctors from nearby hospitals—had come to show support for one of their own. Or to witness his demise. A door opened and three honorable gentlemen entered the courtroom. A draft of fresh air slipped in with them.

"Here's the judge," said a redhead in the front row, taking a quick bite of her sandwich.

The woman beside her slid to the edge of the bench to see better. "Looks like an executioner in that black robe, don't he?" Her eyes gleamed luridly. "Look at all the files he's got on his desk."

"Oh, I'd love to sneak a peek at those. They must be filled with exciting tidbits," the redhead said and giggled. After the last mouthful of her sandwich disappeared between her gaudily painted lips, she wiped her hands on her skirt. They could get started any time as far as she was concerned.

"Whose neck is on the block today, then?" asked a mailman as he squeezed in next to the women. His cap had an oily shine to it, and he put it on the floor in front of him, pulled an apple out of his pocket, and bit into it so hard that the juice spattered the redhead's face.

The woman wiped her cheek and gave the man an irritated look. But then malicious delight took over, and she said, "It's a doctor's wife. Fooling around with her lover in her own house while her husband was working."

"In front of her children," the second woman added as she wiped a sweaty strand of hair from her forehead. "And the doctor's boss, some professor so-and-so, walked in on them. Oh, can't you just picture it!"

"A scandal is what it is!" the first woman said.

The mailman's eyes narrowed viciously. "Well, I'd have whipped her."

The redhead pointed frantically at a petite chestnut-haired woman who entered the courtroom through one of the doors at the front. "Is she the one?"

The second woman furrowed her brow. "*That* pasty thing? Nah, she must be the court scribe." She rolled up the sleeves of her blouse indifferently and scratched at the dry skin on her right arm. A moment later, the redhead jabbed her in the ribs.

"No—that's *her*!"

The audience looked on with a mix of astonishment and fascination as the elegant young woman took her place in the dock, just in front of the judge's bench. A collective murmur rumbled through the room.

"She looks harmless," said the mailman. He sounded disappointed.

"The innocent-looking ones are always the worst!" the redhead hissed.

In the row behind them sat two women who held hands, as if trying to give each other courage. One, Isabelle, was a little taller, also a redhead. The other, Josephine, was blond. They were around the same age, in their midthirties, and dressed in the latest fashions. With their pinned-up hair, chic handbags, and elegant shoes, they looked as if they had taken a wrong turn. They would have fit in perfectly at a café on the Spree or at the premiere of a new play. Unlike the people around them, they were mostly quiet. They only had eyes for the woman in the dock. And in stark contrast to the sensationalism infecting the others, their eyes were infused with affection, compassion, and concern.

"She looks good," Isabelle whispered to Josephine, softly enough so no one else would hear. "Composed."

"I'm proud of her," Josephine whispered back. "When I think of what she's going through to finally be free again . . ."

The accused woman turned around, her brown eyes filled with fear as she scanned the room. But when she saw the two women in the second row of the gallery, relief flickered over her face.

Josephine offered an encouraging gaze to the accused. "You can do it, Clara," she mouthed insistently.

Clara responded with an almost imperceptible nod.

A clerk pounded on the floor with a staff. "Silence in the High Court! The court considers the divorce proceedings of Dr. Gerhard Gropius and his wife, Clara Gropius, née Berg."

"A traveling salesman?" The judge nodded. "Perhaps you would be so good as to tell the court on what business the gentleman traveled?"

"The business of love!" came a voice from somewhere in the middle of the gallery. The spectators laughed, and the clerk banged his staff on the floor in annoyance.

Clara swallowed hard. She'd prepared herself for public malice and had made up her mind to ignore it. If things became too unruly in the courtroom, the clerk would establish order. At least, she hoped he would.

Not one of you has spent a month or a week or even a day in my shoes, she thought bitterly. *Yet you think you have the right to judge me.*

She straightened her shoulders. "He . . . he represented a knife company in Solingen," she said, keeping her voice as steady as she could.

"Knives?" asked the judge, opening his eyes wide in exaggerated shock. The audience instantly broke into outraged hissing.

Clara fell silent. What else was she supposed to say? If she had wanted to stab Gerhard to death, she could have done it with her own kitchen knives—and the judge was perfectly aware of that. Old fool.

"And how often did this traveling salesman visit Berlin?" he asked.

"Once a month," Clara replied.

The women in the front row clucked their tongues and inhaled sharply, and the doctors shook their heads in disapproval. Gerhard Gropius, who sat to the left of the judges' bench with his lawyer, glared at Clara.

"If I understand you correctly, this was not merely a one-time transgression on your part. Once a month, you transformed your lawfully wedded husband's house into a love nest. Is this correct?"

Clara nodded, feeling the blood rise to her face. She wished that the floor would open and swallow her up. Because, despite her confession, she had done nothing of the sort.

Clara had traveled to the other end of Berlin to seek the advice of a lawyer. "How can I initiate a divorce?" she had asked the lawyer, without beating around the bush. It seemed not to be the first time he had heard the question, and together they reviewed the few options available to her. This had all taken place a year earlier, shortly after the death of her parents.

Her husband, the lawyer explained, would probably not apply for a divorce if there were only a one-time indiscretion on her part. From what she had told him about her husband, Gerhard was far more likely to make her life a living hell than divorce her. If she really wanted to "force" him to take such a serious step, then she would have to push the circumstances. An affair, one in which she got caught *in flagrante*, ideally with an honorable guest present as a witness—that would be the deepest disgrace, and her husband would have no choice but to start divorce proceedings.

"But why must I be the guilty one?" Clara had asked desperately. "Why can't I simply tell the truth? My husband beats me, he mistreats me, and his abuse grows worse with every passing year!"

"But is he actually trying to kill you? Only then could you use his beatings as grounds for divorce. However, I would advise against that. Your husband would almost certainly deny everything," the lawyer had explained. And, he added, there were many judges who, instead of a divorce certificate, would give a couple no more than a few sanctimonious words to take away with them.

Sanctimonious words? Clara had heard more than enough of those from her parents.

"Why don't you simply leave him?" the lawyer had asked. "Many couples discreetly lead separate lives. So discreet, in fact, that the separation is hardly recognized by those in their social circles."

Live apart? Clara had shaken her head and laughed bitterly. Then who would play the maid for Gerhard? Who would be his scapegoat when things were not going well with the professors at the university clinic, or with his patients, or with God knows who else? And what of all his pent-up rage? Who would he work that off with, physically, carnally? Gerhard would drag her back home by the hair if she even considered living apart! She would get not so much as a penny from him, and he would take away her children, too, that much was clear.

The lawyer had nodded knowingly at Clara's litany. "Sadly, the rules of law give little latitude in such cases. Where would we be if just anyone could apply for a divorce?" The lawyer laughed at that, as if he had made a joke. But to Clara, it had sounded like a rebuke.

"Simplest of all would be for you to catch your husband in an affair," the lawyer had said.

But at that, too, Clara had shaken her head. She did not know whether her husband had affairs. Because of the children, she spent most of her time at home, so spying on him was out of the question. And at the social gatherings to which he had to take her, she had seen no suggestion of anything of that nature: in public, he played the role of the good husband very well.

In the end, she had left the lawyer's office forty marks poorer but with an important realization: if she wanted to be free of Gerhard, then she would have to compel him to apply for a divorce. Even if it meant branding herself a sinner. Even if it meant receiving no alimony. She would keep her parents' pharmacy, and the money from the lease would keep her head above water. Nothing else was practicable.

Though it had quickly become clear who would appear as her "lover," it had taken her a full year to execute her plan. She had looked for a young, impoverished actor. There were plenty of potential beaus, actors who frequented the city theater in the hope of reading for a role in a new Arthur Schnitzler production. More difficult was coming up with the money she needed to pay the actor. Gerhard gave her barely enough for the household, and she was only occasionally able to save a little off her meager spending allowance. Eventually, she had gathered the money she needed, so all that had remained was finding the right day.

On the first Monday of every month, Gerhard's mentor from his student days, Dr. Kälblein, paid them a visit. The old man and Gerhard would disappear into the library to discuss the world over brandy and cigars.

If she took the children to Josephine for the evening and managed to smuggle her "lover" into the house . . . Just the thought of the farce she was planning had made Clara's knees tremble. Did she really have the nerve to pull it off?

And now, a year later, she sat in the dock of a Berlin court, Clara the adulteress, answering the judge's questions in a steady voice.

After a good hour in the courtroom, the facts were on the table. Clara, guilty of adultery, was responsible for the failure of their marriage—there wasn't the slightest doubt of that, for either the court or the public.

What would my parents say about it all? Clara thought as the judge salaciously read through her transgressions one more time before handing down his divorce judgment. Sophie and Anton Berg, her parents, the respected couple from the pharmacy in the Luisenstadt district of Berlin . . . they would turn in their graves if they knew what their daughter was doing. Her mother had never wanted to believe that Clara was unhappily married.

"If you provoke your husband, it's no wonder he gets angry!" "A marriage is not always a bed of roses." "Other women would be thankful to have a doctor as a husband, but all you do is complain. Ungrateful, that's all you are!" Her mother's words still rang as clearly in her ears as if she had heard them only the day before.

The bruises, the welts on her upper arms, the bald patches from when Gerhard had dragged her by the hair through their apartment—all of it counted for less to her mother than the prestige of having married off her daughter to a doctor. There had been times in the year that her parents had been dead when Clara—the good girl, the pharmacist's daughter—had wished she were dead, too.

She was thirty-two years old. Her son, Matthias, was eleven, her daughter, Sophie, whom Clara had named after her mother, six. She had asked herself a thousand times whether she should stick things out longer for the good of the children. Gerhard was not a bad father. He had not once raised a hand to the children. Only to her. A wrong word here or a thoughtless remark there was all it had taken to bring Gerhard's ire down on her, and over the years, his abuse had grown worse and worse.

". . . to which I will now pronounce judgment . . ."

The judge's words pulled Clara out of her thoughts. She inhaled anxiously.

"Adultery, gross ingratitude, and not the slightest sign of remorse—rarely in any divorce have the facts in the question of guilt been demonstrated so clearly. The application for divorce by Dr. Gerhard Gropius is hereby upheld. No right to maintenance on the part of the guilty party exists," the judge announced in his most accusatory voice. The crowd squirmed feverishly on the benches.

The judge cleared his throat. "Let us move on to the details: the German Civil Code states that the principle of administration by the husband is deemed to apply to the statutory property of the husband and wife. I quote . . ." The judge balanced a pair of spectacles on his nose to help him read, then continued. "By way of marriage, the assets of the wife—that is, the estate brought by her to the marriage—are thereafter subject to the control and the rights of use of the husband. The estate brought to the marriage also includes such assets as may be obtained during the marriage by the wife. In your case, Mrs. Gropius, we are talking about house number fourteen in Görlitzer Strasse as well as the Berg Pharmacy. Both will pass into your husband's possession with this divorce."

Clara could not believe what she was hearing. The house and the pharmacy were her inheritance! She had counted on them continuing to be hers. She needed the money from the lease!

"Custody of the children is to be divided. The son, Matthias, is to reside with his father, and the daughter is to live with her mother. Dr. Gerhard Gropius is obligated to pay support for the daughter." The judge looked with raised eyebrows at Gerhard, who returned his gaze calmly.

Clara looked from her lawyer to the judge and back. The lost house and pharmacy and the threat of poverty were of little concern compared to her children. She would only be getting Sophie? "Children belong with their mother. Most judges, as a rule, will honor that," her lawyer had told her. Clara had been relieved to know that. As long as she could have the children, she didn't care about anything else.

Unrest spread among the public, too.

"Order! I am aware that, at first glance and considering the wanton behavior of Clara Gropius, it would seem appropriate to leave both children in the care of their father," the judge continued. "However, I do not think anyone here would doubt that a six-year-old girl is more urgently in need of her mother than her father. I am thus prepared to make this generous concession. However, I attach two conditions. First, that you, Clara Gropius, may not leave Berlin with your daughter. Second, you are obligated to grant Gerhard Gropius visitation rights at any time, whereby he is *not* obligated to grant you the same with respect to your son, Matthias." The judge removed his spectacles and leaned across his bench in Clara's direction. "I can only hope that you show a greater sense of responsibility with your daughter than you did with your marriage. You have this afternoon to return to your old home and pack your belongings and those of your daughter. After that, you no longer have any right to enter the house of Gerhard Gropius. Do you understand?" he asked sternly.

"But what about my son?" Clara cried in horror. "He needs his mother, too!"

"You should have thought about that sooner," the judge replied, and rose to his feet.

At that, the onlookers jumped up from the benches and began to excitedly discuss what they had just witnessed. "The judge sure gave her a piece of his mind," said the mailman as he pulled on his oily cap.

"That ought to drive a few foolish notions out of some other women's heads," said another man.

"But the doctor got her parents' house and pharmacy, too," said the redhead, frowning.

"It's her own fault," said her friend unsympathetically. "That's what you get for whoring around." She glanced lasciviously toward Gerhard Gropius, whose expression remained unmoved as he pulled on his jacket. "He's a good-looking man, that doctor, wouldn't you say? He'll find someone to console him soon enough."

The women strolled out of the courtroom. What a show!

Chapter Two

The commotion outside was worse than in the courtroom. Spectators, photographers, journalists—they all wanted to see the adulteress with their own eyes.

"There's the hussy now!" People pointed their fingers at her as soon as she walked out of the building. "Shame on you, you tramp!" People spat on the ground in front of her. "Disgusting!"

Clara wanted to turn and run back inside, but she took a deep breath and squared her shoulders. She would survive this, too. Her daughter was waiting for her. Besides, she had to convince Gerhard to give her Matthias as well.

"A photo! A photo, please."

Before she knew it, someone was holding a huge camera in front of her face. A flash blazed, and she flinched. The photographer laughed.

"Mrs. Gropius, an interview for the *Berlin Mirror*?" A heavyset man with sweat marks at his armpits stepped directly in front of her. "Mrs. Gropius, how does it feel to be a divorced woman?"

Relief washed over Clara when she spotted Josephine and Isabelle, pushing their way through the crowd.

"Thank God," she whispered when her friends took her between them.

"Leave this woman in peace!" Isabelle shouted at the pack of journalists.

"Take off!" Josephine snapped at them. "The circus is over. You can all go home."

"Let's get away from here," said Clara, and she took off running. Her friends ran behind her as fast the high heels of their fine summer shoes would allow.

Two blocks away, out of breath and sweating, they stopped at a small oval plaza with a wrought-iron fountain in the middle and, along the side, two wooden benches shaded by chestnut trees. A few young girls played tag under the watchful eyes of a nanny.

Clara was shaking as she sank onto one of the benches. Josephine sat beside her while Isabelle went to the fountain, and dipped a handkerchief in the water. She handed the wet cloth to Clara, then slumped onto the bench herself.

Clara dabbed at her forehead with the cool handkerchief. Dozens of thoughts swirled through her mind.

For some time, the only sound was the twittering of the sparrows in the branches of the chestnut trees. It was Josephine who broke the silence. She slipped her arms around Clara and said, "Congratulations. From now on, you are a free woman again."

"You did what you had to do, and you did it well. I am so proud of you," Isabelle added, also embracing her. "The way that judge was stirring up the audience against you, I felt like slapping the old bastard. But you didn't let him get to you, and that was good."

Clara smiled weakly. The entire process already felt like a bad dream. Had she really just battled her way through a divorce in that courtroom?

"But the judge gave Gerhard the house and pharmacy," said Josephine. "Such an injustice! That belonged to your parents, which makes it your inheritance. You were going to build yourself a new future with that. Isn't there any room for an appeal?" Josephine's eyes gleamed angrily.

"I'll address the properties later," said Clara grimly, standing up again. "Right now, I have to put all my energy into getting Matthias back."

Isabelle and Josephine were instantly back on their feet. "We'll go with you."

The thought of having her friends' protection was tempting. But Clara shook her head. "I think it would be better for me to speak to Gerhard alone. He has no time to raise Matthias in any case, and a boy his age needs his mother. Gerhard has to see that, doesn't he?" Anxious, she looked from one to the other.

Her two friends exchanged an equally anxious look.

Instead of taking the tram, Clara made her way back to Luisenstadt—the district where she had lived until six months earlier—on foot. She needed the time to build up courage to go back to her old home.

Since Gerhard had applied for the divorce at the beginning of spring, Clara had been staying with Josephine. There was more than enough room for her in their large, elegant house in the city, and Adrian, Josephine's husband, had raised no objections to the arrangement. Every day, they had collected Josephine's daughter, Amelie, from school. In the schoolyard, Clara could at least catch a glimpse of her own daughter, Sophie, and was occasionally able to exchange a few words with her. *Mama loves you. She's thinking about you all the time.* Any more than that had been impossible since Gerhard's lawyer had obtained an injunction banning any contact between Clara and her children. She had had no answer when Sophie asked, "Mama, when are you coming home again?"

Without Josephine, who had always been there to console her and give her strength, she never would have made it. And Clara felt even stronger when Isabelle had arrived from France a few days earlier to join Josephine in supporting her through the divorce.

And she had done it. Gerhard would never hit her again. Never again would she have to listen to his derogatory words or humiliating vulgarities. But the price had been high. That day, she had already had a taste of what lay ahead for her as a divorced woman. But she knew, too, that not everyone was as cruel as the spectators in that courtroom. There were those who accepted her decision, like Josephine and Isabelle.

She would pack a few dresses for Sophie, that was all, she decided as she turned onto Görlitzer Strasse. And Sophie's toys, of course. Clara had taken her own things with her when she had left—clothes, a few books, photographs, and some mementos of her parents. There was nothing else she wanted from the house. Nothing except Matthias . . .

When she thought of her son, a deep, inexpressible pain filled her. Over the years, Gerhard had done everything in his power to turn Matthias against her. "Look how stupid your mother's been again." "Your mother doesn't have her head on straight—don't listen to a word she says, my son." And Matthias had, in fact, started to look at her with the same contempt as his father, his mouth twisted in mockery whenever she expressed an opinion. If she tried to stroke his cheek, he stiffened. And every time he did, it hurt so much. But what could the boy do if his father pumped those poisonous ideas into him?

Would he even want to go with me? Clara wondered sadly. Then she pressed the doorbell.

"Madam . . ." Brunhilde Stumpfe, the nanny Gerhard had hired after Clara left, nodded curtly and allowed her to enter.

It was so gloomy inside! How had she never noticed that? A sense of trepidation came over her. *Get away, just get away.*

"I've come to collect Sophie. No doubt my . . . the doctor already told you. Is Matthias here, too?"

14

The nanny shook her head. "Your son is at the music school, like every Wednesday. Sophie is in her room." Without another word, she walked off toward the kitchen.

Matthias had his trombone lesson. How could she have forgotten that? For a moment, Clara stood there, uncertain. What now? Hesitantly, she climbed the stairs to the bedrooms. She opened the door to Sophie's bedroom, and froze with her hand on the doorknob: Gerhard was sitting on their daughter's bed with Sophie on his lap, reading to her.

Clara began to tremble with dread. Despite her agitation, she forced herself to smile at Sophie. "Mama's here to pick you up. We're going to pack your clothes and toys, and then we're going to visit Auntie Jo. Amelie is so looking forward to seeing you." She was already at the dresser, opening the top drawer.

"But, Mama," Sophie squeaked. "I can't go with you."

Clara turned abruptly and frowned at Sophie, then at Gerhard. What was he up to now?

"And why can't you come with me?" Clara asked gently.

Her daughter looked at her sheepishly. "Don't be angry, Mama. But, you see, Matthias is staying here."

Clara stared at Gerhard. "Maybe Father will let Matthias come with us. He doesn't have the time to do any homework with him as it is." Even as she spoke, she realized the futility of the idea. Gerhard would never give up his son.

"And there's something else," said Sophie. "The cat next door, Molly, has had kittens. And Papa promised me I can have one! I'm getting her tomorrow. I'm going to call her Mika. Look, I've already got a basket for her." She pointed to a small cane basket beside her bed that she had arranged lovingly with cushions from her doll's carriage. "Don't be sad, Mama. I'll see you again soon."

"We could . . . take the kitten with us," Clara stammered. From the corner of her eye, she could see Gerhard's sneer.

Sophie shook her head. "Papa says cats need a big garden, and Auntie Jo's house is in the middle of the city where there are lots of cars and bicycles. Mika certainly wouldn't feel very happy there."

Clara could only stand there, thunderstruck. "Would you please come out to the hallway for a moment?" she said to Gerhard, her voice brittle.

"You swine!" she hissed the moment she closed the door. "For years you didn't want a cat or dog in the house, and now this? You're playing the most revolting hand you could!" Her entire body was shaking.

"I changed my mind," Gerhard replied calmly. "If I'd known how much Sophie wanted a kitten, I would have let her have one much earlier." He took a menacing step toward her.

Instinctively, Clara tried to take a step back in the narrow corridor, but she found herself pressed to the wall, with Gerhard's cologne in her nose and her heart pounding in her throat. "Isn't it enough for you to disgrace all of us? Now you want to tear a child out of her happy world? Go live your new life! But leave Sophie here where she belongs. And as far as Matthias is concerned—he's asked me to tell you he never wants to see you again."

The hate in his eyes struck her like hot sparks. But far worse were his last words. Clara's legs felt heavier than they ever had when she returned to her daughter's bedroom. She sat down beside Sophie on the bed.

"Are you sure that you don't want to come with me?" she asked her gently. Sophie was still holding the book Gerhard had been reading to her; pictures of cats adorned the pages.

Sophie looked up and nodded silently. Her violet-blue eyes begged for forgiveness as she said, "Papa is here. And Matthias. And Maria is next door. Can't *you* stay, too?"

"Oh, Sophie . . ." Swallowing a sob, Clara wrapped her arms around her daughter and rocked her gently back and forth. Sophie's silken hair, with its scent of talcum powder, caressed her cheek. Nothing in Clara's life had ever hurt so much. Of course she could assert her legal right and take Sophie with her, but at what price? Her daughter was happy and content there. Did she really want to risk that happiness? Wouldn't a mother's love mean, for now, making do without her daughter? Just for now. She would come back another day . . . but the very thought of leaving her almost tore her heart in two.

Clara closed her eyes. "I love you more than I can tell you. And I only want what is best for you," she said, her voice raw. "If you ever need me, tell Brunhilde, and I will come for you at once! I will always be there for you, always! Do you understand?"

Beaming happily at her mother, Sophie nodded. Then she jumped up and began to rearrange the cushions in the cat basket. "When Mika's here, you *are* going to come and visit, aren't you?"

He was waiting for her in the hallway. Sure of victory, exulting in it.

Clara stopped three feet away from him. With abhorrence, she looked at him. What had she ever seen in the man? His high forehead concealed only arrogance and condescension. His thin lips conveyed scorn and malice. His fingers were so fine, yet so capable of inflicting pain.

"I agree that Sophie can stay here, for the time being. But on one condition—that I be allowed to visit both children at any time," she said, summoning up the last of her strength. Still, she could hear her voice shaking, and she was angry at herself for it.

Instead of replying, Gerhard grabbed her roughly by the arm and pulled her down the stairs and toward the door, which he jerked open. "You don't have the slightest right to demand anything. The children belong to me, now and for all eternity. Now get out of my sight, you wretched whore, before I beat you so hard you won't be able to crawl."

Chapter Three

The house is dark. Everyone but the father has gone to bed. The little brindle cat is tucked into the crook of the girl's arm. Its purring has lulled the child to sleep. They both look content. But when the room suddenly becomes light, the cat, sure of its instincts despite its young age, jumps down under the bed, where it cowers in the farthest corner.

"Didn't I forbid you from taking that cat into your room?" The father's expression is dark, his eyes dangerous.

The girl, jolted out of sleep, tries to swallow, but her mouth is dry as dust.

"What's the matter? An answer, if you please, when I ask you a question," he snarls at the child.

"I . . ." No more than a squeak. Mama. Why isn't Mama here?

"You minx!" The man grasps the girl by the arm, pulls her up, shakes her like a bundle of rags.

Tears run down the child's face. She forces herself to be quiet. Best not to say anything when Father is like this. It only makes him madder.

"Oh, so it's like that! First play stubborn, then come the tears? Just like your mother . . . The apple doesn't fall far from the tree, they say. But I won't have it!" Hot droplets of spittle strike the child's face.

"Father, you're hurting me." The child begins to whimper.

"I'll show you what hurt is, you little beast." He raises his right hand high in the air and . . .

A piercing shriek punctured the stillness of the night. Clara sat bolt upright. Sophie! Where was her daughter? She had to help her. Her heart thumped, and she peered around the room. "Sophie . . ."

A moment later the door opened. Josephine came in with a lit candle and an anxious look on her face. "Clara? Is everything all right?" As Josephine spoke, Isabelle appeared in the room behind her. "Has something happened?"

One look at Clara's distressed face, and it was immediately clear to her two friends that they would not be returning to their beds soon. Josephine made chamomile tea, her remedy for all the upsets of life. A short time later, all three were sitting together in their nightgowns in Josephine's living room.

When Clara inhaled the scent of the healing herb, she actually did feel a little comforted. She wrapped her hands around the teacup and enjoyed the warmth of it. "I could see it in front of me . . . So real. What if Gerhard really does something to Sophie?" Her eyes were wide with fear, and her heart began beating hard again. Hands quaking, she put the teacup back on the tray. "Oh God, and I'm not there to protect her. I've left her all alone." She buried her face in her hands and began to cry. She'd done everything wrong. As usual.

"Oh, Clara," said Josephine gently. "There are a lot of bad things to be said about Gerhard, but not that he was a bad father. You told us yourself that he had never laid a hand on the children."

Clara looked up. "That's true. And if I'd feared that something like that could happen, I would never have tried for a divorce."

"I think we could count on what happened today giving you nightmares, couldn't we?" said Isabelle. "But it was just a bad dream, no more! No doubt Gerhard is sitting in his library with a glass of wine in his hand and congratulating himself on showing you yet again who's the head of his house. But that doesn't mean he would ever do anything to Matthias or Sophie. You can at least rest easy in that."

"A bad dream . . ." Clara looked tenderly from Isabelle to Josephine. She wanted so much to believe them. "And if it was some kind of premonition? Should I have insisted that Sophie come with me?" She began to weep again. "Everything happened so fast. I was caught off guard. And now I think I've made a terrible mistake," she sobbed.

Josephine and Isabelle cautiously exchanged a look. They had been convinced that Clara would return with her daughter. They were both mothers, and neither wanted to imagine what it would feel like to lose her own child. Clara had had the chance to keep at least one of her children, but she had relinquished it. How hard that must have been.

Josephine laid one hand on Clara's right arm and gave it a little squeeze. "You did everything right. Sophie feels good in her home. Leaving her there was proof of a mother's love."

"And besides," said Isabelle, "you have to get back on your feet again as soon as you can. You can only make the decisions you need to make—for you and for your children—when you're self-sufficient."

"What would I do without the two of you?" Clara forced a smile. "I'll visit Sophie as often as I can. Gerhard simply has to concede that. I'll go there again tomorrow and talk to him." She felt a grain of hope appear inside her. Maybe all was not yet lost.

Josephine and Isabelle looked at each other doubtfully. If there was one thing Gerhard Gropius wasn't, it was a man who made concessions.

"That horrible man!" Isabelle suddenly blurted. "Of all the people in this world, why did you have to fall in love with him? Or worse, marry him? It was obvious from the start that he had it in for you. You wasted so many years with him."

Clara recoiled as if someone had struck her with a whip.

"Isabelle," Josephine said in a warning tone. "I'm sure it wasn't all bad, was it, Clara?"

It was a moment before Clara could respond. "At the start, Gerhard was nice. He made all the decisions, and I felt I was in good hands." She looked intently at Isabelle. "Maybe you can't understand that. Your parents always gave you a certain amount of . . . well, freedom. You could get away with things. With your husband Leon, too. But I never knew any other way to live than to obey, without protest. From childhood my mother dictated life for me—everything from what I wore to when I'd been educated enough. I could have gone to a girls' secondary school, like you did! My teacher urged my parents to send me, but Mother wanted me to go to home economics school to learn how to be a good wife." Clara grimaced. "And I really tried to be just that! I wanted to anticipate every wish he had. I wanted to do everything right. And when I couldn't, I looked for the fault in myself. I told myself I was too scatterbrained, too stupid, too forgetful. That I needed to think more before I said something or did something. Listen to Gerhard better. Every day, I tried to become a better housewife . . . a better *wife*. But with every word of criticism, every time Gerhard flew into a rage, all I did was get more nervous and make more mistakes."

"But you're one of the most orderly and efficient people I know," said Josephine. "I still remember how I envied you in school because your exercise books were always so perfect and neat and your school bag was so organized. Mine always looked like a tornado had been through it. I haven't improved much since." She gestured toward the living room table, stacked with magazines, a few empty glasses from earlier in the evening, Amelie's toys, and Adrian's pipe.

All three laughed at that.

Clara took a sip of her tea. "I was never as bold as either of you. And Gerhard destroyed what little confidence I had, bit by bit. It felt like I was dissolving more each day, like an old rag with threads that get more and more fragile. At some point, there wouldn't have been much left of me at all." She laughed sadly. "If I look back on it now . . . every effort I made was a waste of time, because I could never do anything well enough for Gerhard. He didn't want to praise me, but instead to humiliate me, taunt me, lecture me. That's what mattered to him. It had nothing to do with having a perfect house. But I had to understand that before I could do anything about it, don't you see?"

Isabelle and Josephine nodded sympathetically, but Clara doubted that they had really understood.

"Every morning, I had to ask him what he wanted for dinner that evening. He would say potatoes and gravy, for instance. So that's what I would cook. But come dinner, it was possible that he would throw his plate across the room and scream, 'How can you cook such a heavy meal on a hot day like this? Cold meat in aspic would be just the thing for me now!'" She shook her head as if to shake off the memory. "If I took him a glass of beer, he'd want wine, or vice versa. 'Are you trying to turn me into a drunk?' he asked one day. 'Unlike you, I have to work during the day, so it's important that I go to bed with a clear head.' So the next day, all I put on the table was a carafe of water. 'Oh, I see!' he screamed at me. 'I'm supposed to drink water so madam here can drink a brandy in the afternoon with the money I make?'"

"Why didn't you ever say anything?" Josephine whispered. She looked as if she would burst into tears at any moment.

Clara sniffed. "How would that have changed anything? I'd made my bed, and I had to lie in it. Besides, the children were still so small. I couldn't leave them. And you see how hard it is to get a divorce."

For a long time, none of them said anything. The clock on the wall struck two.

"Oh, Clara, if only I could have helped you somehow," said Josephine.

"You did. You were always there for me, and that was enough, even if I didn't always show you what my real life was like," said Clara. "When my parents had their accident, Gerhard was also having problems in his practice. You know how life can be—everything pouring down at once. His best nurse and his secretary resigned at almost the same time, so the office was a mess, and his patients were not shy about complaining. My dear husband was not used to that, not when his female patients worshipped him otherwise. He came home in a bad mood every evening, and he took it out on me. He beat me a lot during that time, and it got harder and harder to pretend my little world was in order. But I still tried to put on my happy smile for the children, to protect them. Still, they must have known something was going on. Sophie began wetting her bed again. She cried a lot and never left my side. Gerhard had turned Matthias against me much earlier, and for the first time I began to think that it could not be good to let the children grow up in such an atmosphere. I had to look for a solution, whatever the cost."

Josephine placed her hand on Clara's arm and pressed gently. "One day, your son will realize what a strong, wonderful woman his mother is. And your daughter will admire you for the courage you've shown."

"Let's hope so," said Clara softly, but she felt doubt creeping over her again. Had the price been *too* high?

Isabelle abruptly put down her cup. The tea was cold. "With all due respect to your tea, dear Jo, now that we're so wide awake anyway, we can just as well end this night with champagne." She stood up and went into the kitchen, returning a moment later with a bottle and three glasses. "Our first Feininger-Lambert, 1901. For Daniel and me, this champagne was the symbol of a new start, and that's what it should be for you, too." She filled three glasses, then raised hers to Clara. "To your liberty!"

"To your new life!" Josephine said. "May everything work out for the best."

Clara gingerly raised her glass to clink with the others. The rose-pink champagne smelled of strawberries and vanilla. "To my new life," she said aloud. Then, to herself: *I will do everything I can not to mess it up.*

Chapter Four

Although it was almost three in the morning when the women went back to bed, they were up again before eight. Isabelle's train left for Reims at ten, and Clara wanted to start looking for work immediately. To make sure that Clara presented herself well, Isabelle was supposed to give her some advice about clothes before she left.

"The black dress? No, much too gloomy for a summer day. And the lacy one is too flirty altogether." Isabelle, legs crossed, sat on the edge of Clara's bed while Clara brought out her dresses for her friend to inspect.

"What do you think of this dark-blue one?" Clara asked cautiously. She didn't have many more to choose from. To her relief, Isabelle approved.

"It's crucial that you look professional and well groomed. Nothing over the top," said Isabelle, well versed in fashion matters. "If you come across as too elegant or seductive, all you'll do is get on the wrong side of the pharmacists' wives."

Clara looked in the mirror. The outfit was a few years old, but the fabric was good quality. The cut was flattering to her slim figure without overemphasizing her curves. The dark blue was easy to look at, and she wore new black shoes as well. But was it enough to make a good impression on a pharmacist?

"Done?" Josephine suddenly asked from behind Clara. Josephine, who was dressed for going out, wore a pale-yellow summer skirt and jacket and a straw hat.

"Because you're both leaving me today, I've decided to go into the shop. Adrian has already gone ahead on his bicycle. Our driver will be here in an hour, and he can drive you, Isabelle, to the station, and then Clara and me into town."

Clara spun around and smiled at Josephine. "What do you think? Can I go like this?"

"You look fantastic!" Josephine said, then turned to Isabelle. "Did you do her hair?" Isabelle nodded. "Well, you should wear your hair that way all the time." Spontaneously, she went over to Clara and embraced her. "Now come on, both of you, let's at least have a little breakfast together!" With one arm still around Clara's shoulders, she led her downstairs. Isabelle, smiling broadly, followed.

"What if you came back to Champagne with me? A change of scene would surely do you good. Daniel would be happy to see you again, too. When you first met, years ago, there wasn't much time for deeper conversations," said Isabelle as they sat together over fresh rolls and coffee. Whenever Isabelle talked about her second husband, her cheeks flushed red with pleasure and desire, and now was no exception.

Clara was so excited by the idea that she all but lost her appetite. "I'd love to visit you on your vineyard, and it would be wonderful to see your husband and Marguerite again. The last time I saw your daughter, she was crawling around the house. And now she's seven!" Clara sighed.

"And you haven't even met the twins, Norbert and Jean. They're already three, you know," Isabelle said, with a tinge of accusation.

"Why do you have to live so far away?" Josephine laughed. "It takes so much just to get there that visits like this are a rare treasure."

"That's absolutely true." Clara nodded. "And, as much as I'd like to travel to Champagne, right now is simply not the right time."

"Not the right time? We've got the picking season coming up. All the commotion of that will get you thinking about other things in no time. Besides, we could visit Raymond Dupont. My dear champagne dealer is still searching for the woman of his dreams. If I remember right, you were once quite taken with him," Isabelle replied.

"Isa! Clara's been divorced for *one* day! And all you think about is matching her up again, just like that?" said Josephine in disbelief.

"It's never too early for a new love," said Isabelle, waving her hand with what seemed like a French airiness.

All three laughed, though there was something forced about it.

The night had been short, and after Clara's nocturnal confessions, they all felt rather vulnerable. Isabelle's imminent departure only amplified the feeling. They had no idea when they would share a moment like this again, the three of them, together. They all felt the burden in their hearts, and it was precisely for that reason that they tried to keep the tone of their conversation light.

"You might not believe it, but I've actually thought of Raymond Dupont and his wonderful champagne business many times. He is a striking man. And then there's Reims—what a gorgeous town that is! A visit to Champagne is certainly tempting," Clara replied, then nibbled at her roll. "But I really don't want to think about a new love in my life now. The first thing I must do is get my life in order. As soon as I've found work and a nice apartment, I'm going to bring Sophie to live with me. And then she can have ten kittens and a dog, too! And who knows? Maybe Matthias will look up to his mother a little again."

"That's the right attitude," Josephine said.

"We women manage a lot more than people give us credit for," Isabelle added. "When I look back at the time of Leon's death . . ." She shook her head. "It all looked so hopeless. I never thought I would ever be happy again. But with your help, I got back on my feet again. And today I have a wonderful husband and three children and a successful company." Her eyes shone with pride and confidence. "The feeling of coping with whatever life throws at you, beating all the odds, is indescribable. It is more intoxicating than champagne."

"You don't know how good it is to hear that." Clara smiled. "When I think about everything ahead of me . . . it terrifies me. Walking into a pharmacy and asking about work? Oh Lord, I might not even get a single word out."

Her two friends protested loudly at that. "But you always wanted to work in a pharmacy," said Josephine. "Now you finally have the chance!"

Clara nodded. "Do you remember? When I was young, I dreamed of studying pharmacology. But at the time it wasn't even possible. And even if women had been able to go to the universities back then, Gerhard would never have allowed it. He ridiculed me when I raised the topic once. Humiliated me." Her expression was grim, but there was determination in her eyes, too. "But that time is over. No one can stop me now. I don't have the money to study, but I can certainly work in a pharmacy."

"Oh, look at the time!" Isabelle cried when she glanced at the clock on the wall. She threw her napkin on the table and stood up. "I hope your driver gets here soon. If we don't get going, I'll miss my train."

Clara and Josephine exchanged a dejected look, then they stood up also. When and where would they see Isabelle again? In Champagne? In Berlin? Only one thing was clear: they had gone through thick and thin together for most of their lives, and the same would be true in the future.

They had almost reached the front door when Clara, from the corner of her eye, saw the daily paper rolled up on a shelf by the coatrack. As if at the command of an inner voice, she stopped abruptly.

"Clara, we have to go," Josephine urged. "Leave the newspaper."

Without a word, Clara unrolled the paper. It was the *Berlin Morning Post*. The front-page headline read **"Divorce! Famous Gynecologist and Unfaithful Wife—She Admits Traveling Salesman Came Once a Month."** Beneath the headline was a photograph of Clara outside the courtroom, taken the moment Clara had looked around, desperately searching for Josephine and Isabelle. She looked disoriented, almost mad.

"This will finish me," Clara whispered.

"Those filthy hacks!" said Isabelle, peering over Clara's shoulder.

"Oh, forget it! Don't lose courage because of something like that," said Josephine vehemently. But a trace of uncertainty tinged her words as well.

"The entire city is going through an upheaval. Unbelievable, isn't it?" said Josephine when they were sitting in the back seat of the carriage. Although it was still quite early in the morning, the streets were already so full that progress was at a walking speed. "You could drive down a street today and come back next week and not recognize anything. They are tearing down whole rows of houses and moving the residents out to other parts of the city, laying tracks for the new tram system everywhere, and even digging tunnels for a new underground railway."

Clara, still shocked by the article in the newspaper, nodded half-heartedly.

"And that's not all," Josephine said, making an effort to sound cheerful. "New companies are springing up all over the place. Little shops, big department stores, mail-order companies, and factories are spreading all over the city. Pretty soon you'll be able to get anything you want in Berlin. And the best part is that more and more companies are being run by women."

"And you were one of the first to risk it!" said Isabelle. "I was so jealous of your independence back then."

"Looking back, it was really very brave of me, but I didn't give it a second thought at the time. I just wanted to show certain people," Josephine admitted with a grin. "When I opened my repair shop in 1896, people were amazed. But just as many berated me. A woman working with bicycles? And running her own business? The general consensus was that I was doomed to failure. Weren't they all surprised when it worked out? Those times are over now, thank God."

"Do you really think things have changed for women in the meantime?" Clara looked optimistically at her friend.

"If you knew how many of these shops have a woman at the helm these days," said Josephine, and spread her hands as if to include the shops lined up like pearls on a string. "Admittedly, most of them are still in the classic female arenas. Hat shops, dressmakers, florists. Big factories and other companies, especially anything to do with technology, are still firmly in men's hands. But who knows what women are capable of?"

"Around Champagne, it's been quite usual for hundreds of years for women to lead major wine-growing estates and champagne cellars," Isabelle added.

"I take so much courage from both of you," Clara said, and she meant it absolutely. "You've achieved so much! The only trails I've blazed have been in the divorce court, and I don't think anyone wants to emulate me for that." She frowned. "Do you remember when we were still so young, and we wished so much that the winds of change would blow through the streets. A turn-of-the-century wind, sweeping away everything old and dusty and clearing a path for new ideas. Sometimes, I think that wind has started, but will it be enough to blow the old cobwebs out of people's heads, too?" Clara's voice trembled a little. The closer they got to the center of Berlin, the stronger the nervous tingling in her stomach grew. What if everyone started pointing at her, like they had the day before in the courtroom?

"Certainly not everyone's head. There are more than enough men around who still think of us as the weaker sex and don't trust us to do anything right. But those are the ones we ignore!" said Josephine as the carriage pulled up in front of the train station.

Isabelle gave Clara's left hand an encouraging squeeze. "It will all work out for the best, believe me. The next time I see you, your life will look very different than it does today!"

Chapter Five

Clara had decided to start her search for work in the center of Berlin. There were more than a dozen pharmacies on Alexanderplatz and the surrounding streets, and she hoped that in the big city, she would be anonymous. She could safely assume that Gerhard had turned all the pharmacists—and their wives—against her in her old quarter. There was probably no one in Luisenstadt who would give her so much as the time of day.

Feeling weak at the knees, Clara opened the door of the first pharmacy. As the door swung open, a shrill doorbell jingled, but it was several moments before the pharmacist appeared from behind a dark-brown curtain.

"How can I help you?" He looked at her disinterestedly.

"I'm looking for work as a pharmacist's assistant," said Clara nervously. *He doesn't seem to recognize me from the newspaper, at least,* she thought, her eyes roaming around the dim interior. The pharmacy looked old and worn out, like the proprietor himself. "My parents used to run a pharmacy, so I'm very familiar with all the procedures. I can make soap, and I've mastered the mixing of creams and pastes as well." She had composed these sentences carefully, and had even practiced them aloud with Josephine. She wanted to sound confident but not overly pushy.

"Why don't you work in your parents' pharmacy if that's where you learned?"

Clara gulped. "Well, I've never done an actual apprenticeship, you see. But—"

"And does your husband happen to know that you're here asking about work?" The pharmacist nodded bluntly in the direction of her wedding ring. Clara's hand flew instinctively to her ring. Blast it . . . Her fingers had been swollen the night before, so she hadn't been able to get the ring off. And that morning, she had simply forgotten about it.

The man frowned at her unpleasantly. "Madam, you are wasting my time." He shooed her out of his pharmacy.

Clara stalked off, angry at herself. She certainly had not carried that off very well. But it didn't matter. She wouldn't have wanted to work there at the best of times! As she walked, she yanked the wedding ring from her finger. She would have loved to toss it into the gutter, but she could not afford a gesture as daring or defiant as that. The gold ring would certainly be worth a few marks. She pushed it deep inside her bag instead.

"Out of the way! Are you blind?"

"Sorry." Taken by surprise, Clara jumped to one side. In the bright sunlight, she had not seen the cyclist coming at all. An accident now—that was all she needed.

Looking left and right, she cautiously crossed Alexanderplatz, picking a path through the tangle of carriages, bicycles, and automobiles. Red-and-white striped awnings were extended over the large windows of the new Tietz department store to protect the goods on display from the sun. Clara found some relief in the shade they offered and looked around, orienting herself. To the right of the department store she saw the Corner Pharmacy, the second on her list. This time, she would handle herself better. "Good morning. My name is Clara Berg, and I—"

The pharmacist interrupted her with an extravagant wave of one hand, like a conductor stopping his orchestra from playing. Then he leaned so far forward over the counter that its edge pressed into his fat belly. "Don't say another word, young lady! I need no more than a single glance to know what it is you need . . ." His eyes glinted lecherously as he looked Clara over from head to toe. After a long moment, he nodded with satisfaction. "You need something to calm your nerves, am I right? Or perhaps to help you sleep? Something for the circulation? Or is it more a . . . woman thing?" Spittle collected in the corner of his mouth as he watched her expectantly.

Clara's brow furrowed. "None of that. I—" But she broke off, and seconds later was standing outside again. The man was crazy!

"No certificate? Not even a reference? Then I'm sorry . . ."

"We don't hire women."

"Work in a pharmacy? Without an apprenticeship? Unheard of!"

"Nothing open, I'm afraid."

Clara's confidence faded with every refusal. She had known all along that it would not be easy, but she had not counted on it being this difficult.

Around midday, her feet hurt so much in her new shoes that she decided to take a break. To try and assuage her guilty conscience as she sat with a cup of coffee and a piece of crumb cake, she reminded herself that most of the pharmacies were probably closed for lunch. But she certainly had not earned such luxury! While she picked dispiritedly at the too-dry cake, she looked at the women sitting at the tables around her. They were in the best of moods, laughing and chatting away. Were these the saleswomen from the Tietz department store, taking their midday break? Or businesswomen from the smaller shops? Or were they just the wives of well-off husbands, there to enjoy themselves? To simply sit in a café . . . it was something that Clara would not have dared do six months earlier—Gerhard would have skinned her alive! But now she sat among all those industrious-looking women. Oh, her feet hurt, to be sure, and her self-confidence had taken a battering, but still, there she was. And it felt good to realize that, in the anonymity offered by the big city, no one recognized her.

With renewed courage, Clara set off again. Just around the corner from the café, she discovered another pharmacy. The sign above the door read "Römer's Pharmaceuticals" in black letters against a white background. *Is this the seventh or eighth today?* Clara wondered. She smoothed her skirt, put on her smile, and turned the door handle.

Inside, it smelled as it once had inside her father's pharmacy, of camphor and lavender, disinfectant and chamomile. How lovely to once again be surrounded by that unique perfume. She felt her strained smile soften.

The pharmacist behind the counter smiled back at her pleasantly. "A wonderful summer's day, isn't it? How may I help you?"

Clara politely put forward her request.

"Well, that *is* fortuitous," said the man. "I am, in fact, looking for someone to help me in the laboratory in back. I've just been thinking about an advertisement for the position." He looked at Clara as if sizing her up. Then he went on: "My former assistant had an accident and will be out of commission for quite a while."

Clara could hardly believe her ears. This was her opportunity.

"My specialty is making medicinal soaps," the pharmacist said. "It's a very time-consuming affair, and when I'm tied up with that, someone has to stand in for me here in the shop."

"Or the other way around," said Clara. "You could take care of the customers while someone else makes the soap. When I was a little girl,

I was already helping my father make his soap. I know every step in the process, beginning to end. Soaps for all kinds of skin conditions, and soaps with lavender and rose perfumes. And abrasive soap, too, and of course simple hand-washing soaps. I know all the different kinds. We used to buy our base soap from the Scheu & Müller soap factory, although I don't know if that still exists."

"It most certainly does. Scheu & Müller is my supplier, too," said the pharmacist happily. His expression was a mix of friendliness and interest. "It looks like I may be able to save myself an expensive newspaper ad. Why don't I take a look at your papers right away?"

Clara swallowed. "When I was helping my parents in their pharmacy, I was still a young girl, and at that time the law did not allow an apprenticeship for women as a pharmacist's assistant. Later, it was no longer possible for me to obtain such an official apprenticeship, so I have no certificates to show you," she said. "But I would gladly work with you on a trial basis so that you can see my technical qualifications for yourself—for free, of course," she added, to be on the safe side.

The man stroked his beard thoughtfully between his thumb and index finger. "I might be worth a try—"

"Karlheinz?" The woman who called out had a voice as shrill as an untuned instrument. The door behind the counter swung open, and a spindly woman with a high forehead and receding chin appeared. "You won't believe it, but that impossible man next door, yet again, has—" She broke off when she saw Clara standing at the counter. "Oh, you have a customer. Excuse me." The woman fell silent, her lips pressed together morosely.

"Hilde, you've come at just the right time," said the pharmacist. He gestured to the woman, who must have been at least ten years older than him, to join him. "Let me introduce Hilde Römer, my wife. This is Clara Berg, and she has just applied for a position as a pharmacist's assistant. Isn't that an amazing coincidence?"

The woman squinted at Clara, making her feel like an insect beneath a magnifying glass.

"Clara Berg . . . I know that name," Hilde Römer murmured to herself. Her high forehead creased.

Clara froze.

"You already know each other?" asked Karlheinz Römer cheerfully.

His wife turned and glared at him, her face stony. "Do you think I'd know someone like her? I don't associate with riffraff like that. There was a big article about *her* in the newspaper. With a photograph! She's the adulteress whose divorce just went through the court. If you read anything but the sports pages, you'd know that!"

"Karlheinz Römer was the only one to show even the slightest interest in me. And then along came his wife and ruined it all."

"That horrible article in the paper!" Josephine said, her voice a mixture of fury and despair. "Someone should be able to ban those hacks from writing about private matters!"

"You wouldn't be happy around people as small-minded as that, anyway," said Adrian, Josephine's husband. "You know that you can come to work for us any time you want. As a secretary in the office. And we need someone else in dispatch, too. The spare parts department has been extremely busy. We can always use hardworking women, isn't that right, Jo?"

Josephine nodded.

"That's nice of you, really, but when it comes to writing letters and invoices, I really don't have any experience to speak of," said Clara, putting down her knife and fork. She had lost her appetite completely, even though Josephine's cook had outdone herself with the roast veal. "What if I'm chasing some sort of vain illusion? Maybe my dream of working in a pharmacy has already expired."

Josephine frowned. "Don't even think it. Today was your first day. You probably just met the wrong people."

"Berlin is big," Adrian agreed. "You'll find the right place soon enough."

"After a start like I had today, I'm not so sure anymore," said Clara flatly. The cook tried to give Clara some dessert, but Clara smiled and shook her head.

"Keep your chin up, Clara," Adrian said. "Today it's you in the headlines, and tomorrow it will be someone else. As soon as that article's forgotten, the world will look like a different place, I'm sure."

The next day, Clara rode the tram to the Spandau district. A new quarter, new luck! But the world looked no different at all in northwest Berlin. Most of the pharmacists said they didn't need anyone, while others said they didn't want to take on a woman. And then there were those who had read about Clara's divorce in the paper.

The following weeks turned into an endless test of Clara's nerves and patience. Whether at the Molkenmarkt or in Dorotheenstadt, in Stralauer Vorstadt or Marienviertel, the doors of Berlin's pharmacies seemed to be nailed shut for Clara.

With every passing day, with every humiliation she had to swallow, she grew moodier, more peevish. She lost weight and twice had to take in the waistline of her dresses. But after a day without success, it was as if her throat had been squeezed closed, and she could not think about food. Her skin took on a gray, unhealthy pallor. This came as no surprise to her: the air in the city was sometimes thick enough to wring out. *As dismal as you look, I wouldn't give you a job, either,* she thought, depressed by her reflection in the mirror.

Plus she missed her children so much that it hurt. Whenever she rang the doorbell at her old home, the nanny turned her away at the door. "Sophie is at her flute lesson." "Matthias is at riding." "They are on an outing with their father." And so on. She was left with no choice but to meet furtively with Sophie in the schoolyard for a few minutes, as often as she could. "Why don't you come home again?" the little girl asked every time. She and her little cat would be so happy if Clara could just do that! But after those stolen minutes, Clara was left weeping and despondent. *It can't go on like this,* she thought, and she decided to send her ex-husband a letter.

> *Dear Gerhard,*
> *As you know, by the decision of the court I could have taken Sophie with me. For our daughter's sake, I have temporarily relinquished that right. In consideration of this great concession on my part, it would be only fair if you were to grant me visitation rights. I miss both children very much. As to the whens and hows, I am sure we can come to an arrangement. You know where you can reach me.*
> *Sincerely,*
> *Clara*

The sun was blazing, and the heat and dust were making people irritable. The black smoke that rose from the chimneys of the surrounding factories hung in the suffocating summer air, robbing Berlin's residents of the last bit of air to breathe. A little bump in a tram was all it took to start a shouting match. The coachmen drove their horses through the sweltering streets with no thought for pedestrians, cyclists, or children playing. Clara was almost run down twice because a carriage shot out of a side street without warning. No apology, no friendly word—both drivers simply ignored her frightened shriek.

The market traders and the street vendors sat lazily at their stands and could only watch as their produce spoiled faster than they could sell it. A simple question about the price of this or that often earned a loud curse.

Why does it have to be so hot? Clara wondered, setting off on her search yet again. Her feet were heavy, and not only because of the heat. There was still no sign of work. And no reply from Gerhard to her request. The waiting and uncertainty was putting her more and more on edge.

"I am looking for work as a pharmacist's assistant. Do you have an open position?" Was this the fiftieth place she'd asked?

"That all depends," said the next pharmacist, who appeared to be a respectable-looking older gentleman until he stared brazenly at Clara's breasts.

"It depends?" asked Clara tentatively.

The pharmacist sighed. "My dear, you know quite well what I'm talking about. A certain . . . reputation precedes you. If I were to employ you, Mrs. Gropius, I would be ruining things with your husband. He would tell his colleagues not to send so much as a single patient here to buy their medications. I might, in certain circumstances, be willing to accept such a loss. You would only have to be a little nice to me." Before Clara knew it, he came around from behind the counter and placed one hand on her breast. At the same time, he grasped her left hand and pressed it against his crotch. "They say you are an open-minded, experienced woman . . ." Shocked, Clara jerked free. Her first reflex was to run away, but instead she swung back her right hand and slapped the man hard on his ear.

"What do you think you're doing?" she snapped at him. "How dare you hold my reputation against me? What shape do you think your reputation will be in when I tell the women who come here that they risk being assaulted by you? Or should I talk to your wife first?" The pharmacist went pale, which gave Clara some satisfaction. "You are repulsive! I would never work for you, not if you ran the only pharmacy in the empire!"

Still seething, Clara walked along the bank of the Spree and thought over all that had happened in the previous weeks. She had done the best she could. Despite the hostility she faced, she had never lost her courage or her manners. But no one had given her a chance. She did not have the slightest idea what to do next. She could not go on living at Josephine's much longer. Nor did she want to! She still had the money from the sale of some of her mother's jewelry—she had had the forethought to give the jewelry to Josephine for safekeeping after her parents' death—but that would not last forever. The chances of the judge returning the house and the pharmacy to her in a second hearing—if she were to appeal the original judgment—were slim, Adrian had told her the evening before. He had made some inquiries with his own lawyer. That meant that she had to earn her own money, and soon. It was the only way that she would be able to afford an apartment of her own. But who would rent her a place was as much a mystery as who would hire her.

As a divorced woman, she had become a leper in the eyes of society. But did that mean she had to accept every vile thing that came her way? Hadn't she been humiliated by Gerhard long enough?

The sun had just sunk below the horizon in a glorious sea of orange and red when Clara made up her mind: though her situation was far from good, from that day on she would never degrade herself again. She would lead her life with her head held high, and take issue with anyone who deserved it!

Chapter Six

With a cup of coffee in her hand, Josephine settled comfortably onto a chair on the cast-iron balcony of their home in the city. It had been a long day, and it was not over yet. Later, after dinner, there was a small reception with the mayor, focused on the arrangements for an important bicycle race the following year. Although it had not been stated explicitly yet, Josephine assumed that the mayor wanted Adrian on his side as both sponsor and fellow campaigner. Josephine had already put out what she wanted to wear, and, without time to see the hairdresser, she would style her hair herself. But first she had to catch her breath. Her daughter, Amelie, was playing in her room, Adrian was still at work, and the cook was preparing dinner. No one wanted anything from her just then, and she could put her feet up for a bit before dedicating herself to the day's mail.

Josephine closed her eyes, enjoying the moment. When she opened them again, the first thing she saw was the Brandenburg Gate, shining golden in the light of the setting sun. Josephine had to smile. The monumental construction held a very special meaning for her: she and Isabelle had ridden beneath it so many times as a landmark on the secret cycling tours they had taken every morning—before dawn, while the world was still asleep—when they were younger.

Today, cycling had become normal. But not twenty years earlier, women who devoted themselves to the sport were met with antagonism and were even pelted with stones! She herself had ended up in prison because of her love of cycling. But it made no difference. Josephine did not regret a single day of her earlier life. She had so much to thank cycling for. Her friendships with Isabelle and Clara. Adrian, the love of her life. Their successful bicycle business. And, last but not least, her old friend Lilo, through whom she had first discovered cycling.

Enough indulging in old memories, Josephine cautioned herself. It was time to get to the stack of mail that she had brought to the balcony with her.

"I don't believe it," she murmured a moment later when she discovered a letter from Lilo in the pile. She had just thought of her! Josephine smiled as she slit open the envelope with one finger. Although they rarely saw each other, she and Lilo were avid pen pals. She would know Lilo's fluid handwriting anywhere, and it made her happy just to see it.

Meersburg, Lake Constance, August 1906

Dearest Jo,
I hope my letter finds you and yours in the best of health.
I'm well, though there are days when I feel like all
the work is eating me alive. I've barely had the chance
to even sit on my bicycle this summer, can you imagine?

Josephine frowned. Lilo was an enthusiastic and extremely successful cyclist, and she had always taken the time for her sport, regardless of whatever else was going on in her life. Curious, Josephine read on.

I never expected my hotel in Meersburg to be such a success, but we have been booked solid since the beginning of March! I already have several reservations for autumn and winter, too. And compared to Friedrichshafen, where the king and his court spend the summer, Meersburg is an insignificant little town! But at the same time, it's beautiful. I am overjoyed that I was right in my judgment, and that in the age of the automobile a few miles here or there doesn't concern most people. Actually, the opposite is true—I think my guests are happy to be able to run their cars along the elegant promenades as far as Constance and Friedrichshafen!

Josephine smiled. Lilo had always been ahead of her time, beginning with cycling. And she had been successful in everything she turned her attention to—including her divorce two years earlier. In contrast to Clara, who had walked away empty-handed, Lilo had received a considerable sum of money from her ex-husband, enough to take over the hotel at Lake Constance. And Lilo seemed not to have encountered any ill will as a divorcée, also in contrast to Clara. Or did she just keep that to herself?

"Josephine?"

"I'm outside!" she said, and pushed her chair backward to make room on the narrow balcony for Clara.

"Well?" she asked, although Clara's expression told her all she needed to know.

Clara sat on the empty chair beside Josephine, swept a strand of hair away from her tired face, and began to talk about her day.

Once Clara had finished, Josephine, truly concerned, said, "That's horrible. Oh, Clara, I'm so sorry you went through that."

"Don't be," said Clara, her voice steady and firm. "It helped me come to an important decision today." Her eyes shone proudly as she said, "From now on, I won't let them get me down. My motto is going to be 'Stay strong and don't look back.' I am going to walk through my life with my head held high, whatever comes."

"Absolutely right," Josephine praised. "You know what I always tell myself when things get tough? 'Keep your chin up, especially if you're drowning.'"

Both of them laughed at that. Clara raised her eyebrows and pointed at Josephine's coffee cup. When Josephine nodded, Clara drank a mouthful of coffee gratefully. Josephine was tempted to ring for the housekeeper to bring them more coffee, but first she wanted to put something else behind her. She handed Clara an official-looking envelope, something that had arrived that afternoon.

"Here, for you. It's probably from Gerhard's lawyer."

Clara's face turned stony immediately. With her lips pressed tightly together, she opened the envelope. When she looked up from the letter, her expression registered both shock and bewilderment.

"It's a court order. They're forbidding me from seeing Sophie!"

Josephine took the letter out of Clara's hand and began to read. "'. . . you did not, as agreed, collect your daughter on the day of the hearing. You have thus convinced the court a second time of your unreliability.'" Josephine looked up, aghast. "Are they mad? You were there! You wanted to take her with you! You only left her behind because Gerhard set you up by allowing Sophie the kitten."

Clara sat and said nothing, as if stunned into silence.

Josephine read on hurriedly: "'The court hereby revokes its original instruction granting you the legal custody of Sophie Gropius. A new instruction takes its place and hereby grants Dr. Gerhard Gropius custody of both children from this day forward. Through your insubordinate behavior, you have also forfeited any visitation rights you may otherwise have enjoyed for your daughter, Sophie, or your son, Matthias. The court orders that from this day forward, you are to approach neither your children nor the Gropius household. Should you violate this order, Dr. Gerhard Gropius is hereby permitted to send for the police and have you removed by force.'" Josephine put down the letter. "Are they allowed to do that? This is just arbitrary!"

"Now it truly is all over," Clara whispered. Tears flowed down her corpse-pale cheeks, and every bit of life seemed to have drained out of her.

Damn them, thought Josephine. Things were getting worse and worse for Clara. Still, she said, "You aren't going to let anyone or anything get you down; that's what you just told me. And now your good intentions are already swimming away on a sea of tears!" Gently, she shook her friend's arm. "Berlin is not the center of the world. The German empire is big. A new start would certainly be easier somewhere else." She felt an old but familiar fluttering spread inside her. It always came over her when new ideas and thoughts came along. A new beginning . . . somewhere else . . .

"Wonderful! So you think I should just jump on the next train to wherever, is that it?" A deep crease appeared on Clara's forehead.

But Josephine was excited now, and she slid forward to the edge of her chair. "No, no! I have something much more concrete in mind! Remember my old friend Lilo?"

Clara nodded, still frowning. "From the Black Forest, the one who introduced you to bicycles in the first place? Didn't you say that she also went through a divorce?"

"Lilo hasn't been living in the Black Forest for quite a while. After her divorce, she moved to Lake Constance." Josephine quickly explained what Lilo had written in her letter. "She's got so much work and her hotel in Meersburg is so successful that she doesn't even have time to go for a ride. What would you say if I wrote to Lilo and asked her if she can use a little help?"

"You want me to go and be a chambermaid at a hotel on Lake Constance?" Clara said. She sounded reproachful. "If you want to get me out of your hair, just say so. I'm sure I can get work as a maid and find a drafty attic room somewhere in Berlin just as easily."

Josephine did her best to ignore Clara's words. "Just listen to what's going on in my head first. Yes, you could certainly help Lilo out with her hotel. At reception, with the rooms, or wherever she needs you to help. But only for half the day! She'd have to offer you free room and board for that. The rest of the time you could go on looking for work. There must be pharmacies around Lake Constance. And no one knows you there. All the prejudice you're battling here won't hold you back down there. Once you're on your feet again and earning good money, you can reclaim custody of Sophie!"

Chapter Seven

Two weeks later, Clara was on a train bound for Lake Constance. In her luggage was everything she possessed: her clothes, a few makeup items, silver-framed pictures of her children and parents. A file of personal papers. A few books. A velvet box that held the few remaining pieces of her mother's jewelry. Her father's thick leather-bound notebook in which he had written down all his recipes for tinctures, pills, and pastilles. Whenever Clara leafed through its pages, browsing the recipes for ribwort cough medicine or peppermint pastilles, all recorded in her father's neat handwriting, she felt very close to him. Maybe the book would be of benefit to her sometime, when she found work as a pharmacist's assistant.

As the train creaked into motion, Clara felt unbearably torn, as if different souls were at war inside her. She was hopeful and frightened at the same time. She was looking forward to Lake Constance, and at the same time her departure from Berlin was painful. And she was leaving the city that had been her home. She, who had rarely ventured out of Luisenstadt in her life. Was she really putting five hundred miles between herself and her children? Was she making a huge mistake, one that could never be put right again? Or was Josephine right when she said that her chances would be much better in Germany's south?

"Travel today is so much more luxurious than it used to be, don't you think?" Not for the first time, the stout older woman sitting opposite her tried to start a conversation.

Clara only nodded. Her inner turmoil was too great for her to concentrate on an impromptu conversation with a stranger. Disappointed, the woman turned instead to the man beside her.

Hour after hour, the landscape rolled past. The pretty Elbe Valley, the hilly vistas of Saxony, the Bavarian Forest. Below Nuremberg, a transformation took place beyond the train's windows: the landscape opened up, the skies grew wider.

Clara suddenly thought of another train journey, one she had taken many years before with Josephine. They had traveled to the Champagne region to help Isabelle after the death of her first husband. Back then, they had shared their compartment on the train with an actress who had told them that she had just come from a three-month sojourn at Lake Constance to "regather her strength" for a new role. Regathering her strength by spending three months at Lake Constance? At the time, Clara had found the lifestyles some people led to be inconceivable. Gerhard would have raised hell if she'd tried to take three *hours* to regather her strength!

Obviously enchanted by the place, the actress had sung the praises of the fabulous landscapes around the lake so vividly that Clara could still remember them clearly. Back home again, one of the first things she had done was look in an atlas to find out exactly where that Swabian Sea actually was. And just a few days ago, she had picked up the atlas again; looking at the map, she had discovered that in the entire empire, there was nowhere more distant from Berlin than Lake Constance.

"A new start at the other end of the empire. It is certainly tempting," she had said to Josephine, who pored over the atlas with her. "But so far away from the children? The very idea nearly kills me."

"What can you do for your children now? You're not even allowed to see them," Josephine had replied somberly, and then promised to keep an eye on Sophie and Matthias, at least from a distance and as best she could.

A new beginning.

Regathering her strength beside Lake Constance.

At last a smile spread across Clara's face.

Two days later, she arrived in Friedrichshafen. It was one of those September days that couldn't make up its mind whether it belonged to summer or to autumn. The sun was shining, but the wind blowing in Clara's face already had a fresh bite to it. The wind—or rather, the air—was the first thing Clara noticed when she disembarked from the train. It was so much clearer than the air in Berlin. Clara inhaled deeply. It smelled of seaweed and algae, of hay and a little of fermented grapes. The air at Isabelle's estate had smelled the same, Clara realized with surprise. But there were no vineyards around, and she had seen nothing of Lake Constance itself yet, either. *I can hardly wait to get my first glimpse of the lake,* she thought as she went in search of a coachman to drive her on the last leg of her journey. She was relieved to see several carriages pulled up directly in front of the station. She had no desire to lug her bags much farther.

"To Meersburg, you say?" the coachman asked as he tied a feedbag for his horse. "I'm sorry, but that's not my stretch." He pointed to two young men rolling heavily loaded barrows his way. "All those goods that come by train from all over the empire? I deliver them to businesses here in Friedrichshafen."

Clara nodded, but she was disappointed. She looked around for another coachman.

The man, noticing her gaze, said, "No point in asking any of my colleagues, young lady. They're like me; they only work here in town. One or two will go as far as the castle over yonder, but no farther."

Clara frowned. "Then how do I get to Meersburg?"

The man looked at her. He seemed a little confused. "Well, by boat, of course."

A little while later, Clara found herself sitting aboard a small passenger boat bound for Meersburg. The coachman had been nice enough to take her and her bags down to the dock and had refused any payment for the service. The boat made regular trips back and forth between Friedrichshafen and Meersburg and had space for twelve passengers. Other than Clara, though, there were only five people—two men and three women—and two goats on board.

Clara nodded a greeting to the other passengers, then moved forward to the bow and gazed out over the lake. She had never imagined just how enormous it was. Like an ocean . . . Clara could not estimate the distance to the opposite shore, but it was certainly far away. Was that Switzerland? And how brilliantly blue the water glittered in the September sunshine. Every single cloud was reflected on the surface of the water.

Holding tight to the railing, Clara kept her face to the wind. As they moved out of the harbor, water splashed against the wooden hull, and a shower of spray splashed her suddenly in the face. She shrieked with the chill shock of it, but a moment later had to laugh. That's what she got for being so enthusiastic!

The boatman, standing just behind her at the wheel, grinned. "You'd best have a seat on one of the benches. You'll stay dry there." The other passengers were already waving to her to join them and shifting to make room.

She smiled her thanks and sat down. "It's so lovely here," she murmured. "You can see so far."

The woman sitting beside her nodded. "I was born by this lake, and I go to Meersburg every week to see my parents. I work at or on the water every day." She spread her hands in a gesture that included the lake and the shoreline they were chugging along. "This beauty still manages to captivate me every single day." She spoke with the same accent and same warm timbre as the coach driver and the boatman; her words lined up gently, like little waves. It sounded so much softer than the hard Berlin dialect.

"It is a wonderful gift not to lose your eye for the beauty of your own life. So many times, another person's fields seem greener than one's own. And one envies the others for what they have," said Clara, and was astonished to hear herself speaking like that. She had spent all the hours on the train solitary and all but silent, her answers to questions monosyllabic, and now here she was chatting with a complete stranger as if they had known each other for decades. She straightened her back and turned her face fully to the warm September sun. Was it the breeze or the expanse of the waters that had made her so talkative?

"The beauty of your own life . . . ," the woman repeated, and the streaming air carried her words away.

Clara looked at the woman. She guessed that they were around the same age, but the woman's forehead and cheeks were raw and creased, and as she swept a few loose hairs from her face, Clara saw that her skin on her hands was deeply cracked, in places a little bloody. *That must hurt terribly,* she thought.

Seagulls crying their sharp cries flew alongside the boat, and one of them landed on the bench directly beside Clara and the woman. At the woman's feet was a bucket in which lay a dozen good-sized fish, and the bird, quick and greedy, eyed them before the woman shooed it away with a wave of her hand.

"Too lazy to go and catch fish itself," she said to Clara and laughed. "But it's not getting any of my catch! My parents look forward to a nice fried trout in the evening."

Clara smiled. "So you're a fisherwoman?" *That would explain the cracked hands, of course,* she thought. Anyone who spent so much time splashing about in the water . . .

The woman nodded proudly. "Elisabeth Kaiser from the Kaiser Trout Fishery." She pointed toward Clara's luggage. "Are you here on holiday?"

"I hope not," Clara declared. "I'm looking for work. And I'd like to live here, too. But somehow, I still can't believe that I'm actually really here." She held out her hand to Elisabeth Kaiser. "I'm Clara Berg."

"You might have done better to come in spring. The tourist season is almost over, so it will get pretty quiet around here," said the woman, returning Clara's handshake firmly. Her voice carried a trace of concern.

With a confidence that surprised her most of all, Clara said, "That will be nice. My instinct tells me that a lot can happen here at Lake Constance." She smiled.

The fisherwoman, who found Clara's enthusiasm infectious, nodded in affirmation.

Clara's eyes swept wide over the lake. Now that the sun was at its zenith, the lake waters shone almost silver.

She was really there. No one apart from Josephine and Isabelle knew where she was. No one at Lake Constance knew her. No one had heard about the humiliating divorce hearing. She was Clara Berg, just one more new arrival looking for work at the lake. No more and no less.

***

An hour and a half later, they reached Meersburg. With the experience of many years, the boatman slowed his craft and approached a quay. The shore beyond was dominated by a large dark-red building.

"That's the Gredhaus. In the past, it was used to store grain, wine, and other goods before they were shipped off to be sold in Switzerland," Elisabeth Kaiser explained to Clara. "It was built in the Middle Ages, like most of the buildings here in the town. These days, the customs gentlemen have made themselves at home there." Her last words carried a trace of grouchiness.

Elisabeth Kaiser stopped to chat with the boatman briefly as they drifted in, and Clara looked up at the picturesque little town that hugged the rising vineyards. Medieval houses, towers, and even some sort of castle huddled close. Clara had not seen any place nearly as romantic looking—not in Berlin nor on her trip south.

The boatman jumped onto the dock and secured the boat before helping the passengers disembark. Clara and the fisherwoman said good-bye as friends. Because Elisabeth also supplied Lilo's hotel, the Hotel Residenz, where Clara was planning to live, they were certain to see each other again.

In Friedrichshafen, Clara had been preoccupied with organizing the last leg of her trip, and she had seen almost nothing of the town itself. Now, in Meersburg, she took the time to at least gain a first impression.

Clara walked along, struggling with her bags, on the street behind the Gredhaus that led directly into Meersburg. It ran parallel to the shore, and she thought that it probably connected Meersburg with the small villages she had seen from the boat. Shops and restaurants lined both sides of the road, and each one was marked by an artistically decorated sign. "Treiber's Emporium," read one, and "Schönbein's Tobacco" the next. Other signs pointed to stores in the narrow roads that ran off the main street. Charmed by everything she saw, Clara spotted a sign illustrated with a brass-colored mortar: "Weingarten Pharmacy, Turn Right in 100 Feet." That was a good start, at least! Clara wanted to go to the pharmacy right away, but she knew she should get to Lilo's hotel first. She stopped a man walking out of the stationery store and asked where she could find the Hotel Residenz.

"See the gate leading out of the low town back there?" The man pointed along the street. "You'll find the Residenz just past that."

Clara thanked the man. Though she didn't have much farther to go, the handle on her old suitcase was cutting painfully into her hand, so she allowed herself a short break. To stay out of the way of the pedestrians and horse-drawn carts, she stood back against a wall. Massaging her sore hand, she looked up at the castle that she had seen from the boat. It loomed on the hillside above the town gate, an imposing medieval construction in gray stone that dwarfed the buildings around it, all solid half-timbered structures housing shops and businesses at ground level and apartments above. *What an extraordinarily beautiful town,* thought Clara after she picked up her suitcase and started walking again. Everywhere she looked—in front of the windows, in large planters, in green areas between the houses—there was a profusion of flowers. The facades of the houses were painted in delicate pastel tones, and the streets were free of trash, unlike in parts of Berlin. And then there was that scent again . . . It was the same that Clara had noticed in Friedrichshafen, the mixture of seaweed and algae, but with a tinge of fermented grape juice.

On the side of the hill that rose above the shopping street, there were small vineyards in between the houses. Here and there, men were harvesting the grapes. Clara thought of Isabelle with a smile. Then, above the vineyards, her eye came to rest on a huge building. It was not as old as the gray castle, which Clara was drawing closer to with every step, and it had something of a baroque style. The wide facade had been painted in a soft pink hue, while the window frames were gleaming white. It looked like a palace for a princess. Who would live so ostentatiously? And what was inside the equally huge bright-yellow building to the right of it, above and behind her now? That must also belong to very rich people.

The closer she came to the gate of the low town, the more Clara understood how Meersburg was laid out. Through the low town was the shopping street that she was walking along, Unterstadtstrasse, from which several short lanes led down to Seepromenade, an esplanade along the lakeshore with a quay wall that dropped into the lake. Clara looked forward to seeing that, too, but it would have to wait for another day. Above the shopping street was another part of the town, centered around the medieval castle. It looked as if there were more shops and restaurants there, too; certainly, there were several elaborate signs that pointed out the various ways to get up there.

Clara was beyond impressed by the town that was to be her new home. When Josephine had spoken of Meersburg, she had made it sound more like a small fishing village. Clara smiled as she resolved that in the future, she would make up her own mind about things, rather than blindly accepting what others said.

Chapter Eight

Clara saw Lilo's hotel straight ahead the moment she stepped through the gate that led out of the low town. It was a classical-looking structure, painted pale yellow with many tall windows framed by pure-white curtains. It was situated a short distance back from and above the waterfront esplanade. On the lake side, there was a long terrace, which would certainly offer fantastic views over Lake Constance. There were white wrought-iron chairs, tables with yellow tablecloths, and white planters overflowing with flowers. On the other side of the hotel where the entrance was, the last roses of the season were in bloom—also yellow.

Lilo has something for yellow, Clara thought. Feeling a little intimidated, she headed for the entrance, which was flanked by two stone columns. She had never expected anything as grand as this!

With her arms open wide, the beautiful and elegantly dressed proprietress of the hotel came to the entrance to meet Clara.

"Welcome! Welcome! When did we last see each other? It feels like half an eternity . . . back when we were still young and stupid, wasn't it?"

Before Clara knew it, Lilo had wrapped her arms around her in a convivial embrace. "Thank you for taking me in," she said with a smile, overwhelmed by Lilo's greeting. If she weren't at Lilo's hotel,

Clara wasn't sure she would have recognized Lilo, whose hair was cut almost as short as a man's. Clara had never seen a woman with such a daring cut, but Clara thought it suited Lilo admirably.

Lilo swept aside a wayward strand of her wheat-blond hair and grinned. "We'll have to wait and see if you really thank me. I need help in the hotel desperately. Some days, I don't know if I'm coming or going. But don't worry, you'll still have time for the real reason you're here. I've already written down the names of several pharmacists, not only here in Meersburg, but in Friedrichshafen and some other places as well." As she spoke, she waved over a young man. Clara guessed him to be in his midtwenties. He wore a dark-blue suit that he didn't quite fill: the sleeves were hanging loose, and a good hand's width of fabric on each leg was piled atop his shoes. The cap he wore was also too big and had slipped low on his forehead. The young man seemed unconcerned by these things and trotted over eagerly.

"I'd like to introduce Fritz. He's responsible for everything that jams, whistles, and squeaks, which means that if you have any problems with a faucet or can't get your door open, he's your man. He also helps guests with their bags. You'll be living back there in the side wing. Fritz will show you where." Lilo pointed to an extension of the main building that Clara had not noticed earlier. "I have an appointment in a couple of minutes. But if you like, we can have dinner together this evening. Before that, you can take your time and look around." She waved her arm as if to include everything about the hotel. Then she kissed Clara on the cheek and was gone. Dazed and fascinated, Clara watched Lilo glide away. What an unbelievable radiance she had! What confidence! And she was also a divorcée.

Clara's room was large, but the leafy trees growing just outside the window also made it rather dim. The walls were painted a light yellow, which helped a little, and a small, pretty chandelier provided a bit of light. Clara screwed up her nose. The smell of mothballs hung in the air, so she went over to the window and opened it. The fresh Lake Constance air streamed into the room. But as far as she leaned out of the window, she could not see the lake itself.

Her children would not be able to spend the night there, she realized, as she sat tentatively on the single bed, which was set up along the narrow side of the room. But she also had no intention of living in the hotel for very long—the sooner she found her own apartment, the better! And then . . . *One step at a time,* she warned herself.

At least her stay at Lilo's hotel would be no hardship. The mattress was good, the down comforter was light, and the sheets were silky and smooth.

There were two chairs, a table, and a wardrobe. When Clara opened the doors of the wardrobe, a few empty coat hangers clattered against each other. A mirror had been attached to the inside of one door. Clara grinned. In the future, she would have to check what she was wearing half standing in the wardrobe. But it didn't matter! She was about to close the wardrobe door again when she caught sight of herself in the mirror. A world separated her in her traveling outfit from Lilo in her fashionable clothes, but she was satisfied with what she saw. Although the journey had been long and stressful, she looked fresh, and her eyes were practically glowing. At the very least, no one looking at her would see the despairing woman she had been just a few days before.

When she had unpacked everything, she knew that she would feel at home there. The picture frames with the photographs of her children stood on the table, and she had stowed her books beneath the bedside table. She only had to find somewhere suitable for her father's notebook, her mother's jewelry, and her own personal documents.

"I hope you were able to get settled in a little," Lilo said when they were sitting together at dinner a few hours later in the hotel's elegant dining room. Lilo had her own table some distance away from the guests' tables and shielded from them by several tall indoor plants. From there she had a good overview of everything going on in the dining room, but she couldn't be seen, and she and Clara could eat in peace.

"More than that. I can't remember the last time I felt so . . . alive. I feel like I could tear trees out by their roots!"

Lilo smiled, and there was something knowing in it. "That's the lake air. Or maybe just living by the lake; I don't know which. I was just the same when I came here from the Black Forest. I felt so cooped up there."

Clara looked expectantly at Lilo, but she already said what she wanted.

"Can your guests rent a safe or lockbox? I don't know what to do with my personal papers and valuables. Not that I have too many of those," Clara said with a laugh.

"Of course. I'll tell reception that they should let you have a box."

As they ate and talked—Lilo asking about Josephine and Isabelle, and Clara asking about life on the lake—Clara's eyes were drawn again and again to the vista offered by the floor-to-ceiling windows. It was dusk, and the esplanade was lit by numerous lamps. Out on the water, boats bobbed with lights of their own, presenting a particularly romantic sight.

"I've never seen anything so beautiful," Clara murmured, her voice laden with emotion.

Lilo smiled. "There's something magical about the lake. It's no wonder that thousands of tourists come here every year from every corner of the empire. We even get the Württemberg royal couple here every year, and they bring all kinds of nobles with them."

"And they stay in the pink castle up on the hill," said Clara confidently. She knew it!

Lilo frowned. "No. The royal palace is in Friedrichshafen. What you're talking about is the residence of the prince-bishops of Constance. Next to that is what they call the Marstall, the royal riding school and stables. Ha! Here, even the horses live like princes! But don't worry, a few baronesses, countesses, and duchesses wander down this way in the tourist season, too."

"Even here, in your hotel?"

Lilo nodded proudly. "Which I'm very happy about, of course, but I treat every guest with the same importance. But let's talk about you now," she said, suddenly businesslike. "Josephine wrote about what you have in mind. And of course I'll help you any way I can. But if I can give you any advice, it's this: don't mention your divorce at all. One does not have to make one's life any harder than it needs to be."

Clara swallowed hard, surprised by the sudden change of topic and, more so, by Lilo's message. "But the people here will ask about my family. Am I supposed to lie? What happens when it comes out?"

Lilo waved off the objection. "Of course you shouldn't lie. Keeping your mouth shut is more than enough. If anyone asks me about my husband, I lower my eyes and do my best to look sad. And everybody thinks they're looking at a grieving widow. It's as simple as that."

"You make it sound very easy," Clara admitted, looking with admiration at the woman sitting opposite her. Lilo was wearing the same dress she had had on at midday, but she had put on long earrings that glittered golden with even the slightest movement of her head. Clara had dressed up for dinner, but she now saw that, compared to the elegant guests and Lilo, she looked like a frumpy housewife. She might have to spend a bit of her emergency money to buy herself something new.

"All beginnings are difficult. I had to go through quite a lot myself before I understood that pearl of wisdom," said Lilo with irony in her voice. "I can't show my face anymore in the small Black Forest village where Horst and I used to live, not as a divorced woman. The people point at me like I'm some kind of thief or other criminal, though it was Horst who had one affair after another. They give *me* a hard time because *I* got divorced! In society's eyes, the only goal worth striving for as a woman is to be a good wife who quietly accepts anything thrown her way." Lilo snorted in a very unladylike way.

"Is that why you left the Black Forest?" It was so good to be able to sit and talk to someone who had been through similar experiences.

"A new start somewhere else, somewhere where nobody knew me, that was the only chance I had to get back on my feet. Horst owned several sanatoriums for lung patients in the area, and I helped him with the management. So I wasn't entirely unfamiliar with how to deal with a lot of guests in one large place. But if I could avoid it, I didn't want anything else to do with sick people."

"So you came up with the idea of opening a hotel," said Clara with respect.

"Of course, I could have taken my friends' advice and kept my eye open for a new husband. But I wanted to try doing something of my own, to stand on my own two feet and *not* be dependent anymore. Do you know what I mean?"

"Only too well. It's just the same for me." Clara nodded vehemently to underscore her agreement. Spontaneously, she reached out and took Lilo's hand. "You don't know how good it is to listen to you talk. For the first time in I don't know how long, I truly believe that a new start might also be possible for me."

"Lake Constance is famous for new beginnings!" Lilo exclaimed happily, and she raised her glass. "Here's to all your dreams, big and small, coming true. And soon!"

Clara lifted her glass, too. "I don't have big dreams. All I want is to find a job in a pharmacy," she said, and drank a mouthful of white wine. "I feel like going straight out tomorrow."

"No one's stopping you," said Lilo. "Let's do this: What would you say to working for me in the afternoons? That would make it easier for me to plan. And if you go off looking for work in Constance or Fried-richshafen or somewhere else farther away, we'll find a solution. Like I said, I've put the addresses together for you already."

"That sounds wonderful!" Clara beamed. "But you have to tell me how I can help you."

"To be honest, I'd like to be able to throw you in wherever I need you," said Lilo. She swung her chin toward the other tables, where the talk, as the evening lengthened, was growing more and more lively. "Tonight, for example, my head waiter is away, which is why we're eating here and not in my own rooms. Like this, I can keep an eye on everything and intervene if necessary. Last week, I had two chamber-maids fall sick at the same time, and the week before that the girl who helped in the kitchen ran off with the dishwasher." She shrugged. "The more staff, the more headaches. That's just how it is."

Clara raised her eyebrows. "And you trust me to jump in everywhere? I hope I don't disappoint you too much."

Lilo patted Clara's hand. "A mother and wife who can run a doctor's household and his practice? I'd trust someone like that to manage quite a bit."

One of the waitresses served dessert. Clara was amazed that she had an appetite for berries and cream. Food hadn't tasted this good for ages!

"I hope you're happy with your room?"

"Oh, absolutely, it's beautiful," Clara said between mouthfuls.

"That's good, then. All the guests want a room with a view of the lake, and I have no reservations at all in fall for the rooms in back. That will change by next spring at the latest, but by then I'm certain you'll have your own apartment."

"Tell me more, and I'll start to believe it myself!" Clara said. She laughed, but then immediately grew serious again. "You're helping me so much. How can I ever repay you?"

Lilo shook her head dismissively. "If I were the one in need, you'd do no less for me. Or for Josephine. Or for Isabelle. We women have to stick together or we'll go under." She raised her glass a second time. "To friendship."

"To friendship," Clara said, delighting in the bright clink of crystal on crystal.

Chapter Nine

It was her first night in an unfamiliar place, but Clara had slept exceptionally well. She wasn't surprised, given the long journey, all the new impressions. Plus, Lilo and she had drunk a bottle of wine over dinner, and there was nothing that would put you to sleep better than that, was there?

Lilo had asked her to help with a birthday party. A guest from Frankfurt was turning fifty and had invited his entire family to Lake Constance for the event. Lilo wanted to set up a smaller secondary hall where the dinner and music could take place. But Lilo didn't need her until the afternoon, so Clara had the morning to herself. There was no better time to visit the pharmacies in Meersburg, so after a light breakfast, she set off. Excited and happy, she hoped she would be able to find the sign with the arrow pointing to the pharmacy.

The Weingarten Pharmacy was set back in a quiet side street and was built so tight against the old medieval castle that Clara got the impression that the castle had taken the little building protectively under its wing like a mother hen. *Does the sun ever shine through these windows?*

Clara wondered as she swung open the door to the little shop. She could not imagine that living so deep in the shadow of such a towering edifice was particularly pleasant.

A bell rang melodically, and a young man stepped out from behind a curtain. He wore a brown suit beneath a white coat. His brown hair was parted in the middle, and a sparse beard covered his chin. His cheeks were flushed, as if he'd just eaten something hot or completed a stiff march.

"Good morning. May I help you?" the man asked, smiling shyly at Clara.

"My name is Clara Berg, and I am looking for work. My parents owned a pharmacy, and I helped my father all the time, so I'm very familiar with most of the processes." Looking more closely, Clara realized the man was not as young as she first thought, but in his midthirties.

"You are from Berlin, aren't you?" said the pharmacist, a little less shyly than before.

"Is it so obvious?" asked Clara, taken aback.

"I'm originally from Potsdam, myself," the man said with a smile. "And as it happens, I am looking for someone. My wife is expecting, and until now she's been the only one I've had to help me in the laboratory. But in the future, she'll have more than enough to do looking after our child."

The pharmacist laughed, and Clara suddenly felt dizzy—jubilantly dizzy—and joined in his laughter. If it were up to her, the pharmacist and his wife would be blessed with twins!

But the next moment, their laughter was cut by a piercing scream that penetrated Clara to the bone. The pharmacist stood as if paralyzed, his hands frozen on the countertop. When a second scream—or more of a drawn-out moan—came, his eyes widened in panic. "Oh God," he breathed. Then he slumped onto the chair behind the counter and stared into space.

"For heaven's sake, what was that?" Clara asked anxiously.

The pharmacist looked at her as if she had spoken in a foreign language.

Another scream, this one even more animalistic, filled the space.

Clara's hesitation only lasted a moment. Someone needed help, and urgently!

She stepped around behind the counter and pushed the curtain aside. On the other side was a kind of parlor. It was quite small, and it smelled of sweat and damp, moldering washing. This was their living room? Clara had little time for such thoughts, however, for there was a red-haired woman cowering on the one armchair in the room. She was in a more advanced state of pregnancy than Clara had ever seen. Her belly, her fleshy arms, her legs, and even her head looked as if they might burst at any moment. *Not even sturdy twins could account for this woman's condition,* Clara thought. The woman was either suffering from edema or carrying far more weight than was good for her, neither of which would make the impending birth any easier.

"Are you a mid . . . midwife?" the pregnant woman whispered, obviously in a great deal of pain. Her face was a pale as a corpse, her forehead was beaded with sweat, and perspiration discolored the armpits of her blouse. A damp patch marked the floor in front of the armchair. Her water had broken.

"The baby is coming! Where's the midwife?" Clara said, turning back to the pharmacist, who was at least on his feet again and standing in the doorway behind her.

"I . . . I have to send for her," he whispered. "Sabine said it was still a long way off."

Clara had had enough of his helpless stammering. "Go and get the midwife. Your wife needs help, and she needs it fast!" she snapped at the man, who ran out of the shop. She turned back and reached out to the woman with both hands to help her. "Can you stand up? It might be better if we got you into the bedroom."

But the pharmacist's wife only shook her head weakly. "I can't make it." She closed her eyes, and a guttural sound crept out of her throat.

Clara stared at the woman helplessly. She should have been in a hospital! Giving birth here, under these circumstances, was life-threatening. Was there a hospital in Meersburg? And even if there were, the woman weighed at least two hundred pounds. How was Clara supposed to get her to the hospital if she couldn't get her into the bedroom?

Clara mustered every bit of resolve she could. "Where's your kitchen?" she asked, putting her handbag aside and rolling up the sleeves of her blouse. "I'll do what I can to get everything ready for the midwife."

The pharmacist's wife waved weakly off to the right.

The kitchen was just as small as the parlor. How could anyone live in such a cramped place, or more to the point, how could anyone that big do so? At least they had running water. And a small fire was burning in the stove. While water heated in a large pot, Clara found a few clean sheets and hand towels. Back in the parlor, she spread one of the sheets on the floor.

"If you can't make it to the bedroom, then lie down here on the floor. Come on, I'll help you. You'll feel better in a minute." Clara half lifted and half pulled the pregnant woman out of the armchair. When the woman slumped onto the floor, the button on her skirt popped off. *That's good,* thought Clara. "Why didn't you say something to your husband earlier? You could have had the midwife here long ago," she said in a somewhat reproachful voice.

The woman's face, previously pale, now turned an unhealthy red. "How was I supposed to know it was coming? My belly's been bucking constantly for weeks. I only knew this time was any different when my water broke." She burst into tears.

"Don't cry. That will just make you strain more," said Clara, trying to placate the woman. Casting accusations at her now wouldn't help anything.

Clara would never have thought that she might wish to see her ex-husband again, but if anyone would know how to proceed in a situation like this, it was Gerhard. Clara tried to recall whatever she had learned in her years at his side.

"Everything will be all right. Don't worry. Until the midwife gets here, I won't leave you," she said softly. She positioned the woman's head on the pillow that had been on the armchair. It was damp and clammy with the woman's sweat. "You'd better put your knees up; that will help you relax a little. Yes, like that. If you'll allow me to, I'll take your underwear off so that it'll be easier for the midwife when she gets here." Clara's own brow was sweating now. As calm and controlled as her voice might have sounded, on the inside she was trembling and agitated. Blast it, where was the pharmacist with the midwife?

The woman launched into another scream, which rose into a shrill screech, then dropped into a wail. Clara pushed the woman's wet skirt and petticoat out of the way, then she unfastened the thin band that held the woman's underwear at the side. *Out of the way, out of the way!* thought Clara as she struggled to pull the underwear down. She was just pulling them off over the woman's feet when she got the shock of her life: between the woman's legs she could see the baby's head!

Clara withdrew sharply at the unexpected sight, but immediately pulled herself together. She'd come this far, and she would finish what she'd begun.

"The baby is already coming. It all looks good and normal. Don't hold your breath! Breathe, yes, like that is good. Spread your legs a little more. Not together, apart! Good . . . You'll be through it any minute!" Dauntlessly, she placed both hands beneath the infant's head. More and more damp hair appeared, then the ears, then the pressed-together shoulders. Carefully, Clara grasped the baby on each side and pulled a little. The next moment, he slipped out as if it was the simplest thing in the world.

On the brink of crying, Clara looked from the newborn baby to his mother. "You have a boy," she said, her voice breaking. Then she laid the child in the woman's arms, and both women burst into tears.

The very next day, Clara was dressed in a white apron, standing in the freshly minted father's laboratory. The pharmacist had no interest in checking Clara's papers or questioning her qualifications. She did not even have to take Lilo's advice and hint at being a widow. It made no difference to Frieder Weingarten if she was married, widowed, or single. In his eyes, Clara was no less than a heroine. He would be forever in her debt, he told her two hours after the birth when he finally returned with the midwife—he had had to go hunting through the entire high town to find her. By then, Clara had retrieved the afterbirth, cut the umbilical cord, and washed and dressed both mother and child. When the midwife arrived, the pharmacist's wife was lying on the chaise longue in a lily-white nightdress, with a cup of hot broth in her hands. Her baby was asleep in a crib in the next room. The midwife examined mother and child and confirmed that both were in good health. "Well done," she had whispered to Clara before leaving.

Well done? The pharmacist had watched the midwife leave with a mixture of dismay and annoyance. Clara had saved the lives of his wife and his son—that much was clear to him! The very least he could do was repay her with a job. Because she had not completed any official training, she would not be able to serve at the counter or advise customers, but she could certainly work in the laboratory. Besides, perhaps Clara would be prepared to help Sabine out a little now and then? For him, that would be the biggest help of all!

Clara was happy with anything. For her, what mattered most was that she would be working in a pharmacy. If that meant making an occasional chamomile tea for the mistress of the house, she'd be happy to do it.

Chapter Ten

Clara could not believe her luck. She had a job! No, she had two jobs. In the morning, she worked at the Weingarten Pharmacy, and in the afternoon she worked at Lilo's hotel. And she was paid for both, the first money of her own, ever.

The pharmacist specialized in making various kinds of herbal drops and lozenges: cough drops, peppermint sweets, pastilles flavored with fennel and skirret. Mr. Weingarten melted sugar in a large copper pot and added herbs, then he poured the mixture into a press that could be fitted with various molds to produce differently shaped sweets. When the sweets were cool, Clara filled small bags with them and labeled the bags. She was amazed to see how many sweets the pharmacy sold in a day. Among tourists, Weingarten pastilles were considered an insider secret, and they were often bought as souvenirs to take back home. Clara was disappointed to find that Mr. Weingarten made practically no creams or medicines at all, ordering them instead from two suppliers in Munich and Mannheim. How dearly she would have loved to dip a spatula into a pure-white hand cream again or to stir a thick ointment that smelled of chamomile or some other healing herb.

Some days, business at the pharmacy was so slow that Frieder Wein-garten asked Clara to spend time with his wife. Then Clara would do some ironing or cook a light meal, and sometimes she just chatted with Sabine. Once the woman told Clara that she and her husband had tried many years for their child, but even as she rocked her baby back and forth, Sabine did not seem happy. Instead, she was introverted and gloomy, which came as no real surprise to Clara: the young mother had no visitors, and she never left the house by herself. It was as if she were afraid of the world outside. Mr. Weingarten even took care of the grocery shopping, and did so without complaint. This all seemed strange to Clara, and she could not imagine that the air in the little house, with its persistent odor of mold, could be good for the infant. Mother and child were both in urgent need of getting out of those four walls, she felt, after observing them for a good two weeks.

"When I went down to the basement to find something for your husband, I found a baby carriage," she said, flipping the pancakes Sabine had asked her to make. "If you like, I'll bring it up for you. You could go for a walk along the esplanade. The fresh air by the lake would do you and your baby good." The esplanade was Clara's new passion. Ever since she had discovered the pretty street with its restaurants and cafés, she strolled there every day, enjoying the view over the water, feeding the ducks, and people watching.

Sabine looked at her in utter horror. "But I don't know my way around here at all!"

"What do you mean, you don't know your way around here?" Clara frowned in bewilderment. Mr. Weingarten had told her that he had spotted the advertisement announcing the sale of the Meersburg pharmacy in the *German Pharmacist* magazine three years earlier. The Weingartens no longer had any relatives in Potsdam, so without much hesitation and backed financially by a small inheritance, they had embarked on this adventure. "You've been here almost three years. You must know Meersburg inside out by now."

Instead of answering, Sabine tore off a piece of pancake with her fork, smeared it with marmalade, and stuffed it into her mouth.

"If you went for a walk, you could stop somewhere for a cup of coffee and a piece of cake." Clara hoped that the mention of coffee and cake might shake the woman out of her complacency.

"Go into a café? I couldn't do that." Sabine Weingarten shook her head vehemently. "Oh, no. I still don't understand half of what the people around here say. Don't you think the southern dialect is terrible?"

Clara, who loved the soft sounds of the local vernacular, said nothing. She flipped another pancake onto Sabine's plate. "Then wait until your husband closes up in the evening and you can take a walk together. The early autumn evenings are still lovely."

Sabine Weingarten laughed loudly. "My husband is happy to get away from the Meersburgers after he closes. The carriage was his idea, and not one of his best, if I may say so."

Clara gave up. To all appearances, neither of the Weingartens were interested in getting involved with their new home.

It was another gorgeous Sunday morning. Things were still quiet in the hotel, but Clara, an early riser, had been awake for two hours. Instead of getting up, she lazed in bed and read *The Sisters* by Jakob Wassermann. The book had been published that year and told the stories of three women—Johanna von Castile, Sara Malcolm, and Clarissa Mirabel—who, Clara thought, were at least as different from one another as she, Isabelle, and Josephine. The sun splayed golden bands across her bedspread and illuminated the open pages of the book. Clara sighed contentedly.

Gerhard had never liked to see her with her nose buried in a book. "If I'd wanted an intellectual for a wife, I'd have looked for one," he said—at best. On bad days, if he caught her with a book, his reaction had been far more violent, so Clara had limited her reading to when she was alone in the house. She read books that she had pilfered from her father's bookshelves, wanting to find out more about salves and tinctures, chemical formulas, and medicinal compounds. Just as secretly, she had used Gerhard's name to borrow specialized books from the library and thus had learned about human digestion, circulation, infections of wounds and their treatment. Once, she had discovered a book about dermatology; that had excited her a good deal! Beauty care in ancient Egypt, in India, Japan, France—Clara had wanted to keep the book, like so many others, forever. Instead, she had laboriously copied the most interesting passages into a notebook that Gerhard had bought her to manage the housekeeping. Some Sundays, when he was home and she could not pick up any other book, she had—undisturbed by Gerhard—leafed through her "housekeeping" book until she had committed many of the passages to memory.

Being able to read without fear—that was a special pleasure in her new life. Admittedly, the hotel library with its large collection of light, entertaining novels and women's magazines was not exactly to her taste, but the small library in the high town had a good selection of literature, and that was where she had found the new Jakob Wassermann.

Clara did not know from where her thirst for knowledge, her hunger to learn new things, came. Was it because her desire to study had been slighted by Gerhard and her parents? There were days when she still dreamed about going to university, but she was realistic enough to know that that would forever remain a dream. She was thirty-two years old and hardly a woman of means. Her children were her priority, and for them and for herself, she needed financial security and a place of her own.

Around eight, Clara was sitting in the hotel dining room with a handful of other early risers. The lake gleamed a pale morning blue, and there were not yet any boats in sight. A few seagulls turned in lazy circles in the sky, searching for fish for breakfast. Clara still could not say which time of day by the lake was loveliest. The early morning hours, when the world was still as if made for her alone? Or the evenings, when the lake and its people settled down again? Clara turned away from the floor-to-ceiling windows, determined to write the letter to Josephine that she had been putting off for so long.

As the dining room slowly filled, her pen fairly flew over the stationery decorated with delicate roses that she had treated herself to. Her arrival at the lake, Lilo's hotel, the unexpected way she had landed her position in the pharmacy . . . There was so much to tell!

> . . . the work in the pharmacy is certainly not particularly demanding, but I am enjoying it immensely. Though the Weingartens, I have to say, are a little strange. They have lived here for three years but have practically no contact with any of the local people. Poor Mrs. Weingarten is so lonely and unhappy that she is constantly gorging herself. But I doubt she really finds any consolation in that . . .

It was unlikely that Josephine would ever meet Sabine Weingarten, so Clara did not feel guilty for writing so candidly about her employer.

> In any case, I have decided not to be like that at all. Whenever the opportunity presents itself, in the hotel or on my walks around the town, I try to talk with the people. The Meersburg locals are so friendly and engaging that I feel at home here, although I cannot claim to have made any real friends yet. I miss you so much, dear Josephine!
>
> I am therefore all the happier to be with Lilo. She doesn't have time for long chats over coffee, of course, but I am learning so much from her. Like you, Lilo is a wonderful businesswoman, and it doesn't bother her at all if

I look over her shoulder a little. I'm starting to think that she only assigns me the best and most interesting tasks. Yesterday, for example, I helped her write invitations for the end-of-season party. And the day before, she had me tie up small bouquets and lay them in the guests' rooms. Once, I spent an entire day in charge of reception. You can imagine how nervous I was, but Lilo said she knew I would manage everything fine.

Dear Jo, I am gradually coming to believe that everything can turn out well for me. But for that I first had to travel to the other end of the empire. If you had not been so insistent, I would not be here today, dear Josephine. I will always be grateful to you for that. For the first time in my life, I am earning my own money. That is such a good feeling . . .

Smiling at her own words, Clara read through what she had written. She could not believe herself how her life had turned around in the few weeks she had been in Meersburg. To get a job in the first pharmacy she visited—she would never have dreamed it possible.

Of course, I miss my children above all else, but I have to be strong. At the moment, there is little I can do about Gerhard and his court orders. It is for the best that I concentrate on creating a secure livelihood for myself and . . .

Clara looked up when a shadow fell across the stationery. It was Lilo, standing beside her with wet hair and a towel over her arm. "May I join you?"

"Of course," Clara replied happily, and turned to wave over the waitress. But the girl had already seen her boss and hurried over with a breakfast tray specially prepared for Lilo: an apple cut into slices, a slice of lightly buttered brown bread, and a cup of tea. No wonder Lilo was slim!

Lilo nodded in the direction of Clara's pen and paper. "Another letter to your children? I will bet that your ex-husband intercepts every one of your letters and that the children haven't read a single line you've written."

Clara's expression darkened. "I fear you're right . . ." To distract herself from the depressing thought, she pointed to Lilo's wet hair. "Is something broken in the bathroom? Did you take a quick wash in the lake?"

"I was swimming," Lilo said matter-of-factly.

"You were what?"

"Since I don't have the time for cycling anymore, I go swimming every morning. Half an hour, or an hour if I can spare it. After that, I feel fit for the day," said Lilo, and took a hearty bite from her slice of bread. "But I was a bit late getting out today. Normally, I make sure I get back into the hotel unseen."

Clara was speechless. She didn't know a single woman who could swim. And Lilo talked about it as if it were the most obvious thing in the world.

"But how do you know how . . . I mean, swimming is not exactly safe. The lake is very deep, I've been told. Aren't you afraid of going under?" *And what if a fish started to nibble at you?* The thought made Clara shudder.

"Go under? The water holds you up. You float in it. It's a fantastic feeling!" Lilo laughed. "I've got an idea. A little exercise would do you a world of good, too. You spend all your time working, reading, and writing letters, and that's not healthy. You need exercise and fresh air! And swimming is really very easy."

"Oh, for heaven's sake, I'm the least athletic person in the world!" said Clara, horrified. "Just think of my first attempts to ride a bicycle. I fell so badly that I broke my leg." If it hadn't been for that accident, she never would have found herself in the hospital and probably never would have met the young doctor, Gerhard Gropius. Her life would have been completely different.

"Cycling was simply the wrong kind of sport for you," Lilo said resolutely. "But swimming is harmless, and you don't have to be athletic to do it. Besides, why else is the lake there? The water is still nice and warm, and you have to make the most of it while you can." She lifted her cup of tea as if proposing a toast to Clara. "Bright and early tomorrow! Six o'clock at the gate on the terrace, the one that leads to the shore."

***

What am I doing here? Clara asked herself while she stood shivering at the agreed meeting place, a towel over her arm, at six o'clock on the dot the next morning. She had to be at the pharmacy at nine, so she could still be curled up in her toasty bed.

Patches of thin fog drifted across the lake, and she could only make out the Swiss shore as a distant hazy line. A light breeze blew over the water, and it was decidedly chilly. Clara pulled her cardigan a little closer. So cold, and she was supposed to get undressed and go into the water? She didn't even own a bathing suit! And she was afraid of the lake . . . Why had she let Lilo talk her into such a silly idea? She wanted to go back inside.

But just then Lilo appeared, striding along and wearing a huge smile. "We have to go to the right," she said by way of a greeting, and off she marched before Clara could even object.

After just a few hundred yards, the well-made path that followed the shore away from the Hotel Residenz petered out into nothing. Here, tall reeds and other water plants lined the water's edge and made it difficult to get through. The path trodden through the reeds by Lilo and perhaps other walkers was so narrow that the women walked single file. Clara's cardigan was constantly getting caught on reeds poking out into the path. *Might as well throw it away as soon as I get back,* she thought grumpily. And whenever a water bird, disturbed by their passing, flew out with a shrill cry from among the clumps of reeds, she jumped. Her mood grew worse and worse. She could not see how anyone could freely submit themselves to such tortures every single morning.

After a ten-minute march, the reeds thinned out and they came to a small bay. Lilo stopped and threw her arms out wide. "My very own beach!"

Gravel crunched under Clara's feet and glittered colorfully in the light from the rising sun. Instinctively, she crouched and picked up a singularly lovely gravel stone. It felt warm and smooth in her fingers. Small waves sloshed onto the shore, almost as if they were stroking it.

"It feels as if we're the only people on earth," Clara whispered almost reverently. How warm it was there, where the sun didn't have to fight the breeze. How silent and tranquil.

The magic of the moment was interrupted abruptly by Lilo, who said, "Come on, get undressed! You can swim naked if you want. No one can see us here."

Clara looked at Lilo aghast. Naked? She had never in her life undressed in front of another person. Not even Gerhard. "I'd prefer to keep my petticoat on, if that's all right," she said with embarrassment.

Lilo shrugged. She undressed, piled her clothes together neatly, and deposited them at the edge of the little bay. Then, stark naked, she stepped into the water.

"You can go out a good thirty feet here and the water will only be up to your chest, so you don't need to worry. Come on, we don't have all day."

With her face turned away toward the reeds in mortification, Clara took off her clothes. But Lilo was not looking at her. With powerful strokes, she was already swimming out into the lake.

Clara dipped one toe in the water to test it. She was surprised to find that it was almost warmer than the air, and so clear that she could see the bottom. Lilo was right—it wasn't very deep there at all. Clara took a few steps forward and, a moment later, was standing knee deep in the water. Small waves lapped at her petticoat, which clung wet and heavy to her legs. Maybe she would feel better when she was wet all over? Screwing up all her courage, Clara crouched, but when she was completely enveloped in the water, she realized that it was, indeed, quite chilly. Her heart beat harder. It all felt a bit scary.

Before her anxiety could get the better of her, Lilo appeared beside her. "Really, swimming isn't hard at all. Look, you move both arms like this . . ."

Clara watched her friend carefully. It didn't look too difficult. With her feet still touching the bottom, she tried to do the same as Lilo.

"Very good! Now all you have to do is take your feet off the bottom and paddle them up and down in the water, like this."

Clara, encouraged by her initial success, tried to imitate the way Lilo tread water. Clara lifted her left leg. The right stayed on the bottom like lead. And if she raised her right leg first, and then the left?

"I don't trust myself!" she cried out, giggling hysterically. "Can you still swim if you're standing on one leg?" If she rowed strongly with her arms and hopped along the bottom with one leg at the same time . . .

"You're not a stork, silly! If you want to swim, you need both legs, so get those shanks up!" said Lilo with a laugh. Then Clara felt Lilo's hand against her stomach. "Don't worry, I'll hold you. Now give it a try."

Clara had no choice but to overcome her fear and lift both legs. When she could no longer feel the firm lakebed underfoot, she let out a little yelp of fear, but Lilo's hand held her up securely, and Clara relaxed again. Rowing with her arms, paddling with her feet, and being supported by Lilo, Clara crossed the width of the little bay. Before the water got too deep, Lilo turned around with her, and Clara "swam" back. She tried to say, "This is fun," but as soon as she opened her mouth for the first word, she swallowed water.

"Well done! You're a natural at this," said Lilo when they returned to their starting point. Then she let go of Clara, who immediately poked around for the bottom with her feet. "Now do it without me."

Clara hurriedly paddled with her arms back toward shore. "Isn't that enough for today? You already said that I did well for a beginner."

But Lilo shook her head.

It took a very long time before Clara dared to lift her second foot off the bottom of the lake. But finally, after a lot of frantic squealing, splashing, and swigs of lake water, she managed to do it.

"Now swim! Swim, go, move!" Lilo spurred her on.

And Clara moved. At the start, her arm movements were as hectic as the kicking of her legs. But to her own astonishment, it wasn't long before her movements became smoother and more deliberate. She didn't have to splash like a madwoman to stop herself from going under. The water supported her as Lilo's hand had before.

"This . . . this is amazing!" she said, then coughed out a mouthful of water.

Ten minutes later, both women were back on the shore. Clara felt as exhausted as if she'd just spent hours shoveling coal. Her arms were shaking, and her legs felt like jelly. Yet at the same time, she felt a sense of happiness she had never known before. She actually swam in Lake Constance!

Laughing, she wrung the water out of her hair with both hands. "My skin feels as soft as a baby's," she said in astonishment.

"That's the lake water. It's a blessing not only for the skin, but for your well-being generally," Lilo explained as she pulled on her clothes.

For Clara, however, it was a struggle to get out of her wet petticoat before she could get her dress on again. "Next time, I'll go without my petticoat," she said, but more to herself than to Lilo, who just smiled.

Respectably dressed again, they stood for a moment longer and looked out over the water, where boats were starting to appear. Fishing boats, but also passenger ferries and a pleasure steamer, its wake churning into large waves. The magical hour in which the lake belonged only to them was over.

"Thank you," said Clara softly. "Me and swimming—I never would have thought it possible. If you don't mind, may I come with you another time?"

"What are you talking about?" Lilo frowned. "Swimming is something one should do regularly. The best thing for you would be to swim every day. All the way into November, by the way. The water will get colder week after week, but that will toughen you up! And it frees your head for new acts of courage."

"New acts of courage? It took all the courage I have just to come to Meersburg, thank you."

Lilo laughed out loud. "That's what you think! The lake air doesn't just free one's mind; it makes the people around here downright feisty. You'll surprise yourself."

Chapter Eleven

In the last days of September and into October, Clara settled more deeply into her new life. Along with her work at the pharmacy and the hotel, Clara went swimming with Lilo in the early morning and passed the evenings reading, with the exception of one night a week. On Wednesday evenings, she went with Elisabeth Kaiser, the fisherwoman she had met on the boat, to sing in the church. The choir was in urgent need of new voices, Elisabeth had said one day as she delivered a supply of trout to Lilo's hotel. Lilo had immediately begged off—too much work. But Clara had no excuse, and to her astonishment she discovered almost as much pleasure in singing as in swimming.

By mid-October, many guests had departed, and the town grew quiet. The steamboats that carried passengers across the lake almost hourly in summer shut down for the season. The lake turned gray, and only fishing boats dared the choppy early-morning waters. After a week of steady rain, the lake had become distinctly chilly. Driftwood and weeds floated on the rough surface, and the bottom of the lake was only occasionally visible. Clara had to steel herself to get into the water, but within a few strokes she was overcome by the feeling of happiness she felt the first time she went swimming with Lilo.

Every morning when the two women met, they were accompanied to their bay by a sense of wistfulness. Would today be the last time? At the start of November, it came. "That was it for this year," Lilo announced when they teetered out of the water, covered in goose bumps again. For better or worse, Clara agreed. In recent days, it had taken her a long time to feel relatively warm again after bathing in the lake.

"I'll miss the swimming," Clara said.

"What about going for a run instead?" Lilo immediately suggested. "You'll certainly be warm enough, and you'll stay fit, to boot."

In her own way, Clara took up Lilo's idea. Dressed in her coat and with a wool cloth wrapped around her ears, she went walking every morning: up to the vineyards, along the paths that led through the reeds, or along the esplanade by the lakeshore. Walking like that, taking in the sweeping views across the lake, she felt a calmness, a peacefulness, fill her. Day by day, she felt freer, and she allowed herself thoughts that she had subdued for a very long time. Who was she really, when it came down to it? For many years, she had been the good daughter of Sophie and Anton Berg; she had said and done everything they had asked of her. Then she became the wife of well-known gynecologist Gerhard Gropius and suffered at his hands. And finally, a devoted, self-sacrificing mother. And now? Who was she today, here and now? What was inside her? That was hers to find out.

It was a drab November day, the kind of day that didn't want to brighten at all, when Clara unlocked the door to one of the guest rooms overlooking the lake. Although it was only three in the afternoon, she switched on the light. Erika, the chambermaid who normally cleaned the rooms in this wing, was in bed with the flu, so Lilo had asked Clara if she could jump in. Of course Clara had said yes. It wasn't many rooms, and neither the guests nor Lilo minded that she could only tend the rooms in the afternoon.

Calm had settled over the Hotel Residenz, too, and of the forty rooms available, only ten were in use—regular guests who, for various reasons, spent the winter by the lake. One was a writer who wanted to finish the book he was working on in peace and quiet. There was an elderly couple there to escape the bitterness of the Black Forest winter. And there was also an older woman visited often by a Swiss gentleman, who usually stayed the night—Lilo and the workers in the hotel turned a blind eye and went about their business.

Clara had no idea what had moved the woman whose room she was currently cleaning to come for an extended stay at Lake Constance. Besides, she had other things on her mind. The pharmacist's little boy had spent the entire morning coughing piteously. This did not surprise Clara in the slightest. The old house wasn't warm enough now that winter had come; despite a fire burning in every room, an unhealthy, cold, damp climate prevailed. The baby needed to see a doctor urgently, Clara had advised his worried parents. But instead of doing that, the pharmacist had cooked up a cough mixture of honey and ribwort that he and his wife had then administered to the child. After that, Clara had not voiced her opinion that it would definitely be for the best if the young family were to find a more comfortable apartment. *Was that a mistake?* she wondered now, as she wiped invisible dust from the white-lacquered dresser with its makeup mirror. Should she have been more insistent with them? They were both extremely unworldly in the most everyday matters. A small pot of cream beside a comb and brush atop the dresser caught her eye. "Healing ointment," it said in black letters on a yellow label. "White lead, camphor, lanolin, and other ingredients," she read on a smaller label on the back. *Strange mixture,* she thought, then her thoughts returned to the Weingartens. Maybe it was better if she said nothing. Who was she, after all, to give well-meaning advice to other people?

The next moment, her thoughts were abruptly interrupted when the room door swung open.

"Don't let me disturb you," the woman said to Clara. She was around seventy years of age, and she wore a shawl around her shoulders and felt slippers. "We're playing bridge in the library, and I'll be gone again in a moment. I just came up to put on a spot of cream." As she spoke, she opened the pot of cream on top of the dresser and dipped her right index finger in. Then she lifted her hair away from the back of her neck.

"Stop!" Clara cried as she saw the woman's neck, the now-exposed skin covered with pustules.

The woman paused.

"I do beg your pardon." Clara paused, embarrassed. "But with your skin condition, that cream is far too strong. You need something gentler, with mild ingredients." A chill ran through Clara as she spoke, but her face flushed hotly at the same time. What in the world had gotten into her? Just this morning, she was lecturing the Weingartens, and now she was laying down the law for Lilo's guest!

The woman looked from the daub of cream on her finger to Clara and back. "And how would *you* know what is good for *my* skin?" she asked in a haughty voice.

"I'm the daughter of a pharmacist," Clara whispered. "My father was an expert in all kinds of healing creams. I learned some things from him. Camphor is indeed good for reducing the swelling of an abscess, and your skin certainly seems a little swollen, but more than anything else, it is irritated and inflamed. The camphor and the white lead in that cream will only make the problem worse. I . . . happened to see the label." With every word Clara spoke, her confidence grew. These were things she knew something about.

The women scrutinized her for a long moment. Then, with her clean hand, she took a handkerchief out of the dresser and wiped her smeared finger clean. "You may be right. Since I've been using this cream, the spots *have* gotten worse. My neck itched so much last night it nearly drove me mad."

Clara exhaled with relief. If she were lucky, the woman would not complain to Lilo. "I work in the Weingarten pharmacy. If you explain your condition to Mr. Weingarten, I am sure he will prepare a good cream for you."

The woman picked up the cream pot and dropped it in the trash basket. "No, young lady, I have a much better idea. Because you seem to understand these things so well, *you* can prepare a cream for me." She turned to face Clara directly and planted her hands on her hips. "Now when can I expect this wonder balm?"

Clara had never before cleaned the hotel rooms as fast as she did that day. And all the while, as she wielded her dust rags and buckets, her mind rattled and clattered as if a procession of steam trains were rolling through it.

It was nearly five thirty in the evening when she finally pulled off her apron, put on her street shoes and jacket, and hurried up the alley to the pharmacy. When she threw the door open, Mr. Weingarten was already busy tallying up the day's revenue. He looked up in surprise. "Mrs. Berg! Is everything all right? No problem at the hotel, is there?"

Clara shook her head vehemently. "No, everything is fine. It's just that—" She broke off with a frown. In all her haste, she had not actually thought about what to say. How would Mr. Weingarten react to her request? Would he be angry? The pharmacist was still watching her. Clara took a deep breath.

"I would like to make a cream. I need a few ingredients."

"What, exactly?" Mr. Weingarten replied, as if her request were perfectly normal.

Clara felt a load lift from her heart. "Well, I thought of white wax as the base. Then I would need almond oil, a few drops of genuine chamomile oil, and rosewater." As she spoke, the pharmacist made some notes. "And if you have it, spermaceti!" she added. Spermaceti was a fatty substance obtained from the head of sperm whales. It added a pleasing coolness to a cream—but it was not an ordinary ingredient. Although Clara had been working in the pharmacy for two months, she had no idea what they had on hand. Only Mr. Weingarten had access to the pharmacist's cabinet, where he stored all the ingredients for the medications he produced. He had already started rummaging through the drawers in search of what Clara needed. "You're in luck; it's all here," he said, setting out an array of bottles and receptacles on the counter. "May I ask what kind of ointment this is supposed to be?"

"Not an ointment, but a cream. It's for one of the guests at the hotel. The woman has irritated skin, and I thought of a soothing, delicate cream that would still allow the skin to breathe. We talked this afternoon, and when she found out I was a pharmacist's daughter . . . of course, I recommended that she come here. But she insisted that I prepare the cream for her myself." Clara shrugged apologetically.

"So it's not an ointment for healing as much as a cosmetic cream." The pharmacist waved dismissively. "My dear Mrs. Berg, in your free time, you can do whatever you want. And if one looks at the matter conscientiously, your background *is* in the profession. Besides, the manufacture of creams and ointments was never my favorite métier, which is why I specialize in lozenges and the like."

Clara sighed. "Thank God. I thought you would be angry with me." She smiled sheepishly.

"I could never be angry with you," Mr. Weingarten declared emphatically. "If you would like, you are more than welcome to use my laboratory. You only have to promise me that you will never breathe

a word about it to anyone, because—regrettably—you have never officially trained as a pharmacist, after all."

"That would be wonderful!" Clara exclaimed. "And I promise I'll
leave everything as clean as a whistle." She had envisaged herself working in the hotel kitchen between the soup pots and sinks.

"Who says I'm going to let you work alone?" said Mr. Weingarten
with a smile. "If I may, I would gladly look over your shoulder. Maybe
I can learn something myself!"

Clara carefully melted the wax in a glass beaker over a very low flame
until all of it had turned into a translucent liquid. Later, when it cooled,
it would take on its white color again and look like freshly whipped
cream. Next, using a glass spatula, she mixed in the almond oil, then
added the spermaceti, and finally the rosewater.

"You do that so deftly, as if you did nothing else all day," said
Mr. Weingarten, standing beside her.

Without looking up from her work, Clara replied, "My father prepared cosmetic creams for my mother for most of his life. I learned
everything I know from him. The creams you normally buy are often
very thick and heavy, and they smell bad. For my mother, at least, they
were not good enough. But my father's creams were light and cool and
smelled marvelous. Then, when I—" Clara broke off abruptly. *Good
heavens!* She had almost given the game away and told Mr. Weingarten
that she had prepared creams for herself when she'd been married! "I
helped my father make creams until his death, so I really can claim a
little skill," she said instead, although it wasn't entirely true. Without
doubt, Gerhard would have given her a piece of his mind, or worse,
if he had caught her in her father's laboratory. No, she had prepared
creams for her own use secretly, in her kitchen, when her husband was
out of the house.

Clara squinted hard, as if by doing so she could rid herself of the memories. Then she lifted the beaker and waved the rising fumes to her nose. The rosewater was clearly there; it was the merest hint, but it was all the rose she wanted. "Maybe a little lavender? Or maybe chamomile would be better?" she murmured to herself.

A moment later, Mr. Weingarten handed her two small dark-brown bottles. "Lavender oil and chamomile—but don't use too much oil or the cream will separate."

"True. And that would be a waste of these precious ingredients," said Clara, then added one drop from each of the bottles to the beaker. The perfume immediately took on a note of lavender and chamomile. "This preparation is my father's own recipe, and I've followed the quantities precisely. The components should come together nicely," she said, stirring the mixture carefully. The cream maintained its delicate consistency and now exuded a warm, full scent.

"Done!" said Clara, and turned the flame off.

That night, sleep was a long time coming, but Clara's sleeplessness came from exhilaration, not worry. Again and again, she turned over in her mind the way that she had mixed the cream. It had been delightful to work with all the fragrant, fine ingredients. It had made her feel very close to her father again. And being able to work in Mr. Weingarten's laboratory had been exceptionally helpful. What a wonderful man! Instead of sticking his nose in—as she herself was always doing with him and his wife—he had simply looked on curiously, apparently quite enthralled by the whole process.

Suddenly, Clara could no longer lie in bed. She jumped up and crossed to the table where she had left the pot of newly made cream. The container itself was white milk glass and looked very pretty. Clara had not even known that Mr. Weingarten possessed such pretty jars. The pharmacist had just shrugged and said that his predecessor had left behind boxes of them. "He probably used them for his ointments," Mr. Weingarten speculated. "But they're not much good for my pastilles."

Almost reverently, Clara unscrewed the glass cap. The white cream would practically melt on her skin. She wanted so much to dip her finger inside and try a tiny daub on the back of her own hand. But she resisted the temptation, of course. When she gave the cream to Lilo's guest the next day, it had to look flawless.

She screwed the lid closed again, then went to the cupboard and opened the door with the mirror.

It would be her birthday in a little more than a month. She was a Christmas child, born on December 24, almost thirty-three years earlier. Her skin was still that of a young woman of twenty. Unblemished, unlined, not even the smallest hint of a pimple. And very pale, as well. She had never had to douse herself in stinking rice powder or some other whitener to conform to the porcelain-pale ideal of beauty. Other women were not as blessed, especially those who were naturally red-cheeked, or who had freckles or a tan complexion, and who did everything they could with this or that cream to cover up their flaws or get rid of them altogether.

Slowly, Clara pulled her nightdress off over her head. Since she had begun swimming with Lilo, she was more comfortable naked than she had been before. Her legs were still rather thin, but swimming in the lake had added some muscle. Her waist, too, was as slim as a young girl's. Compared to the rest of her petite body, her breasts, which had nourished two children, were large and heavy, but passably firm. Would a man ever see her like this? With Gerhard, it had been enough for her to take off her underpants for sex. Any more than that had made Clara exceptionally ill at ease. Slowly, she stroked her right hand over her breasts, and her nipples puckered pleasantly at the touch. Would a man ever touch her like that? A shiver ran down her back. *What strange thoughts you have . . .* She quickly climbed back into her bed before she was chilled through.

Chapter Twelve

The next morning, Clara knocked on the elderly woman's door. The woman didn't answer. She was among the early risers, Clara knew, and was probably already at breakfast. A little disappointed, Clara took her master key, opened the door, and left the cream on the dresser.

It seemed that almost everyone in Meersburg had caught a cold, and the town's year-round residents descended on Weingarten Pharmacy in droves, looking for decongestant, cough medicine, and throat lozenges. At the hotel, too, the guests were sniffling and coughing. Clara had a sympathetic word for everyone, and she brought the guests various medications to soothe their symptoms.

"I've noticed that you get along well with the guests," Lilo said over dinner one evening. "What would you say to working for me full-time? As my manager, you would be a second point of contact for the guests, and that would be a great relief for me. I might even be able to go off traveling myself for a few days."

Clara was surprised by Lilo's offer, and she was thrilled to be asked. Still, she did not accept immediately but promised Lilo that she would think about it. Her work in the pharmacy, although not exactly what she had dreamed it would be, was still a source of pleasure for her. She wasn't sure about simply giving it up.

Between the illness and the turnover of hotel rooms as some guests left and new ones arrived to spend the new year at the lake, there was quite a lot of hustle and bustle. So Clara was happy and surprised when, a few days later, the woman for whom she had prepared the cream came up to her during dinner and embraced her and kissed her on both cheeks in front of all the other guests.

"Look at my skin!" she exclaimed so loudly that even those at the farthest tables could hear. She yanked off the scarf she had wrapped around her neck against the cold. "No more sores, no more redness. With a complexion like this, I could star on stage at the Royal Theater!" She laughed louder than anyone at her words.

Clara could hardly believe her eyes. It was true: the woman's skin was flawless! And she was smiling from ear to ear.

"Thank you a thousand times," said the woman, shaking Clara's hand emphatically as if she would never let go. "Now, please, you must tell me what this wonder cream costs so I can finally pay you for what you've done."

Clara reddened. She hadn't given a thought to the price, and had no idea at all what the ingredients or the container cost. Mr. Weingarten had simply said that he would deduct the total from her next paycheck.

"Well, it's like this . . . ," Clara said tentatively.

"Mrs. Berg will leave the bill in your room sometime today," said Lilo in a businesslike tone. She had observed the exchange from some distance and was now standing beside Clara.

Clara gave Lilo a grateful sideways glance. Just then the older woman who received regular visits from the man from Switzerland approached them. "Excuse me, young lady."

"Yes?" said Lilo with a friendly smile.

The woman looked at Lilo politely for a moment, then turned to Clara. "I couldn't help but overhear your conversation, and you have piqued my curiosity. If you were to cast your eye over my skin . . ." With an exaggerated gesture, she pointed to the countless fine lines that framed her eyes and furrowed her cheeks.

Clara nodded vaguely. "Your skin is mature, of course. A little dry, but otherwise it looks healthy to me. You should use a face cream every day, though. That will bring a new suppleness to it."

"I would do just that, my dear, but until now I cannot claim to have had any good experiences with face creams." Clara raised her eyebrows, prompting the woman to continue. Lilo and the guests were all listening.

"One smelled very peculiar, and another just would not spread very well. A third made my cheeks feel like they were on fire! But at my age, I think another attempt is perhaps worth it. So, to be perfectly honest, I would also like to try a wonder cream like that."

"And I'd like another ten jars of it to take home with me!" said the first woman.

Clara was suddenly so dizzy that she looked around for something to support herself on. "But I don't even know if I can find the time for it. Things are so busy in the pharmacy, all the cough medicines and pastilles and—" She stopped when she saw the elderly women's disappointed expressions. "All right," she said, raising both hands in a gesture of surrender, "I'll prepare the creams after hours."

"You look so cheerful," said Elisabeth Kaiser to Clara when they were walking together through Meersburg the following Saturday. Over the previous weeks, Clara and the fisherwoman had started to become friends, and they sometimes went for coffee together, as they did today. Clara wanted to use her day off to buy Christmas presents for her children. She thought it might be best to send them to Josephine and to ask her to give the gifts to Matthias and Sophie. A pair of white stockings and a doll for Sophie, and for Matthias a book about airships. She would write a short letter to go with it and mention that she had already seen a number of zeppelins herself.

"I'm feeling fine," said Clara, and her voice carried a trace of amazement. The first Christmas without her children—shouldn't that make her feel wretched? But her good cheer came from knowing that everything she did was for her children. For a future together. Her gaze moved from the lively esplanade to the lake and back again. "I can hardly believe that it's been just three months since I arrived. Before I came here, I was miserable, utterly miserable! I thought everything was over forever."

Elisabeth nodded sympathetically. Like most people, she believed Clara to be a widow. True, Clara had never spoken about the death of her husband, but no could fault her for that.

Clara's eyes shone as she went on. "I never would have dreamed that everything could turn for the good in such a short time. Three months ago, I had no work, and now I have so much that I can hardly keep up with it all. Half the day in the pharmacy, the work in the hotel, and I'm producing my creams on top of everything." She shook her head as if she could hardly believe her luck. "Someone wants a cream for rough elbows, another for her cracked lips—my room is starting to look like a laboratory." She laughed.

She had begun to make the creams on the table in her room. Mr. Weingarten had obtained the equipment she needed for her concoctions: various containers for melting and mixing, a scale, a Bunsen burner, and jars for the finished product. He had offered her the use of his laboratory, but Clara had no intention of exploiting his kindness. Her creams, after all, were not ointments intended to heal, and they were not sold in the pharmacy, so she felt it was better to separate the two. Besides, Clara didn't want the pharmacist to find out just how much she was now producing.

"I never expected anyone to come to me for advice," said Clara. For years, all she had heard from Gerhard was how stupid she was. In the end, she believed it herself. And when she had gone looking for work, she had heard again and again that women were worthless when it came to working in a pharmacy. But now, suddenly, the things she said mattered.

"I'm not surprised at all that the women are lining up to see you," the fisherwoman replied and held out her hands to Clara. "Look. All the painful cracks in my skin have healed! I put up with them for years, and then you came along and whipped up a cream for me, and suddenly my hands are normal again. I'd wager that if you had a stand at the market, your creams would be sold out in half an hour." She hooked her arm in Clara's amiably. "And now I'd like to invite you to a glass of sparkling wine. What is it they say? Celebrate when you can."

"My friend Isabelle says that all the time," said Clara with a laugh, and together they entered a small café.

An hour later, the two women went their separate ways. Elisabeth went to visit her parents and Clara to buy the presents for her children. Who would have thought that she'd ever drink sparkling wine in the middle of the day, Clara mused happily as she walked to the small store where she had seen the pretty stockings for Sophie. When she bought them, she treated herself to a yard of purple lace. She would sew it carefully to the collar of one of her older dresses. So far, she had spent hardly a cent of her two salaries, and while she could certainly afford a new dress, she could not so easily shake off the thrift that Gerhard had hammered into her for years.

She was on her way home when a sign over a door on Höllgasse Lane caught her eye, suspended perpendicular to the facade. "Coiffeur," it read, and there was an illustration of a pair of scissors and wild swirls that might have represented curly hair. Was the shop new? Or had she simply not noticed it before?

Curious, Clara peered in through the front window, which was arched at the top and flanked by two light-green shutters. A young woman was cleaning brushes in soapy water. She had red-blond hair pinned close to her scalp, but Clara could see no customers. She hesitated a moment longer, then stepped inside.

"Good morning, I—"

"You'd like a wash? And a fresh trim, perhaps a nice hairdo?" said the hairdresser eagerly before Clara could say another word. "I can even dry your hair with this. It's the latest thing, look!" Hastily, she hoisted a metallic, dangerous-looking piece of equipment into the air.

Clara laughed and nodded.

"You couldn't have seen my shop before, because I've only been open a week," the young woman, who had introduced herself as Therese Himmelsreich, explained. "But *I* have been to the pharmacy where you work, several times. I get my soap from Mr. Weingarten, but it does have rather a strong smell, unfortunately. But I've never seen you in there, either."

"I work in the laboratory," said Clara. "I don't have any contact with the customers at all."

"That's a pity," said the hairdresser. "As pretty and charming as you are, I think the customers would love to see you behind the counter."

Clara blushed. Pretty and charming?

"I don't have anything to do with making the soap, either," Clara said. "If I did, the soaps would have a delicate perfume of lavender or roses, as they used to at my father's pharmacy. I have been making some creams—the sort I also learned from my father."

Once Therese had washed Clara's hair in a large porcelain basin, she set to work with her scissors. "Not long ago, I was a chambermaid for a

Flemish countess. She and her husband always spent their summers here at the lake, and that's how I first came here." She took a step back and scrutinized her work through narrowed eyes. She seemed satisfied, then went back to snipping and chatting. "The villa my employers rented in Friedrichshafen was a dream. But then the count started looking at me, and that was less dreamy. And, idiot that I am, I didn't say no, though I knew full well it would only cause trouble." The hairdresser underlined her words with a particularly furious bout of snipping at the back of Clara's head.

Clara, worried, looked in the mirror, but her hair was still below her shoulders.

"What had to happen . . . happened. I got pregnant. And suddenly, the fine count wanted nothing to do with me anymore." The hairdresser shook her head indignantly.

Clara was speechless. She had never in her life heard a woman speak so openly about such things. But everything about Therese Himmelsreich was unique. Every word she uttered, every gesture she made showed an appetite for life and highlighted her untroubled, easy spirit. In the winter light falling through the window, Clara saw that Therese's red-blond hair was as fine as the fluff of a newborn chick. With hair like that, it would have been impossible to create an elaborate hairdo or fancy braids, but Therese had done the best she could with it. Clara smiled. What was the old saw? The cobbler always wears the worst shoes . . .

"And then?"

"He threw me out. Before his darling wife found out anything about his 'lapse,'" said Therese in a sober voice. "At least he was decent enough to pay me a good severance. It held me over while I figured out a new way to make a living. It took a little while, but now I've opened this shop with the rest of his money. There, finished," she said, and laid down her scissors with a flourish.

"But your child? Where is . . . I mean . . ." Clara bit her lip. "Excuse me, it's none of my business." Just because Therese was so open about herself did not give Clara any right to go asking questions like that.

"I lost the baby after just a few weeks," said Therese, and she shrugged indifferently. "That was not good. Very sad, really, and I did cry a little, of course. But I had to move ahead."

After that, they stopped talking because Clara's head was engulfed in the hot air that swirled from the howling hair dryer. Five minutes later, when the torture was over, Clara was more than relieved.

"Abominable machine," said Therese as she put the heavy device down. "But very helpful." With quick movements, she began to arrange Clara's hair. She paused now and then to explain what she was doing. "If you twist your hair like this and then pin it, you can do this chignon yourself. If you ask me, it's far more elegant than the old-fashioned bun you walked in here with. See for yourself!" She held a mirror behind Clara's head so that she could admire herself from all sides.

Her hair had taken on a beautiful luster, and having her hair pulled up gently at the sides showed off her fine cheeks to advantage.

"You have magic in your hands," said Clara admiringly.

"Tell that to all the women you meet, please. Then my little shop here will be booming," laughed Therese.

While the hairdresser swept up the hair, Clara remained in the chair a moment longer, thinking. She had worn a chignon like that once before, when she had visited Isabelle in Champagne. It had not been a very happy time . . .

"What's the matter, Mrs. Berg?" Therese asked, and her water-green eyes widened with concern. "Don't you like your hair like this?"

Clara stood and rested one hand soothingly on Therese's arm. "Don't worry. I was just thinking of something, and it made me sad."

"Well, if you're looking for something to cure sadness, come to me," Therese said, looking Clara in the eye. "I know from experience that it does not pay to spend long brooding on things. Life is far too beautiful for that. Maybe you should think about opening a place of your own. You could make and sell your lovely soaps and creams. Then you'll have no time left to think about sad things." She looked at Clara critically. "You don't need to be someone's helper any more than I do."

"Me? Self-employed?" Clara let out a shrill laugh as she surveyed the inside of Therese's parlor. Looking at it more closely, she could see that the place was scantily equipped. One hairdresser's chair, a basin on the wall, the monstrous hair dryer, and a shelf on which stood various shampoos and dyes. Was that really all one needed to be a hairdresser? *That and magical hands,* thought Clara, wondering if she had her own kind of magic. In a brittle voice, she asked, "How has business been?"

"Up to now, pretty slow. At the moment, I'm paying out more than I'm making," Therese admitted openly. "Either the women of Meersburg have their hands full getting ready for Christmas, or they're not vain enough to think about getting their hair done. My job is to convince them that prettifying themselves is worth it!"

Clara laughed.

"Come next spring, when the tourists arrive, I'll have my hands more than full," Therese went on. "I know that the king of Württemberg and his royal retinue spend summers at the castle in Friedrichshafen, but many noblemen rent villas in the surrounding towns. Here in Meersburg, too."

"My friend Lilo owns the Hotel Residenz, and she told me that there are several high-society guests who stay there," Clara said. "If you like, I could promote your shop a little at the hotel."

"That would be wonderful!" Therese grasped Clara's hands. Clara was thrilled at the mutual pleasure of their meeting.

With her hand on the door handle, Clara let her eyes roam the room one more time before she walked out. Seen from the door, Therese's hairdressing counter and equipment mostly occupied the left side of the shop, but to the right, the place was essentially empty, and the two large show windows in front were undecorated. In fact, the space was far too big for what Therese was doing with it . . .

Chapter Thirteen

"You want to *what*?" Lilo, sitting across her desk from Clara, looked at her with surprise.

Clara had burst into Lilo's office as soon as she had returned to the hotel. There was no one she would rather share her idea with than Lilo!

"Open a shop for my creams. A . . . shop of beauty," Clara said, not sure what else to call it. She felt the heat in her cheeks, but she wasn't sure if it was from her excitement or from the icy west wind she'd walked against. "I could officially sell my creams. The hotel lobby has been lucrative, but I know it can't work as a salesroom in the long term." She could not stop smiling. "I'll offer soaps, as well—delicately perfumed soaps. I learned how to make them when I was a girl. And face lotion. A small selection to start with." Clara was so excited that she had to take a deep breath before she could go on. "Therese thinks that the women in Meersburg aren't very particular about beauty care, and that one can't expect to make a fortune, but that business will pick up nicely when the tourists come back in spring. That's what I'll be counting on, at least."

Just moments earlier, on her way to Lilo's office, she had been approached yet again about her creams. The young pianist that Lilo hired for the holidays wanted to take a jar home to his mother in the new year.

"Who is this Therese, again?" Lilo asked. "And exactly where is this business of hers?"

Clara told her all about Therese Himmelsreich's hairdressing shop and how it had more than enough room to house a second business. "An amazing coincidence, isn't it?"

"Therese seems to know her trade, at least. Your hair looks fantastic," said Lilo, then she stared off into nothingness for a moment.

Is she thinking about it, or angry at me? Clara wondered. "I haven't talked with Therese about it, yet. Nothing's been decided . . ."

"Not yet," said Lilo. "But now I'm looking forward to paying a visit to the new hairdresser's, where your wonderful creams will also be on sale." She broke into a broad grin.

Clara felt a weight lift from her heart. "So you're not mad at me? Not mad that I have to turn down your manager offer?"

Lilo stood up, strode around her desk, and threw her arms around Clara. "Nonsense, I'm happy for you! This is a huge opportunity, take it from me. Haven't I always told you that the lake opens your mind to new ideas? I just didn't think it would happen to you quite so fast. Congratulations!"

"I can hardly believe I'm thinking so fearlessly," said Clara a bit later as they sat in the restaurant, celebrating Clara's plans with a glass of champagne. "I'll talk to Therese tomorrow. I just know she'll be happy to have me move in and share the costs of the place with her."

"You're starting to sound just like a businesswoman. Who would have thought?"

Clara soaked up Lilo's admiration. "There's something else," she said slowly. "If I really start the business, I don't think I'll be able to work for you anymore, not even on an hourly basis. But can I keep on living here? I'll pay, of course! And it would only be until I find a small apartment of my own."

"Oh, don't worry about that. The wing you're in has to be renovated before I can rent the rooms. And I won't start with that until the middle of January, at least."

Another load off Clara's mind. "How much would the rent be?"

Lilo waved one hand dismissively. "If you let me have one of your creams now and then, we'll call it good. I know the place on Höllgasse Lane, by the way. The building itself belongs to Alfred Schrott, one of the town councilors. He's one of Meersburg's honorable citizens, but I find him extremely disagreeable." She shivered.

Clara looked at her inquiringly, but instead of explaining her remark any more, Lilo said, "It's a nice place, and well situated, if not exactly a prime location. There used to be a fabric store there. It belonged to Alfred's wife, Lydia. She had wonderful fabrics. Look, I bought this velvet from her." Lilo held out one arm to Clara, who felt the sleeve of the night-blue dress between her fingers. "But it was no fun to visit her shop. Mrs. Schrott is grumpy and miserable all the time, and she seems to think she has to take it out on somebody. It was enough to put off even her most patient customers. She had to close up shop completely a year ago because the Meersburg women preferred to go to Friedrichshafen than put up with so much unfriendliness."

"*I* plan to be friendliness personified. It's all about giving good advice, if you ask me. So I'll be telling my customers precisely how to use the products and—" Clara stopped when she realized it was far too soon to think about such details.

"You can hardly wait, can you?"

Clara shook her head. "I really can't. The only thing that really worries me is telling Frieder Weingarten."

"Then why don't you keep the job in the pharmacy a little longer? Now that winter's here, it's very quiet by the lake. As you've said, it might be slow until spring."

"Maybe you're right," said Clara thoughtfully. "But I feel like I've already wasted so much time in my life that I *have* to focus on the shop now, and there is so much I need to do to get ready to open. Don't ask me where this sudden impulse comes from. I don't know. But . . ." She faltered, searching for the right words. "It *feels* like the right thing to do. Do you know what I mean?" She would still offer to help Mr. Weingarten in an emergency.

Lilo smiled. "I know *exactly* what you mean," she said softly. "Here's to your shop of beauty!" she said then, more loudly, and lifted her glass of champagne.

"To the shop of beauty," Clara repeated. The clink of crystal was the most exquisite music to her ears.

The next morning, Therese was just opening up when Clara went hurrying up the hill. She had been so excited the night before that she had hardly slept. Now, out of breath and with a tremor in her voice, she laid out her plan to the hairdresser.

"That is the best idea I've heard in a long time. If one of us has to run out for a minute, the other can keep an eye on the store. That's good for both of us," Therese said, and she hugged Clara gleefully. "When did you want to start, Mrs. Berg?"

Clara felt dizzy with relief. "Tomorrow?" Therese nodded, and Clara stepped back and held out her hand. "And please, call me Clara."

***

The weeks that followed were exhilarating and exhausting. Frieder Weingarten accepted both her departure and her promise to help if needed with good grace. And even without the work in the pharmacy, Clara was on her feet from early morning to late evening, every day, setting up her half of the shop. The first thing she did was hire a carpenter, Mr. Bastian, who constructed a kind of wooden screen at the back of Clara's section. She would set up a work area behind the screen where she could mix her creams and tinctures without being disturbed. Clara also had him build a partition in the center of the room. Therese's hairdressing studio was on the left side of the partition and Clara's realm was on the right, so each woman could attend to her customers privately.

When the carpenter had finished his work, Clara painted the walls on her side in a pale lavender that Meersburg's only professional painter mixed especially for her. She was exhausted from the physical labor, but when she stood back to inspect her handiwork, the room looked so airy and feminine that she imagined she already had the scent of lavender in her nose.

That evening, Clara and Lilo had a moment to enjoy a glass of wine together, and Clara was eager to describe the carpentry and the new paint. "I am so pleased with how it's turning out. Now I just need some sales counters and a few shelves to show off my products. And I was thinking that a small table and two chairs would be ideal for a customer who prefers to sit during her consultation."

"My storeroom is filled to the brim with furniture that we don't need in the hotel anymore," Lilo said. "Maybe you can find a shelf or something else for your shop? Most of it is a little worn, I'm afraid, but with a bit of pepping up . . ."

Clara didn't hesitate. Later that evening, she found Fritz just as he finished repairing a small leak and asked him to unlock the large storeroom for her. There she found the furniture stacked to the ceiling. Ignoring the dust and the sharp stench of mothballs, Clara rummaged through the narrow aisles, and Fritz helped move things around, pointing out a cupboard here, a shelf there. Two large shelves with peeling gray paint, a sideboard with broken panes of frosted glass, a pair of small tattered armchairs, and a round table with a turned base—Clara was pleased with her loot. No doubt the painter could tell her how to strip the old paint from the shelves. Then she would repaint them in a muted lavender. And she would reupholster the armchairs . . .

"Fritz, do you know what that is?" She pointed to something green on top of a high cupboard.

Fritz frowned. "No idea. Let's take a look." He climbed onto a chair and began to tug at the green object that had been wedged between the cupboard and the ceiling. The next moment, layers of green fabric came tumbling down on top of them.

"Whoops!" Clara laughed, then kneeled to examine the rolls of fabric more closely. It was a ribbed material, a light shade of lime green, and creased and crumpled from being poorly stored. Clara's eyes gleamed as she smoothed it with her hand. "Do you think Lilo would let me have this, too? I'd even pay her for it." If she reupholstered the dainty armchairs with this fabric, the lime green would complement the lavender walls perfectly. And maybe she could line the interior of the sideboard with it also.

"I'm sure the boss has no use for that old stuff. Besides, she said you could pick out whatever you wanted. Why don't you just take all the rolls with you? If you like, I'll bring everything up to Höllgasse Lane in a cart."

"You'd do that for me?" Clara gave Fritz a grateful smile. "What would it cost?"

"A jar of your cream for my fiancée would be plenty!"

***

With her right hand wrapped protectively in an old rag, Clara smashed the damaged panes of glass out of the old sideboard. Then she carefully put the shards of glass in the trash. She was pleased with her handiwork: the sideboard was far more appealing without the frosted glass. Next, she held up the material she had used to reupholster the armchairs. The green background would show off her white glass jars to their fullest advantage, so she set to work measuring and cutting the fabric she would need. She had always been good with a needle and thread, and she had an eye for color, cut, and form—in her old home, she had made all her own clothes and her children's. Considering how tight Gerhard had been with the household money, she had had no choice. She never would have guessed that the skills she honed as a housewife would come in handy for something like this.

"That's going to be very nice," said Therese, who had come up behind Clara. "If you have any of the green fabric left over, you could use it as a liner for the basket where I keep my curlers. Then they wouldn't rub on the willow so much."

Clara replied with a noncommittal nod. *I wanted to reserve the green-and-lavender color scheme for my side of the shop,* she thought, a little put out. If she did line Therese's basket, then she would do it in a different color. But she had enough to take care of for her own shop first. "If I want to open just after the new year, I really have to keep at it over here," said Clara, but more to herself than to Therese.

"So, what are you going to call your shop?" Therese asked while she buttoned her coat.

Clara paused with the scissors in mid-snip. "A name? You don't think 'beauty shop' is enough?"

Therese screwed up her nose. "It's not exactly an elegant name, my dear. I don't call myself a hairdresser; I'm a *coiffeuse.* I think the French lends it a certain *je ne sais quoi.* Just some food for thought." She checked her hat in the mirror to make sure it was sitting perfectly, then said, "I'm off for the day. One of my customers has invited me to a concert at her house. A good opportunity to meet interesting people and spread the word about my business. See you in the morning!" With a friendly wave, Therese disappeared through the door.

Clara glanced at the clock that hung over the entrance. It wasn't even three in the afternoon. "What if someone comes in?" Clara called after Therese, but she was already too far away to hear.

Clara frowned. It wasn't the first time Therese had left early or gone off in the middle of the day—whether to accept an invitation to coffee, try on some clothes, or take a ride with her admirer, who picked her up in his horse and carriage. Clara did not find that behavior businesslike; for her own shop, she would keep regular business hours.

She had just finished with the first section of the cabinet when the bell over the door jangled. Clara was worried it was one of Therese's customers, who would be disappointed the hairdresser was gone for the day. But when she turned around, she saw a man whose belly was so rotund that it preceded him by a good foot and a half. *This is all I need,* Clara said to herself.

"Well, I go away for a week and look what happens."

"Mr. Schrott, already back from your trip?" Clara forced a smile. He *would* show up just then, when she was all by herself.

It was the second time that she had met the owner of the building. The first time had been ten days earlier, when, with Therese at her side, she had gone to see him about sharing Therese's shop. The Schrotts lived in an apartment directly above the storefront. Mrs. Schrott had not been present at that first meeting, and Mr. Schrott had looked Clara over from head to toe; his probing gaze had made her extremely uneasy. "What could I have against having not one but two pretty women as my tenants? As long as the rent comes in on time," he had said before laughing loudly.

Therese had joined in with his laughter affectedly, while Clara stood beside her, feeling unsure of herself. She could not claim to find the man very agreeable, but she was glad that he had not objected to their arrangement.

"Don't worry about him," Therese had said dismissively when they were outside the Schrotts' stuffy apartment. "He's always spouting hot air like that. Just try to ignore him. And his wife, too, if you possibly can. Lydia is an old battle-axe, I can tell you! She sticks her nose in here every day, wanting to know and see everything. I bet she even has a key and pokes around here at night."

Clara had grinned at that. But she had still chided Therese: "Just don't be rude! We have to get along with our landlords."

Therese had merely shrugged.

"I hope that wall isn't permanent." Mr. Schrott strode to the partition and shook it. "Aha, freestanding."

"Just like the screen at the back," said Clara. "We're handling everything very carefully, don't worry."

"It doesn't surprise me at all that a fine woman like yourself has caring hands," said the landlord. "Maybe I should have you take care of *me* a little, when everything here is done?" He snickered and stroked his bulging belly lecherously.

Clara smiled painfully. She hoped she would never have much to do with him.

Chapter Fourteen

"My God, did you empty every drawer in the Weingarten Pharmacy? That must have cost a fortune," said Therese the next morning when she looked behind the screen. Clara had outfitted her laboratory with a chemist's scale, glass beakers, stirring rods, wooden spatulas, scientific thermometers, a mortar and pestle, and various other implements.

Clara, wearing a pure-white apron, smiled ruefully. "It did. But I can't make creams or soaps without this equipment. Let's hope the investment pays off." She knew she sounded confident, but that wasn't how she felt. After the equipment had been delivered the previous afternoon and she then spending hours arranging everything, she had lain awake half the night, fearful of her own courage—but she was excited, too. And then she had come in at eight in the morning, before it was even properly light, to get started on her products.

"What are you making first?" Therese asked, her eyes roaming Clara's workbench.

Clara smiled. "Soap! The stuff you can buy in the pharmacy or a department store isn't what I'd call a delight." The corner of her mouth turned down. "My soap will have the most delicious perfume and will foam luxuriously. Rose, lavender, peppermint—if you'd like a particular scent, let me know," she added.

"You really sound like you know what you're about," said Therese, honestly impressed.

Clara set to work opening a large brown package. "This is the base for all kinds of soap. I ordered it specially from Scheu & Müller's soap factory in Berlin," she explained. "Look!" She pulled back the last layer of wrapping paper, and a large whitish block appeared.

"It already looks so silky smooth! So fine and pure, much nicer than anything Mr. Weingarten sells." Therese reached out to touch the block of soap, but Clara pulled it back out of reach.

"Please don't. When you make cosmetics, hygiene is always first and foremost. I've already disinfected my hands with alcohol." She turned back to her base soap and carved off about a third of the block, then divided that into smaller pieces again. Clara was not sorry to see Therese—expecting her first customer—retreat to her side of the shop. As much as she liked the hairdresser, at that moment she wanted nothing more than to be left completely alone. Would she remember every step in the process? Strangely, she felt quite certain that she would.

She felt a lump forming in her throat as she looked around at all her collected tools and ingredients. She had never believed that, after all these years, she would once again be able to do this. Without warning, she felt herself transported back through time.

She had been a young girl, perhaps twelve or thirteen years old, when she had helped her father in his laboratory, and often in secret so her mother didn't catch on. Sophie Berg preferred to see Clara doing fine embroidery or crocheting curtains, something more appropriate for a young girl. But Clara was much happier helping her father make soap in his laboratory—where no one other than the two of them was ever allowed to set foot.

"Did you steal the mincer from Mama's kitchen?" she had asked him one afternoon as he screwed a similar device to his workbench. It was the first time that she had been allowed to help him make soap.

"Now why would I do that? No, this little device is for making my pharmaceutical soaps and nothing else. It's a kind of grinder, and it turns the raw soap into small chips. Watch!" Anton Berg picked up a few chunks of soap that Clara had cut and pushed them into the opening. Then he put the metal lid in place and began to turn the handle. Small white flakes dropped into the glass bowl at the other end of the machine.

Clara had watched in fascination. "Can I turn it?"

Anton Berg had furrowed his brow. "Your mother would put me out on the street if she knew I let you do this. You can help with the measuring. We need four pounds of raw mass for forty bars of soap, and then we mix the medicinal additives into it."

While Clara weighed the crumbled soap, her father pulled out another machine, far bigger than the grinder.

"This is called a rolling mill. Without it, you can't make perfect soap. After I've mixed the soap chips and the additives, I put the mixture in here, at the top."

Clara had watched in silence as her father worked. So many steps, just to make soap! Until then, she had not given much thought to her father's work. She never could have imagined how much fun it was to mix an ointment. Or how wildly her heart would beat when the water and oil portions of a cream bonded together. And that her hands, so often jerky and impatient when made to do embroidery, would be so calm when cold-mixing a salve. But as a girl she already knew this was her world. She could already see herself wearing a white coat and standing behind a counter, asking customers what they wanted, giving them advice. She had pictured herself studying at university to become a pharmacist.

But her mother had had other plans. She didn't want her daughter to waste her life studying. She wanted her to be a good wife, with everything that implied: marrying well, a pretty house with a *bel étage*. Then, at the right time, two children, and a nanny to help her look after them. And one or two girls as servants, of course. A good life in the better circles, that was all.

The doorbell jangled when Therese's first customer entered, jolting Clara out of her memories. "Mother, if only you knew . . . ," Clara murmured, her tone ironic.

***

Christmas came and went. On Christmas Eve, Clara sat with the other guests in the hotel dining room and sang the old, familiar Christmas songs. It was her birthday, too, and with the holiday, she couldn't have been more lonely. She missed her children terribly, of course—so much so she cried in her sleep that night. But Josephine had sent her a small card that both Sophie and Matthias had signed, and that helped, at least a little. It seemed that Josephine had managed to get on the good side of Gerhard's new nanny. She was able to visit the children occasionally and then report to Clara later. She had also managed to give Clara's Christmas gifts to them.

Being so busy during the holidays was a help, and Clara spent the days between Christmas and New Year's with final preparations for opening her shop. Lilo had advised her to send a personal invitation to all the wives of the town dignitaries. The mayor's wife. The priest's wife. Count Zeppelin's chief designer's wife. So Clara had bought lavender-colored writing paper in the stationery store and sent the invitations Lilo had suggested. She also sent invitations to Josephine in Berlin and Isabelle in France, but, sadly, neither could come. Josephine could not get away from her own business, and Isabelle hated the idea of traveling so far in the winter. But she had sent Clara two crates of champagne. *For your grand opening! I will open a bottle myself and raise a glass to your success,* she had written in a card, words that had warmed Clara's heart. Where would she be without her friends?

It was the seventh of January. The night was clear and bitterly cold, and at eight thirty in the morning, the land around Meersburg still shivered beneath a layer of frost. The lake was dark gray and still, and small ice floes had formed along the shore in places where the water was particularly shallow.

Clara buttoned her lavender dress with feverish haste. Then she put on the lime-green lace collar she had embroidered during the holidays. Lime green and lavender purple—the colors of her brand.

She was checking her hair one last time when there was a knock at her door.

"Ready?" Lilo asked as she stuck her head into Clara's room.

Clara nodded and said, "I am so happy you'll be giving me a helping hand today." Her mouth was dry with excitement and she could hardly speak.

Lilo sniffed dismissively. "Giving you a helping hand? I'd much rather be there for your first triumph! A grand opening on January 7, 1907!"

Arm in arm, the two friends made their way up Steigstrasse. "I can hardly wait for spring to get here so I can finally go swimming again," said Lilo, and every word ascended into the chill winter air like a little cloud.

"How can you even think about swimming today?" Clara laughed. "I'm so cold, I'm wondering if I should serve hot punch instead of champagne."

They had just turned into Höllgasse Lane when Clara pulled up short. Lilo, her arm still hooked into Clara's, was forced to stop as well.

"I don't believe it," Clara whispered, and she pointed to the crowd gathered in front of the shop: a throng of women, chatting excitedly and all in their finest dresses, among them several guests from Lilo's hotel. "Have they really all come to see me?"

Even Lilo looked surprised.

"Come on, we really have to get a move on," said Clara, who took a step forward, but Lilo held her back by her sleeve.

"You have to explain one thing to me. How in the world did you come up with that name? It's very pretty, I admit, and it fits perfectly, but it's certainly unusual." She pointed to the sign that hung directly beside Therese's: "Bel Étage" was printed in white letters on a lavender background.

Clara laughed gently. "It's a long story. But, in a nutshell, my mother always wanted me to live in a big house with a *bel étage*, a lovely second floor with a drawing room or a library, perhaps a music room. Unfortunately, I'm not much good on a grand piano. But now I *do* have a Bel Étage."

"It smells so good in here!"

"I'd like a jar of the face cream."

"What's this light-green one for?"

"Would you have something for the crow's feet around my eyes?"

"Oh, what gorgeous jars you have."

"Champagne? So early? Don't mind if I do!"

Although Clara, Therese, and Lilo did what they could, they were unable to answer every question. The crush was simply too great. When Frieder Weingarten arrived to offer Clara his congratulations and, simultaneously, to hand over some things she had ordered, the chaos was perfect.

Elisabeth Kaiser, who came carrying a bouquet, took in the situation at a glance. "Where can I put my coat?" she asked Clara, who nodded frantically toward the back in response. As if she had done nothing else her entire life, the fisherwoman then took over with the champagne, opening one bottle after another. She rinsed the used glasses and poured fresh ones for newcomers.

Clara glanced appreciatively at Elisabeth before turning her attention to a customer asking for advice about the little red veins traversing her cheeks. "I don't have anything in stock for that today," Clara said politely. "But perhaps you could come by again at the end of the week? I can make a special facial toner just for you by then."

The woman's cheeks grew a shade redder as a joyful smile spread across her face. "I'll be back; you can count on it! And for today I'll take one of the small jars of cream and a bar of soap."

"While you're there, I'd like half a dozen bars of soap. The lavender scented, please!" added another customer.

Around twelve, the landlord's wife put in an appearance. She looked more bad-tempered than ever, the deep creases framing her mouth even deeper than usual.

"This noise is too much, really. I can hear the clomping around upstairs," said Lydia Schrott, and she looked around Clara's shop with envy. "Just once, I would have loved to find a crowd like this in my fabric shop."

Clara laughed. "It's just because it's opening day. I'm sure things will quiet down tomorrow," she said. Then, from a shelf, she took a jar of cream with a delicate vanilla perfume and handed it to Lydia. "For you. To make up for the inconvenience."

Without a word of thanks, Lydia took the jar and left the shop.

"There isn't a cream in the world to save a face as pinched as that," said Lilo, who had followed the exchange.

Clara waved it off. "There isn't anyone or anything that can ruin my good mood today," she said, then she picked up two champagne glasses.

"We haven't even drunk a toast yet!" she said, holding a glass out to Lilo. Laughing, they raised their glasses to each other and took a sip, but the next moment, Lilo had to go back to her duties at the register.

Clara took a moment to look around. Beside her, the mayor's wife was testing a hand cream, and she sighed with pleasure when she smelled its rose perfume. At the front window, Elisabeth Kaiser smoothed a peppermint-scented lotion onto a townswoman's temples, both of them talking excitedly. Another woman gathered up several pots of cream and marched over to the cash register.

Clara smiled. If things continued like this, she would have to start making new stock that very evening. Then she filled her mouth with Isabelle's turn-of-the-century champagne.

Chapter Fifteen

Northern Italy, autumn 1907

It was not the people themselves that Roberto loathed more with every day he and his brother traveled. It was their smell. The smell of poverty. Of hunger, decay, disintegration. It was wearing him down more and more.

He had been in business as a *caviè* for five years, which meant traveling every fall, September to December, and always with his brother, Michele. He didn't know if it was the same for his brother, but Roberto had learned to recognize every odor in the small, cramped huts they visited. It made no difference where they roamed—Veneto, Trentino, or the Po Valley. There was always the warm stench of chickens or rabbits in a kitchen corner, awaiting their day of slaughter. The fetor of damp shoes and jackets, the rancid stink of goat bones and potato peelings boiled too many times. Fumes from a fireplace with a chimney that drew badly or barely at all. Soot-blackened walls spattered with cooking grease. The miasma of too many bodies sleeping, making love, having babies, and dying in confined spaces. Bare tabletops rank with beer and fat. Full diapers. Oily, unwashed hair. The men who lived in those huts reeked. Their coarse, pocked skin gave off a stench of unwashed asses, of piss, of farting, of semen. None of it made much difference to Roberto. As soon as he and his brother knocked at a door, the men retreated, as if they did not care about the sacrifices their wives and daughters made. As if they did not want to see how close the good-looking brothers came to their women.

For Roberto, that moment—when he laid his hands on a woman—was a moment of both triumph and sorrow. And it was about to happen again, because they had arrived. A smell that had nothing to do with filthy clothes or sooty huts found its way into his nose. It was the smell of the women themselves. The sour tang of armpit sweat, the metallic residues of fresh or dry menstrual blood, scabbed skin oozing decay.

The cheap soap the women used did little to make the patchwork of odors more bearable. Now and then, he met a woman who still gave off the scent of youth. Or perhaps the lingering perfume of lilies of the valley was just from a nicer soap a lover had given her some time ago. Roberto was tired of thinking about such things.

From inside, his gaze wandered longingly out through the small, grimy windows, where, above the summits, the sun shone and the snow draped a virginal veil over the ridges and mountains of the Piedmont. So much beauty out there. Yet here the people seemed locked in, almost as if buried alive.

Michele impatiently cleared his throat, drawing Roberto out of his thoughts. Roberto looked at the group gathered around the open fire, and four pairs of eyes looked back, expectant and fearful. Three daughters, aged from eighteen to twenty-four, and their mother. Roberto guessed the woman was no older than forty-five, though she was as careworn and haggard as an old *nonna*. It was the mother who spoke first.

"Do women give up their hair in other villages, too? Just like that?"

Roberto and Michele nodded in unison. "The women are happy to be able to earn money in a simple, honest way," said Roberto. "Hardship is everywhere, *signora*. Please believe me when I say that no one must feel ashamed of that. Poverty has many faces, but none as beautiful as those here in your house." He insinuated a bow to the three daughters, who giggled in embarrassment at the gesture.

"We pay good money," Michele added to entice the women. He cast a quick glance at the father of the three young women. He was sitting in one corner, smoking his pipe in silence by the stove. A woman's hair was a woman's concern. But the mention of easy money was never out of place if the man of the house was present. "Money you can put to good use. Enough to buy some sacks of rice or rolls of cloth. Tools. Shingles to fix the roof. New shoes, lamp oil . . .You know best what to spend your money on." With an extravagant motion, Michele pulled something shiny out of his bag. "But such practical matters aside, why not a beautiful necklace for the *signorine*?" He dangled the necklace of Murano glass beads seductively before the daughters' eyes, then he put it in the oldest daughter's hand. Instinctively, he and Roberto had already identified her as the one they needed to convince; the other two took their cues from her.

"Necklaces like this are in style all over Italy right now," Roberto said, underscoring his words with a pompous flick of his hand. "We've heard many a young woman say that with all this glitter, the men now only look at her bust, and not at her tatty old dress. Hiding one's poverty is an art in itself, isn't it?"

The three young women cooed over the necklace, and even their mother glanced furtively at it. Then they took turns putting it on and rolling the glass beads with their fingers.

Roberto leaned back on his hard chair. He had all the time in the world. A hut as full of daughters as this farmhouse in a remote corner of Piedmont was a rare gift. The only other locations with so many women in one place were the gloomy nunneries high in the mountains. More often than not, all the brothers found in the houses they visited was an old woman. Of course, they still took her thin gray hair, but they could earn far more with the beautiful tresses of young women like those in front of them now! Best of all: two of them were ash blond, the most popular color of all.

The oldest daughter, a stalwart, pretty woman with thick dark-brown hair, handed the necklace back to Roberto. "But isn't our hair also a jewel that we can wear with pride?" she asked with an undertone of defiance, and she ran one hand over the thick braid pinned close to her scalp.

Roberto nodded slowly. "The most beautiful jewel of all. And because of that, we pay so well. Ten lire for one braid, imagine that! So much money, so easily," he said almost devoutly, as if impressed himself.

"And hair grows back quickly," Michele added. "When we come back in two or three years, you'll have it all back. And in the meantime . . ." Once again, he dug into his bag, this time retrieving a stack of colorful cotton headscarves with different patterns. "In the meantime, you simply wear one of these as a headdress. A gift from us."

The mother and her daughters exchanged a long look. "If we were to agree . . . what will become of our hair?"

That was the moment when Roberto knew that they had won. As if reading Roberto's mind, Michele said, "We've got them," in Occitan, the old language of Piedmont, a language hardly anyone except the hair traders still understood. It was the secret language of the *caviè*. Roberto glanced at him, annoyed: don't unsettle these three beauties any more than they already are. He looked at the women with large, honest eyes.

"First, we take all the braids we've bought to Elva, our hometown. It's a small village high in the Maira Valley," he explained. Experience had taught him that the more information he gave, the more trustworthy he appeared. "Then my sisters and my mother sort the hair by color and length. And then we sell the hair to a dealer, who sells it to wigmakers all over Europe." His expression grew concerned as he said, "Not every woman has been as blessed by God as the three of you. You have inherited your mother's beauty. Other young women are heir to more than a hooked nose." He made a face and formed an extra-large nose with his right hand. The three young women and their mother giggled. "Others have large warts on their faces." He tapped one finger at his cheeks and forehead. "And the worst thing of all is that some women are not only ugly, but also have practically no hair on their heads at all. Their husbands revile them and call them 'baldy.' They are beaten and humiliated, and many are abandoned by their husbands."

The women were watching Roberto curiously, but he also could see there was some satisfaction: there were women in this world who were worse off than they were, there, on their little farm.

Roberto looked for the words to really put the icing on the cake, but nothing occurred to him, and Michele, too, was silent.

Instead, rather weakly, Roberto finished with, "Those poor women are endlessly grateful if they can buy a wig. But for that they need women like you, who are prepared to sacrifice their hair."

"You would be doing something good, and earning a lot of money at the same time," Michele added. The brothers were a good team.

"But . . . if you cut off my hair, I'll be a 'baldy' myself!" said the youngest of the sisters nervously. She had the loveliest hair of all—as if spun from the finest gold, a heavy blond braid hanging past her hips. "Who will look at me at the spring festival then? I'll shrivel up like an old maid and never find a husband!"

Roberto and Michele, used to such objections, smiled mildly. "*Signorina*, nothing could disfigure your beauty. Just look at yourself." Roberto produced a small mirror and held it up to the girl's face. "Your perfect lips, your beautiful pink cheeks, your violet eyes . . . Nothing will change you. The young men at the spring festival will be fighting to have the first dance with you." Roberto was glad to see that the young woman smiled, albeit uncertainly. Tears at the decisive moment only made his work harder.

He leaned forward and tugged a few strands of hair free from her thickly woven braid. The girl, he was relieved to note, was one of those who smelled of lilies of the valley. "Look. All this hair on top will still be yours. We only cut the hair from the back of your head. If you wear a scarf, no one can see what is missing . . ."

With determination, he pulled a pair of scissors out of his bag. Now or never.

"Who'll be the first?"

Michele held up the colorful scarves, but unlike the necklace, he did not hand them over. Not yet. "Whoever's first gets first choice of these fine cloths."

For a long, tense moment, no one spoke. The father cleared his throat nervously.

"I'll do it," said the mother. She wore a sorrowful expression on her weather-beaten face, but she was determined. "Our last harvest let us down. Money is tighter than ever. And our roof leaks. When it rains, I have to put out five buckets to catch the water. If we can repair that . . ." She looked over at her husband. He shrugged almost imperceptibly.

"A wise decision!" Roberto praised. It was a start.

Michele let the woman choose a scarf while Roberto positioned a chair so that her daughters did not see the devastation he would wreak with a few snips.

With some hesitation, the woman sat down. "Not every woman has the opportunity to earn money so easily," Roberto repeated, and his scissors made a soft ripping sound. No dandruff, no lice, very good. "So many times, we have to go away empty-handed because the woman's hair is far too thin. Or so curly that one would suspect it came from some other part of the body. Who would want to wear a wig like that?"

As expected, the women shrieked with laughter. A dirty joke now and then never hurt, in Roberto's experience. He made use of the moment to make another snip with the scissors. It was important to cut the hair very close at the nape to preserve the braid in all its fullness.

"Done!" With a flourish, Roberto immediately tucked the cut-off hair inside his traveling case. It was not necessary for the women to see it again.

Michele, positioned beside him with the headscarf in his hands, now tied the cloth expertly around the mother's head. Then he held the mirror up for her. "Take a look, *bella signora*. Nothing unusual to be seen."

The woman examined herself critically in the mirror. It was true: her gray fringe still showed from beneath the scarf, and the silky hair at her temples, too. She nodded.

"And here is your ten lire. You've earned this for yourself." With a grand gesture, Roberto began to count ten coins into the woman's hand. As he did, he sensed the unease that now spread among her daughters. Who would put her hand up next?

A short time later, the brothers were on their way with four braids in their bag. They had turned down the mother's invitation to stay for dinner. Misery would descend the moment that one of the women lifted her headscarf, and neither of the brothers wanted to be there when that happened.

"Four perfect braids. I'd call that a good day!" Satisfied, Michele clapped Roberto on the shoulder. "If the father hadn't been squatting there in the corner, we'd have got even more. The middle daughter had her eye on me . . ."

"Women are all the same in that regard. A few pretty words and they're all yours," said Roberto. None of the young women had appealed to him particularly. He had seen some true beauties during his travels, and both brothers had experienced his share of what women had to offer.

Michele laughed. "When I think about that girl in Murassone . . ." He sighed. "You know, we have the best job in the world! We can do what we like, and no one at home ever finds out. We don't have to buy any expensive supplies or carry any heavy tools with us, like a blacksmith or a knife grinder. And we see a lot of the world. All we need is this little bit of magic!" Triumphantly, he took his scissors out of the bag and made a few snips in the air with them.

Roberto found himself smiling. He could not completely comprehend his older brother's enthusiasm, but he liked to listen to him. When Michele told a story, any story, a thousand sparks glittered in his eyes. Hardly a woman they visited could resist his charm, and he made a good impression on most of the men they met. But Roberto was not second to Michele in any way. On the contrary—compliments came even easier to him. Not that he would ever lie through his teeth to the women he met. That would have been beneath him. But a long time ago, Roberto had realized that compliments that possess a grain of truth are far more effective than exaggerated flattery. If he looked closely, he could find something beautiful in any woman, so when he offered his compliments, he believed them himself. Maybe that was the true art.

It didn't hurt that the two brothers were very good-looking. They were tall and fit. Michele had brown eyes and dark, unruly hair, while Roberto had straw-blond hair and dark-blue eyes. The Totosano brothers were a successful team.

"How many braids have we cut this season?" asked Roberto. Although he thought he knew the number, he wanted Michele's confirmation.

"Two hundred and a few more. This will give us a decent profit. I estimate at least four thousand lire, assuming the Sorris have brought home the amount they usually do. Papa will be proud of us."

At the mention of their father, Roberto's mood darkened. "The Sorris! I can't believe Papa still works with them. It's absurd! There probably isn't another partnership like it anywhere, and if you ask me, it's unfair and unjust. It makes me so angry!" At the thought that, in just a few days, the two families would meet to settle their accounts for the year together, Roberto balled his hands into fists in his jacket pockets.

"Calm down! You know it's an old tradition in Elva that our families divide the hair trade," said Michele, unconcerned. "And frankly, I think that's good. When the hair goes into one big pile at the end of the season, we know what work the Sorris have done, and vice versa. No one can fool anyone."

"And do you also think it's good that we have to split the profits, although the two of us bring home more braids than Federico, Martine, and Antonio put together?" The three Sorri sons were not only lacking in good looks, but they had no charm at all. No wonder they convinced fewer women to give up their hair.

Michele shrugged. "What's a few lire more or less? At least there's no envy or resentment. I, for one, don't want trouble with my father-in-law. And if you marry Gaia soon, you'll see things the same as I do. Everything stays in the family one way or another."

Roberto stopped walking. "Who says I'm marrying Gaia? She's a nice girl, but that's all. Is Papa making deals with Lorenzo for that? If he is, he'd better not count on me. I won't let anyone force me into anything, never!"

"Roberto," Michele said calmly. "Take it easy. No one wants to force you to do anything. But you have to admit that you should have been married long ago. You're twenty-eight. And Gaia is very attractive, even prettier than my Marta. She looks up to you, and I think she might even be a bit in love with you. What would be wrong with marrying her? We all have to go through it sometime, don't we?"

Roberto said nothing, but the brothers started walking again. It was not that he was fundamentally against marriage. Or that there was anything not to like about the younger of the Sorri daughters. What gnawed at him was the fact that his father and Lorenzo Sorri shared a conviction that they could decide the fates of everyone and everything around them. Yes, he was twenty-eight years old, a grown man and a good businessman—but he had no more say in things than a schoolboy. How long would the reign of the two powerful fathers last? And who would succeed his father? Michele, perhaps?

Roberto reached up to his collar and opened the top button of his shirt, as if to get a little more air to breathe. So he was supposed to marry Gaia . . . and that would weave the net of mutual control a little tighter.

"So far, Papa only made one small remark, just before we left. Nothing's been decided yet. Just forget I said anything at all," said Michele, as if he could read Roberto's thoughts. "What would you say if we try to convince Papa not to sell the hair to that agent in Dronero, but to go out and sell it on the market ourselves?" Michele asked. "Our profits would be much higher, and we could go off traveling again in summer instead of breaking our backs in the fields."

Surprised by the question, Roberto gave his brother a sidelong look. "I wanted to suggest just that to Papa. Not that I think he'll go for it. We know him better than that—*now don't go messing with the old customs . . .*" Roberto's voice carried mockery and scorn.

"Still, it's worth a try," said Michele. "You'll see, it will all work out."

Roberto mumbled something he knew Michele would take as agreement. There was no need to start arguing on the last day of their travels. His brother was as caught up in the whole system as he was. Perhaps the occasional affair, the betrayal of his wife—Lorenzo Sorri's older daughter—that Michele allowed himself when they were out in the country was his way of defying the power others had over their lives. Roberto still had not found anything like that for himself. But didn't they say that thinking was free? That was something, at least.

Tomorrow, they would head home. The very thought made it harder for Roberto to draw breath. He stopped walking again.

"We've done well today. Why don't we stay somewhere decent to mark the occasion? Enough sleeping in barns and eating dry bread for supper. On our way here I saw a guesthouse that looked good, with a lot of carriages parked in the yard. Let's celebrate!"

Michele cheered.

***

The guesthouse was located at the junction of two well-used roads. From there, travelers could go to Dronero or farther to the larger city of Cuneo, and then on to the Ligurian coast. But it was also the gateway to the wild and sparsely populated highlands surrounding Monte Chersogno. The brothers' hometown, Elva, lay in the shadow of the high mountain. Roberto looked up at the mountain; he'd give anything not to have to hike back up there the next day.

A clamor of voices and the heavy scent of garlic and cooked offal greeted the brothers as they entered. The guesthouse was crowded, and Roberto looked around, feeling a little self-conscious until he saw two empty chairs at a large round table toward the back. Four chairs at the table were already occupied—two by men wearing exceptionally elegant suits, and two by younger men in breeches and coarse leather boots.

Roberto steered Michele toward the table, where one of the elegantly dressed men—in his midforties, Roberto guessed—was talking. The other three listened attentively.

". . . and then I said to my business contact, 'Listen, my man, you won't get away with games like that on me!' But that's the Milanese for you. Think they're better than everyone else, ha!"

Roberto cleared his throat. "Pardon me, are these two seats available?"

The gentleman paused his storytelling and looked from one brother to the other. He must have liked what he saw because with a sweep of his arm, he waved them closer. "Join us! What about a glass of wine? On me, of course! Alfonso Scavize, at your service. I was just telling . . ."

Before Roberto and Michele knew it, each had a large glass of red wine in front of him and they had ordered pasta dinners. They exchanged a happy look. "Looks like we picked the right table," Michele whispered to Roberto in Occitan.

"In Milan, there will soon be more cars driving around than horses and carriages. Next time I visit the city, I'm going to rent one and drive it to the Scala!" Scavize looked around for approval of his plan. He was on his way home to Genoa, he then told the brothers, something the others at the table already seemed to have heard. But he said nothing about the purpose of his trip or how he earned his money.

He doesn't seem too hard up, at least, Roberto thought as he admired the fine cloth of Scavize's suit. Then, instinctively, he looked down at his own old suit, tailored from coarse linen. His mother had sewn the jacket and trousers for him, and they fit well enough, but no one would ever call his outfit smart.

"To the Scala in Milan with an automobile? Isn't that a little vulgar? I'd be happier with a decent four-in-hand with silk benches, gilded lamps, and a uniformed coachman," said the man beside him, who had introduced himself as Gianfranco de Lucca. He was a fabric merchant from Naples who had been in the German lands on business. Good business, by all appearances, because he immediately ordered another round of red wine for the table.

"You have no idea! The automobile is the vehicle of the future. Let me tell you, in Vienna, where I come from . . ."

Roberto ate his pasta in silence. He had never seen an automobile. A machine like that must be a breathtaking sight.

Michele pushed his empty plate away and patted his stomach. "You don't see a fine meal like that every day, I'll tell you. That's the good thing about traveling on business."

The man beside him, who looked young and athletic and up to then had said very little, looked at Michele with a frown. "What's so special about pasta and Bolognese sauce?" He and his companion were eating venison stew.

"It's just a figure of speech around here," said Roberto hurriedly. He looked irritably at Michele. Couldn't his brother at least act as if he had some sophistication?

"Ah, you're from this region, then? Where, exactly?" asked the athletic man. Neither he nor his companion had touched their glass of wine but drank water instead.

"From Elva," Roberto answered.

"Isn't that the village of the hair traders?" asked the Genoan merchant. "Creepy business, that. Cutting the hair off poor young women . . . just the thought of it!"

Roberto and Michele exchanged a look. They were used to people looking down on their line of work, and they had put up with their share of ridicule and derision. In the eyes of outsiders, it made no difference that they earned very good money from it, and the brothers, as a rule, said nothing to anyone about what they did for a living.

"What brings you to the region?" Roberto asked, a distraction, and he turned to the two young men wearing breeches.

"We're from Rome, and we want to climb Chersogno," one said.

"That's right," the other added. "Is it true that from Elva it takes six hours to climb Chersogno?"

Roberto shrugged. "I think that would do it. But there is still snow up there. Do you have the right equipment?" Why anyone would voluntarily climb a high mountain was a puzzle to him.

The two men grinned. "We've got the best equipment money can buy. And more than enough experience, don't worry."

Michele, who had only listened to the exchange until now, joined in. "Pardon me for asking, but . . . *why* do you want to climb Chersogno at all?"

Roberto smiled to himself. It happened often that one brother thought something and the other put it into words . . . but the next moment, his smile froze.

"Because I can," said the climber, confident and cool.

Roberto's hand rose to his right ear as if someone had slapped him there. He could have lived with any other answer. If the young Roman had said "Because I love nature" or "Because I want to test myself" or

128

"Because I'm competing with my friend," Roberto would simply have nodded and shrugged and been content with that.

"Because I can"—with those three words, the man had demonstrated the gulf that existed between them. It wasn't that one was from Rome and the other from Elva. Or their different professions. No, it was that the Roman was free, and he, Roberto, was not.

Because I can . . .

Chapter Sixteen

Clara had never been as aware of the seasons changing as she was at Lake Constance. At first she believed that late summer was surely the loveliest time of year at the lake. Everything was so buoyant and alive: the vibrant lakefront promenade, the water as if speckled white with all the boats. Then came autumn with its vibrant colors, then winter, and the memory of the bustle of the summer months gave way to calm and quiet. Swathes of fog enveloped the lake like a lace scarf. Some of the locals complained about the foggy winters and how they could make for melancholy, but Clara perceived it differently. For her, the fog softened everything hard, quieted everything loud. Besides, there were still days when the air was so clear that one could see every silhouette on the Swiss shore opposite—it looked almost within reach. There wasn't much snow, but the frost lay like a sugar coating over the dried-out stalks of the reeds and the seaweed. On such days, the lakeshore seemed especially enchanted.

Now when Clara went for her morning walk beside the water, she was alone except for a few ducks and some dogs with their owners. The peace and quiet and the exercise helped her at least partly to clear her head, which was buzzing with a thousand ideas. *Could the lake be any more lovely than it is in winter?* she wondered.

"You haven't yet been here in spring," said Lilo one evening in late February when Clara was telling her about her impressions. "When the tulips and daffodils are blooming in every garden and in planters along the promenades, when the petals from the fruit trees are coming down like fresh snow, when the first green leaves appear in the vineyards— for me, that is the most beautiful time of year. And besides"—Lilo grinned—"I can finally go swimming again."

Clara nodded fervently. She missed swimming, too. She could not remember ever looking forward to the spring as much as she was now.

But there was still some time before spring would arrive, and she wanted to make the most of it. To distract herself from how much she missed her children, and staying true to the motto "Hard work, light heart," she redoubled her efforts in the shop. If there were no customers, she disappeared into her laboratory to test a new ingredient in a cream or to try out a new recipe for a facial toner. "Lavender Water," "Rose Crème," and "Peppermint Tincture"—every time Clara walked past the shelves displaying her products, she was overcome with a feeling of happiness. Her creams, soaps, and tinctures were not only the highest quality, but also very attractively packaged. And her customers, it seemed, felt the same way. It wasn't exactly as if the women of Meersburg were breaking down her door, but she had between five and ten customers every day. Considering that she had only opened at the start of January, Clara was happy with the business she had. She could pay her share of the rent and buy ingredients for new products, and she still had a little left over for herself. She consoled herself with Therese's prediction that visitors would arrive along with spring. "Then your register will really be ringing, you'll see!" said Therese, and her eyes gleamed in anticipation.

***

Winter retreated. The birds twittered joyfully. The sun shone from a radiant blue sky, and the lake glittered more brightly than Clara had ever seen. Meersburg woke from its hibernation. Troughs of flowers were planted, window frames given a fresh coat of paint, and the owners of the cafés and bars put out small tables and chairs for those guests who preferred to drink their coffee *al fresco*. In the hotels, the maids and handymen were busy from morning to evening with spring cleaning and repairs. The Meersburgers waved cheerfully to the new carriages appearing on their streets, and even more cheerfully to the occasional automobile. Meersburg was ready. The season could begin!

"In the *Southern Germany Illustrated News*, it says that in the big cities, more and more hairdressers are offering what they call a permanent wave. It's new; a man named Karl Nessler introduced the process only last year." Therese looked up from what she was reading. "What do you think? Should I add an electric permanent-wave machine for this season?"

Clara, who dreaded more noise similar to that made by the hair dryer, said, "You already get very lovely curls with those curlers of yours. Why do you need a machine? Besides, a thing like that would cost a lot of money, wouldn't it?" She took a step back from her show window and looked at her new display: a pyramid of jars of cream and a bouquet of purple tulips. She thought it looked vernal.

"But I could really use it to *wave* to the seasonal guests, you know?" Therese laughed at her wordplay. "With the new technique, I could create long-lasting curls instead of curls that only last for a night . . . I'd do one for you for free, naturally."

"What if something goes wrong?" Clara did not like the thought of having toxic or burning chemicals on her scalp at all. And anyway, she had grown so used to her classic chignon that she could no longer imagine having her hair done any other way.

Therese laughed her carefree laugh. "Then my name will really be mud. But that won't happen."

Clara joined in the laughter halfheartedly. Instead of chemicals and machines, Therese could boost her business by replacing the dry fir tree branches left over from Christmas and making her shop window a little more springlike. "Fantastic idea, I'll do it," Therese had assured Clara the week before, but nothing had happened since.

"Oops, customer!" said Clara, glancing toward the door. Therese immediately jumped up and wiped a dust cloth over her mirror, while Clara went to the stove and put on water to warm for a pedicure. They had agreed it was not good for customers to catch them idling.

The door opened with so much force that the glass rattled in its frame. "Made it!" said Roswitha Maier, who ran the Green Tree restaurant, as she sank into Clara's treatment chair, completely out of breath. "I ran as fast as I could . . . I hope nobody saw me."

"What would be so terrible if they did?" Clara asked Roswitha, and not for the first time. "You don't have to feel bad about visiting my shop. It just shows that you care about your appearance." She pulled over a stool, sat in front of Roswitha, and began the pedicure Roswitha treated herself to every four weeks. It was Roswitha Maier, in fact, who had got Clara thinking about pedicures in the first place. "With all due respect to your creams," Roswitha had said the first time she visited, "when you see my horrible, chapped feet, you'll know that a cream alone won't help." With one look at the woman's maltreated feet, Clara had had to admit she was right.

"You say that, my dear Mrs. Berg," Roswitha said now. "But the people here love to talk, and in the end the proprietress at the Green Tree turns into a vain and lazy creature."

Clara felt compelled to laugh along with her customer; in truth, however, she did not find that kind of talk very funny. It would have been better for her business if women like Roswitha Maier were less concerned about what others said about them.

While Clara went back to the stove to finish preparing the footbath, Roswitha chattered away. "They say that the first of the nobility will be coming this week. I heard it from Veronica, the maid at the Bellavista."

Clara was suddenly all ears. "This week? Already? But it's still April. I thought the nobility only came to the lake in mid-May." She glanced inquisitively over toward Therese, but the hairdresser only responded with a shrug.

Roswitha laughed. "Once upon a time! Oh, yes, the king and his immediate retinue are still up in Stuttgart or somewhere else right now. But the other nobles are coming earlier and earlier every year, which doesn't surprise me! It's especially lovely here now that everything is turning green and starting to flower. I told Elisabeth Kaiser to deliver three times as many fish starting next week. And I've already hired two more wait staff for the season. I'm well prepared." Roswitha sounded very pleased with herself.

Clara frowned. If only she could say the same.

Advertising matters! Print some attractive leaflets and leave them at tourist spots and hotels. I'm sure Lilo, at least, wouldn't object to a stack of them in her hotel, Isabelle had advised in a letter. Clara had been impressed. Leaflets advertising her business! Why hadn't she thought of that?

Whatever advertising you do, make sure it has a personal touch, Josephine had advised. She and Clara had also been in regular contact. *Anybody can put an ad in the local paper, but handwritten invitations are far more effective! Make the effort to find out who is arriving and when, and where they will be staying. And then send every important guest a personal invitation.*

Clara had hurriedly sent off letters of thanks to her more experienced friends and assured them that she would put their ideas into practice.

***

That's all well and good, thought Clara as she shaved a layer of callused skin from Roswitha's right heel. She had bought some good paper, a fresh bottle of ink, and new pens, but she had not yet written a single invitation. Nor had she gotten very far with the leaflets: though she had commissioned a small printer with the job weeks earlier, the proprietor had not told her when she would receive them. At the time, Clara had believed it would be a while before the high-society visitors arrived, so she hadn't pressed for a deadline.

Now, suddenly, it was urgent. She massaged her oiliest cream into Roswitha's dry feet. "You should do this every evening at home. The chamomile in the cream helps to heal the chapping, and the marigold makes the skin supple," she said. "And don't you think you might like a facial? Now that spring is here, our skin loves to be pampered." Clara made an effort not to stare at the woman's wrinkled cheeks.

"I don't know . . . ," said Roswitha uncertainly. "I need my feet every day just to get around, but my face? Wouldn't it be a waste of money?"

"Oh, certainly not," Clara said with a smile. "You want to look appealing to your guests, don't you? And to your husband. And to yourself! Every woman has the right to look as nice as she can." She stood up, went to a shelf, and came back carrying a jar of cream. "Smell this." She held the jar under Roswitha's nose. "Doesn't it smell like an expensive perfume? And the ingredients are so beneficial. Your skin will thank you."

Roswitha sniffed at the cream and sighed extravagantly. "Something like this is much too fancy for me. But I will take a jar of foot cream."

When Roswitha stepped out the door, Clara sighed. "It's a shame, the way the women here do so little for themselves. She spends the entire day on her feet, toiling away in her restaurant, and I am willing to bet that she takes care of her household, too. Yet she's too miserly to do anything good for her skin. Why is that?"

Therese sniffed. "Her hair is certainly in need of some attention, too. But with Roswitha Maier, there's no point talking about it. All she has in her head is her restaurant."

Clara nodded. If she stopped to think about it, she had been just the same in her old life. She had spent every spare penny on the household, or had bought new clothes or a toy for the children instead of treating herself to something nice.

Although Clara could now support herself with sales of foot creams and face lotions, she wasn't earning enough to start a savings. Expensive facials and courses of treatment over several weeks would bring in good money. She was convinced that, with such courses of treatment, she could work wonders for the women here. But she needed the right customers—upper-class women who not only had access to the money, but were prepared to spend it for the sake of beauty. Only then could Clara afford to travel to Berlin to see her children.

"You said the nobles would only start to arrive in the middle of May. Now, suddenly, the first ones are on their way, and I haven't even written a single invitation!" If only she had spoken to Lilo about the arrival of the nobles instead of Therese!

"Calm down," said Therese. "I can help you write the invitations, although I doubt the effort will be worth it."

"I'll gladly take the chance," Clara said. Isabelle and Josephine would not have advised her to do it if it were a waste of time.

Clara snatched her coat from the coatrack. "I'm going to run down to the Residenz and get my writing paper and ink. I want to get started straight away." She already had her coat buttoned when the doorbell jangled and the door opened.

"Well, what do we have here? Leaving my lovely shop in the middle of the day? Earned enough already, eh?" With his thumbs hooked behind his suspenders, Alfred Schrott stood inside the store, rocking back and forth on the balls of his feet and gazing at Clara's breasts. He stepped closer. Clara could smell the onions on his breath.

She shuddered. "Urgent errand," she said, and was about to push past her landlord and escape when she felt Therese's hand on her left arm—stay!

"How can we help you?" Therese asked, and her voice sounded unusually tinny.

Alfred Schrott grinned. "What makes you think I want anything from you? I came by to check if everything is in order. You know that if there's anything I can do for the ladies . . ."

From anyone else, such an offer might have sounded friendly and helpful. But from Schrott, the words carried an insinuating tone. Nothing explicit, but unmistakable, and Clara shuddered again.

"Everything is perfectly all right," she said stiffly. "We're getting along just fine by ourselves, aren't we, Therese?"

The hairdresser nodded vehemently. She was all but hiding behind Clara.

"Ah. Good then." The disappointment in his voice was unmistakable. "But in case there's anything you—"

"Alfred? Alfred!" Lydia Schrott, her voice shrill and demanding, called out from the doorway.

Some days just get worse and worse, thought Clara when Lydia Schrott stepped inside. Clara gave the landlord's wife a pained smile. Lydia nodded curtly and, without a second glance at Clara or Therese, said, "I searched the whole house for you! You were going to help me take down the curtains on the top floor. And the garden gate needs oil. It squeaks so loud it gives me a migraine."

Clara watched with relief as Lydia Schrott pulled her husband out of the shop.

"Those two really are peas in a pod, aren't they?" said Therese, and they both smiled.

Then Clara's smile turned to a worried frown. "I find that man so repulsive, but we can hardly tell him he can't come in." It bothered her especially that he had described the shop as his, and she told Therese so.

"What was that supposed to mean? We pay him good rent, after all, and we should say what goes on here," Therese said firmly. "But he thinks he can get away with anything. He came here a few days ago, too, you know. If I remember right, you'd gone out to Treiber's. I was washing towels. 'Oh, what's that I see? Has the basin sprung a leak?' he said from the doorway. I knew straight off that all he was doing was looking for an excuse to squeeze up close. I told him everything was fine, but he was already standing next to me. Shameless bastard put one arm around me as if he were checking something on the sink and then brushed against my breast!" Therese wrinkled her nose in disgust.

Clara exhaled sharply, horrified. "Why didn't you tell me straight away? That's monstrous!"

Therese snorted. "I'm more annoyed that I was so startled. Next time I'll rap him over his knuckles; you can quote me on that!"

"What now?" said Clara, still taken aback by Therese's disclosure. Normally, she was the one left alone in the shop while Therese went off to enjoy herself. The idea of a run-in like that Schrott was anything but pleasant.

"Best we can do is ignore him," said Therese. "His charming wife usually makes sure he keeps his distance from us. Other people tie a dog up in their yard. But Alfred Schrott has a dragon in his house!"

A short time later, when Clara returned with the writing paper, envelopes, and a bottle of ink, Therese was standing by the door ready to go out herself.

"Finally! I thought you weren't coming back at all."

"And I thought you were going to help me write the invitations?" Clara watched as Therese pulled her hat down over her forehead so that only her left eye was still visible, a jaunty, daring look. The next moment, Therese gave her a kiss on the cheek.

"I'll help you tomorrow, promise! But Hubert was just here—you know, Count Zeppelin's engineer, the manager? He's in a champagne mood, he said, and he wants to take me out to dinner. I couldn't really say no, could I?"

Therese and the engineer had met on New Year's Eve, and the man had shown up at the shop several times since with flowers and chocolates or to take Therese on an outing. Given his occupation, Clara couldn't imagine how he had so much free time. "Oh, Hubert is such a treasure!" Therese sighed dreamily. "Do you think I should tell him about the permanent-wave machine? As an engineer, he's a very forward-thinking man, and technically knowledgeable, of course. I'm sure he can tell me what he thinks of this invention. Maybe he'll be prepared to help me out a little with the purchase . . ."

"I don't know," Clara said, furrowing her brow. "Don't you think you'd be putting the gentleman in an awkward position? I mean, what if he doesn't want to finance a machine like that for you?"

"Then he just has to say so," said Therese, as if it were the most obvious thing in the world. "And so you don't think I'm selfish, I'm going to ask Hubert if he can wrangle an invitation for both of us to one of Count Zeppelin's parties. We could do a little quiet advertising. Once we have one or two fans in the better circles, more women will follow suit. Soon everything will be running like clockwork, you'll see!" She gestured with a gloved toward Clara's writing implements. "And you can save yourself the effort of writing invitations." With a happy wave, she was gone.

Clara watched her leave with dismay. "What if someone comes in and wants a haircut?" she called, but Therese wasn't listening anymore.

Chapter Seventeen

The spring weather held, and the skies remained cloudless. More and more open carriages were out on the streets around the lake—excursionists out enjoying the attractions of the region; some of them were just there for a day or two, but there were also guests at the local health resorts, some there to spend the entire summer. There were rumors that members of the royal court in Stuttgart had already arrived. Nobody had actually seen any high-ranking nobles in Friedrichshafen or anywhere else, but that didn't stop Meersburg's rumor mills from grinding at top speed.

Lilo's Hotel Residenz was fully booked, and when Clara entered the breakfast room, there were often only one or two tables free. Rather than taking a table from a paying guest, Clara decided to have breakfast either in her room or at a café along the esplanade. "You don't have to do that, you know. I'll always have space for you," said Lilo when Clara hadn't appeared for breakfast for a few days. Clara appreciated Lilo's words, but she thought Lilo might have been relieved by her thoughtfulness.

***

Clara breathed deeply, filling her lungs with the clear morning air, and looked out over the water as she sat on the café terrace, waiting for her breakfast to arrive. She knew how lucky she was to have her first meal of the day in the open air close to the water. The slap of wavelets washing against the quay wall was both calming and invigorating.

A waiter had just set a cup of coffee, a roll, and a small pot of marmalade in front of Clara when, behind her, she suddenly heard laughter and a babble of voices speaking French and a language she did not recognize. She turned as surreptitiously as she could in the direction of the esplanade to see the source of the commotion. An older woman of extraordinary girth was at the center of her personal entourage. She lumbered along with the aid of a walking stick. A small white dog with dark button eyes scurried so excitedly around her feet that the big woman nearly tripped over it, but she caught herself at the last second with surprising agility. Instead of chastising the dog, all she did was laugh.

She makes Sabine Weingarten look as petite and spry as an elf, Clara thought.

The woman wore at least ten long strings of pearls around her neck, and with every step she took the pearls bounced on her enormous bust as if they were trying to jump free and return to the depths of the water from which they had originally been fished. Wearing a fortune like that around her neck in broad daylight! Clara was surprised. The woman's entourage was composed of much younger women—Clara guessed they were in their midtwenties to early thirties—and all, without exception, were extremely attractive. A group of actresses, appearing at a theater near the lake? Or dancers, perhaps? They were elegantly and elaborately dressed, and even the youngest among them wore flamboyant jewelry and large hats decorated with veils, flowers, and feathers. So these were the famed summer guests of whom Lilo, Therese, and so many others spoke with such admiration.

As the dazzling group came closer, Clara pretended to be lost in thought, gazing out over the water. The women sat at the table directly behind her. The legs of the cast-iron café chairs scraped across the floor, and then Clara heard a threatening, groaning sound—as if something were about to break apart. The corpulent dame and the small, ornate chairs—Clara preferred not to think about the combination. She listened with amusement to the lively conversation and laughter behind her. One of the women tried to order coffee, and another called out for champagne. Then a third shouted, "No, hot chocolate for everyone!" The little dog yapped out its approval of each.

"Please bring all the drinks you have," said a deep female voice in a decisive tone. Clara assumed it was the big woman who spoke.

The question of what the women wanted to eat then took a great deal of discussion.

Clara grinned to herself, thinking how she, Josephine, and Isabelle were so tame compared to these women! She bit off a mouthful of her roll as the little dog trotted off across the esplanade to the quay wall.

"*Bijou, ici!*" called several women simultaneously, but then they ignored the dog entirely.

The little creature put its head between the bars of the railing that was meant to prevent pedestrians from accidentally falling into the lake below. A loud burst of barking followed, but whether it was just a few ducks that had got the dog so excited or something else, Clara could not see. *The dog isn't going to jump, I hope,* she was thinking, when exactly that happened.

"*Excusez-moi, votre chien . . .*" Clara turned around in her chair and waved her hand excitedly toward the water behind her. "Your dog . . . it's fallen off the quay!"

"*Bijou! Mon Dieu!*" One of the woman's hands flew to her throat in fright, then she laboriously rose to her feet and shambled with her walking stick over to the quay wall. Her fashionably attired entourage and Clara followed close behind. The little dog was paddling helplessly in the small waves, whimpering piteously.

The women were shouting in various foreign languages, but that didn't stop Clara from understanding that none of the woman's entourage could help in any way. There was no dock worker, no policeman, no official in sight along the esplanade—and what if there were? Who would get wet for the sake of a little dog? But one could not simply look on calmly while the little creature died!

Should she? She could swim, after all. But the lake was still freezing cold at this point in the spring. She would almost certainly catch a cold. If she got drenched now, she'd have to hurry back to the hotel to change to have any hope of making her first appointment at Bel Étage at nine.

"Why isn't anyone helping?" the corpulent woman shrieked. Her entourage wailed and sobbed.

While Clara's thoughts were in a turmoil, one of the Lake Constance ferries passed by, and the dog was caught in the vortex of its wake and pulled farther away from the shore. Its little white head was barely visible anymore.

She couldn't hesitate any longer. Clara pulled off her jacket and shoes, climbed over the railing, took a deep breath, and jumped into the water. The cold hit her like a wall of ice, and for a moment she could not breathe at all and was afraid her heart would stop. Then her arms and legs instinctively began to move. Her petticoat and dress clung to her skin, and the weight of all the material pulled her down. Only with a huge effort was she able to make any headway in the ice-cold lake. She frantically scanned the water stirred up in the wake of the ferry. Where was the dog? Was she too late?

"The dog! Where is it?" she called, turning back to the quay for help.

"Over there, to the right!" the big woman shouted and pointed, then she waved her hands frantically and helplessly in the air, and the other women did the same.

Clara's teeth were chattering uncontrollably as she swam in the direction the woman had pointed. There! The dog!

The next moment, she reached the tiny ball of fur. Bijou's eyes were wide with fear when he caught sight of Clara.

"It all right, little dog. Everything will be all right," Clara murmured in the tone she used whenever one of her children came home with a scraped knee. Gently, she put the dog over her right shoulder, and began to swim back toward the shore.

"I will never forget what you've done!" the woman said, speaking German now. Her face was streaked with tears as she pressed Clara and Bijou to her titanic chest. "Thank you from the bottom of my heart, my dear, thank you! You saved my little darling's life."

Her companions looked at Clara with a mixture of admiration and horror. "Don't mention it, really," Clara murmured, pushing her wet hair out of her face. Shivering, chilled to her core, she freed herself from the big woman's embrace. She needed to get into some dry clothes urgently, or she would catch her death!

"I have to go . . ."

"But I haven't even thanked you properly! What's your name? Where do you live? Stay, please!" the woman called after her, but Clara was already rushing away to her warm, dry room.

Luckily for Clara, she could sneak into the hotel through a rear entrance so that no one would see her in such a state.

Three-quarters of an hour later, with dry hair and fresh clothes, she made it to Bel Étage with five minutes to spare. Smiling and courteous as ever, and trying to act as if nothing had happened, she served her nine o'clock customer, who happily reported that, thanks to Clara's cream, the spots on her décolletage had disappeared. Clara was pleased with the progress, but recommended a supplementary cleansing lotion to maintain the benefits. Still chilled through, her bones ached. *Now don't start whining. You've only got yourself to blame if you're feeling miserable.*

But Therese noticed that something about Clara wasn't quite right. "Have you caught a cold? Don't infect me if you have!" she said when the customer left.

Clara was about to tell her about what had happened at the lake when the door opened and an enormous bouquet of flowers appeared. The young man barely visible behind the bouquet was having trouble keeping the arrangement from falling.

Clara and Therese looked at each other, eyebrows raised.

"My Hubert, how sweet . . ." Therese sighed, and went to take the flowers from the messenger. But right away she turned and looked at Clara in confusion. "It's not for me at all. It's your name on the envelope."

"That's not possible," Clara said. "Who would be sending me flowers?"

The messenger cleared his throat and shifted his weight impatiently from one foot to the other. "D'you ladies happen to have a bucket or somethin'? This is gettin' a mite heavy . . ."

"Countess Zuzanna Zawadzki has invited you to her spring ball?" In disbelief, Therese looked from the card that came with the flowers and back again. "How, may I ask, did you pull this off?" Therese asked with more than a trace of envy in her voice.

Clara's shrug quickly transformed into a bout of shivering. As briefly as possible, she related the incident that morning. "But I didn't even tell the woman my name," she said.

"You didn't have to. Countess Zawadzki has the connections and money to find out. Finding out your name would have been child's play for her. Congratulations, you rescued just the right lapdog from the lake!" Therese said stiffly. "At the spring ball, you'll meet ladies and gentlemen of the nobility who spend the season at the lake. And lots of other high-ranking types, to boot. After that, you won't ever have to worry about your business again. Once people find out that the Russian czarina likes you, they'll be knocking down your door."

"That would be nice," said Clara rather doubtfully. "But how is it that you know the countess?" She looked at the enormous bouquet. Roses, lilies, tulips—the cost of those flowers would have fed a family well for a week.

"Countess Zuzanna Zawadzki and the man whose money paid for me to open this shop move in the same circles. Our paths have crossed several times, which is not to say that the countess would ever lower herself to talk to me, so I really can't tell you too much about her. But she is rather a flamboyant personality, and impossible to overlook."

A flamboyant personality—those were exactly the words to describe the countess. When Clara realized that Therese was miffed, she said, "Oh, come on, cheer up a little. If you're right and the countess really does become one of my customers, that would be good for your business, too. The question is just"—she frowned—"will I go to the ball at all? I don't even have anything decent to wear."

"You bet you're going to that ball!" said Lilo sternly that evening. "Turning down this invitation would be a fatal mistake."

"But—" Clara began.

"But nothing," Lilo cut her off immediately. "Besides, I'm also one of the lucky ones to get an invitation, so I'll be there for support. Now all we need is something pretty for you to wear, and everything will be fine." Lilo beamed. "I would say we have roughly the same figure. I'm sure we can find something in my wardrobe for you."

***

A little while later, Clara and Lilo were drinking wine in the dining room at the Residenz.

"Would you tell me a little about our hostess for the ball? I still don't know anything about her."

"Countess Zawadzki . . . It's a tragic story," said Lilo. A thin fog had gathered over the lake, and in the dim light cast by the street lamps, couples could be seen strolling hand in hand along the shoreline. The sight triggered a sense of longing in Clara.

"Zuzanna married into high Polish nobility when she was still very young. Back then, I've heard, she was as slim as a Silesian birch and a real beauty. Her husband, Count Szymon Zawadzki, owned gold, silver, and copper mines throughout Poland. But anyone who thinks Zuzanna married Szymon for money is mistaken. Her own family is immensely rich. It was true love for both of them."

"You're talking about the count in the past tense," Clara said, suspecting the worst.

Lilo nodded. "Six or seven years ago, Szymon was killed in a mining accident. Ten men died with him. I don't know the whole story, but it's said that Countess Zuzanna was so deeply affected by her husband's death that she wanted to take her own life. She drank poison . . ." Lilo looked meaningfully at Clara. "It was only because her dog would not stop barking—the same dog you rescued so heroically this morning—that the servants noticed that the countess was sleeping much later than usual. They managed to save her at the last minute. Then, in her grief, she started to eat. The finest food, more and more of it. I've been told that the countess never wants to fall in love again."

Clara's brow creased. "After my divorce, I can honestly say I'd had enough of men, but still, I find it terrifying to think that I might never again be held in a man's arms."

Lilo only shrugged. "Self-imposed celibacy . . . I would not like that, either. But every person is different. These days, Countess Zuzanna prefers to surround herself with pretty young women. They swarm around her like butterflies around a sweet-smelling flower. Zuzanna . . . in a way, she continues to take part in life through them."

"The young women also seem to enjoy the countess's company very much," said Clara, but her mind was still on Lilo's first words. So Lilo had no interest in celibacy, either? Not for the first time, Clara wondered whether her friend might have a secret lover, but she did not feel confident enough to ask her.

"Does that surprise you, considering the countess's generosity? Before she bought the Villa Carese, she spent two summers living here in the Residenz. She and her hangers-on drank so much champagne every evening that I could hardly keep enough in stock." She smiled openly at Clara. "I can tell you this—this coming Saturday evening will be unforgettable."

Chapter Eighteen

The Villa Carese was a long two-story structure built among the vineyards above Meersburg. The architect had taken his inspiration from Italian mansions: small bay windows, a miniature tower, and several balconies graced the building. A wide staircase led from the forecourt up to a loggia that stretched across the width of the building. Pure-white marble columns lined the loggia; in between, lemon trees bloomed in white ceramic tubs.

"Ready?" Lilo whispered. She was wearing a magnificent ball gown of emerald taffeta. Like all the other guests, she had hired a carriage to drive them up the mountain. They joined the line of guests moving toward the entrance.

Clara nodded. She felt dizzy, but was not sure if it was because of her excitement or the smell of the lemon blossoms. "You'll stay close, won't you?" she whispered. She smoothed the skirt of her dress. Maybe she should have accepted Lilo's offer of a dress after all, she thought, looking at the elegantly attired women around them.

"The countess is an exceptionally extravagant woman," Lilo had told her, offering her the most eye-catching dresses she had in her collection.

"Cut so low? And isn't the color a little overpowering? I'm sorry, but I'm much too modest for something like that." Clara had laughed, turning down everything Lilo offered. She was wearing a dark-blue dress that she had sewn herself from heavy, expensive taffeta a few years earlier. It fit perfectly and had a timeless appeal. To give the dress a festive touch, Clara had added a lilac-colored lace collar around the décolletage and sewn the same lace around the cuffs. She used what she had left to spruce up her old evening bag, a black taffeta accessory from the days when Gerhard had taken her to the opera or theater. Her outfit was not exactly the latest fashion, but in it Clara felt true to herself. If the countess didn't like it, that wasn't in Clara's power to change, she reminded herself when they reached the entrance at the top of the steps.

The ballroom was on the second floor, and its many windows looked out toward the lake. Spring flowers tied in lavish garlands surrounded every window like expensive picture frames. Industrialists with their beautiful wives, artists in dramatic outfits, actors, and a host of other colorful characters. Clara could not remember ever seeing such a dazzling crowd, not even at the glamorous birthday party thrown by the famous champagne dealer Raymond Dupont to which Isabelle had taken her. Guests greeted each other merrily and talked animatedly, a trio of violinists played along, and the tinkling of champagne glasses heightened the convivial melody.

Clara clenched her glass and acted as if she were on her way to greet someone she knew on the other side of the room. But she knew nobody. She had not even seen the countess. And Lilo had disappeared five minutes after they arrived when she spotted an old friend. *So much for Lilo's support,* thought Clara, a little annoyed. She found a spot by one of the bay windows and felt more comfortable in that half-hidden niche than in the open ballroom. She had just set her glass down on the windowsill when three young women stopped beside her. Like everyone else, they were elegantly dressed.

"Next week I'll be starting at the university. I'm a little worried, certainly, but I'm not the first woman to venture into that male bastion, after all." She lifted her glass and took a good swig, as if drinking in some courage.

"Never fear, dear, you'll show the men how it's done," said the young woman beside her.

"And if you need any encouragement, come to me. Winterthur is a stone's throw from Zurich. I can't leave my new gallery alone for days on end, but I can always find time for a cup of coffee with a friend," said the third.

They laughed then, each obviously familiar with the others. And suddenly, Clara felt more alone than before. If only Isabelle and Josephine were there.

"Jean-Luc wants me to learn to drive an automobile. What do you think? Should I?" the first young woman said.

"Oh, absolutely! I've been thinking about it myself . . ."

Women studying, running galleries, driving automobiles. Women who dared to do things!

My God, thought Clara. *Our turn-of-the-century wind isn't just blowing here; it's* whistling *through the room!* She had to write to Isabelle and Josephine about it soon.

At the thought of her friends and all they'd accomplished, Clara straightened up, squared her shoulders, took a deep breath, and smiled. She had no need to hide from this colorful assemblage of strangers. Wasn't she herself one of those women who dared to do something?

"Oh, my dearest Clara Berg, here you are! I've had people looking all over for you!" Countess Zuzanna bore down on Clara, and the guests standing around quickly cleared her path.

Before Clara knew what was happening, she found herself crushed to the countess's ample bosom. "Thank you, and thank you again! I will never forget what you've done for me. Bijou was the last present my beloved husband ever gave me. I would never have gotten over it if I lost him before his time, too," she whispered in Clara's ear. The next moment, she let Clara go, then turned and called so loudly that the entire room could hear, "My dear friends, this woman is a true lifesaver! When it really mattered, Clara Berg was more intent on the welfare of my little Bijou than her own. A toast! A toast to a dauntless woman!"

Suddenly, waiters were moving through the ballroom, delivering fresh glasses of champagne on silver trays.

"To Bijou's savior, Clara Berg!" Countess Zuzanna raised her glass so energetically that Clara was momentarily afraid that she would toss it behind her in the Russian fashion. Instead, she drank it all in one draft.

"To Clara Berg!" everyone else called.

Clara was so embarrassed by the attention that she wanted to crawl away. With a pained smile, she sipped at her own champagne to complete the toast.

Before Clara could put her glass down, the countess took her by the arm. "Now tell me, my dear Mrs. Berg, what your little shop is all about. Bel Étage—that sounds so mysterious."

"Well, what I do really is a little mysterious," Clara said. "I make beauty creams, lotions, and toners. And soaps that smell wonderful— the soaps are one of my specialties."

"I've never heard of such a thing," said a young woman who had linked arms with the countess on the other side. The gesture showed familiarity, but the young woman was also clearly staking her claim. "Most soaps smell sour and unpleasant. What is it that makes your soaps smell so nice?"

"That varies," Clara said. "In winter, I like to mix rose perfume with cinnamon and vanilla. Now that spring is here, I love the scent of flowers like lilac and honeysuckle, and a hint of lavender." She paused. "Just yesterday, I tried something brand new—peppermint with a touch of lemon."

With every word Clara spoke, the countess's deep-blue eyes grew more covetous. "I don't know of any soaps like that. Do you?"

The young woman shook her head. "Peppermint and lemon . . ." She sighed rapturously. "Does the perfume stay on your skin?"

"Of course," said Clara. "I also have lily of the valley–scented soaps in stock at the moment."

"I would like these soaps. All of them!" the countess said.

"*What* is it you'd like, darling?" asked an elderly woman who joined them just then, and the countess told her about Clara and her profession.

"A beauty shop? They have that sort of place in Paris and on Fifth Avenue in New York, but I've never been inside one. To be honest, I'm skeptical. Isn't beauty God-given? And fleeting, besides?" said the newcomer.

"Oh, not at all," said Clara. "I believe that any woman can be beautiful, at any age. She only has to take the time to look after herself. She needs a good cream, one that suits her skin—and also the circumstances of her life—and a little nurture. Half an hour a day can make a huge difference. But so many women lack just that, half an hour for themselves."

As Clara spoke, more and more women gathered around. They were mesmerized. A shop dedicated to beauty . . . they thought it sounded wonderful and very tempting.

A woman in a showy dress and hat said, "How right you are. The children, the staff, the house, and, of course, the husband—there's always something demanding a woman's attention. Sometimes I get to the end of a day and I find myself wondering how I've managed to get through it at all."

"Maybe it would be worth it to find the right moment to think only of yourself?" Clara replied.

"Absolutely right!" the countess rumbled. "You only get to live this life once."

"What did you mean when you said that a cream has to suit a woman's skin?" asked one of the women.

"Well, the air and wind here at the lake, for example, are different than in a city. It's important to take that into consideration when choosing a skin cream and—" Clara broke off when she felt a small jab in her back.

"Mrs. Berg's products are the best I have ever tried. Personally, I never want to be without them again! She is a pharmacist's daughter, and she has spent years building her knowledge to the point where she is now a true expert in beauty matters." Lilo paused dramatically to let her words sink in.

Embarrassed by all the attention, Clara smiled and lowered her eyes. "My customers have to decide that for themselves. But I do believe that the very best is only just good enough for the women who come to me," she said. "That's why I start every consultation with a thorough examination of the skin."

"Sounds almost like a visit to the doctor," a young woman said, giggling.

"It sounds sincere and rigorous to me, and I like that," said Countess Zuzanna. "Too often, we women are not taken seriously at all."

"Wise words, Countess, and true," said Lilo, then she turned to the women around them. "Ladies, I am sure you will understand that Mrs. Berg can only pass on a fraction of her knowledge just now. Why don't you visit her at Bel Étage? That would be best, wouldn't it, my dear Clara?" She put her arm around Clara's shoulders as a sign of their closeness.

Clara stiffened at Lilo's touch. Suddenly, she felt as if she were back in earlier times. With Gerhard at a reception or party. For Clara, there never had been anything fun about such events—only anguish, with Gerhard's right arm clamped around her shoulder. He would speak to someone, saying, *"An invitation to your country place? We'd love to! Best if you give it directly to me. My wife is a little scattered. She might forget about your party altogether . . ."* Or *"Clara? Supporting the fine arts? My wife can barely handle a pen and ink. She's a messy little writer, aren't you, Clara?"* And he would squeeze her shoulder tighter and smile as if he were her best friend.

He had belittled her like that so many times that he had worn down and crushed the last bit of self-confidence she had possessed.

"Clara?" Lilo said, when she didn't reply right away.

Clara blinked, forcing away the images from the past. Damn it, the old days were over! The people here were on her side, and they valued what she had to say. "You are all welcome to pay me a visit, any time you like," she said to the women around her.

"You already have one new customer in me!" said Countess Zuzanna. "My days as any kind of beauty are long past, but I would love to sample all your fragrant lotions and potions."

Clara's heart instantly beat faster. The countess, in her shop! When Therese found out about that, she would burst with envy!

"A beauty shop . . . I think I'd find a place like that interesting, but what if someone saw me there?" said the woman wearing the hat.

"What of it?" the countess rumbled. "Why shouldn't they see that you think something of yourself?"

"There's nothing disgraceful about it," said the elderly woman. "All the best people visit the Paris place that I mentioned. It's very much *en vogue* to be seen there!"

"And it's just the same for us," said Lilo.

"In that case . . ." The woman with the hat took a deep breath. "I would like to make an appointment with you."

"So would I!"

"But my dears, I am first in line!" boomed the countess.

Clara looked helplessly from one woman to the next. She was about to say, "Don't worry, I can make appointments for all of you," when she suddenly stopped herself. Clara remembered something from the trip she had gone on with Isabelle to try to sell her champagne. Isabelle's business had been on the verge of going under, but when she met her American customers, she acted as if her stock were very limited indeed, and as if she would be doing the men a favor if she were to sell them anything at all. It made the Americans want Isabelle's champagne even more.

"The season has just begun, but my appointment book is already rather full. Before I can say yes to anyone, I will need to take a close look at my calendar," she said, and the women around her responded with looks of dismay, almost shock.

Clara smiled to herself.

The very next day, Countess Zuzanna came to Bel Étage with half a dozen young women. Within an hour, she bought up all of Clara's stock and ordered three dozen bars of lavender soap as gifts for guests to her upcoming soirees. In the nights that followed, Clara hardly slept at all. Hour after hour, fatigued but happy, she stood in her laboratory and replenished her supply of soaps, creams, and lotions. Long hours aside, she still swam every morning without fail: it refreshed her and prepared her for the day.

Word soon circulated among high-society circles—and the summer tourists as well—that the Polish countess had fallen for Clara Berg's products. Hardly fifteen minutes could pass without the bell over the front door ringing, and Clara's calendar was booked with "skin consultations." As popular as her services and products had become, there were still women who did not want to be seen in a beauty shop, and they went to great lengths to arrive stealthily. To Clara's relief, though, there were also many women who had no such concerns. "I've heard that a visit to your place here is very much *en mode*," said one, while the next openly stated why she was there: "My husband is very . . . demanding. I want to look young and pretty for him, to make sure he doesn't go looking for a younger lover."

Many clients combined their visit to Clara with an appointment with Therese, who also had her hands full keeping up with demand. While the hairdresser kept her customers entertained with stories from her own life, Clara instead listened patiently to the needs of her clients and offered at least one solution to nearly every problem. But many of her skin-care recommendations were so new that, at first, her customers resisted her advice.

"You want me to splash water on my face like a farmer's wife? How vulgar!" The woman who had been wearing the hat at Countess Zuzanna's spring ball was clearly shocked by Clara's recommendation that cold water would improve the circulation in her skin. Clara, who had heard this objection before, demonstrated what she had in mind at her washbasin. She formed her hands into a bowl, dipped them in the water, and splashed it onto her face. She repeated the process several times, then asked the woman to try it. The woman needed some coaxing at first, and she shrieked at the shock when the cold water splashed against her skin, but Clara insisted that she keep going.

Finally, after sloshing the chilly water on her face half a dozen times, the woman said, "That isn't too bad. Actually . . . it feels wonderful." She looked in amazement at her rosy cheeks in the mirror. She hadn't looked so healthy in years.

Clara smiled and recommended her rose-scented cream. "Of course, it would be best if you came to me regularly during your stay here. I could pamper your skin with steam baths, herbal wraps, and face massages."

Even as Clara spoke, the woman took out a small leather-clad book. "When can we start?"

When another woman objected strongly to using a generous amount of cream on her skin because of the smell, Clara nodded. "I don't like the medicine smell of those old-fashioned creams, either. But try this one." She held out one of her small jars and waited for the woman's reaction. She was not disappointed.

"That smells like morning dew in spring!"

"You'll see how good it is for your skin. Before I started using it, my skin got so tight that it hurt, especially in the evenings. Now that tension is gone completely," said Clara, and patted her own cheeks to demonstrate.

The woman nodded admiringly. "You have the skin of a young girl. If that comes from the cream, then I'll buy two jars here and now."

"Well, try it first," Clara laughed. "You can always come to me for more."

"I will. I'll also take the toner, and a few bars of soap. Presents for the ones who couldn't come with me."

Others were harder to win over.

"As young and lovely as you are, you're the best advertising your products could have. But still, who's to say they would work for me? And how is it that you know so much about these things?" one dubious customer asked.

"As a pharmacist's daughter, I've always been interested in the skin's needs," Clara explained. "There's no secret behind beautiful skin, just regular care with good products."

The description "pharmacist's daughter," combined with Clara's white laboratory coat, worked wonders, even with the skeptics.

***

By August, the Bel Étage was so busy that Clara could no longer take care of everything alone. Although it wasn't easy for her, after much consideration she decided to take on an assistant. Sophie Bauer was Elisabeth Kaiser's niece and had previously worked for free in her parents' guesthouse. But in the next year, she and her fiancé planned to marry and set up a home of their own, and for that they needed money. For that reason, and several others, Sophie explained that working for Clara seemed like a heaven-sent opportunity: The lovely shop! All the fragrant creams! And no more scrubbing floors sticky with beer, as she had had to do working for her parents.

On her first day, Sophie Bauer turned up at the shop in a crisp white apron and with her hair pinned up tightly—just as Clara presented herself in the shop. Clara congratulated herself on her decision. She took it as a stroke of good fortune that her young assistant had the same name as her own daughter; every time she said Sophie's name, she automatically thought of her daughter, and it made her feel a little closer.

At twenty-five, Sophie already had a lovely way with people, and she was very keen to learn. There was only one thing that Clara did not like about Sophie: she tried so desperately to hide her freckles with rice powder that it looked as if she was wearing a mask. On her first day, Clara forbade her to use the stuff again.

"It smells horrible, and it's like a layer of dust on your skin that stops it from breathing properly. You have beautiful skin, but if you keep using that powder, all you'll have is pimples and sores."

"I just want to hide my freckles. Do you have a better powder?" she asked Clara hopefully.

"I don't. Not yet. Although I do have an idea for a new kind of face powder, one made with mineral pigments. As soon as I have a little time, I'll get to work on it in my laboratory. A powder that smells good and doesn't make you look like you're wearing a mask would almost sell itself, I'm sure." She wanted nothing more than to get to work on it that minute, but she made herself be reasonable. "Meanwhile, don't worry about your freckles. You're pretty just as you are. Now let me show you what's what before the customers start to arrive.

"When a woman comes in for a skin consultation, I bring her over here." Clara walked toward the window, under which a small chair had been placed. "This is where I have the best light and can examine the customer's skin properly." She patted the magnifying glass that lay on a small table next to the chair.

"Now this place is even more like a doctor's office, with *two* doctors!" said Therese, who just had entered the shop and was hanging up her coat.

"May I introduce Sophie Bauer, my new assistant?" said Clara with a smile.

After the two women greeted each other, Clara said to Therese, "You'll just have to get used to the sight of two lab coats. Cleanliness is absolutely crucial for what we do. For our clothes, the laboratory, and the patient chair." She looked over pointedly at Therese's side of the shop, where hair from the previous day was still lying on the floor.

But Therese was immune to such criticisms. "Patient chair, pfff! It's as I said—like visiting the doctor," she said as she admired herself in the mirror. She was wearing an elaborate lacy dress that was better suited to a night at the opera than a day styling hair.

"Are you going out again?" said Clara when she saw that Therese did no more than straighten a few things that were lying around before pulling on her coat again.

"Terrible, isn't it? But Thierry insists that I go over to Switzerland with him. He wants to show me his chalet." She sighed rapturously. "Oh, the day is simply too nice to spend it in here! Only two customers have booked for today . . . They will just have to come back tomorrow."

"Thierry?" Clara raised her eyebrows. "What does Hubert have to say about you going off with another man?" Once again she would have to tell Therese's customers that the hairdresser wasn't at work. She found the situation impossible. But Therese was who she was, and she did whatever she liked.

"Hubert!" Therese waved her hand dismissively. "In all the months we were together, he didn't manage to get an invitation from Count Zeppelin even once. I'm fairly sure that Hubert was leading me up the garden path about his position. Thierry, on the other hand . . ." She sighed again. Then, with a sidelong glance at Sophie, she said, "I'll tell you about him another time."

Clara nodded. Her eye was drawn unconsciously to the permanent-wave apparatus that took up an entire corner of Therese's side of their shop. It had taken three men to unload it from the wagon and drag it inside, where it stood in its corner like a torture instrument. Hubert had paid for it—for that, at least, he was still good enough.

Chapter Nineteen

Berlin, September 1907

Dearest Clara,
I hope this letter finds you well. Before I write another
word, I must thank you for the wonderful package you
sent! Your creams are getting better and better all the
time. I found the verbena skin cream especially good,
and I use the verbena facial cleanser every day now. You
remember how I always had a few ugly little spots on my
forehead? Well, now they are gone. Thank you!

Clara smiled. Josephine had never bothered much about her
appearance. She was a natural beauty, but it made Clara happy to know
that her friend, who was always so busy, was finding at least a little time
to pamper herself.

Nothing much has changed here in Berlin. The
weather this summer has been miserable, raining all the
time, and Amelie and her friends have been spending all

day inside and going mad with boredom. And we had been looking forward so very much to going cycling and going on outings to Wannsee lake.

As she read, Clara felt the familiar stab in her heart. It happened every time anyone she knew so much as mentioned their children.

The bad weather is also the reason that I can't tell you as much about your children as you would probably like. Amelie and Sophie spent a lot of time playing together in the park in spring before the weather turned, but all through this wet summer, they have not seen much of each other. A few days ago, out of sheer desperation, I went for a walk along your old street. As discreetly as I could, of course.

Clara smiled, but the pain in her heart grew. Dear Josephine.

It was one of the rare sunny days we've had. And in your front garden, I saw a young woman sitting on a blanket playing with Sophie and her dolls. No sign of the old nanny Stumpfe at all! I was so surprised that all I could do was stand there and stare and wonder who she was. Oh, Clara, Sophie has grown so much this year! She has legs as long as a foal's, and she moves with a natural grace that my Amelie could only dream about.

A tear splashed onto the stationery. Clara blinked.

I didn't feel comfortable watching like that, but I stayed anyway and hoped that Gerhard was at his office and not at home. Then Sophie spotted me. She came running over to me holding the young woman's hand. I introduced myself and discovered that the young woman is the new nanny. Old Mrs. Stumpfe has moved in with her son down in Märkische Schweiz. "She even lives in the house with us!" Sophie said about the new nanny, and she smiled from ear to ear. The nanny's name is Marianne Klein, and I must say she made a very good impression on me. She was very nice with Sophie, who really seemed to like her, too. I didn't see Matthias, however. When I asked about him, Miss Klein said that he was away at a summer camp and that he was apparently having a wonderful time.

Matthias? At camp? Clara imagined tents standing in water, children wrapped up in sodden blankets. Tin plates half-filled with watery soup. Rough manners and a rougher atmosphere. Wild games in the woods and on the field. Clara could not imagine her delicate son being very happy there at all. It must have been one of Gerhard's attempts to "make a man out of the boy," Clara thought, simultaneously angry and helpless. Her hands shaking, she went on reading Josephine's letter.

Dear Clara, I thought for a long time about whether I should write all this to you at all. I'm sure my few lines offer you some consolation but that they are also very painful. Still, I think that anything to do with your children must be of great interest to you. I am convinced that children never forget their mother! Sophie, of course, asked after you immediately. I gave her a kiss on her forehead and told her it was from you. I hope it was all right to do that? Oh, Clara . . .

Clara let the letter sink onto her lap. Her cheeks were wet with tears, and there was a lump in her throat so big it was hard for her to breathe. As wonderful as her new life might be—her days so self-determined and fulfilling—her longing for her children was like a thorn that dug deeply into her skin.

"Do you know that it's been exactly a year since you arrived in Meersburg?" said Lilo one morning as they undressed in their private swimming area.

"A year ago? Today?" Clara stretched her arms in the air to loosen up. "I'm surprised I didn't think of it myself." She shook her head. "It's strange. On the one hand, it feels like yesterday. On the other, it's like I've lived here all my life."

"That just proves that you feel good here," said Lilo, and she splashed water onto her legs. Clara followed her example. The water already had become quite cool. They would not be able to continue their daily swims too much longer.

"It's true. I've never been happier anywhere in my life than I am here," Clara said, and she meant it. Then she added, "As long as I don't think about giving up my children."

"You haven't given them up. Not forever," said Lilo. "You must remember this is only temporary. You are doing everything you can to ensure that is the case."

"That's true. I never would have thought that I'd be running my own business one day." Everything about the Bel Étage still felt like a dream. Neither her parents nor her husband had ever thought she would amount to much, and now she was completely responsible for the fate of her successful company!

"Anything is possible here at Lake Constance." Lilo smiled. "On three . . . ," she said, and took a deep breath. "One, two, three!"

And both women dove, slipping gracefully into the water.

***

It was midday when Clara spontaneously decided not to let her one-year anniversary slip by uncelebrated, but to enjoy it with friends instead. Elisabeth Kaiser, Lilo, the Weingartens, and Therese—they all had contributed to her finding her feet in Meersburg, and now it was time to thank them. A fine dinner, a few bottles of local wine . . . What a wonderful idea!

"Do me a favor and deliver a few messages for me, would you?" she asked Sophie, who was wiping nonexistent dust from the shelves. As the season drew to a close, the daily rush of tourists visiting the Bel Étage had fallen off. "Start at the Residenz and ask Lilo to reserve a table for me. Then . . ."

Thankful for any distraction, Sophie whipped out a small notebook and made a list of her errands.

Sophie had hardly left when Clara went into her laboratory, where large quantities of fresh raw materials were waiting to be put to use. Clara had spent the summer listening carefully to what her customers wanted: an avid skier wanted an oil-rich facial cream to protect her skin against the cold; another woman wanted a cream that would lighten age spots. Countess Zuzanna had raved about the scent of damask roses and believed it would be ideal for a facial toner.

Clara had kept copious notes, and she wanted to use the quiet months to try out her new ideas and surprise her customers the following spring. She would not, however, be able to fulfill every wish, because although Mr. Weingarten, from whom she continued to buy all her ingredients, did all he could to obtain everything she wanted, he was not always successful. An essence distilled from old damask roses? Something like that would only be available in Grasse directly. Grasse, in France, was *the* town when it came to special fragrances, he told her.

"A trip to Provence, where the real lavender grows. Or to Grasse on the Côte d'Azur . . ." The pharmacist had sighed, gazing into space at the idea. When he saw Clara's look of surprise, he added, "A man can dream."

She was mixing rose and orange blossom water together for a facial toner when the doorbell rang. Clara, with a small, frustrated sigh, pushed everything to one side, straightened her apron, and went out.

"Ah, the good woman at work in her witch's kitchen, I see?"

"Mr. Schrott," said Clara, as politely as possible. Her constant flow of customers had protected from her landlord for most of the summer, but now that things were quieter, he kept finding reasons to come by more often. Therese and Clara were normally able to get rid of him quickly, but Sophie downright feared the man. Clara was glad her assistant was not there at that moment.

"So the season's over, is it? And the golden well's run dry again?" As always, he stood uncomfortably close to her. She *hated* how he formulated almost everything as a question, and the way he always brought up her earnings was only slightly less annoying.

"My next customer is due any minute. I'm just getting everything ready for her," she said, patting her apron.

The man looked at her doubtfully. "And your pretty little assistant is out? Not everyone can afford a salary for a helper . . ."

"Miss Bauer will be back later," said Clara. "Is it something urgent, Mr. Schrott? If not, my time is tight." She pointed at the round clock hanging on the wall between the two halves of the shop.

"Oh, but you will have to take a little time for this." He extracted a crushed envelope from his pants pocket. "It is a written notice that I am raising the rent. Now that you count so many prominent people among your clientele, the minimal rent I charge you is laughable, wouldn't you say? The shop's worth a lot more now."

Clara had to laugh. "And *why* is it worth a lot more? Because I'm running it!" She did not know herself where she found the audacity, but she did not stop. "And before we talk about raising the rent, would it be too much to ask you to fix all the problems?" She stepped over to the front window. "The rain practically pours in here, and you can feel the draft coming through these cracks from across the room! The plaster is peeling off the walls in the back storeroom. And—"

"Easy, young lady, easy, all right?" Alfred Schrott raised his hands appeasingly. "Why don't we go around and you can show me everything that needs plugging or oiling? You might not know it yet, but I'm very good with my hands." He gave Clara a lewd grin and waggled his hands playfully in the air. Clara mentally rolled her eyes. *Oh, nicely done!*

"I'm afraid we're going to have to postpone that tour. Like I said, my next customer will be here any minute." If only the doorbell really would ring and a customer would step inside.

"If that's how it is." Mr. Schrott frowned, but his expression brightened again instantly. "I might be prepared to forego a rent increase altogether. You only have to be a little nice to me."

Before Clara could reply, the man wrapped his arms around her. She felt his hot breath on her face, his hungry kisses on her cheeks, her mouth, her nose, and his hands grabbing painfully at her breasts. "Let go of me, right now!" Clara screamed, writhing frantically, trying to free herself from the man's grip. The man had taken leave of his senses!

"Now don't be like that. You want it, too, a woman like you, without a man; it's only natural you would want this . . ."

***

Neither Alfred nor Clara had noticed Lydia Schrott standing at the front window with her forehead pressed against the glass.

So she'd been right! Clara did have her eye on her husband, but it was something else to see for herself the minx seducing Alfred now.

There! They were embracing! And look at that Clara Berg, snuggling against Alfred. Shameless it was, shameless! Lydia knew that men were helpless against a trollop like that, and her kindhearted Alfred more than most. Oh, yes, that ointment-mixer from the north was a hussy, through and through. Making eyes at her Alfred in the hope that he would get rid of Lydia for her. Wanted to get her oily fingers on the house and the shop, no doubt.

Oh, she could barge in and take the slut to task there and then, but she would probably just try to blame Alfred. No, she had a better idea. *Just wait, missy. I'll show you who's in charge here,* thought Lydia as she marched away. Inside the shop, Clara stomped on Mr. Schrott's foot as hard as she could, and he abruptly stopped pawing his shocked and disheveled tenant.

***

It was Lilo who had inspired the trip with her suggestion, at the end of the long tourist season, that she and Clara find some time for themselves and take a vacation in Baden-Baden. It was Lilo's hometown, and there was a luxury hotel, the Hotel Belle Époque, that she was eager to try. Plus there was the added draw of seeing Countess Zuzanna, who had moved from Meersburg to Baden-Baden for the winter.

As appealing as a Baden-Baden vacation had sounded for all the reasons Lilo had pointed out, Clara had known right away that there was a more urgent trip she needed to take.

Laden with two suitcases and a leather travel bag, Clara arrived at Görlitzer Station in Berlin early in the afternoon on October 30, after more than two days of travel. She had not gone ten steps along the platform when she felt her stomach begin to churn. Berlin . . .

She stopped on the sidewalk in front of the station and looked around. To her left she was relieved to see the Schreimann Hotel, where Lilo had arranged a room for her.

While Lilo had helped her plan her trip, Clara had not told anybody in Berlin that she was coming. She wanted to surprise her children right away and then, that evening, Josephine. She had brought gifts, of course: for Sophie, a beautiful porcelain doll and a small case packed with doll's clothes, and for Matthias, a miniature steam engine. For Josephine, she had her complete new skin-care series, and for Josephine's daughter, she brought another doll.

Clara sighed. Wouldn't her children and Josephine be surprised to see her!

There was no one at the hotel reception desk. Clara rang the bell forcefully. She had no time to lose. Finally, finally, more than a year after she left Berlin, she was going to see her children again.

An hour later, Clara approached her old home. It was two in the afternoon, and she had chosen the time carefully. Gerhard was at his office during the day, and when he closed his practice on Wednesday afternoons, he always went out with a group of other doctors. Sophie and Matthias, she hoped, would already be home from school but would not yet have gone off to any afternoon activities. The only other person to deal with would be the young nanny that Josephine had mentioned in her letter, and she would certainly not mind if Clara spent a long afternoon with her children. Clara began to walk faster.

The house looked as it always had. The curtains that she had taken so long to crochet were still there. The garden was in good order, if rather drab because it was November.

Strange, thought Clara, setting down the bag with the gifts. She had spent so many years of her life there, but apart from the deep longing to see her children again, she felt nothing. No connection to the house itself. Not the slightest trace of regret. No sadness.

She pressed the bell and jumped when the door immediately opened wide. "Come in, come in. The broken stovepipe is in the kitchen," came a man's voice from the hallway.

Gerhard! Clara's hand flew to her throat. The fear went through her so quickly that her knees began to tremble. She wanted to turn and run away, far away, or to make herself invisible. But before she could take a single step, she heard Gerhard's voice again. "Is there a problem—" The next moment, he was on the doorstep in front of her. His face turned to a scowl. "You?" His eyes moved quickly down from her head, past her elegant traveling outfit, and to the tips of her toes. He glanced at her large bag. "What the devil are you doing here?"

"What a friendly greeting," said Clara. "I would like to see the children. I am still their mother, after all." Her voice was shaking, and her hands, too. She made fists of them. He did not look any different. Handsome, arrogant, and callous.

Gerhard snorted with laughter, but when he spoke he all but spat. "Oh, you would, would you? What makes you think for a moment that I would let you see my children?" He took a step toward her threateningly, and for a moment Clara thought he might try to hit her. *Don't you dare,* she thought, holding her ground despite her fear.

The next moment, a woman's voice came from inside the house. "Gerhard, what is going on out there?"

And then another voice, softer and more girlish: "Mama? Is Mama here?"

"It's just some good-for-nothing that strayed onto our street, that's all. Marianne, send the children to their room!" Gerhard shouted over his shoulder. Then he turned back to Clara. "Have you forgotten that the court banned you from having anything to do with both of the children? You have no business here, so go—now—or I will send for the police!"

"Gerhard, please! Half an hour, that's all! I've missed them so much . . ." Clara pressed her lips together hard to stop herself from crying.

"The state of your feelings does not interest me. Leave now! And take your trash with you." He kicked the bag that Clara had set down, and there was a crunch that Clara felt sure was the head of Sophie's doll breaking.

***

"It was so horrible," Clara sobbed an hour later. "I couldn't even say hello to them, and I even heard Sophie calling out to me." She covered her face with her hands.

Helplessly, Josephine put one arm around her weeping friend. "Don't cry. Things will get better again." She was trying to console Clara, but she knew how hollow her words sounded. Sometimes, nothing gets better again.

She and Adrian had been ready to go out when the doorbell rang. *The driver,* Josephine had thought, and had picked up her hat and gloves. They were planning to spend the afternoon looking at an empty factory hall with a large adjoining open area in Berlin's north. Once they had decided to risk a foray into the automobile industry, they urgently needed more space.

But it was not their driver. It was Clara, standing on the doorstep. One look at her bloodless face and Josephine knew that something bad had happened. She and Adrian had looked at one another.

"You stay here. If I think the property might be what we need, we can go and look at it together another time," Adrian had whispered to her before leaving.

Josephine smiled sadly. Adrian was so understanding and sympathetic. Why couldn't Clara have been as lucky?

Josephine led Clara into the sitting room, and the two friends sat together on the sofa. "It's been over a year since I last saw either of my children. Some days, I've wanted to see them so much that I was overcome by pain. When it finally was clear that I could travel to Berlin, I thought I might perish from the ache." She looked at Josephine almost as if it were all her fault. "Why did Gerhard have to be home today? Why today?"

Josephine had nothing to say.

"What must Sophie think of me? She heard me. Maybe she even saw me from the window," Clara said, with panic in her voice.

"Oh, Clara," said Josephine weakly. She could have told Clara from the start that Gerhard Gropius would never allow her to see the children, but she hadn't thought it would be necessary. Now, though, she was amazed at Clara's naïveté, at how she could assume that such a spontaneous visit would even be possible.

"I've been working so hard, morning to night, to build up my business, to earn a livelihood of my own. And for what? Without my children, it's for nothing. I might as well jump in front of a train. At least then the misery would end."

"Now stop it!" Josephine said vehemently. "Gerhard's won the last battles, but not the war." She tugged lightly at the bell pull that hung beside the sofa. When her maid appeared, she said, "Ludovika, make us a pot of coffee, please, and a bring a few slices of *gugelhupf*. The carafe of cognac and two glasses, too."

At first, Clara resisted. She did not want to eat or drink anything. Josephine pressed the glass of cognac into her hand. "Take it, drink it. No talking back!" To add emphasis to her words, she raised her own snifter and swallowed the contents in a single draft. The golden liquid ran warm and harsh down her throat, and she felt its heat spread through her.

"I never want to hear about an idea to jump in front of a train or anything like it, is that clear?" she said severely when Clara also had drained her glass. "You've already achieved so much in your life, and you will get through this crisis as well. Expecting Gerhard to treat you fairly, by the way, is like expecting to jump into Lake Constance and not get wet." She saw that her remark drew a tiny smile from Clara.

"If Gerhard were a sensitive, compassionate man, you would never have divorced him. But he isn't. He's cruel, and he has always enjoyed watching you suffer. Why would that have changed since your divorce? Just think about the humiliation you inflicted on him with that."

Clara shrugged helplessly. "But what does that mean for me? That I can never see my children again, ever?"

Josephine knew she needed to tread carefully, but she said, "Of course you will see them again. But you have will to be a lot more clever about it than you were today. Maybe you should hire a lawyer?"

"A lawyer?" Clara suddenly sat at attention, and some color came back to her face. "Do you really think a lawyer could do something?"

Josephine thought of the lawyer who had represented Clara—ineffectively—during her divorce trial. "A good lawyer could at least examine the legality of the court's original decision. But the time may not yet be ripe to take that step," she said with a little more reserve. Pensive, she crumbled a piece of cake into her plate. "You are an independent businesswoman now, earning your own money. That's a big step forward. But you're still stained by the affair you created to get away from Gerhard. And by the divorce." Despite Josephine's ironic tone of voice, Clara winced. Josephine went on quickly. "If you really expect a lawyer to make any headway for you, he will need strong evidence that you have an impeccable reputation. Earning a good living, by itself, won't be enough, nor even will your successful business. Living in your own apartment instead of a hotel room, per-haps even a new husband . . . *that* would show the court that you can offer your children stability." She did not mention that Gerhard was doing everything he could to offer exactly that kind of stability for his children. So far there were only rumors, but people were saying that the new nanny had become more to him than an employee.

"And I'm supposed to just conjure up a new husband out of my hat?" Clara snorted indignantly. "No, thank you. I've had enough of men."

Josephine laughed. "That's exactly what Isabelle said after Leon's death, remember? And then she went and fell in love after all, and with two men at once."

"That must have been the French air. Or all the champagne," Clara said. "But you don't fall in love in Lake Constance quite so fast."

Both women laughed, but they quickly grew serious again.

"Forget my suggestion," said Josephine. "Getting married only to get a judge to give you visiting rights to your children isn't the solution. But somewhere, sometime, you are going to fall in love again, and then . . ." She shrugged. "I understand that, for now, you want to prove that you can get your own life in order. But pushing too hard and acting rashly won't help. You have to move cleverly and cautiously—and be patient!"

"Be patient, when all it does is tear my heart apart?" Clara replied, tears again brimming in her eyes.

***

The girls collected pinecones, acorns, and beech nuts beneath the trees on the edge of the park. Their braids swung wildly, the moist air causing the ends to curl and crinkle. It was a cool, windy early November day, and apart from a few people walking their dogs, the park was empty. But the girls were so involved in their collecting that they forgot about the cold.

Josephine called the girls over to her to show them something. Amelie immediately ran to her mother, Sophie just behind.

Clara pushed aside a few branches to be able to see better from her hiding place. When she realized what Josephine had made for the girls, she had to smile. Josephine had used a small knife to carve a hole in an acorn and had then pushed a small branch into the hole. Her handiwork looked like a pipe. And, in fact, Josephine lifted her creation to her mouth and pretended to smoke.

The two girls squealed with glee.

The young woman who had come with Sophie said something in an admonishing tone, but she, too, was smiling. She looked very nice. Tall, blond, and pretty, with an open, friendly face. Sophie's new nanny looked as if she would not hurt a fly.

Sophie tugged trustingly at the woman's skirt. "Can I have a pipe like that, too? There are lots of fat acorns back there." Sophie gracefully bounded off toward the trees, and the nanny followed.

"I don't think we should tell your papa that you want to smoke, though. He could get the wrong impression about how I'm caring for you," the nanny said, smiling back at Josephine.

"Men don't need to know everything," Josephine said, with a conspiratorial wink back.

Clara pressed her hand over her mouth to stop herself from sobbing out loud. That could have been an exchange between her and Josephine.

How grown up her daughter was. She would turn eight in January. A schoolgirl now, not a little child anymore. Her brown-and-white checked skirt stopped just above her knee. It was about time someone sewed a frill along the hem of the skirt to lengthen it. Or crocheted a lace border. *Red,* thought Clara, *that would match the brown nicely.* She felt a pang in her heart. It took all the strength she had just to stay out of sight behind the cherry laurel bush. There were just a few yards between her and her daughter. To take her in her arms, to kiss her, to hold her tight . . . to reassure her that her mother loved her. She would have given anything. Anything! But she didn't. She couldn't. So she stayed hidden in the bushes like a thief.

A few hours later, she was on the train, heading back to Lake Constance. She was so exhausted that she could not imagine even changing trains at the next stop. All she could picture was Sophie's too-short skirt. She never would have allowed her to wear anything that she had grown out of. A mother had an eye for things like that. It didn't matter how nice the nanny was; she was no replacement for a mother.

What had she done, getting the divorce? Why hadn't she just kept putting up with Gerhard's cruelty? Her children would have been worth it ten times over.

Her thoughts were as grim as the landscape passing beyond the window of the train. This entire trip had been a mistake. She had been so stupid, so thoughtless, that it was doomed to failure from the start. Nothing like that could ever be allowed to happen to her again. Never again!

At some point, Clara had had enough of her own silent accusations, and she felt herself gripped by such a destructive fury that she could barely stay in her seat. She wanted to get up and smash the train compartment to pieces. Or hit somebody. She was scaring herself, she realized. What kind of law was it that ordained that a mother could no longer see her children just because she was divorced from their father? Why was the law always on the side of the men, and never on the side of women or justice? Wasn't it time to change that, and not just swallow every injustice uncomplainingly? Wasn't it time to defend herself?

It would not be the first time, after all. Back then, in court, she had defied Gerhard. She had spent weeks refining her story of the traveling salesman, and only when every detail was in place did she tell the court her story. It was only because of her clever, careful preparation that the judge had granted the divorce.

"Acting rashly won't help. You have to move cleverly and cautiously—and be patient!" Josephine had advised her. Now Clara could see just how right her friend was.

She would fight for her children! She would scrutinize every step she took to see if it would help that single-minded cause. No more impetuous, ill-considered decisions like this trip to Berlin! No. She would continue to build up her business to give herself a solid, reliable income. And she would look for a good, large apartment. Josephine had been right about that, too—a judge wouldn't look favorably upon a hotel room as a home. But if she had an apartment of her own, perhaps then the court would allow the children to visit her during their vacation.

Clara smiled dreamily. She would take Matthias to Friedrichshafen, and with a bit of luck they would be able to watch the zeppelins rising from their enormous hangar. And Sophie was certain to find the Bel Étage fantastic. She could take both of them to the lake, and they would be amazed to see how well their mother could swim!

The next moment, her smile vanished, and a thin line appeared on her forehead, between her eyes. The battle would take longer than she wanted it to. Gerhard would throw every obstacle he could find in her path. But that was just how things were. She would show him how resilient she could be.

Chapter Twenty

"So how was business?" Clara asked as she hung up her coat at Bel Étage. She inhaled deeply, luxuriating in the perfume of lavender and rose, and looked around her shop. It was good to be back.

"What business?" replied Sophie.

Clara laughed as she straightened the lime-green velvet armchair her customers used during their skin consultations.

"It's true there are some customers who only want to be seen by the boss, but we have a lot of women who know that *you* know about beauty treatments, too." She smiled benevolently at her young assistant, then went to the cash register and opened it. She blinked, confused. If she were not mistaken, the register held exactly fifty-five marks—the same amount she had handed over to Sophie before she had gone away, and not a pfennig more.

"I don't know how to tell you this." Sophie shrugged helplessly. "Since you left, not a single customer has come in. I've been going mad, checking the door ten times a day to make sure I hadn't accidentally locked it." She shook her head. Clara frowned. "Has anything special happened in town? Something that's been taking up all the ladies' time?" She couldn't imagine herself what that might be.

Sophie shook her head. "At my parents' guesthouse it's business as usual, and I haven't heard about anything else."

"And Therese? Where is she?" said Clara, narrowing her eyes in the direction of the abandoned hairdressers.

"Sick. She caught a cold when she was out boating, and she's been in bed ever since."

Clara's frown deepened. Was it a cold or a new suitor that was keeping her in bed? She dismissed the thought. She would deal with Therese later. "Maybe everyone's come down with a cold?" That would explain the lack of customers.

But Sophie simply shook her head. She looked as if she were close to tears.

"Now don't fret," said Clara consolingly. "In winter, without the tourists, we're bound to have some quiet days." But even on the quietest days, a handful of customers had found their way to her shop. Had her run of luck with the business run its course? Had the demand for good creams and lotions evaporated? The very thought was so terrifying that Clara quickly pushed it aside. *No doubt the rest of Meersburg is just as quiet,* she thought, trying to encourage herself.

"You know what?" she said with forced cheerfulness. "You make us both a cup of tea, and I'll pay a visit to Fabienne in the flower shop. Some nice flowers on the counter will get rid of the November blues. They will be good for the customers, too." The florist was a notorious chatterbox, and Clara was certain that she would find out from her what was going on.

The fog lying over the lake like an eiderdown, the choir where they both sang on Wednesday evenings, the approaching days of Advent—all of Clara's attempts to start a conversation with the florist failed. Without a word, Fabienne Alber tied the tea roses that Clara had chosen into a bouquet.

"Did my cream help with your chapped hands?" Clara finally asked. She extended one hand across the counter invitingly. "May I see?"

But instead of showing her hands to Clara, the florist took a step back. "My hands are fine, thank you. That comes to four marks fifty. Can I get you anything else?"

Clara left the florist's shop more confused than when she went in. She had never known Fabienne Alber to be so uncommunicative. Worse, she had been downright unfriendly!

Clara had almost reached the Bel Étage again when she thought better of it and walked a block farther.

"I need some new stationery," she said to Elsbeth Treiber, who was redoing her window display when Clara entered the shop. "Now that winter's here and everything has slowed down, one finally has a little more time to devote to letter writing, don't you think?"

"*I* really can't complain about a lack of work," said Elsbeth, and Clara thought she could hear a caustic undertone in the words. Elsbeth took several kinds of stationery out of a drawer and set them out in front of Clara. "Let me know when you've chosen something," she said, and went back to her window.

I've had far better service here, too, thought Clara as she flicked through the different papers unenthusiastically.

***

"At first, I couldn't believe it when Sophie told me not a single customer had come in to Bel Étage for days. But it's true! Yesterday and today, too. No one! You'd think a cholera epidemic had broken out," said Clara to Lilo three days later. Lilo had only returned the previous evening from her trip to Baden-Baden. Clara had been looking forward to seeing her friend again. She had wanted to tell her about how difficult her return to Berlin had been, but all she could talk about now was the inexplicable disappearance of her customers.

She pushed away her plate of soup. "I'm sorry, but I've lost my appetite. It isn't enough that everyone seems to be avoiding my shop, but I get the feeling they're avoiding *me*, too. Even the customers I've had the best relationships with turn away in the street to avoid talking to me." She looked at Lilo. "What have I done wrong? I can't think of a single mistake."

Lilo said nothing. Then she waved over one of the waitresses to take their soup plates. When the girl left, Lilo refilled Clara's wine glass. *Diversionary tactics? That's strange,* thought Clara.

"Lilo, do you know something I don't?" she said, and the hollow feeling in her belly told her she was about to hear something she would not like.

"I was away, too. What am I supposed to know?" Lilo said defensively and drank a mouthful of her wine. But when she saw Clara's despairing expression, she slowly added. "All right. But I can't tell you anything concrete. It's just a rumor, that's all."

Clara nodded impatiently. If Lilo talked about a rumor, she could assume that it contained more than a grain of truth.

"I haven't spoken to many people yet, but it seems likely you can thank your landlady for your disappearing customers."

"Lydia Schrott? She's behind this? But I don't understand . . ." Clara swallowed.

Lilo leaned across the table conspiratorially and whispered, "It seems that Lydia Schrott has been spreading word around Meersburg that your creams contain a dangerous poisonous acid and that they gave her a bad rash."

Clara jumped up so suddenly that she bumped the table, nearly knocking over the wine. "That's outrageous! First, her husband forces himself on me so vigorously that I was lucky to escape, and now his wife is spreading lies?"

"Calm down and talk quietly. Everyone is looking!" said Lilo, urging Clara to sit.

Clara's heart was pounding and she was shaking with anger. "I feel like wringing Lydia Schrott's neck," she hissed. "What does she get out of it? If I can't pay my rent anymore, it only hurts her."

"Maybe she *wants* you out," said Lilo. "Her lies and her husband's interest in you might be connected. Have you considered that? The woman is jealous!"

Clara snorted. "As if I'd ever give that repulsive beast husband of hers a second glance. Besides, Alfred Schrott chases every skirt in town. It's not as if I'm the only one he's after. Do you really think . . .? And the people have nothing better to do than believe the words of that jealous old hag? They think Lydia Schrott is more trustworthy than I am?" Clara's voice was growing loud and shrill again, but when she saw Lilo's raised eyebrows, she quieted down. "Sorry. But it's like a knife in the back. I always thought the women here trusted me."

"Against malicious gossip, you don't stand a chance," said Lilo with suppressed fury. "I found that out for myself a few years ago. My ex-husband's business partner, Kurt, didn't like me 'sticking my nose in' all the time. He and I had a different opinion about every single important decision. The man hated me!" Lilo laughed bitterly. "And I, idiot that I am, thought that because I was Horst's wife I was immune to his attacks. But I was wrong. At some point, Kurt began spreading rumors that I was sleeping with the male guests at our sanatoriums."

"Your husband didn't believe it, I hope?" Clara forgot about her own situation as she listened in horror to her friend's story.

"Not at first," said Lilo. "But backstabbers like Kurt—and Lydia Schrott—are very clever. It seems that Kurt was constantly dropping insinuations, things that cast me in a bad light. In the end, it got so bad that I couldn't bear the endless fights and having to justify myself all the time. That was when I left town."

"But I thought you left of your own accord?" Clara didn't know what to believe anymore.

Lilo sighed. "You can look at anything two ways." She waved one hand as if throwing something away. "Old history. Enough. I'm glad those times are over. And as far as you're concerned . . ." She took Clara's right hand in hers and squeezed it. "I hope with all my heart that you defend yourself better than I ever could."

Chapter Twenty-One

Northern Italy, early 1908

The meeting was taking place at the Old Jug Inn. A week earlier, Giacomo Totosano had reserved the side room in Elva's only tavern, and a day later Lorenzo Sorri had shown up with the same request. Anna, the proprietress, had known perfectly well that a meeting between the hair-trading families was to take place in the room, but she still allowed herself the fun of saying to Lorenzo, "*Scusi*, but everything is booked for that evening." Only after Lorenzo Sorri started pulling at his beard did she tell him that it was actually his business partner, Giacomo, who had booked the room. For *both* of them.

When he heard that, Anna had sensed Lorenzo's blood was boiling, but the hair trader presented his usual friendly self. "Well, then, good old Giacomo . . . how prudent of him."

Anna had grinned to herself. As much as the Sorris and the Totosanos liked to emphasize how well they cooperated and how happy they were to do so, everyone in the village knew that the two families were locked in eternal competition. And some of the villagers took great pleasure in stirring up the men—and their wives. The wealthy hair dealers believed they were a notch better than the other villagers, and they were quite willing to show it, so a touch of revenge felt good.

The proprietress stared at the closed door and wondered what the meeting was about. Was there another wedding in the offing? Roberto Totosano and Gaia Sorri had become engaged the previous autumn, after all, and Anna was not the only person in the village wondering why a wedding date had not been announced. Certainly, her tavern could use a big wedding celebration. Anna glanced outside through the tiny window. The roads and houses of Elva were still buried beneath heavy snowdrifts. *Like a fairy tale, where everything has fallen into an eternal sleep,* she thought. She sighed heavily, but then it occurred to her that the hair traders might be planning the wedding for after Easter. Most of the snow would have melted by then, or at least Anna hoped that would be the case. Not a sound had come from the room since she had served the drinks and food they had ordered, and Toni Sorri had shut the door behind her. *No sign of a heated dispute this evening,* Anna thought with disappointment.

***

"As all of you know, for years we've been selling our hair to the dealers in Dronero," said Lorenzo Sorri, looking around at the group with an air of importance. "We did the same last year, too."

Roberto cast his father a disparaging glance. Why wasn't he speaking? Why did he hand over the reins to Lorenzo?

"And as all of you also know, those dealers earn a pretty penny with the hair we collect. They sell it on the open market, shipping it off to America and England, and they make many times what they pay us."

It was an effort for Roberto to stifle a snide laugh. Did Sorri really believe that he was telling any of them anything new? Michele and he had been saying the same thing to their father for years, trying to convince him that it would be far more profitable to circumvent the dealers and sell the hair on the market themselves. But Giacomo Totosano had never wanted to hear a word of it, and they could just forget Lorenzo Sorri! Everything ran fine as it was. The old order, ad nauseam.

The old order! Roberto felt as if an iron ring were clamped around his chest, making it hard to breathe. The old order also meant the sons and daughters of the two families obediently married each other, deepening their mutual dependence. Not a word about love or affection. At the same time, Michele and Marta's marriage appeared to function very well indeed. And their sister, Elena, seemed satisfied with Federico Sorri.

Roberto looked over at Gaia Sorri, his fiancée. This year, he would have to convince himself that it could work with her. A shudder ran through him.

Gaia was pretty, certainly, and she had strong legs and large breasts, but she also had a sharp tongue, and there was something tomboyish about her that did not appeal to Roberto. He could see that, in just a few years, she would fall apart like a cheap string of pearls. Just like her mother. Instead of drinking wine and listening to the men's discussion, Gaia had brought a sack of comb-hair with her. She had spread it all out on the table in front of her and was going through it, patiently sorting it into its various lengths and thicknesses. It almost drove Roberto insane. The sight of the dusty hair nauseated him. He felt like letting out a powerful sneeze and "accidentally" blowing the hair off the table, but he didn't think he could pull it off. He wondered whom Gaia was trying to impress with her fake industriousness. He would have preferred it a thousand times over to see his bride-to-be stitching some pretty embroidery instead.

Comb-hair was hair that had fallen out or been combed out rather than cut off. It was a waste product, collected over the course of a year by the residents of the houses that Roberto and Michele visited: picked from pillows, the floor, the wash basin, wherever it landed. When the hair traders came to buy hair, the residents usually handed over a small sack of comb-hair as well, and the brothers paid only a few pennies for it. Sorting the loose and usually foul-smelling hair was hard work, and it brought little profit because it was no good for wigs and only used to weave cheap hair brooches and rings. Roberto could not imagine who would voluntarily wear such a piece of jewelry on their lapel or finger. But the Sorri and Totosano women sorted the comb-hair gladly, because they were allowed to keep the money from its resale for themselves and could spend it how they liked. That, too, was the old order.

The old order. Roberto would have given anything for a terrible avalanche to come roaring down the mountain and sweep away all the old laws and rules and bury them forever. Why was he the only one concerned? The Sorri brothers—Federico, Martine, and Toni—sat there, drinking their wine, adding nothing, not even a yes or no, to the discussion. Not that he'd contributed much himself. But no one expected it from him any more than they did from any of the sons. It was only their fathers who showed off with big speeches.

"The hair trade in Elva has worked very well for a very long time, mainly because our families cooperate. And that's the way it should continue." Lorenzo Sorri's gaze moved from one person to the next, and everywhere he looked heads nodded in agreement.

What was the old man getting at? Roberto wondered. He turned and looked peevishly at Toni Sorri, sitting next to him and stuffing his face with a dish of pickled kidneys and onions as if he hadn't eaten in days, which Roberto knew was not the case with a mother who cooked like Toni's did. The biting smell of the food mixed with the stale atmosphere of the room, and once again Roberto felt as if he could not get any air.

Toni's long hair fell in his face, and strands caught on his lips, greasy with onion broth. If Toni kept on like that, he'd have trouble getting women to part with their hair at all—they would not like the idea of handing over their locks to a pig like him, Roberto thought. He and Michele took a completely different approach. Even on days when they'd had to spend the previous night in a stable, not a piece of straw remained on their clothes. The Totosano brothers always looked neat, and that simply made a better impression.

"They can't be serious," said Michele, on the other side, and he gave Roberto a jab in the ribs. "Did you hear that?"

Roberto had been so caught up in his thoughts that he had stopped listening to Lorenzo Sorri. He shook his head, momentarily confused.

"But we've always dreamed of reselling the hair ourselves!" Michele said, perplexed, misinterpreting Roberto's shaking head.

"Oh, yes, of course," Roberto grumbled, angry at himself for losing his concentration. Were the patriarchs actually making a break from the old order? He looked at his father and, with as much composure as he could muster, asked "So, what exactly do you have in mind?" hoping that that topic hadn't already been discussed.

His father and Lorenzo Sorri exchanged a look and smiled, then Giacomo said, "Naturally, Lorenzo and I have considered this important step carefully. And we have decided to do things the usual way." He nodded, satisfied with his decision.

The usual way could mean many things, not all of them good. His father seemed to expect more than silence from him, so Roberto asked, "What does the usual way mean?"

Giacomo seemed pleased to hear the question. He nodded again, then said, "Lorenzo and I, in the usual way, have decided together to open a kind of subsidiary—a shop—in Zurich, from where—"

"From where, in the future, we will do business directly on the Zurich hair market," Lorenzo Sorri interrupted. "And that's not all. In our shop, we will also sell wigs. Zurich is a rich city with rich citizens, and we think we can count on good revenues," he added, his chest puffed up proudly.

A shop? The hair market? Doing business themselves? A wave of unrest rumbled through the offspring of both families. What did that mean for each of them?

"And because we want to continue with the cooperation that has served us so well in the past, we have decided to send one son from each family to Zurich. My choice is you, my dear Toni"—Lorenzo looked at his second son—"and from the Totosanos, Giacomo has selected Roberto to be his representative."

For a moment, Roberto thought that he would never breathe again. He was going to Zurich? But that meant . . . The iron ring clenched around his chest suddenly released with a bang. Away from that stifling village. Out into the big, wide world. It might even mean putting off his wedding or dissolving the engagement altogether! He would be free. He almost let out a whoop of joy. For the time being, he pushed aside the thought that he would have to travel with fat Toni.

"Why not me, Papa?" Michele asked then, with a pang of jealousy. "I'm the eldest, and I'd be good for a job like this."

"Or even better—why not let Michele and me travel together? We're a good team, a successful team!" Roberto suggested, earning a grateful look from his brother.

"Now wait just a minute until you've heard the whole plan," said Giacomo, and he rapped Roberto on the top of his head as if he were an unruly four-year-old.

"When do we go?" asked Toni indifferently, pushing away his empty plate.

"As soon as the snow has melted and the trails are passable again. Between now and then, Giacomo and I will prepare everything," Lorenzo said. "Each of you will lead a packhorse, and you will be carrying six hundred and fifty pounds of the highest-quality hair. When you get to Zurich, the first thing you will do is look for a suitable storefront. Our two families will provide the capital you will need. As for the journey itself, I will give Toni enough money to get to Zurich, and Giacomo will do the same for Roberto."

Roberto's father nodded. "Until then, our women will do nothing but make wigs. We want to have a lot to offer in the shop, after all."

Selling wigs in Zurich . . . In his mind's eye, Roberto could already picture beautiful women stepping into the elegant boutique, where he would be standing behind a fine walnut counter, ready with advice for every customer. No more lice-ridden farm girls whose hair he had to cut off. No more rundown mountain huts. Instead, city style and rich people.

"Of course, we expect regular reports—one letter a week from each of you. Once you have our shop up and running, which we calculate should take no more than six months, you will go different ways. Toni will stay in Zurich, and you, my dear Roberto, will return to Elva. Michele will then go to Zurich in your place."

Michele's face brightened.

Roberto looked at his father with incomprehension. "You want me to come back in six months?" From the corner of his eye, he saw his fiancée glaring venomously at him, but he ignored her.

His father grinned. "In the fall, you'll go back to the mountain villages. No one is as good at buying women's hair as you. We simply can't do it without you. And besides, don't you want to get married this year? As you can see, my son, we've thought of everything."

***

From that day on, the first thing Roberto did every morning was look out the window. The snow was relentless, and he was beyond morose. He wanted nothing more than to be on the road. But the snow was still more than three feet deep, and the earth beneath it was frozen hard, the mountain trails impassable. When old Elena, three houses down, died at the beginning of February, the undertaker had no choice but to store her body in his shed until the earth began to thaw. The previous autumn, he had simply dug too few graves, which was another way of saying that he had not counted on winter's grip lasting so long.

Roberto could have screamed in his frustration. In conditions like that, no burial could take place, and no journey could begin.

Plip. Plip. Plip.

Roberto rolled over grumpily on his straw mattress. What was that strange, monotonous sound, ruining his sleep, annoying as a stone in a shoe?

Plip. Plip.

The next moment, he sat upright in bed. Then he jumped to the window, tore the curtain aside, and squinted out into the colorless morning light. Drops of water. Blessed drops of water. Roberto's bad mood vanished instantly. Finally.

The yard-long icicles dangling from the roof had started to melt.

Their route would take them via Turin and Milan to Monza, and from there onward to Como and Lugano, then Locarno on the shores of Lake Maggiore. After that, they would cross the Alps, following the road to Andermatt, then travel north through Switzerland until they reached Zurich. No one could tell them exactly how far that was or how long it would take them. Was it three hundred miles? Five hundred? It made no difference to Roberto if they had to travel three or five or ten weeks. For him, all that mattered was going! Gaia had been getting more and more clingy and weepy in recent weeks. "Why don't you take me with you?" she had asked Roberto one evening. Roberto had made an excuse about helping his father with an urgent repair, and quickly made his escape. Away! Just get away, get out of there, breathe again!

"These leather boots are useless! My feet are already burning again. It's like I'm walking on hot coals," Toni grumbled. He leaned on his packhorse's reins, letting the poor beast practically pull him along. It ducked its head, suffering under Toni's weight.

"We're nearly there," said Roberto, gritting his teeth. He would have given almost anything to walk in such comfortable leather, but all he had on his feet were thin linen boots. Though the patriarchs were intent on presenting everything as equal between the families, truth was that Giacomo did not like to part with the money that Roberto and Michele brought in, and Roberto was suffering for his father's tight-fistedness.

"That's what you always say, and then it still takes hours before we arrive," said Toni, sounding even more aggrieved than usual. "I'll starve to death by then. The hole in my belly is so big, I'll soon disappear into it myself."

"Then eat twice as much later," Roberto shot back. He wanted to give his detested traveling companion a good punch in the face. What a whiner Toni was!

Roberto never would have believed that the journey could be so strenuous. But it wasn't the distance traveled each day that pushed him to the edge. Nor was it the responsibility he felt for the packhorses—his had thrown a shoe on the second day. What got to him most of all was Toni's ceaseless moaning, which was worse than any prissy girl's. When the sun shone, it hurt his eyes. When it was hazy, he couldn't see clearly. Instead of being grateful that his packhorse was hauling two hundred pounds instead of him, he complained that his father had not given him a horse to ride as well. And every day, from midday on, he grumbled and groused about how tired and hungry he was.

Roberto's loathing for his companion grew with each day. Lorenzo Sorri had equipped his son with everything one could want for such a long march: a jacket with an inner sheepskin lining that could be unbuttoned and removed in warmer weather—Roberto had never seen anything like it. Robust leather boots. A leather hat that kept rain, snow, and sun from Toni's poor head. By contrast, Roberto had to wear his old traveling clothes: a threadbare suit, an extra jacket, and a battered cap.

As for the money for food and lodging along the way, Toni's father had given Toni substantially more than Roberto's father had given him. At every guesthouse, Toni ordered the most expensive food and drink. Rich meat dishes and the best red wine. But Roberto had to make do with a daily plate of pasta or bread and ham, washed down with water. It didn't help that Toni was about as bright as a rock. Not a day went by without Roberto having to rescue his companion from at least one predicament. Once, Toni left his money bag on their breakfast table. Roberto turned back one last time before they left the guesthouse to make sure that he'd left nothing behind. And it was at just that moment that he saw the maid stowing Toni's money bag in her skirt. When she saw Roberto coming back, she returned it immediately. Toni hadn't even said thank you, and he didn't buy so much as a jug of wine to share that evening. Next time, Roberto decided, he'd just walk away.

Another time, Toni forgot to tighten his horse's girth. If Roberto hadn't pointed it out, the entire load would have slipped and likely spooked the horse or caused it to fall. And every junction brought a discussion. "We have to go left," Toni might say, whereas the map that Roberto was following clearly showed that they had to go right. With every day, it grew harder for Roberto not to lose his temper. But deep inside, his anticipation at seeing the big city pushed him onward. Zurich. As soon as he reached Zurich, he knew the world would look like a different place.

"Drink, lad, drink. They're voting this summer to ban absinthe, and if the confederates get their way, our 'green fairy' could be prohibited by the end of the year!" Laughing, the man—a local sawmill owner— tipped his head back and poured the cloudy, greenish liquid down his throat.

Toni and the others at the table followed his example. But Roberto only pretended to drink. Green fairy? More like a green devil. He had never liked the bitter taste of wormwood, but the men at their table seemed to be sworn devotees of the drink, and one of them was already ordering another round.

After three weeks on the road, they had arrived in Andermatt, a small village in the Ursuren Valley in Switzerland. The Reuss River, swollen by snowmelt from the surrounding mountains, tumbled noisily down the narrow valley. Roberto and Toni had been following its banks since midday.

"Madam, the next round is on me!" Toni shouted. His cheeks were red, his eyes unfocused, his voice too loud.

"Remember that we have to tackle the pass tomorrow," Roberto said. "If you keep drinking like that, I don't like our chances."

"I don't like our chances with you either way, you miser," Toni slurred. "Why don't you buy a round for once?" The men at the table joined in Toni's raucous laughter. "*Salut!*"

Disgusted, Roberto stood up and went outside. It was a clear night with the promise of spring in the air. From the stable came the happy whinnying of his horse. Roberto grinned. He and the brown had become a good team. For the sake of the horse, he had called a rest day more often than he otherwise would have, though it lengthened their journey. But he didn't want to change horses along the way; he had taken the brown too deeply into his heart for that. He couldn't really afford such sentimentality, he thought, as he whistled softly to the horse through the open window. He had big plans. And time was ticking away.

Reaching the railing of the bridge that spanned the river, Roberto looked up to the sky. Here and there stars glittered, and for a moment he had the feeling that they were sparkling auspiciously just for him.

Once they cleared the pass the next day, they would have the hardest part of the journey behind them. After that, they would manage the rest easily. Maybe, for a change, without Toni complaining.

Roberto could hardly wait to get started finding a suitable shop and trading directly on the hair market. He, the *caviè* from the Maira Valley, trading hair on the exchange . . .

He thrust away the nagging thought that all these thrilling prospects were supposed to come to an end after just a few months. He was out of Elva. Now it was up to him to convince his father to let him stay in the city. Michele could go to the mountains in the fall and cut hair!

Off to Roberto's right, one star glinted especially brightly. A lucky star? No doubt. Roberto sighed, satisfied. He did not know where his inner confidence sprang from, his sense that life held more for him than what his father envisaged. But he felt that, somewhere down the road, he would be a rich and important man, one who had a say in how things ran, and who did not just dance to his father's tune.

"I've never felt so sick in my life," said Toni when they led the horses out of the stable the following morning. It was already ten o'clock, and Roberto had hoped to be on the road much earlier than that. But no matter how hard he shook Toni, his companion simply would not wake up.

"If you hadn't drunk so much, you wouldn't feel so wretched now, so stop whining," said Roberto, checking his horse's harness a final time. Unlike Toni, the animals were well rested, which was good, because the trail over the mountains would take all the strength they had.

Roberto could not believe it when he saw Toni trying to swing himself onto the back of his horse. "Are you crazy? She's got enough to carry!"

"Shut your damn mouth," Toni growled, and he swung his right leg up once again, boxing the mare roughly on the flank as he did so. The horse shied, and Toni punished it with a sharp jerk on the bit.

Without a word, Roberto marched off. Toni, leading his packhorse by the reins, trudged after him.

As expected, the route was steep and winding. In some places, it was as wide as a road, but most of the time it was a narrow track, and when it was, Roberto led the way, his horse following behind, cautiously, step by step. Apart from them, there were few travelers, since most of them crossed the Alps at the Gotthard Pass. With a horse and cart or an automobile, Roberto would also have preferred the Gotthard Pass, but leading a packhorse, he felt more comfortable on the quieter route.

Crusted snow crunched underfoot, and the snot froze in his nose in the damp chill. Roberto was used to the mountain air in Piedmont, but this climb up to the pass at seven thousand feet was taking it out of him. He was even happier now that he had not drunk too much the previous evening, and he did not want to imagine the extent of Toni's suffering. He looked back occasionally and saw that his companion was falling farther behind. When they had started out that morning, he stopped frequently and waited for Toni to catch up, but whenever he stopped, his sweating horse began to shiver in the cold. Roberto knew they couldn't keep going this way, and he was about to call to Toni that he would go ahead to the shelter at the pass when he saw that Toni was once again trying to mount his packhorse, and on a particularly narrow stretch at that. Roberto shuddered. One false step by the horse would be enough to send both man and animal into the abyss.

"Get your foot out of the girth—" But his warning was lost in the skittish whinnying of Toni's horse as it frantically tried to shake free of its overweight master. The next moment, its left rear hoof stepped into emptiness. The two-hundred-pound load on its back slipped and pulled the horse over the edge so that only its front legs and stretched belly and chest lay on the path. The mare let out a shriek and scrabbled at the snow and earth, trying to find a footing. Toni, his foot still caught in the girth, was sliding with it.

"*Dio mio . . .*" In a panic, Roberto sprinted back down the narrow trail. He was only a few yards short when mare and man tumbled into the chasm.

"Hey! Toni?!" Roberto's heart was beating in his throat as he leaned out and gazed down into the gorge. But he could see neither Toni nor his horse, just rugged crags, loose boulders, and crusted snow.

"Toni! Where are you? Are you all right? Answer me!"

He heard a pitiful moan. Toni was alive, at least. A wave of relief washed over Roberto. "I can't see you. What's going on down there?" he yelled.

"My leg . . . I think . . . it's broken." Another moan, very quiet.

A broken leg? Roberto did not want to think about what that would mean. "What about the horse?" Frowning, Roberto waited for an answer. When none came, he called out again, "Toni? Can you hear me? Say something!" His heart beating hard, he leaned out a bit more, but still could see nothing. Either they must have fallen very far or were lying in a cleft in the rocks that he could not see into. The mountains there were full of such deep gashes, cut into the rocks over millennia.

Roberto forced himself to breathe and dropped into a crouch. He bit his lip. He was at a loss. What now? Should he try to climb down? Would he even be able to find a grip on the icy rocks with his thin linen boots? And what was he supposed to do with his own horse in the meantime? God forbid it should wander away with its valuable cargo or be stolen by some passing traveler.

Roberto turned away from the chasm and looked up to the pass ahead. The station at the pass was an hour's hike, probably less, he guessed. Best to get up there as quickly as he could and find help, he was thinking, when a second, very different thought crept into his mind: What if Toni died before he could get back?

The rescue was difficult and was still going on after nightfall. Torches lit the steep trail while Toni, his right leg almost certainly broken, was hauled inch by inch up the mountain by the men from the pass station.

Roberto stood anxiously to one side. The men had assured him that it wasn't the first time they had pulled someone out after an accident. With God's blessing and a little luck, they would be able to rescue his friend.

"You're really not going to come?" Toni looked up tearfully from the stretcher. His right leg was, in fact, broken, and they suspected a broken bone in his right wrist. And, of course, he was grazed and bruised all over. His horse had not survived the fall, and they had left the cadaver in the cleft in the rocks. Luckily, the men from the station had told Roberto that they would recover the load the horse was carrying.

Roberto hated to think what would have happened if they'd lost the valuable hair and wigs as well, and he said to Toni, "What am I supposed to do in Elva? You can lie back and let yourself heal there, but I'm needed elsewhere." *How much would it cost to buy another packhorse here in the mountains?* he wondered while Toni's stretcher was lifted onto a wagon.

"But it was never agreed that you should go to Zurich alone. Our fathers won't like it at all," Toni grumbled.

"And it was never agreed that you'd be idiot enough to get drunk on absinthe and break your leg," Roberto snapped. "What about our plan to open a shop and take the sale of our hair and wigs into our own hands? Are we supposed to give that up because you're a fool?

Our fathers would be furious if I went back with you. But . . . there is one thing," Roberto said, and he cleared his throat. "I need the money from your father. Otherwise I won't have nearly enough to open a shop or even buy a new packhorse.

"You want me to hand over my money? All of it? What if you run off and take the hair and the money with you?" Toni's expression, usually so lethargic, was suddenly alert.

"Now there's an idea," said Roberto with a laugh, and he clapped Toni Sorri companionably on the shoulder.

Chapter Twenty-Two

It was the pharmacist, Frieder Weingarten, who gave Clara the crucial tip. It was New Year's Day, 1908. Christmas had come and gone, her second without her children. Again, she had sent presents and cards for them via Josephine.

"There's a shop on Unterstadtstrasse that will soon be vacant," the pharmacist said when he and his wife visited Clara in the Hotel Residenz. "In the first row, where all the better shops are."

"What good does that do me?" Clara asked while Sabine Weingarten, rather shyly, offered her a homemade New Year's pretzel. Clara was so inwardly nervous that she almost put the pretzel aside untouched, but then she thanked Sabine and turned back to Mr. Weingarten. "Do you really think anyone in town will rent me anything after all the slander?" Although she did her best to sound calm, she could hear the tremor in her voice. What if someone really . . .

The pharmacist only smiled. "I already talked to the owner of the building and told him what an absolutely reliable and exceptionally clever woman you are. If it had been necessary, I would have told him not only that I would rent you a shop myself, but that I entrusted you with my wife and child!" He smiled fondly at his wife, who was pregnant with their second child, then said to Clara, "If you like, we could go and see the place right now. Mr. Schmidt is expecting us."

"Now? On a holiday? Really, are you serious?" She was fighting back tears. It was so good to have friends! She felt like giving the man a kiss on his cheek in sheer gratitude, but what if Sabine took it the wrong way? Where men were concerned, Clara never again wanted to find herself in a situation that could be misconstrued or in which her reputation was compromised.

So instead of a kiss, she stiffly shook his hand. "Thank you so much!" Then she hooked her arm into Sabine Weingarten's and laughed gaily. "What are we waiting for?"

The pharmacist cleared his throat. "Sabine ought to be getting home, actually. In her condition, an outing like this would be too strenuous altogether."

"But—" Sabine began. Her disappointment was obvious.

"Sabine," said Mr. Weingarten in a doting voice—but firmly—and his wife nodded.

"You're right, Frieder. I'll put my feet up for a bit, then I'll get dinner started."

Clara watched unhappily as Sabine left. Situations like that were all too familiar to her.

Heinrich Schmidt was eighty-three years old, and until recently had run a tobacconist's shop there. Clara could still smell the tobacco when Mr. Schmidt showed her around. There was a spacious sales room at the front, and, behind a tattered curtain, there was a small kitchen and a slightly larger storeroom. Like the place on Höllgasse Lane, the sales room also had two large front windows, with the entry door situated between them. Clara hoped that Therese would move her business so they could share this space, too. The hairdresser was a bit flighty, but she was sincere, likeable, and straightforward—traits that Clara appreciated very much, and which ultimately meant more to her than perfect punctuality or a beautifully polished mirror.

"I'm moving to Switzerland next year to be with my daughter," said the old man, interrupting Clara's train of thought, "so I'm looking for someone to rent the shop and eventually for a tenant for my apartment on the second floor. It's more than a year away, but would that be of interest to you? If not, I will still rent you the shop, and I'll look for someone else to rent the apartment."

She blinked, taken aback. Had she heard right? An apartment of her own! That would be a big step toward being able to offer her children a place they could call home. *Please, God, don't let this be a dream,* she prayed, as the New Year's sun filled the salesroom with golden light.

"I would very much like to rent the apartment also," she said, her voice trembling with excitement.

"I will still need to live here until April or so next year. It's a long way off, but one step at a time, as I always say."

Clara nodded. One step at a time—wasn't that how she had done things herself? As much as she wanted to establish herself, she knew she had to be patient.

"Don't think I haven't heard what the people in town have been saying about you. That your creams cause rashes and damage the skin," Mr. Schmidt said unexpectedly. "But when I see your flawless skin, I know that can't be true. Besides, I've never put much weight in other people's gossip." He patted Clara's arm awkwardly. "When I look at you, I can see that you are an honest sort. I haven't seen a single woman in town with a rash, but I *have* seen some with nothing but envy in their eyes when they talk about you, the successful businesswoman."

"Successful businesswoman." Clara laughed bitterly. "I can't say I feel like one right now."

"It will all be yesterday's news before you know, take my word for it. If you like, we can make a deal. And your business partner, the young hairdresser Mr. Weingarten told me about, would also be welcome, of course."

The next day, Clara and Therese moved out of the space on Höllgasse Lane. They could hardly wait to get away from their unsavory landlord and his witch of a wife.

Their new shop was in such good condition that it only needed a few small repairs. Still, the next week was a whirlwind of packing up, cleaning, moving out, moving in, and painting. As in the old store, Clara decorated her half of the shop in lavender and lime green. When they celebrated their opening day on January 7, the rooms still smelled faintly of paint. They would not have managed it at all without working together, and Clara saw how capable Therese could be when it really mattered.

A new beginning in a new year. And on the exact same day she had opened her first shop. If that wasn't a good omen, nothing was!

On opening day, Clara hung a sign in the shop window advertising a free cream for every woman who booked a facial treatment. Since her return from Berlin, she had thought almost single-mindedly about how to win back her reputation and her customers. She was certain that if she could get the women back in her shop, she would be able to convince them once again about her trustworthiness and the quality of her products.

Isabelle, whom she had reported to at length not only about her miserable return to Berlin and having to spend another Christmas without her children, but also about her professional dilemma, had written back: *You have to offer your customers something for free! Nothing brings people in and gets them to buy products as much as free samples. I know from my own experience that the more champagne you pour for your customers at a tasting, the more they buy afterward.*

Isabelle's advice had come as a revelation to Clara, and because of it—even before it was clear that she would move into the shop in Unterstadtstrasse—she had begun stocking up on her creams. From the first day, pretty glass pots of delicately scented creams filled the shelves in her new place of business.

Whether it was the sign that drew the women of Meersburg back into Clara's new Bel Étage or just plain curiosity, Clara did not know. Whatever the reason, what mattered was that the customers who had deserted her were now back. Fabienne from the flower shop came in for a face massage, and after her came Roswitha Maier from the Green Tree. The mayor's wife arrived with a woman from the town council, and all of them were happy to take Clara's free gift. No one said a word about how her creams might damage their skin; instead they looked curiously around the brightly lit, elegant sales room.

"You feel like you're on a throne here," said Fabienne when she took her place on Clara's treatment chair. She ran her chapped hands almost reverently over the arms of the chair, which Clara had had gilded.

"I think every woman, in her way, is a queen," Clara replied. "You are the Queen of Flowers. But I'm afraid your hands look more sorry than sovereign. Luckily, I've developed a brand-new hand cream that will be just the thing. I'll give you a hand massage with it, and then you can see for yourself. Now relax. You work so hard, you've more than earned a little rest."

The florist looked at Clara gratefully. "No one's ever said that to me before. And you'll really give me a cream to take with me?"

Clara smiled and nodded.

Though it would be months before the tourist season began, Clara's appointment book was so full that Clara and her assistant, Sophie, were kept busy from opening time until well into the evening.

***

If Count Zeppelin succeeds in his bid to convince the military of the performance of his dirigibles, nothing more will stand in the way of an important contract. That would mean a meteoric boost for the airship business at Lake Constance. In summer, Count Zeppelin is planning to undertake a twenty-four-hour test flight with his LZ 4 airship, and the entire Lake Constance region is keeping its fingers crossed for him and his engineers!

Three months after opening her new Bel Étage, Clara looked up from the newspaper. She was at the Esplanade Café, where she had breakfast every morning, and she looked out over the lake in the direction of Friedrichshafen, where Count Zeppelin had his factory. In some way she felt oddly connected with the man. The business aspirations of the Zeppelin factory were characterized by a constant change of fortunes. Every success was followed by a setback, and every setback led to the next triumph. The ups and downs were no different for her and Bel Étage, she thought as she finished her coffee. She paid her bill and had just left the café when a loud honking sounded behind her and made her jump. She turned around to see who the driver was, and when she saw who was behind the wheel, she almost jumped a second time.

"Lilo?"

Her friend grinned, then reached across to open the passenger door for her. "Come on! Come for a spin."

Clara laughed aloud. "I'd love to, but I have to get to the shop."

"You don't have to do anything of the sort," Lilo said. "You have half an hour before you have to be there. And if you are a few minutes late, your customers will wait."

"What kind of car is it?" Clara asked as soon as she sat in the passenger seat. The interior smelled of leather and luxury.

Lilo laughed. "It's a Brennabor Type A1. I didn't want a Daimler, and the Brennabor is much sportier. The company has its headquarters up in Brandenburg. They want to open their own racing arm this year and win some big races, and I'm sure they'll do it. My car, for one, is very fast. Want me to step on the gas?"

"Better not," Clara said quickly while Lilo swung her new toy daringly around a corner. "Why didn't you tell me you were going to buy a car? And where did you learn to drive? I imagine it must be very complicated." Clara pointed to the buttons on the metal dashboard, which glinted like pure silver in the sunlight.

"And you probably thought that driving was only something that men do, right? Ha!" Lilo was beaming. "Driving is fantastic. It makes me feel so carefree, just like I used to feel when I was cycling."

Clara smiled and leaned back in her comfortable seat. Yes, driving an automobile was wonderful, she thought as the buildings of Meersburg flew by. As was everything else: the Meersburg shops with their splendid displays, and one of them was hers. The show of flowers along the lakeshore and the violet-blue sky. The cheerful mood that had rolled through town with the arrival of the first tourists. Business was booming everywhere, one marvel of technology followed another, and there was a steady stream of premieres in the theaters. People were celebrating themselves and their inventiveness, champagne bottles were popping in drawing rooms, and the newspapers carried stories about the Belle Époque. For Clara, it was enough to say: life was beautiful.

Half an hour later, Clara was at her new shop. And her heart gave a small joyful leap to be there, just as it had every day since she and Therese had moved in in January.

"I can't wait to hear what the Countess Zuzanna has to say about our new shop," Clara said to Therese as she took a moment to simply stand at the window and admire her shop and the view. Through a small gap between two houses opposite, they could see the lake glittering—Clara found the sight just as enchanting then as she had on the first day in their new location.

"Zuzanna? But she isn't even in town," Therese lisped, a collection of hairpins between her lips as she did her best to pin up her thin, rebellious hair. "I've heard a rumor that she may not be coming at all, and that she's going to stay in Baden-Baden."

Clara's face fell instantly. "That would be a shame." She had been looking forward to seeing her patron again. She had produced a cream especially for her, with the scent of damask roses.

But that was not the only thing new to Clara's range—her shelves were practically overflowing with new products: a cooling cream made with peppermint, a facial toner with the perfume of lemon blossoms, a new hand cream that the skin absorbed more quickly. And even though her product range was already substantially bigger than the year before, Clara dreamed all the time of creating new beauty products. "Here, sniff," she said, and held an elegant carafe of almond oil under her friend's nose.

"Hmm, that smells as if someone had just peeled an orange," said Therese. "May I?" Without waiting for Clara's answer, she poured a few drops of the oil onto the palm of her left hand. Then she rubbed both hands together and ran them through her hair, which immediately became shinier and more obliging.

Clara watched with interest. "Yes, there's orange to scent the almond oil. That's actually meant to be a body oil. But you've given me an idea . . . Maybe I should be thinking about hair products also?"

Therese groaned and handed back the carafe. "Clara, you always manage to give me a bad conscience! Shouldn't it be *my* job to rack my brains about hair care?"

"It should. So any new ideas?" Clara asked with genuine curiosity, but all Therese did was groan louder.

"No, and no plans to get any, either. My customers are satisfied with what I already give them. Besides, life isn't just for working, even though someone seems to have drummed that into you. Believe me, my dear, life is so much lovelier if you simply enjoy it!" She blew a kiss first to her reflection in the mirror, then to Clara, then she pirouetted across the shop like a ballerina.

Clara laughed. "If I ever need a lesson on how to enjoy life, then I'll come straight to you." She flipped open her dark-blue leather appointment book to see who her first customer was. Emmaline Möricke. She did not recognize the name. A new customer. Sophie must have made the appointment.

Therese grew serious. "I know what drives you, you know," she said quietly. "My child would be almost three years old now, if God had wanted her to be. Believe me, I would have done anything for her, too. Which is to say—work hard only to give your ex-husband as good as he's given you, and the sooner the better. And if I can ever help you do that, in any way, tell me. I'll always be on your side."

"Thank you. That's very nice to hear," said Clara, her voice a little husky. She wasn't sure how Therese might help her, but it felt good just to know that the offer was there.

In a weak moment, Clara had told Therese everything. Lilo and Therese were the only ones who knew Clara's secret. Everyone else in Meersburg believed she was a childless widow.

Therese's cheeky expression returned. "Even so, I'm not going to stop until you've enjoyed at least a little of the good life! And if you ask me, that works best when you have a generous lover who pays for it all. Picture it—then you could work just because you felt like it, like me," she said, plucking hair out of the bristles of a brush. "Tomorrow evening there's a dance at the Lakeview Hotel. Thierry and I will be there, and I'm sure he won't have anything against you coming along. There will be plenty of dashing young men there." She batted her eyelids flirtatiously.

"Dashing young men! Listen to you! I'm not twenty anymore, in case you hadn't noticed," Clara laughed. Then, more seriously, she said, "Besides, if word ever reached Berlin that I was running around with dashing young men, I can forget all about visitation rights for my children. Quite apart from that, though, I have no intention of living off any man, certainly not when I can stand on my own two feet. Besides, I don't have the time to fall in love. As soon as we close for the day, I have to start on the creams and lotions, or I won't have anything to sell tomorrow."

Just then, the bell jangled, and a woman Clara had never seen before tentatively stepped inside.

"Good morning. Can I help you?" said Clara with a friendly smile.

"Good morning. I'm Emmaline Möricke. I have an appointment for a skin consultation," said the woman, who did not look up. "My skin is so thin and pale, especially my cheeks. Look." With two fingertips, she pinched the skin on her cheek; it looked almost lifeless. "My husband says I look like a specter . . ." Her last words were no more than a whisper. "Sometimes I think he doesn't like to look at me anymore."

"Oh, I can't believe that. An enchanting woman like you?" said Clara consolingly though she was churning inside. Why were some men so incredibly insensitive?

Clara asked the woman to sit in her gilded chair, then she took her magnifying glass and looked at Emmaline Möricke's skin more closely. "You don't have the slightest sign of pimples, nor any other impurities," she said. "Your skin does have a gray sheen to it, but we'll soon take care of that." *She hardly ever gets outside,* Clara thought. Back in Berlin, she often walked past a shoe factory, and at shift change, the women who worked there came streaming out after twelve hours of work, and their skin looked just as tired as Emmaline Möricke's. *And if the skin looks so miserable, how must the woman inside it feel?* Clara wondered.

"A fresh toner to cleanse the skin, regular massage with a firming oil, and a light cream for everyday use. That will do you a world of good," she said, putting the magnifying glass aside. She took the woman's hand and squeezed it comfortingly. "But even better would be for you to get out now and then during the day. Get outside in the fresh air, every day, even just for a few minutes. A short walk by the lake, the spring breeze—that will help the blood flow to your skin. And it will do even more for your well-being."

The woman looked at Clara through tired eyes. "That would be nice. But from early in the morning until the evening, I can't get out of our office. My husband runs a large hardware business, and we supply all the factories around Friedrichshafen. With the bookkeeping and looking after the house and children, I'm busy all the time."

"You do all the housekeeping as well?" Clara asked.

Emmaline Möricke nodded. "Franz thinks it isn't worth employing someone to help in the house, and as soon as we close up for the day, I cook, clean, and iron. There's really no time at all to go for a walk. I've stolen today for myself, more or less. Franz is off with the Friedrich-shafen businessmen at a spring picnic."

I'd like to give that Franz a piece my mind, thought Clara. Men had no idea how hard it was to manage a household.

"You haven't stolen today at all. You've *earned* it," she said resolutely. "I'll let you try out all my different creams today, and you can decide for yourself which one you like the most. Then I'll give you a face massage, and show you how to do it yourself at home. You'll feel much better after that, I'm certain."

Her encouraging tone must have had some effect: for the first time since entering the store, the woman smiled.

Two hours later, Emmaline Möricke left Bel Étage with radiant skin and a promise that from then on, she would take at least half an hour a day for herself.

Clara was not sure that the woman would keep her promise or her follow-up appointment. Would her daily routine start to wear her down again as soon as she opened the front door? "For every woman who works in a factory, for every secretary, the working day comes to an end sometime. But what about for you?" Clara had asked, and had felt like adding: "How long are you going to let your husband exploit you like this?" But that, of course, was not a question she could pose. Still, she had had the feeling that Emmaline Möricke had been asking herself the same question for a long time. Would she push it aside or make room for it?

Despite her doubt, Clara hoped that she had helped the woman, at least a little. Ultimately, though, everyone had to be responsible for themselves. Clara knew that better than anyone, but sometimes it helped to get a little push from outside.

With a sigh, Clara began to soak the towel and brushes she had used for the facial in lukewarm soapy water.

Who knew what the coming season would bring? As she dried her hands, she had the feeling that a very special summer lay ahead. But living off a man—Therese could keep that piece of advice for someone else.

Chapter Twenty-Three

Once Roberto left the Alps, the path became easier. The new packhorse, for which he'd paid a ridiculous sum at the pass, was good-natured and strong and quickly adjusted to working with Roberto's brown. Now that he no longer had to put up with Toni's endless griping, Roberto should have been able to enjoy the journey, but with every step he took, his inner struggle intensified.

In a few days, he would reach Zurich. What then? Should he carry through with the plan that his father and Lorenzo Sorri had worked out? Or should he take the unique opportunity that Toni's accident offered him? If he handled it cleverly, no one would find him, at least not easily. A new town, preferably with a new name . . .

As he led his two packhorses through Zurich's magnificent center, he was still uncertain about what he would do. Zurich, with its huge guild houses, spacious squares, and beautiful stores was clearly a wealthy, vibrant city. Running a shop there would bring with it a great deal of prestige and respect. But for whom? Not for him, because he would have to return to Italy in the fall to once again cut off women's hair.

And his brother, Michele, would be the one enjoying the advantages that Zurich had to offer. It was perfectly clear to Roberto, however, that his *own* life would be very different, and the notion horrified him.

The Zurich town hall beside the Limmat River came into view. Everyone intending to stay in the city was supposed to register there.

Roberto turned to his horses and clucked his tongue.

"All right, you two, let's pick it up! We've still got a long way to go."

He laughed then, free and loud.

From then on, the inner voice that previously only had whispered its ambivalent messages became clear and unequivocal. Winterthur, Frauenfels, Konstanz—Roberto journeyed farther and farther with his horses. To live a new life, a life of his own, he could not stay in Switzerland. The danger of discovery was too great. But in the German lands, he was sure no one would suspect him, so Roberto boarded a ferry in Konstanz and set off for the far shore of the lake. The ferryman told him that he would disembark in a town called Meersburg. From there, his fellow passengers told him he could quickly make his way to Friedrichshafen. Or to Lindau or a dozen other German towns. Roberto nodded vaguely. He didn't recognize any of the names they mentioned.

The German shore came closer, and Roberto could make out a collection of buildings set among grapevine-heavy hillsides. The buildings had something medieval about them, and their facades were brown, yellow, and dusky pink. Roberto had seen similar structures in the northern Italian mountain villages. Meersburg did not look especially large or as if it were the place to find a new life! But it was already afternoon, and he decided to look for a place to spend the night and take the time to think about where he wanted to go next, now that he had set himself free.

As Roberto climbed onto the dock at Meersburg, the ferryman told him that he could house the horses in the Marstall at the prince-bishop's castle. And for a little more money, he could store the goods the horses were carrying in a lockable room in the castle. It was standard practice for those traveling through.

A prince-bishop's castle? In this little town? For a moment, Roberto thought that he had misheard the man. His earlier travels had taken him to regions of northern Italy where German was spoken, so he understood the language, and while he wasn't fluent, he could speak it reasonably well.

Still surprised, he turned away from the ferry dock to the lively esplanade, where one café after another offered respite to pedestrians.

"The tourists are here," said the ferryman, who had followed his gaze. "Just like every year, they come and rain gold over Meersburg."

Raining money? Tourists? Roberto was suddenly all ears. "What do these tourists do here in Meersburg?" he asked in halting German.

The ferryman laughed. "That's a strange question. Look around! Meersburg has everything that the nobility and other well-heeled visitors love. The shops, the water, boating parties and regattas, strolling along the esplanade and up through the vineyards, concerts in the park, horse riding around the lake. And every evening, they're in their villas or the hotels, carousing the night away. To tell the truth, I could use a little of that kind of summer myself," said the man with a sigh.

Roberto's senses were more alert than usual as he walked through the well-paved streets in the direction of the stables. All the automobiles driving around! Roberto admired a fine silver auto as it rumbled past. What must it feel like to be Count-this or Lord-that and sit at the wheel of such a contraption?

There were many people out walking, and Roberto heard languages other than German being spoken. So tourists came from other countries to visit Meersburg? That surprised him. As he made his way through the narrow streets with his two packhorses in tow, occasionally a woman glanced in his direction. But Roberto was accustomed to attracting female attention, and apart from that no one seemed to take much notice of him at all. The Meersburgers seemed to be used to foreigners in their midst. And Roberto noticed something else: the people there were dressed just as well as the rich citizens of Zurich. The women wore colorful, elaborate outfits with matching hats and parasols. Small handbags dangled from their wrists, looking well filled with coins.

And then there were all the beautiful shops! Tobacconists, stationers, a gentleman's tailor and a shoemaker, several emporiums and—what was that? Roberto pulled up short in front of a small business. There were two huge front windows, one of which was beautifully decorated around a display of beauty products, and the other of which showed a sign for a hairdresser. A hairdresser that sold beauty potions? Roberto had never before seen such a shop. Should he stop by for a visit later? A chat with whoever ran the business might help him with his own plans. Somewhere, somehow, he would have to sell his wigs. Names, contacts, information: anything would be useful to him in his current situation. Maybe he could get them to cut his hair while he was there? He hadn't seen a barbershop or men's hairdresser anywhere else in Meersburg, and he was long overdue for a haircut. The last time, Gaia had done it for him in Elva, and it was certainly not among her strengths.

Elva . . . it already felt like a place from another life. Roberto was only interested in what was right here. The town smelled of money and wealth, and there was a cheerful mood that Roberto found infectious. Whistling a little tune, he climbed the last short stretch of the hill on which the Marstall was situated. As soon as he secured his goods and stabled the horses, he would have to find a guesthouse for himself. After that, he would take a closer look at this extraordinary town.

***

Berlin, April 1908

Dear Clara,
As always, I hope this letter finds you in the best of health. I
would so love to be there at Lake Constance, to go strolling

along the shore with you and enjoy all the beautiful flowers
that you described so vividly in your last letter.

Clara smiled wistfully. Every time she received a letter from Isabelle or Josephine, she felt a pang of longing for her friends. Would she manage to see them again that year?

Spring has come to Berlin again, and the old chestnut
trees along the boulevards are all bursting into bloom.

Strange, thought Clara. It wasn't like Josephine to write so much about trees and flowers. Was her friend turning into a romantic? Clara smiled to herself.

A shadow moved across the front door, then moved on. She sighed, relieved it wasn't a customer. She wanted to read Jo's letter to the end.

Clara, I'm happy to say that your children are well.
Sophie and my Amelie are going to violin lessons together,
which means I get to see your daughter at least once a week.
She is content, and she laughs all the time. Though neither
she nor Amelie seems very fond of playing the violin . . .

Sophie and the violin? That was hard for Clara to imagine. She breathed deeply, as if that might ease the little stabs she felt around her heart. If anything, she would have suggested the tambourine. That would certainly have been more suitable for her spirited daughter.

Sophie has told me that Matthias feels at home in his
new school, and that he's at the top of his class.
There's something else that I heard from Sophie. Oh,
Clara, I don't know how to break this news to you gently.

Gerhard has married again. It was last week, and his new wife—would you believe it!—is the young nanny. Sophie was all smiles when she told me he was getting married and that they had bought her a new dress for the occasion.

Clara lowered the letter to her knees. She sat for a moment without moving. Her mind was empty, and her heart beat slower than usual. That . . . couldn't be, could it? Sophie must have made it up. Children came out with the craziest stories sometimes. Her hands trembling, she picked up the letter again.

At first, I didn't want to believe her. I laughed and told her the new dress must be for some other occasion. I'm afraid I rather confused the poor child.

Clara swallowed. Poor little Sophie . . . What did they do to them, the grown-ups?

But on the same day, the Berliner Evening Post *published an article about how the divorced Dr. Gerhard Gropius, treated so despicably by his first wife, had found a second chance at happiness, and that the ceremony was to take place at the town hall among a small circle of close friends. Dear Clara, believe me, the very thought offended me.*

A wedding. A small circle of friends. Sophie and Matthias with a new mother.

Dearest Clara, I have done something I am not especially proud of. On the day of the wedding, I hid behind a pillar in the lobby at the town hall. It had nothing to do with curiosity, please believe me, and certainly not with sensationalism. I had to see it with my own eyes, or I simply would not have been able to believe it. I hope this news does not break your heart, but if I were in your shoes, I would want to know everything, so I will write everything I saw as completely as I can. The children were both there. Matthias wore a suit, which made him look very grown-up indeed. And Sophie had the most adorable pink ribbons in her hair. Both of them were very excited, and Sophie was hopping from one foot to the other. Gerhard looked fit to burst with pride and self-satisfaction. The bride wore a pink dress. She looked so young and innocent that it made my heart ache to see her. I wonder if she has any idea whom she's marrying. Such a lovely creature, giving herself up to a dog like that . . . Your history is repeating itself, Clara. Isn't that awful?

Clara sobbed aloud. The letter fell to the floor and tears flowed down her cheeks. The doorbell rang, but Clara didn't care.

"Sorry I'm so late. My hair was driving me mad again. It took me half an hour to get it this far. If this goes on, I'm going to start wearing a wig!" With an effusive sigh, Therese threw her summer coat over the back of a chair. Only then did she look over to Clara. A moment later, Therese was holding her in her arms. "Clara, sweetheart, what is it?"

"It's all over, all of it," Clara blurted. "Gerhard has married again. Sophie and Matthias have a new mother . . . I don't have a ghost of a chance anymore. What judge would ever give me custody of the children now? I—" She burst into tears again just as the doorbell jangled a second time.

***

Roberto took in the atmosphere of the place even before he had fully crossed the threshold. Gloom, sadness, and something else—hopelessness?—hung in the air. None of that seemed to fit with the chic interior of the business or the two attractive women, one of whom was dabbing tears from her eyes with a handkerchief. She sat there, the picture of misery, while the younger woman consoled her.

Did the pretty store belong to these women and not to a man? He cleared his throat meekly and said hello.

The younger woman stood up and said, "I'm Therese Himmelsreich, the hairdresser here. What can I do for you, sir?" She had thin red hair that looked as if a bird had built a temporary nest in it, but it did not detract from her allure, and she seemed well aware of that. When Roberto did not reply immediately, she added coquettishly, "Are you seeking a gift for your deserving wife, or can I help you some other way?" The redhead swept her hand wide, a gesture that encompassed the entire shop. Roberto noticed that the shop was not only decorated with exceptional elegance, but also divided into two parts. The left side was clearly for hairdressing, while the right side . . . he wasn't quite sure what it was, but the shelves and cabinets were well stocked with jars and bottles, all for sale.

Roberto said, "Perhaps it is more that I can help you. My name is . . ." He hesitated for a moment. Then, before he had a second thought, he continued. "Stefano Santo. I am a hair trader from Italy." *Stefano Santo. Where did that come from?* With a flourish, he produced one of the wigs that he had put in his bag before storing the rest of his goods. The wig was fashioned from chestnut-brown hair with a tinge of red, and styled into a voluminous bun. As he spoke, he turned the wig toward the front windows, where the sunlight that streamed through showed off the red shimmer of the hair to its best advantage. From the corner of his eye, he saw that he already had the full attention of both women.

"May I?" he said, and set the wig on Therese's head as he spoke.

"Wait, I—" she said, but fell silent the instant she caught her reflection in the mirror. The wig fit perfectly, and she stroked her newly

220

opulent hair almost reverently. Two seconds later, she burst out laughing.

"A wig! See, Clara? Some wishes come true faster than you think." She giggled.

Roberto, now Stefano, smiled with satisfaction when he saw the other woman's face brighten just a bit.

"The wig is perfect for you, *signora*. If you will allow me to, I would like to give it to you, as my gift. For a man, it is a great joy to be able to please a woman," he said, and bowed slightly to both of them.

"But there are also men who like nothing more than to make a woman unhappy," said the woman named Clara, and then both women laughed loudly.

Stefano raised his eyebrows and waited.

"Please excuse us," said the redhead after a moment. She was still wearing the wig. "You must think we're a pair of hysterical old women. Just before you came in, we—" She gestured dismissively. "It doesn't matter. So you're a hair trader?" she asked, and again she stroked her new hair admiringly. "Such a lovely gift, but I cannot accept it, Signor Santo."

"I would be deeply disappointed if you were to turn it down, Signora Himmelsreich," Stefano replied engagingly. "My family is one of the biggest traders in women's hair, which is even used to make wigs for the lords in the English upper house. Imagine that! Until now, we have only sold our hair through intermediaries in Italy, but that is about to change. I've been sent to set up a base for us in Germany, somewhere where we can sell what we make directly. I really should have been on my way again long ago, but when I saw your shop here, I had to come in and look around." He glanced at Clara. She was even more beautiful than her partner. But what fascinated him even more than her looks was her radiance. She seemed at once strong and fragile, inwardly calm but also agitated, and he realized that he had to get to know her better. But at the same time, a voice of warning sounded in his ear: *Roberto, what do you think you'll do? You'll be moving on tomorrow, on to a bigger city.* To which Stefano silently replied, *Who's Roberto? There is no more Roberto, but his departure means a thousand new opportunities.* He forced himself to turn away from Clara and back to Therese Himmelsreich. "If you like, I could leave you with three or four more wigs." He was already pulling them from his bag. "You could do them up artfully and display them on mannequins in your window. Then the people could see immediately that they are dealing with a woman who has mastered her craft."

"What a wonderful idea!" cried both women simultaneously.

"And you would finally have some nice decorations in your window," Clara added.

Therese gave her a slightly miffed look, then said to Stefano, "So what would these wigs cost?"

"Did I say a word about selling them? Maybe I could entrust them to you, just like that," Stefano replied. "Beautiful hair is a woman's greatest gift. I'm sure you are talented enough to make your customers see that."

"You bet I am! I have a wonderful braid I can try on this blond wig, and I'd pin up this brown hair so elegantly. On what conditions would you entrust them to me, Signor Santo?"

"I only have one condition, and it is not complicated . . ." Stefano looked from one woman to the other. "It is such a glorious day. May I invite you both for coffee?"

"Come back when we close for lunch, and you certainly may!" said Clara, before Therese ran off with Stefano there and then.

It was eight in the evening before Stefano sat down to eat dinner at the Star guesthouse, which belonged to the parents of Sophie Bauer, Clara Berg's assistant in the Bel Étage. Stefano had realized that the world was small in Meersburg. He wasn't yet sure whether that fact would help him or hurt him.

Either way, his day had certainly been interesting. Over coffee with the two women, he had learned that the first tourists of the season were already in town and that many more were expected through the season, which would last until late autumn. Therese Himmelsreich had added willingly that one could earn a lot of money from the tourists who came to visit.

He had been planning to head toward Friedrichshafen or Lindau and to look into opening a shop there. Or perhaps to go on as far as Munich or Frankfurt. But maybe this small town beside Lake Constance would be well suited to his business. He had asked the two women whether, by chance, there was a shop free in town, but neither knew of one.

It didn't matter. He would find out everything he needed to know, he thought, as he drank a mouthful of Lake Constance white wine. He looked thoughtfully at the glass in his hand. The wine was fresh and fruity, similar to wines he had drunk back home. Was that an omen? A sign that Meersburg would become his new home? The small town was busy and vibrant, but there was nothing hectic about it. And because of the many tourists, he did not stand out, which, in his case, was not a bad thing. If he played his cards right, he would be safe here. Why would anybody in Italy ever think to come looking for him there?

The biggest question was what he was supposed to do with all the hair and wigs. He could not possibly try to sell them openly. If he were selling apricots or fabric, that would be no problem at all. But his line of trade was so exotic that word would spread quickly if he opened a shop there. What had made him give the hairdresser the wigs so impulsively? It would be better if no one connected him with the topic of hair in the future. Which meant that he had to come up with another plan to support himself, and soon.

They can certainly cook here, at least, he thought, pushing another forkful of the butter-fried fish into his mouth. It tasted delicious.

But his acquaintances that afternoon had been even more delicious, he thought next. Therese Himmelsreich and Clara Berg. The two women seemed to make a good team, as he and his brother once had.

Clara Berg. She was beautiful and, by all appearances, she was also a shrewd businesswoman. Earning money with the beauty of women—that she had even come up with the idea was astounding to him. It was not so far removed from what his own family did. Something told him that Clara Berg was only at the start of her success, and then it occurred to him that the hairdresser must also have recognized that Clara was destined to succeed, and that was why she had become her partner. But such partnerships were not written in stone. Every alliance had its weaknesses. Petty jealousies, different business perspectives . . .

An idea came to him abruptly. He set aside his cutlery, blinked, hastily gulped down a mouthful of wine. What if *he* were to join forces with Clara Berg?

His smile vanished when he suddenly heard Italian being spoken at the next table. He lowered his head instinctively and covertly looked over. Three older men. Faces he had never seen before. Stefano relaxed a little.

What are you afraid of? he chided himself. The *famiglia* couldn't find him. Roberto Totosano no longer existed. Zurich and Elva were far away. His name was Stefano Santo. And as Stefano, he had nothing to fear.

He finished his wine and signaled to the waiter that he wanted to pay. It couldn't hurt to be a little cautious while he sounded out his chances with Clara Berg. And there was something else he had to make sure of—what he had said to Clara and Therese could not be unsaid, but that was as far as it could go. He would never mention the hair trade to anyone else, because a trade so unusual would attract far too much attention.

He cast a final glance at the Italian men. *Attention—that's something I don't need.*

Chapter Twenty-Four

In the weeks that followed, hardly a day passed without Stefano dropping in at the Bel Étage. His search for a suitable shop was proving more difficult than anticipated. Meersburg was small and the number of shops limited. He had something in mind, but good things took time, and he needed to be patient. For the time being, Stefano had more time on his hands than he wanted.

Sometimes, he brought fresh strawberries. Others times, roasted almonds or sweet pastries. Clara, Therese, and Sophie, who were so busy some days that they had no time even for lunch, descended on his gifts ravenously. He always had some cheerful quip at the ready and could make the three women and all their customers laugh.

"What a lovely man," sighed Fabienne from the flower shop while Clara applied a facial mask. Stefano had just left the shop with a bright *"Ciao, bellissime!"* "If I weren't married . . ."

"Then a good-looking businessman like Stefano wouldn't be after you," Therese said, impudent as ever. "I think I could get used to him myself . . ."

"Ha! As if Stefano Santo would even look at a hairdresser," the florist shot back. "Clara, a little more of that wonderful mask, please! And if it comes to that, *I* still look fabulous."

Although Clara said nothing, she had wondered more than once why he came by so often.

One beautiful evening in May, Stefano came by just before closing time. He wanted to invite the three women to a glass of wine down on the esplanade. But Therese was already going out with Thierry, and Sophie had plans to visit her fiancé, which left only Clara.

"I don't actually have the time right now. I need to make more creams tonight," she said regretfully, for which she earned a sharp jab in the back from Therese.

"You can do that tomorrow evening," said the hairdresser.

"Absolutely. And I'll help you," Stefano added. "Of course, only if you let me take you out now."

And so it happened that Clara, for the first time in many weeks, did not spend the evening in the laboratory, but instead went for a glass of wine and then a walk alongside Lake Constance with Stefano. At ten o'clock, he escorted her back to the Hotel Residenz, said goodnight, and gallantly kissed her hand. Clara, almost remorseful, watched as he walked away. She had not enjoyed herself so much for quite a while.

"So I hear that Stefano Santo has his eye on you," said Lilo when they set off to go swimming the next morning.

"What? Where did you hear that?" said Clara, aghast. "We just had a glass of wine."

"Ah. I see," said Lilo with a knowing look. "And a little bird has told me that he drops into your Bel Étage every day."

"Lilo, there's nothing there, believe me," said Clara with a laugh. "Until his business takes off, he simply has too much free time. That's all. And he doesn't know very many people in Meersburg yet."

"Oh, you're mistaken there. A man like Stefano can make contacts very fast." Lilo pushed aside some reeds crossing the path. "A few days ago he ate at the Residenz. He sat at a table with three other men, businessmen who were at the hotel for only one night."

"Did he?" asked Clara, as casually as possible. Where had she been that evening? No doubt hard at work in her laboratory.

"And Estelle Morgan, the American actress living in the hotel right now, told me that she bumped into Stefano a few days ago down at the marina. It seems that she was on her way to a private party, and she asked him to go along."

Clara furrowed her brow. "Did he go?"

Lilo let out a small laugh. "I don't actually know. But what I'm trying to tell you is this: if a man like Stefano Santo is spending so much time with *one* woman—you, in this case—then it definitely means something."

Clara's heart beat a little faster, but she shook her head resolutely. "I think you must be wrong. You said it yourself—Stefano could have anyone he wants! What would he see in me? A woman my age, with children she can't even see, a divorcée . . . if he knew all that, he'd run away as fast as he could."

"A woman doesn't have to reveal all her secrets at once, does she?" Lilo raised her eyebrows and said no more.

Two nights later, Clara was making a rose-scented facial toner when someone knocked on the glass front door. Was it Stefano? Was he going to keep his promise and help her in the laboratory? Clara smiled at the thought. She was a little confused by the nervous fluttering she felt in her heart as she unlocked the door and stood facing him.

"Clara, I apologize, but I would very much like to kidnap you again. I have rented a rowboat. The sunset out on the water is so beautiful—would you make me a happy man and come out onto the lake with me?" His eyes sparkled with anticipation.

"And here I thought you wanted to help me with my work," Clara said with a smile as she untied her white apron. She could make the rosewater toner in the morning just as easily.

A short time later, they were gliding through the water in the rowboat. While Stefano pulled at the oars as if he had never done anything else, Clara dangled her hand in the water. It felt good not to do anything at all. Not to speak, not to think . . .

It surprised her to realize that apart from once or twice on a ferry, this was her first time out in a boat.

The sun was settling orange over the lake.

"Look at the houses. They look as if someone's dipped them in gold and bronze," said Clara, emotion in her words. "In all the time I've been here, I've never really looked at Meersburg from the water. It's truly beautiful, and very different from walking through the narrow streets."

Stefano grinned. "Sometimes looking at things differently pays off." He steered toward a small bay. "If you like, we can stop here. I had a small picnic prepared for us."

"A picnic by the lake—you really are spoiling me," Clara said. "I'm going to start feeling like a rich tourist any minute."

"Forget the tourists," said Stefano dismissively. "I want you to feel like a queen."

A blanket, bread and cheese, and a cold bottle of champagne—Stefano had thought of everything.

"I'm starting to feel downright royal," said Clara, sipping cautiously at her glass of bubbly. The next moment, she laughed out loud. "Oh, if my friend Isabelle had seen me doing that! She always says that champagne should be drunk in *large gulps*, because that's when its aromas really shine."

"Then let's give it a try." Stefano raised his glass and clinked it with hers. Then he drank a large mouthful and said, "Your friend knows about champagne?"

Clara nodded. "Oh, more than knows about it. She owns a very important winery in the Champagne region, and she and her husband are always winning prizes for their champagnes. And as if that's not enough, my other best friend, Josephine, is just as successful, maybe even more so." She shrugged, a staged look of concern on her face. "Compared to them, I feel almost pathetic."

"You can't think anything of the sort, Clara," Stefano said vehemently. "Your Bel Étage is something very special. In all my travels, I've never seen another shop like it. You'll go far, I'm sure of it." He spoke the last words quietly, then looked out silently over the lake.

What is going on inside him? Clara wondered, and she felt her stomach tighten nervously. When they had taken a walk a few nights previous, Stefano had told her that he still hadn't found suitable premises. But every day, he was making new contacts, and he hoped that something would appear on the horizon soon. His family in Italy was counting on him, after all, and he had said he couldn't even contemplate being unable to accomplish what they wanted of him.

The mood had been light and easy just a moment before, but then she'd started showing off with her oh-so-successful friends, and that had set him thinking. How stupid of her! Maybe Gerhard hadn't been wrong when he used to accuse of her speaking without thinking.

"Signor Santo has rented his room indefinitely," said Sophie when Clara told her that, the day before, he had picked her up from work once again.

"Indefinitely?" Clara repeated, her voice trembling a little. What did that mean?

She would really have preferred to talk with Therese about Stefano and how she feared that if he didn't find the right place in Meersburg soon, he would move on. But the hairdresser was spending less and less time there—very much to Clara's chagrin, not to mention that of Therese's customers. And Clara would just have to make do with Sophie. The young assistant was clearly enjoying her role as Clara's ear-piece. She leaned forward and said, "He seems to have enough money, at least. Mother says he always chooses one of the more expensive dishes on the menu, and that he drinks a glass of our good wine every day."

Clara smiled wistfully. "I can believe it. Stefano Santo is the kind of man who can enjoy life to the fullest. I've never met anyone like him. I find him simply refreshing. In everything he does. Just imagine, when we went walking yesterday, he insisted on taking me to the Brettschneider Café. You know, Fabienne had just canceled her appointment at short notice, so I had a free hour. But if I'd known what he was planning . . ." Clara shook her head, but she was practically beaming.

"What?" Sophie almost screamed.

Although the shop was empty and no one could overhear them, Clara lowered her voice. "Stefano asked if I would like cake. And I said yes, but you can't imagine what happened. The waiters brought out more and more plates of cake. Chocolate éclairs, cream-meringue pie, tarts, fruit cake—the table was covered in cake! Sabine Weingarten passed by just then, would you believe, and her eyes nearly popped out of her head at the extravagance." Clara smiled. No man had ever spoiled her like Stefano.

"You've got it good," said Sophie, sounding a little envious. "I'd be happy just to have Ernst treat me to a cup of coffee now and then. But he thinks anything like that is a waste of money. It's not like we can't eat and drink in my parents' guesthouse for free," she added ironically. She gestured tragically. "Free? We're there for two heartbeats, and my mother suddenly discovers a hundred things for me to do. Before I know it, I'm standing at the sink in the kitchen, and Ernst is putting his heels up at his usual table. He's my sweetheart, but he doesn't understand that *I* would like to be the one getting served occasionally."

"Then I wonder if he's the right man for you?" Clara said, only half joking.

Sophie sighed. "I'd like a Stefano of my own. Doesn't help, though; he's only got eyes for you."

"Nonsense," Clara said. "Our outings are just a way for him to pass the time while nothing's happening with his business. He still doesn't know many people here."

Sophie Bauer glanced sidelong at her boss.

On her way home that evening, Sophie could not stop thinking about what Clara had told her earlier. As clever as Clara was in some things, in others she seemed utterly naive. Anybody could see that the good-looking Italian was trying to win her for himself. And who could miss that Clara had fallen head over heels for him, too?

Chapter Twenty-Five

What a morning! It was nine thirty as Clara hurried from the Hotel Residenz toward her shop. First, she overslept and was late meeting Lilo for their early-morning swim. Lilo was already far out in the lake when Clara stepped into the water. But the lake was magnificent and the water deliciously warm! Afterward, though they both had a busy day ahead, they sat on the sun-warmed gravel shore and let the sun and the breeze dry them. Sunshine, the gentle rippling of the water, the whispering of the undulating reeds—Clara could not remember the last time she had felt so good.

"Did I tell you? Isabelle sent a letter. She's planning to visit sometime this summer," said Lilo. "She's going to see a specialist in Munich with her daughter, then bring her to spend a little time with us. She promised to book a room as soon as she knows when she's coming."

Clara, who had her eyes closed and was enjoying the sun's warmth, was on her feet in a second. "Isabelle is coming here? Then we have to get Josephine to come down, too. We must!"

"The four of us together again, just like the old days? How fantastic! We could . . ." And they had gotten so caught up with talk and plans that they had completely forgotten the time.

Before Clara met Stefano, she would never have been late for work. But now she was less strict with herself. He had awakened a lightness in her that she never knew existed. *Cause for concern? Or something to celebrate?* Clara wondered as she looked longingly toward the Esplanade Café. She was so late that she would have to get by without breakfast. Her first appointment—with Baroness von Böttinger—should actually have started at nine thirty, so Clara would be at least ten minutes late. She knew, though, that Sophie would have had the presence of mind to apply a cleansing mask for the baroness.

She had just passed through the gate that marked the entrance to Unterstadtstrasse when she saw the small crowd gathered in front of the shop, Sophie and Stefano among them. *Oh, what now?* she wondered, and her good mood evaporated.

"Mrs. Berg, finally!" Sophie cried. "Therese hasn't come, and I don't know where she is. And I don't have my key. Therese borrowed it yesterday because she forgot her own."

"Unheard of! Forgotten like the dead, that's what we are!" grumbled Baroness Viola von Böttinger.

"Oh, a few minutes is neither here nor there, is it?" said a second woman, who had an appointment with Sophie. "Mr. Santo has been showing us some excellent breathing exercises while we have been waiting. Very good for cultivating one's beauty, he says."

"Not that you would need that, dear lady," Stefano demurred. "Nor you, Baroness. But I'm sure you could teach them to your less attractive friends, couldn't you?"

"Aren't you the charmer!" the baroness laughed, and she whacked him playfully on his arm with her fan.

Clara's hand trembled with suppressed anger as she inserted the key in the lock. It was the second time that month that Therese had failed to open up as agreed.

"Sophie, please light the stove so we can warm water quickly."

"I can do that," said Stefano, and he strode off toward the back room before Clara could stop him. But she was grateful, and relieved to have him there. She turned her attention to Baroness von Böttinger.

"Please, take a seat," Clara said, indicating her gilded armchair. "My assistant, Sophie, will pamper you with a hand massage while I prepare everything for the skin consultation." She smiled at the second customer and offered her Therese's empty hairdressing chair. "Madam, if you wouldn't mind taking a seat, Miss Sophie will be with you in a moment and—" She was interrupted by the tinkling of the doorbell as three women entered. They came hand in hand and seemed to be the best of friends. New customers.

Normally, Clara would have been thrilled to have three new customers, but now she felt a touch of panic. And she hadn't even begun to deal with the three women when the doorbell jangled again and one of Therese's regular customers came in to have her hair curled, as she did every Friday.

Perfect chaos. For a moment, Clara didn't know whether to laugh or cry. She glanced outside frantically. Where was Therese?

"*Che belle signore!* How can I help you this morning?" Stefano said, addressing the three women before Clara had even had a chance to greet them properly. The women giggled while Stefano opened a sample jar of hand cream for them to try and misted some facial toner on their faces.

He seems so knowledgeable, thought Clara, surprised and a little in awe. It was as if he had never done anything else. She looked back to Therese's customer.

"If you wouldn't mind taking a seat, Miss Himmelsreich will be coming soon, and I'll be happy to wash your hair before that."

"Pardon my interruption, but Miss Himmelsreich is ill," Stefano contradicted her. "I fear that we will have to arrange a new appointment for you."

"Which is it?" the woman asked, looking from Clara to Stefano in annoyance. "Is Therese coming or isn't she?"

Stefano held up his arm gallantly for the woman. She accepted his offer and he accompanied her to the door. "Isn't it a glorious day? On a day like today, why spend hours at the hairdresser? There are so many other things you could be doing. Your hair won't mind; it looks beautiful just as it is."

Clara could only look on speechlessly as the woman gave Stefano a happy smile and strolled away. He had the women all but eating out of his hand. How did he do that?

"Mrs. Berg, you should attend to Baroness von Böttinger!" Sophie whispered beside her. "I should see to my customer. She's giving me dirty looks."

Clara reached for a small basket that was standing on the counter and took out a small jar of hand cream. "For your customer. To make up for the time she's had to wait. A gift from us."

***

Three hours of good deeds was enough, Stefano decided, and he went to Clara, who was massaging lotion into a customer's forehead and temples.

"The fire in the stove is burning well, three pots of water are warm, and the register's been ringing nicely. *Tutto è bene*," he said softly, not wanting to disturb Clara's customer. "If you don't mind, I'll go down to the Sommer Patisserie and get us a little something. A bite to eat after such a busy morning can't hurt."

That could not have gone better, he thought happily as he walked to the bakery, and counted himself lucky that lazy Therese had slept late! Like this, he could easily endear himself to Clara. She'd been impressed by the way he had her customers eating out of his hand. And he'd been surprised at often the cash register had rung. He'd seen his supposition—that beauty could bring in a lot of money—confirmed in spades. And he had realized something else: he'd lost none of his skill with women.

"I don't know what I would have done without you this morning," Clara said as she polished off the last of the strawberry cake Stefano had brought back. "That was the first thing I've eaten all day, and I was almost dizzy with hunger." Stefano was relieved to see that Sophie had gone home to her parents' guesthouse for lunch. He needed time alone with Clara.

"I had a good time this morning," he replied. "I have missed that kind of contact with customers." He tried to inject a yearning tone into his voice, and it must have worked, because a shadow crossed Clara's face.

"Oh, now I've got a guilty conscience. You wanted to spend this morning working on your own business, didn't you?"

He leaned closer and looked at her seriously. "You, Clara, are a thousand times more important to me than any business. I want to see you happy, laughing, and free of cares, and not facing the kind of stress you had to earlier."

She slid back on her wooden chair, away from him. *Aha, that was too far.* He was left with two possibilities: retreat or attack. Who knew when he would have such a good opportunity again? "I can see that my candid words have frightened you, and I apologize for that. But sometimes, Clara, sometimes, when I see you, it feels as if my heart all but bursts with joy." He was absolutely sure that his gaze at that moment was warmer than the sun outside.

Clara sighed softly. For Stefano, her excitement was palpable. *Now don't overdo it!* he warned himself. He sensed that one more declaration of love would push her away rather than bring her closer. He did not know much about her past, but he suspected that she had not found much happiness with the men in her life. He would have to move forward slowly, with caution.

He cleared his throat and adopted a more businesslike tone. "May I ask you something?"

Clara nodded.

"Why do you bother with Signora Himmelsreich at all? She can be exceptionally charming, but she is also fickle and unreliable."

"I'm sure she really is unwell today," Clara defended Therese automatically, but Stefano could hear in her voice that she agreed with him.

"You are too kind, dear Clara. In private matters, that is a good thing, but in business it can only cause harm. I fear that, at some point, Therese's unreliability with her shop will have a negative effect on your Bel Étage, too. Do you really want to risk that?"

"What can I do about it?" Clara replied, her voice despairing. "Therese and I rent this shop together. I can't force her to keep to her opening times. Besides, she took me in as her tenant first, and I will always be grateful to her for that."

"Which is one of your best traits, and no less than I would have expected," he said calmly. "Forget what I said. I'm probably a bit too rigid about things like a good reputation, punctuality, and honesty." He waved one hand dismissively.

Clara frowned. She seemed about to say something but didn't, probably for fear of sounding disloyal to Therese.

Step one, Stefano thought triumphantly.

***

It was later in the afternoon, just after Stefano left, that Therese finally walked through the door. She did not excuse herself for her absence, but said instead, "I just bumped into Stefano. He had a real spring in his step and looked like the cat that got the cream. Did he finally admit he's head over heels for you?"

"Not here, Therese," Clara said. She nodded toward her customer, the last of the day, who was bathing her hands in warm almond oil, then beckoned Therese into the back room and said, "Do you have any idea what happened this morning when you didn't open the shop? What was it this time?"

"Oh, Clara, you know how it is sometimes." Therese looked imploringly at her. "I really meant to be here, believe me. But . . ." Her expression changed and her eyes sparkled mischievously.

"It simply isn't fair to leave Sophie and me alone like that! It was chaos in here, and I don't want it to happen again!" Clara said, making an effort to keep her voice down. Then, seeing how crestfallen Therese looked, she raised her eyebrows and went on. "And I don't think I want to hear the 'but' . . ." Therese probably had yet another lover. Clara was always amazed by how easily her friend managed to attract men. But perhaps she had that talent herself, at least a little? She smiled. "Now that you've brought it up—Stefano actually did admit that he's in love. That's how I understood it, anyway." In a low voice, she told Therese about her talk with Stefano at midday.

"See? It was good that I wasn't here," said Therese. "So what now?"

"Nothing. Nothing at all. Naturally, I didn't give in to his advances." She heard a loud snore and glanced out from behind the curtain. Her customer had fallen asleep in the comfortable armchair. The woman had seemed exhausted when she trudged into Bel Étage, so a few minutes of rest would do her good.

"I don't understand you at all. An attractive man comes knocking on your door, and what do you do? You act like an old prune!"

Clara screwed up her face. "Thank you very much," she said. "But you're right; I did act like that. What does a young man like that see in someone older like me?"

Therese sniffed dismissively. "These days many women have younger boyfriends. Countess Zuzanna, believe it or not, has a young lover herself, which is the reason she's in Baden-Baden for the summer and not here. They say he's twenty years her junior, so what difference does the few years between you and Stefano make? Besides, you look younger than you are. I'm sure he doesn't think you're a day over thirty."

Clara said nothing. Since moving to Lake Constance, she did feel younger, and certainly nothing like a thirty-four-year-old divorcée. She could no longer deny that she liked Stefano.

She sighed deeply. "I have no idea how to feel or what to think. After everything that's happened, I never would have believed I could fall in love again. But since I've known Stefano, I'm no longer sure of that. He's so considerate, so nice to me. It's lovely to be spoiled by him. It's something I've never experienced before," she said. She smiled as it occurred to her that Stefano must certainly know how to spoil a woman in bed, too, and she felt herself blush at the thought. "Honestly, I feel so much different around him. So wonderfully warm . . ."

Therese giggled.

Clara grew serious again. "But I still don't trust any of it. Stefano is not just good-looking, but also a successful businessman. A man like him could have any woman he wanted. Lilo told me that Estelle Morgan, the actress staying at the hotel, has her eye on him. She's rich, famous, and beautiful. Next to her, I'm nobody. And anyway, I know hardly anything about him. He's probably married with a wife and three children back in Italy. And he knows nothing about me. If he ever finds out I'm not a widow but a divorced mother of two, he won't want anything else to do with me."

"You old trout! Number one"—Therese held up her right thumb— "if Stefano was interested in Estelle Morgan, he'd be spending his time with *her*. Number two"—Therese held up her right index finger—"a man like Stefano can easily imagine that you had a life before you met him. And number three"—up went her next finger—"you think too much. Since you don't know, why don't you find out? Just ask Stefano exactly where he comes from. Get him to tell you about his Italian home and his family. Men like to talk about themselves, and they like it when you sit and listen to them. You'll be amazed how much he'll talk. And I'm certain that everything you hear will be good."

"And what if it isn't?" Clara asked. But Therese was suddenly distracted. She waved her hand toward their front window and cried, "Where are the two wigs? Were they stolen?"

"No! Stefano sold them. He put the money in your register," said Clara.

Therese broke into a broad grin. "How fantastic! I like the man more and more. Stay on his good side, Clara!"

Two days later, Clara accepted Stefano's invitation to dinner. They sat out on the terrace at the Hotel Residenz. Dozens of candles were placed along the terrace wall and on the tables, and they cast their soft light on the faces of the guests, creating an atmosphere of warmth and romance. After they had finished their outstanding meal, Clara worked up her courage to ask Stefano to tell her a little about his life in Italy.

"Instead of trying to teach us something from our mistakes, my father preferred to reach for his stick. As children, my brother and I were beaten often. It's a miracle most of our bones are intact. We learned very quickly not to talk back and to do what Father told us. What else could we have done? Our village is in a narrow valley, and everyone knows everyone else. Our father is a wealthy, respected man there, and no one would have dared stand up to him. Besides, the people there believe that a father has the right to beat disobedient children."

Clara felt her throat tighten. *"Why do you have to upset your husband so?"* She suddenly had her mother's voice in her ear. *"You're such an insubordinate wife. It's no wonder Gerhard sometimes loses his temper."*

"In our village, the only thing that matters is what my father and Lorenzo, his business partner, think. Those two men determine everything. But what *I* want to do with *my* life—nobody ever bothered to ask me that. Being a hair trader is probably the last thing I would have chosen . . ." Stefano's gaze wandered toward the lake, blue-black in the night. His face was filled with pain, and in his she could see he was struggling with old demons. "Sometimes, I felt like I'd been buried alive. A marionette dancing to my father's whims, unable to take a single step without him. My father had even found a wife for me, but I defended myself. If I ever marry, it will be for love." He took Clara's hand and looked into her eyes for a long moment.

Clara swallowed. Therese had been right; Stefano had been very forthcoming indeed about his past. And she appreciated his openness very much. But at the same time, their conversation felt almost too intimate.

"Did your brother suffer as much with your father being so strict?" she asked. She hoped her question would break the spell of the moment.

Stefano let himself be distracted. "My brother is cut from softer wood," he said. "He married Lorenzo's daughter, just as my father wanted him to. And he finds it easier to be the obedient son in other ways. But I think that for him, too, the only truly good times were when we went off traveling together." He recalled something then, and it made him smile. "But they were not carefree times. We lived with the constant fear of not being successful enough, of coming home and having to face our father's wrath again."

"Apart from wigs and the hair, do you deal in anything else?" Clara asked. "I'm sure you must have told me, but just now I can't seem to remember."

She watched as his face, until now so animated, dulled in the space of a heartbeat. "Would you think less of me if we didn't talk about business? It brings up so many memories. Painful memories . . ." He voice trailed off as Lilo appeared at their table with a fresh bottle of wine.

Oh, now I've managed to hurt him with all my nosy questions. Clara looked up gratefully at Lilo, then turned back to Stefano. "I can sympathize with so many of the things you've told me about," she said, her voice raw. She wanted to take him in her arms, to drive out the gloomy memories. But instead, she said, "No one ever asked me what I wanted out of life, either. When I was girl, I wanted so much to become a pharmacist, but then it was impossible. Perhaps it would be easier for a woman today, but—" She broke off, lifted one hand, and let it fall again. "Life has taught me that it's better to leave some dreams behind. There are still enough things that are worth fighting for. But to come back to you." Deliberately cheerful, she asked, "What do you want from life? What would you do if you could choose, and if you had the freedom?"

Stefano looked at her with a serious expression. "I've never asked myself that question. Freedom? I never experienced it before this journey. Since I arrived here at Lake Constance, I've felt free and light of heart." He smiled shyly. "But I do believe that my high spirits have a lot to do with being close to you."

"Stefano . . ." Clara, abashed, looked away, but her heart was beating hard. "It frightens me a little to hear you speak like that." Where was it all supposed to lead?

"But if it's the truth? I've never felt better in my life than in the days I've spent in your presence and in your beautiful shop." He sighed deeply. "I admire what you do more than I can tell you. The kindness with which you treat your customers impresses me newly every day. You give them your attention or, really, something like devotion. You return to them what life—and maybe men, too—have taken away: their sense of who they are, their beauty, their youth or at least the memory of it. With every jar of cream, you give them back so much."

Clara gulped. "You made it all sound very lovely," she said, her voice a little husky. "I would never dare describe my work like that myself. All I do is sell creams and scented lotions. Most people probably find that extremely superficial and useless, actually." What would her father have thought of her profession? Might he have been just a little proud of his daughter? After all, he had instilled in her a love of making soaps and salves.

"You do nothing but good for women. Who else can claim that?" A shadow, as sudden as a summer shower, darkened his face. "I wish I had a calling like that myself. I feel so unnecessary."

"What are you talking about?" Clara said vehemently. "Didn't your family send you to Germany to set up a business? That's—" She broke off when she saw a crease appear between his eyes.

"Yes, my family sent me," he said. "But every day I sense that I have to find my own way. I don't care if my family hates me for it for the rest of my life. I don't want anything to with the old business, not anymore."

Clara bit her lip thoughtfully. "So what will you do now?" she asked hesitantly, almost fearfully. He didn't want to leave Meersburg, did he?

"First, I'm going to sell all the hair and wigs I brought with me the best way I can, and send the money home. It's important for me to make a clean break. I don't want to cheat anyone. And then . . ." Stefano shrugged. "Clara, I don't have the slightest idea. I have to believe that I still have some undiscovered talents."

"I don't doubt it for a moment. I've seen how well you deal with people," said Clara with conviction. "I only have to think about how you handled Baroness von Böttinger when she was so upset, and how helpful you were when the shop was overflowing with customers and I didn't know which way was up. Stefano, you have salesmanship in your blood, and I'm sure that's not all."

He laughed at that. "Now you're flattering me. But you're right about one thing: I feel at home in the Bel Étage. Enough about me. A toast to the here and now!" He raised his wine glass. "And to you, dear Clara. Or may I say, to us?"

With a trembling hand, Clara lifted her glass. She felt a warm tremor pass through her. "To the here and now," she said quietly, feeling the cool wine run down her throat.

"So!" Stefano abruptly set his glass down. "Now it's your turn. I want to know everything about you, every secret. I want to see into every corner of your beautiful soul."

Clara's heart began to race. Should she reveal her secrets? The truth, once spoken, could not be taken back. But he had revealed a lot about himself. Didn't she owe him the same? And didn't she need to know how he would react to her past and what she was working toward for the future? If he could not accept that, it was best to know sooner than later.

She began to speak, haltingly at first. About her marriage to Gerhard. About the beatings. About the many humiliations, large and small, he had heaped on her. About how she had been worn down, how she became fearful and small, just as he wanted her to be. She told him about her divorce and her children and her irrepressible desire to one day have them live with her again.

By the time Clara finished, most of the other tables were empty. "Now I really have let you into every corner of my soul," she said. "I hope I haven't shocked you."

"You have," Stefano replied, to Clara's horror. "It shocks me to the bone to hear what a miserable hand life has dealt you. And how, apart from your friends, nobody helped. From now on, I want to be there for you! I want to lift every care from your shoulders and help you get your children back. Bambini belong with their mama."

"Oh, Stefano," said Clara, sad and happy at the same time. "I'm afraid only I can help myself. The business has to grow. I have to earn a lot of money to be able to afford a nice apartment and good lawyers. Of course the business is off to a good start, and an apartment is in the works. But I am a long way from leading a respectable, stable life, at least in the eyes of the court. And I would so much like to do more, today, here and now! But what?"

"Your love for your children, how much you miss them . . . these things are making you impatient. I know exactly what you're feeling," said Stefano. "But don't be so hard on yourself. You have achieved so much already. Be proud of that."

Clara nodded, but she said nothing, fighting back tears. She had rarely felt as understood as she did by Stefano. He had a way of seeing everything so clearly that it made her own heart feel lighter.

He cleared his throat. "I don't want to put my nose in any more than I should, but maybe you will allow me a word about something I've observed in the last few weeks." He paused. When Clara said nothing, he went on. "Is it true that most of the people who visit Bel Étage are guests in the hotels here in town?"

Clara looked at him in surprise. What made him think of that now? "Yes. Most of our customers are summer visitors. Hotel guests, or they've rented a villa by the lake."

Stefano's eyes were bright. "Have you ever considered opening a second beauty shop here in Lilo's hotel? You'd be going to your customers rather than having them come to you. You'd have greater capacity. You could serve more women, and earn more money."

Clara had to laugh. "A Bel Étage in Lilo's hotel? How did you come up with that?"

He shrugged lightly. "To me, it seems a natural step. Your treatments make women happy, so if more of them had the opportunity, well, that would be a good thing."

"A second Bel Étage . . ." The words tripped hesitantly over Clara's lips. "When I think about it, I can already see the room I would want to use." The storage room where she had found some of the furniture for her shop. It would do the job nicely. And surely Lilo would like the idea of earning rent for the room—it wasn't being used for anything important, after all.

Clara eyed Stefano inquisitively. "A second business would mean twice as much work. I would have to hire and train another assistant, maybe even two. I would have to produce substantially more of my products. I'm the only one who knows the recipes, and I want to keep them secret, so I can't contract that work out." She shook her head. "As tempting as it sounds, I don't think I'll be able to do it."

"And if I help you? You and I would make such a good team, we could coax the moon from the sky," Stefano said, looking so deeply into her eyes that she felt almost giddy.

Lilo was thrilled about the idea of a Bel Étage location in her hotel. "And you can use the old laundry next door, too. Ever since we added the catering wing, we haven't used that laundry. There's running water, two wash basins, and an old tub for washing your towels. But no daylight, I'm afraid. You'll have to work by lamp."

Clara could hardly believe her ears. "Oh, Lilo, thank you so much!" she said.

"Don't thank me too soon, because I have *one* condition. Either you manage to get set up and moved in within four weeks, or you'll have to postpone the entire project until the fall. A construction site is the last thing I need in the high season. It would unsettle my guests too much."

Clara gulped. Four weeks to turn an old junk room into an elegant beauty shop? *"And if I help you? You and I would make such a good team."* Stefano's voice echoed in her ear. If she stayed in the shop and Sophie took over the treatments in the hotel, it could work.

She held out her right hand. "It's a deal! Four weeks from today, we celebrate the opening of Bel Étage–Residenzia."

"Residenzia?" Lilo raised her eyebrows. "That sounds very Italian."

Clara laughed. "Do you think so? The name just came to me, and you know what? I think it sounds very chic."

Chapter Twenty-Six

Clara insisted on decorating the Bel Étage–Residenzia in the same colors as her shop in Unterstadtstrasse. She found the combination of the light lime green and the lavender both invigorating and calming; plus, it had become something of a trademark.

The painter, the carpenter, then a visit to Friedrichshafen to visit a man who dealt in used furniture—each day from early morning until late evening was filled with a breathless buzz of activity. But Clara was not alone. She had Stefano by her side.

"Go choose the fabric for the curtains. I'll keep an eye on the painting," he would say. Or "Let me come along to the furniture place. I'll get a good price for you!" Clara kept all his help and suggestions in mind. They spent more and more time together, and grew more and more familiar with each other, but there were no more advances from Stefano, no declarations of love . . . perhaps because, when she thought their conversation might be moving in that direction, she quickly steered them another way.

Sometimes, late at night, with the day's work finished, they sat together with a glass of wine, and Clara wanted nothing more than to have him put his arm around her. How would it feel to kiss him? His lips on hers . . . She felt her body begin to vibrate slightly whenever she was near him. Was it just her imagination, or was she more alive when she was with him? But would she say yes if he asked her to marry him? When she thought of that possibility, she still felt unsure, so she was thankful for the reserve he showed. Time would tell how things went between them. For now, it felt good just to be together.

It felt good, too, not to have to make every decision by herself. Stefano dealt with the craftsmen, paid invoices, kept track of deliveries—there were so many things he took care of that otherwise would have drained her time.

But even with Stefano's help, there were days when Clara hardly knew which end was up. She was making do with five or maybe six hours of sleep each night, because when she was done with her appointments and everything needed for the new shop, there was still the daily work of making creams, soaps, and lotions.

When, late in the evening, Clara fell into bed exhausted, she often cast a glance at the stack of books lying neglected on her bedside table. When was the last time that she had turned a page in *Cleopatra's Beauty Secrets*? Or learned something new from the *Atlas of Diseases of the Skin*? She had always cherished reading.

And yet, Clara had rarely felt as good as she did these days. Slowly, she began to believe that she was no longer the little gray mouse that had crept out of her Berlin suburb, a little mouse only able to oblige her husband. Slowly, she grew used to the fact that she was a successful businesswoman, just like Isabelle, Lilo, and Josephine.

***

"Most important of all is to cleanse the face thoroughly. Unfortunately, the upper-class women still believe—quite wrongly—that washing with water is something only the lower classes do. Nothing cleans the skin as well as water does, but you really have to splash it on. Look." Clara dipped both hands into the basin and demonstrated what she considered to be the best face-washing method.

Evi Förster, who was twenty years old, and Ruth Stein, who was a year older, watched closely. Clara was training them to be beauty assistants. They were supposed to start work the following week in Bel Étage–Residenzia, where Clara's first assistant, Sophie, would take them under her wing.

It was Stefano who had suggested taking on the young and exceptionally attractive young women. Previously, they had worked as waitresses in the harbor restaurant. Stefano had noticed them when he was there for lunch.

"The prettier and younger your assistants are, the better. Customers will want to be just as young and pretty," he had explained. When Clara had met with the two young women, she was sure they would work out well.

"Now try washing your face like that yourselves," Clara encouraged them. "You have to know what it feels like before you can recommend it to a customer."

Both assistants washed their faces as Clara had. Stefano smiled. Clara was good at training them.

Clara handed Evi and Ruth towels. "Once the face has been cleaned, we can start with the treatment. It's best to recommend no more than one face cream and one facial toner. Anything more seems to confuse most women. Beauty care should be simple and fun."

Stefano's smile vanished. What was Clara telling them? Why sell just one or two products when women were prepared to buy several at once? He was about to interrupt, but he stopped himself.

"Any cream has to be massaged deep into the skin. This must be done with sensitivity, with small circular movements, like this," said Clara, and demonstrated her technique. "The worst thing you can do is be rough. Never beat or pull. We're not rubbing fat into a roast. We're handling delicate female skin."

The two young women laughed. Stefano, too, had to smile. Clara certainly had a vivid way of describing something.

"Show each customer how to do the massage themselves at home. Then they can get the most benefit out of my creams. So far so good?"

Clara's assistants nodded enthusiastically, and Stefano's eyes narrowed.

"Why is it actually so important to you to explain so much to your customers?" he asked Clara when she was finished with her lesson for the day. "All you're doing is loading them down with knowledge unnecessarily. They should be the ones coming to you. They should be relying on your advice and your expertise. If you go turning them into experts, all you'll do is lose their loyalty."

"I see it differently. I would like every woman to be able to ensure her own well-being. Starting when we are very small, women are brought up to care for others. But when it comes to caring for ourselves, we hesitate. That is something I would like to change. If that means that my customers take my advice and, at the same time, use other creams and tinctures, then so be it. That's something I have to accept."

Stefano had rarely heard such nonsense! But again he managed to stop himself before he said too much. "It's late, darling," he said, as mildly as possible. "Let's have a little to eat and a glass of wine."

But Clara waved off the offer. "I'm running out of my orange blossom water. I have to make more, urgently. I also want to do a couple of experiments with bath oils so I can add them to my line. After all that, I *really* have to write the invitations to the grand opening next week." Her forehead creased with concern. "I had been hoping so much that Countess Zuzanna would come to Lake Constance this summer after all. I'm sure that I could have won some new customers among the nobles through her. Now that I have the second business, having more customers is more important than ever."

"It is just as important to keep your existing customers as loyal as possible, darling!" said Stefano, and he kissed her hand to take the edge off his words.

A short time later, Stefano was eating soup at the restaurant by the harbor, which the tourists, a little pretentiously, called the marina. But for the local people it was simply the harbor, and the so-called yacht club was not a private club but a small, modest restaurant with a few tables and fewer dishes on the menu. Still, it remained a popular meeting point not only for locals, but also for rich tourists, who could tie up their elegant boats right outside the windows. Stefano, too, liked the place. He enjoyed the banter with the rich and beautiful, and he enjoyed buying a bottle of champagne or sparkling wine. As long as he still had money from selling the hair and wigs, he could be generous.

The previous week, he had managed to sell all the hair and wigs for a good price across the lake in Switzerland. He had left his two horses there, too, but had made the brewery owner who bought them promise to take good care of the animals. He had been a little sad to see the man lead the brown away. But in his new life he needed neither wigs nor horses. Because from that day forth, he was banking everything on a different horse.

Clara Berg.

When his own money began to run low, he would be able to draw from the deep well called the Bel Étage. At least, that was his plan. But his plan had developed a small crack that day.

Had he been mistaken about Clara's talents as a businesswoman? What if the well ran dry faster than he thought? If things went south with his source of funds, then he would be married to a woman who he did, indeed, hold in high regard, but did not love. And he would have a business that was far less profitable than he hoped, a millstone around his neck. He imagined a far different future for himself than that!

Clara had to make her customers loyal to her. All those fine ladies were supposed to come back hungry for more of Clara's expensive products. But if Clara kept handing out her selfless advice, and if she trained her assistants to do the same, the women would pursue their beauty care themselves—no matter what Clara believed.

While he grumbled to himself about all of this, he looked around to see who was at the restaurant that evening. Estelle Morgan was sitting at one of the tables along the side. As usual, the actress was surrounded by a group of young admirers. They laughed at all her jokes, sighed when she sighed, groaned when Estelle told them to. Stefano sniffed contemptuously. Lapdogs, all of them.

The next moment, the American actress looked in his direction. Stefano smiled and nodded, then he withdrew a notebook from his vest pocket and pretended to write something down. Funny coincidence that Estelle was there. He had been planning to invite her to the opening of Bel Étage–Residenzia, but right now he preferred to keep his own company. He had to think some things through.

Clara was simply too good-natured. That was the problem. He pushed his empty soup bowl away. All those years at the side of her despotic husband had made her soft and weak, though the image she showed to the outside world was that of the strong businesswoman.

But what did that mean for him, for their future together? Did his big chance lie precisely in her weakness?

If he succeeded in winning her heart, and if, after that, he managed to keep her as far away from her customers as possible, and away from the meddlesome Therese . . . and as long as Clara stayed in her laboratory stirring her pots of cream . . . then she couldn't start babbling the kind of nonsense she had that afternoon.

He glanced over again at Estelle's table, where everyone was laughing affectedly. A shudder ran through him. Was he even one notch better than Estelle's lapdogs? He, too, thought carefully about every word, every sentence, that he said to Clara. *Don't push too hard. Move with caution.*

The previous week, he had tried to steer their conversation to the topic of getting engaged. But before he could even get the words in his mouth, Clara had hurriedly changed the subject. Like a horse shying at an obstacle.

"Because I can!" Suddenly, he had those words in his ear. When and where had he heard them? It took him a moment to remember the mountain climber that he and Michele had met on their last journey into the mountains together. Michele had asked the young man why in the world he wanted to climb Chersogno. "Because I can," the climber had replied. As simple as that.

And what could he do? Stefano wondered as the whir of voices around him grew louder. In the past, he had always believed that he had a way with women—he was not the most successful *caviè* for nothing. Had he overestimated himself and his talents? There was still no engagement, no promise of marriage. And what he had to say carried no weight in the Bel Étage without Clara's backing, as much as he might like it otherwise. Now and then, Clara pressed some cash into his hand so that he could settle the invoices from the carpenters and other craftsmen. When he skimmed a little of that for himself, no one noticed. But should he be satisfied with that?

Piano, he chided himself. *Go slowly.* It wasn't as if he were just marking time. In most things, Clara already took his advice. He resolved to have a tighter grip on the reins by the end of the year. His good looks, his charm, and the perfect manners his father had beaten into him— women appreciated all of it. He had the rich wives of Meersburg and the smug young dames and duchesses eating out of his hand just as he had with the farm girls whose hair he'd cut off. It was ridiculous to think that his charm would fail him with Clara.

His thoughts were interrupted by a group of elegantly dressed gentlemen when they sat down at the only available table. Chairs scraped across the floor, the table shifted . . . They were speaking Italian. Stefano felt fear run through his body. What if someone recognized him, the runaway *caviè*? Instinctively, he lowered his head so that no one could look him in the face. But even as he did so, he told himself that his fear was completely unfounded. After all, even if they were Italians, why should they have anything to do with the hair trade?

The men ordered their food. Stefano ordered another glass of wine. He took a deep breath and exhaled. It calmed him; no, he would *not* run from the restaurant like a criminal.

"She will be arriving in two days," said one of the men in Italian. "Are her lodgings prepared?"

"*Sì*, Signor Battista. The villa has been rented for the entire summer and has been cleaned from top to bottom. All the guest rooms have been fully outfitted. Her Highness and her retinue will have nothing to complain about."

Her Highness? Her retinue? Stefano almost choked on his wine.

"And the arch? And what about the lemon trees and orange trees?"

"A dozen have already been set out on each of the terraces, on the lake side and in the courtyard. And a magnificent archway has been constructed at the entrance of the villa."

Stefano could hardly contain his excitement. He knew which house they were talking about! On his daily walks, he had been watching the elaborate preparations taking place at one of the last houses on the lakeshore, just a few hundred yards from the Hotel Residenz. Stefano had stopped several times to chat with various workers, but none of them had known who was moving into the villa.

Stefano gave a little cough and shifted his chair so that he could hear the men better.

"And what about the palm trees that are supposed to line the road?"

"That, admittedly, was more of a problem," said the second man. "The mayor had to be convinced of the need for such an extravagance. We managed to obtain his approval in the end."

Stefano saw the man shrug casually. The third man said nothing, but took copious notes in a small book. That reminded Stefano to act like he, too, was busy writing down important information. He didn't want to be spotted as an eavesdropper, after all. But he was growing more excited with every word he overheard. Damn it, who were they talking about?

"Our honored guest will feel like she's in Rome."

Rome? A high-ranking guest from Rome. Stefano relaxed. The men had absolutely nothing do with Elva.

"Our honored guest is not meant to feel like she's in Rome, but as if she is in her *own home,*" the first man admonished his counterpart. "Is an automobile at her disposal? And if so, what kind? I hope very much that it is one of the newest and best. Our guest is well known for her exceptional love of automobiles. It would be unforgivable to present her with something that smokes and rattles."

Why did the men keep using "honored guest" instead of calling this woman by her name? What—or whose—secret were they hiding?

"Rest assured that we could not have organized a more luxurious automobile for our honored guest than what is right this moment standing in the garage of the Palazzo Margherita," replied the second man coolly.

Palazzo Margherita. The answer hit Stefano like a blow to the head. Suddenly, he knew exactly who they were talking about. He flipped his notebook closed and put it away, threw a few coins on the table, and rushed away.

***

Clara yawned. Because she was alone, she didn't make the effort to hold one hand politely over her mouth. Instead, she stretched both arms up over her head. She was tired: her bones ached, her eyes were burning. It had been a long day, but she had achieved a lot. At the

Bel Étage–Residenzia, everything was going according to plan, and she was looking forward to opening in two days. Her two young assistants were coming along nicely, the orange blossom water was finished, and tomorrow morning she and Sophie would fill the new, elegant bottles she had ordered especially for it.

Another yawn, and she looked at the notes, bills, and papers scattered across her desk. She had no desire to tackle the bookkeeping so late, but then a reminder from Mr. Eckard, the painter, caught her eye. Strange. Hadn't Stefano paid the man on the spot? *It must just be an oversight,* she thought, and put the reminder to one side. But then she changed her mind. It was best not to postpone anything when there was so much to do, so she looked over the bills that had come in the last two days. *Window sealing compound, 2 marks and 50 pfennigs, paid cash.* Clara shook her head. She didn't have any windows. Both rooms in the new beauty shop were in the interior of Lilo's hotel! Was the sealing compound used for some other repair? That must be it. She put the bill on top of the painter's reminder.

"Clara! I'm so glad you're still here!" Stefano came charging in.

Did he miss her so much that he couldn't wait until the next morning? She felt a pleasant warmth spread through her. "How nice of you to—"

"Clara," he interrupted her. He crouched until he was on eye level with her, then he took her hands in his. "You have to listen to me very carefully. What I'm about to say to you could change our lives forever."

"Yes," Clara breathed, and her heart was pounding. A proposal! In the middle of the night.

Stefano had already tried several times to find his way to a proposal. And every time she had quickly turned their talk to another subject. She was in love with Stefano, but was she ready to commit herself forever? Maybe today . . .

"I've discovered something sensational," Stefano said, his exhilaration making his voice shaky.

"Yes?" Clara breathed again. Not a proposal?

"The mother of the Italian king is coming to Meersburg! She always travels with an entourage of ladies-in-waiting." Stefano swallowed again. "Clara, this is *the* chance! Weren't you just saying that you wanted more customers from the nobility? Well, there's no woman in the world more noble than Margherita of Savoy-Genoa."

"Stefano." Clara blinked. Was she dreaming? "That's . . . that's fantastic. But what makes you think that, of all things, the king's mother needs my services?" she asked. She was having difficulty recovering from her previous thoughts, but Stefano was back on his feet and looking around frantically.

"Where is your orange blossom water?"

"In the other shop, at the lab," said Clara.

He nodded. "Then let's go there. Margherita loves oranges and lemons above anything else. We'll prepare welcome packages for her and her court ladies and add an invitation to the opening of the Residenzia. That's how you get the nobility as clients." There was triumph in his voice.

"But I don't speak any Italian at all!" Clara suddenly cried out, infected by his excitement.

"But *I* do," said Stefano with a laugh. He kissed Clara on the lips before she knew it.

> *We are pleased to welcome our Italian summer guests from the lakeside villa to the Bel Étage–Residenzia. On 15 June from 5 p.m. onward, our beauty shop will be at your disposal—we guarantee absolute discretion. After such a long journey, treat yourself to a few relaxing hours and let yourself be pampered by my staff and me.*
>
> *Your beauty expert,*
> *Clara Berg*

Clara had written the text by hand on heavy cream-colored hand-made paper. No recipient names were mentioned anywhere, a point that Stefano considered paramount. And Clara followed his stipulations, although "beauty expert" sounded a little forced. She was appeased, however, when Stefano told her that the expression in Italian sounded particularly beautiful: *esperta di bellezza.*

At Stefano's suggestion, Clara also filled a dozen small baskets with a selection of her products. "Expensive advertising," said Clara. What if Stefano had got it wrong and someone else had moved into the villa?

But Stefano was absolutely sure he was right.

"I don't know how these things work in German countries, but if you want to get the Italian nobility on your side, you have to offer them something."

Clara nodded vaguely. She did not have the slightest idea how it worked with the German nobility, or any other kind, for that matter. But suddenly, Isabelle's voice came to her. *"Nothing tempts the rich like a free gift!"*

"All right. Nothing ventured, nothing gained," she said. She gave him the small baskets so that he could hand them over personally at the gate of the villa.

"Orange blossom water, a beautifully packaged bar of soap, and a jar of lavender cream. Very good, Clara! But what's this—an orange?" said Stefano, and he looked with a frown from the basket to Clara.

Clara laughed. "That's called a scented pomander!" She picked out one of the oranges—it was spiked all over with cloves; she had added the pomanders to the baskets on a whim—and held it under Stefano's nose. "Smell it. It's wonderful."

"But you're not selling oranges, are you? You're selling soaps and creams." Stefano shook his head disapprovingly, but Clara would not let herself be swayed.

***

The day of the grand opening arrived. Almost all of Clara's loyal customers came by, and Sophie and the other assistants served sparkling wine. "It looks just like our Bel Étage!" was the enthusiastic response. Clara smiled with satisfaction. It was exactly what she'd intended.

Lilo and most of the women staying at the hotel stopped by as well. Clara, Stefano, and the assistants performed one demonstration after another, and dabbed samples on the women's wrists. Soon, the air was infused with the scents from Clara's products, and the women, even any who had been skeptical, relaxed as they soaked up the products and the luxurious atmosphere that Clara created.

Skin consultations, hand massages, foot baths, and advice—Clara's appointment book was completely filled for the days to come. Estelle Morgan came in with two young women in tow and strolled around as if it were the most natural thing in the world. It seemed that a beauty shop was nothing new to her, and she wanted an appointment for the following morning.

"I'm very sorry, but the first opening I have is the start of next week," said Clara, and she exchanged a satisfied look with Stefano. They were off to a good start.

Late in the afternoon, the crowd began to thin, and only the occasional new customer stopped in. Clara took a moment to eat a little food and drink a cup of tea. She had been on her feet for ten hours. In the whirlwind of the opening, she had forgotten about Stefano's Italian noblewoman, and her promise that at five o'clock she would close her shop to the general public.

When the door opened at five and an elegantly dressed older woman entered followed by a number of other women a few steps behind, Clara was not immediately aware of who she had in front of her. She greeted the new arrival with a shake of her hand as she had everyone before her, friendly and welcoming. Only when, from the corner of her eye, she noticed Stefano hurrying two remaining women out of the shop and closing the door behind them did she realize that she had just shaken the hand of the mother of the king of Italy.

"How nice that you . . . could come," she croaked while she attempted to regain her composure. Wasn't she supposed to say "Your Highness" at some point? She was glad when Stefano appeared at her side and greeted the women again, this time in Italian.

His greeting met with a torrent of Italian words in reply.

Stefano laid his right hand on his chest and, smiling, made a small bow.

"Our guest says that she and her ladies-in-waiting were very happy to receive your welcome gift," Stefano translated. "She also says that she would very much like to learn how to decorate an orange in such an original way." He seemed somewhat bewildered.

Decorate an orange? "Oh, the pomander!" She smiled at the king's mother. *How strange that it was the small gift that the woman liked so much,* she thought. She went to the counter, where oranges and lemons were piled high in a silver tray as decoration. She picked an orange, then took a small linen bag of cloves out of a drawer.

"You can actually make a scented pomander very easily." Under the interested eyes of the older woman, she pricked the cloves into the orange in the shape of a crown, as she had with the oranges in the gift baskets. "You can put the pomander on the windowsill during the day. It develops its scent especially well in the sun," she added with a smile when she was done.

"Che carina! È permesso . . . ?" said the king's mother effusively.

Clara looked questioningly at Stefano.

"She'd like to try it herself," he said.

"But of course," said Clara, and she handed the noblewoman another orange and the bag of cloves. "Please ask the other women if they might like a face massage or footbath while they're waiting," she said quietly to Stefan, who quickly translated. "They are welcome to try out more of the products, if they want to."

They wanted to.

While the king's mother eagerly decorated another orange with a snake of cloves, Clara ran to find Lilo, who was at the reception desk.

"Lilo, the champagne! Bring two bottles, or no, better make it three! And could you have them serve the bread with the marmalade right away? Thank you!"

Lilo stopped what she was doing immediately. "Champagne? What for? I thought Isabelle was bringing some with her?" she asked with a frown.

"Isabelle?" Clara, confused, shook her head. "What made you think of her? I need the champagne for an important guest!"

"I see . . . and can you tell me which important guest is in my hotel?"

But Clara shook her head again. "No names, I'm sorry. All anonymous."

It was almost eight o'clock when Margherita of Savoy-Genoa and her retinue left, each of the ladies-in-waiting carrying a well-stuffed bag. They had all but emptied Clara's shelves. The former queen, however, had chosen only a single hand cream for herself.

"I do not know from which mouth certain indiscretions escaped, but I do know that *you* know who I am," she said to Clara before leaving, while Stefano translated.

Clara felt herself blushing. She searched feverishly for something to say, but the king's mother held up her hand: no need to say anything.

"And I must say that I am extremely grateful for *your* discretion, and that you have treated me like any other guest. You know, at my age, beauty is no longer very important to me. But I had a lot of fun with the oranges and cloves, and I have every intention of showing it to my grandchildren." She sighed deeply. "In another life, I would have loved very much to work with my hands. As you do, my dear Mrs. Berg."

Clara laughed, abashed. "You are welcome to come back anytime," she said. Spontaneously, she reached up to the shelf behind her and took down a small lace bag of dried lavender. "For you."

Charmed, the older woman took the scented bag. "This also has such a lovely scent. Would you show me how to make these, too?"

Clara smiled and nodded eagerly. "And if you like, you can come to my laboratory when I make my soaps. That might be interesting to you," she offered. She lowered her eyes and glanced at Stefano. No doubt he would accuse her later of giving away her knowledge for free. But she should make a king's mother happy, shouldn't she?

"Lei è una donna molto amabile." Margherita of Savoy-Genoa embraced Clara spontaneously, and at the same moment there was a loud rattle on the glass door. Clara looked over the woman's shoulder to the door. Then, with a squeal of joy, she freed herself from their embrace.

"Isabelle!"

"The specialist thinks that we can use some special exercises to increase Margie's concentration. He gave me a list with all kinds of coordination games and puzzles." Isabelle grimaced. "I can only hope *I'm* coordinated enough to do them."

The church bells rang ten o'clock. After her long day, Clara should have been exhausted, but Isabelle's surprise visit had banished all trace of weariness.

After a late dinner with Stefano and Lilo, Isabelle and Clara were now sitting together on the bed in Clara's room. *Just like when we were girls,* thought Clara. Isabelle's daughter Marguerite, whom everybody called Margie, was asleep in the next room, and every fifteen minutes Isabelle jumped up to check on her.

"Of course you are. You do everything for your daughter." Clara smiled. Margie had red-blond hair, pale, freckled skin, and a small rosebud mouth that looked as if it were always on the lookout for someone to kiss. At first glance, she looked like any other child, but when you looked closer, you could see that she was special. Not long after her birth, the doctors had diagnosed her with Down syndrome.

"My own Christ child. Just like you, born on Christmas Eve. Can you believe she'll be ten this year?" Isabelle smiled blissfully. "I would do anything for her. I would cut out my own heart for her if I thought it would help. Margie is such a good child, and happy, too. You never hear a bad word from her, unlike from my devilish boys." She rolled her eyes theatrically.

"Boys are just boys," Clara said. The tricks that Isabelle's twin sons, Norbert and Jean, got up to now filled half her letters. "Oh, Isabelle, I'm so happy to have you here," she said, and squeezed her friend's hand.

"It's just a pity I couldn't come any earlier in the day. I heard from Lilo that you were celebrating your big opening today, and I wanted to surprise you. But then the appointment with the doctor ran much later than expected. And . . ." She shrugged.

"Some things are just more important than others," Clara said softly.

Isabelle nodded, then said resolutely, "Enough about me. Was that really the mother of the king of Italy earlier? And what about Stefano and you? And is there any news about your children? I want to know everything, my dear, so you'd better get started!"

They talked through half the night, jumping from one topic to the next as only the closest of friends can do: Isabelle's children, Clara's children, Josephine, the work in the vineyards and winery and in Clara's shops in Meersburg, Lilo and her hotel, Clara's wish to move into the apartment above the shop in Unterstadtstrasse as soon as she could . . . and naturally, Clara wanted to know what Isabelle thought of Stefano.

She had rarely seen such an attractive man, Isabelle answered, then added that it still wouldn't hurt to take things slowly. If she had followed properly what Stefano had said, then he had originally planned only to stay in Meersburg briefly. But then he had decided to establish his own business in the town. And now that plan had been filed away, too? For Isabelle, that all sounded a little strange. Erratic. Vague. What did the man really have in mind? Did he have *anything* in mind? Or was he all talk and no action?

Clara swallowed hard. Such skepticism from Isabelle, of all people? From the friend who risked everything for love?

"Stefano is not erratic!" Clara said. "He never had any love for the hair trade. It was only for his family's sake that he had anything to do with it at all. Now he's sold all the wigs, sent the money to Italy, and told his family that they should rely on his brother or someone else. He wants to stay here at Lake Constance." *With me,* she added silently.

"Which is fine," said Isabelle. "But what's he going to do? How's he going to live? And what's he living on right now?"

"Am I supposed to interrogate him?" Clara said, knowing she sounded petulant. "If you think that Stefano is living out of my pocket, I can assure you he isn't. He spoils me rotten, and he doesn't seem to lack the money to do it. And for now, I'm enjoying his attention very much. He's a great help to me with many things. But that's as far as things have gone." She sighed. "Though I should say that he has tried to bring up certain subjects. But whenever I've gotten the feeling that he's steering the conversation to a point where he might propose, I've always changed the subject. I'm a chicken, I know! Being married again, sharing my life and my bed with a man—it's something I *do* want, but I'm also terribly frightened of taking that huge step. Marriage and me—it's come to grief once already."

"Sometimes it takes a second start," said Isabelle, and she smiled peaceably. "And speaking of spoiling, I can hardly wait to get my facial tomorrow morning. Thank you so much for fitting me in! Living out on the land like we do, I never get to enjoy anything like that."

Clara was glad Isabelle had changed the direction of the conversation. "Who knows? Maybe I'll open a beauty shop near you in Reims one day." She pulled her legs up closer beneath her. "You know, there's an idea that's been buzzing around in my head for a while. Most of my customers only come to Lake Constance in summer. In spring, they go to the horse races in Baden-Baden, in autumn they go off to a spa somewhere, and the opera premieres in Verona are on most of their calendars, too. They're like migratory birds. Perhaps I should migrate with them?"

Isabelle nodded thoughtfully. "It could make sense—and be very profitable—to have shops in towns that get a lot of visitors, especially when they are your devoted clients." She looked at Clara in admiration. "You continue to surprise me. I honestly never suspected that such a smart and spirited businesswoman was hiding inside you."

Clara laughed. "I'm just toying with the idea. But Countess Zuzanna, who was one of my first customers, asked me in her last letter whether I could visit her in Baden-Baden to give her facial treatments. She would pay for everything." There was pride in Clara's voice as she said it.

"Now that would be an exclusive house call! So? Are you going to do it?"

Clara shrugged. "If both my Bel Étages are running well and they can spare me, why not? I've never been to Baden-Baden. They say it's a lovely town." Maybe Stefano would go there with her. It could be a romantic trip for the two of them.

"Reims is also very lovely. If anywhere, you should think about opening a shop there," said Isabelle. "The women of Champagne are well off, and you could earn good money with us. But until then, you still have to send me my creams regularly. Promise?"

"Promise!" Clara said happily. "Tomorrow, you can take your time and see what you like. I've got a new cream that has the most wonderful lavender scent." She thought of something and suddenly frowned.

"If the new cream is so wonderful, why are you frowning?" Isabelle asked.

"It's something that has been on my mind a lot lately." Clara sighed. When she saw Isabelle's expectant expression, she continued. "When it comes to my fragrances, I have to admit that I've been growing dissatisfied. All my creams smell of rose, lavender, citrus, or violet. Don't misunderstand me—I only use the best ingredients. And just having a cream or a soap that smells good at all is new for a lot of my customers. Many of them only know the bitter smell of soft soap." Clara raised both arms in a helpless gesture. "But I want something more lavish! Fragrances that develop little by little on the skin of the woman wearing it. Like a good perfume."

"Then there's only one place to go. Grasse, in France," said Isabelle immediately. "The best parfumiers in the world are there." She sat forward excitedly. "I've got an idea. What would you say if we went together? I could translate for you, maybe find out a few good addresses in advance. And it would be wonderful to go on a trip together. And exciting! What do you think? Although the trip would have to wait until after the harvest."

Clara smiled. "Then we have that in common: you have to deal with the grape harvest and I have to get through the tourist season." She chewed her lip for a moment. "Grasse . . . ," she murmured, and she found that the name alone sounded promising. She wondered what Stefano would think of the idea, then she looked back to Isabelle and her face lit up. "Let's do it! But next year. This year, I really do have to make sure that my Bel Étage–Residenzia is a success."

"If the mother of Italian king has already graced you with a visit, I wouldn't worry," said Isabelle. "All right, then. Next year," she added with a laugh, and they shook hands on it. "Clara, I hardly recognize you

anymore, you know? You're so energetic, so fearless, so . . . modern!"
Isabelle said. "Maybe Stefano Santo has had a good influence on you
after all? Or was it just getting out of Berlin?"

Is it Stefano's influence that has made me so fearless and modern? Clara
wondered as she lay in bed trying to sleep after Isabelle had gone to
her room. His encouragement, advice, and help were good for her.
And they certainly had a modern relationship. Most of the people
around them would probably describe their relationship as ambiguous
or socially unacceptable. But she didn't care. The tentative, fearful Clara
who was always worried about what other people thought of her was
long gone. Starting with the move to Lake Constance, she had begun
to strip off her old fear. She had freed herself like a butterfly emerg-
ing from its cocoon. What she had been through in Berlin—Gerhard's
abuse, the abyss after her divorce, and the loss of her children—was the
worst that could happen to her. What did she have to fear now? Things
could only get better.

Chapter Twenty-Seven

Thirty pots of chamomile extract hand cream were finished, along with three dozen bottles of scented body oil. Now she had to prepare the next batch of face cream. And she must not forget the cleansing rosewater. Clara looked up at the calendar hanging on the wall. It was December 18, 1908. The calendar had served her well all year, reminding her of appointments, deliveries, and pay-by dates. Now it hung gray and limp from all the steam it had been subjected to. Gray and limp—Clara felt just the same. So few days until the end of the year, so much work still to do . . .

She stifled a yawn, then she gathered the ingredients she would need for the face cream. As tired as she was, she was happy for the work. The busier she was, the less she had to think about her children.

Christmas. She used to love this time of year. She had glued golden stars to the windows of her home in Berlin, baked Christmas cake, and knitted socks for everybody. But the days of Advent had become the hardest and loneliest for her. She had written letters to her children. She had bought small gifts and sent everything in one package to Josephine, though she was not sure that her friend would manage to get it all to Sophie and Matthias or if the new Mrs. Gropius would even allow the contact. Day after day, Clara waited for news from Josephine, but so far she hadn't received any. It would be Christmas Eve in a week . . . Maybe Josephine was planning to give them the gifts and letters then? Christmas Eve. And her birthday, too. Clara had always thought the holiday itself brought her such gifts. In the glow of the thousand candles on the Christmas tree, Sophie had always looked like a little blond angel. And Matthias singing "Silent Night." Would his voice have broken already? Would he sing "Silent Night" or just croak the words?

Clara wiped away a tear. Someday, she was sure of it, she would be reunited with her children. But until then, she had to stay strong. Work would always be a useful distraction, and—

Laughter came from the front room, jolting Clara from her thoughts. A moment later, Therese and Stefano walked into the laboratory. Therese was wearing an elegant black outfit with a pretty brooch shaped like a Christmas tree and set with dozens of green stones. "You haven't even dressed for the Christmas party!" Therese cried. "We are supposed to go to the yacht club."

Clara put on an apologetic face. "I didn't think the work would take this long."

"The host has prepared a wonderful buffet. Are you really going to miss it?"

Stefano added, "There's supposed to be an excellent band playing. In all the time we've known each other, we haven't shared a single dance. *Mia cara*, are you really going to make me dance with other women?" Stefano looked disappointed. "You can't do that to me. Besides, without you, the evening will only be half as good."

For a moment, Clara was tempted to yank off her apron and go with them. But her good sense won out. "Go ahead, I'll come a little later," she said, and gave her two friends a reassuring smile.

"Uh-huh," said Therese, entirely unconvinced. "I know you, and once you get your nose into your creations . . . You can take one night off. Isn't it about time you just had some fun?"

"Why should I? You've been having enough fun for both of us for weeks," Clara answered. It was supposed to sound funny, but Clara could hear the edge of reproach in her voice. Lately, Therese had only been showing up for an hour or two in the middle of the day. She spent the mornings sleeping and recovering from her partying the night before, and she needed the afternoons to get herself ready for the next party, dinner, or visit to the theater. "New man, new happiness," she would say with a laugh whenever Clara asked what she was doing. "My own great love is just around the corner. And then I'll put away my scissors once and for all. Doing other women's hair has never been much fun."

Clara could not subscribe to *that* attitude at all.

Stefano turned to Therese. "Go ahead. I'll help Clara, and we'll come a little later."

The moment they were alone, he went to Clara and kissed her affectionately on the nose. At the tender gesture, a lump formed in Clara's throat; in recent days, she'd been more sentimental than usual.

"Stefano . . . I don't want you to help me right now," she said, her voice thick with emotion. "You do so much for me. Don't give up the Christmas party on my account, too." In truth, she wanted to have him close to her, and she wished that he would stay. But she did her best to push this feeling aside. In recent months, she had kept Stefano at arm's length as best she could, not wanting to commit herself; she could hardly demand such sacrifices of him now.

He took her in his arms and whispered in her ear, "Bella Clara, I worry about you. Therese is right; you work too much. Can't we forget the creams for today?" He nodded in the direction of her work area. "They will still be there tomorrow."

"I would love to," Clara said, taking pleasure in the warmth he radiated. "But tomorrow night I have to make a new batch of soap. And the day after that there will be something else. I would never have predicted that business would be *so* good this Christmas. But if I don't produce anything tonight, I won't have anything to sell tomorrow. It's as simple as that."

Stefano nodded. "Even so, things can't go on like this. All this work is wearing you down. I'll come up with some way to help!"

Clara smiled. "Why not call up a conjurer to secretly fill my shelves while I sleep like a baby? Or maybe Santa Claus can do that kind of thing?"

Stefano laughed at that, but was quickly serious again. "Speaking of Christmas . . . for me, this will be my first Christmas without my family. I would like very much to spend Christmas Eve with you. We could go to church together, then drink a glass of champagne under the stars. Wouldn't that be a nice way to spend your birthday? But where would we celebrate? You live in the hotel, me in my guesthouse—neither of us has a homeland, or a home."

"Well, I don't think of myself as not having a homeland," Clara replied with a laugh. Stefano was so dramatic sometimes. "On the contrary, actually. I feel quite at home in Lilo's hotel. Right now, this is the best solution for me. And when the apartment above the shop is free next year, I'll have a real home of my own." She held her breath, as tense as ever when their talk turned to future plans. Did they have a future together? If yes, it was still somewhere off among the stars.

Stefano ran one hand through his hair, and his handsome face was transformed by a grimace. As if he could read her thoughts, he said, "Clara, so much between us is unresolved. I wish I could offer you more. A beautiful home, a ring on your finger, a future. But until I know where things are going for me professionally . . ." He shook his head. "I understand very well that you don't want to accept my courtship. I'm a nobody, after all."

Clara sighed. It was not the first time they had had this conversation. She reassured him, as she always did, that he was one of the most important people in her life, and that he was important to the customers, too. "And you do all the work for me without accepting a cent for any of it. I'd feel much better if you would at least let me pay you." It was not the first time she had said that, either.

Stefano shook his head. "I'm would never let you pay me! The things I do for you, I do for love, Clara. And love is not something you pay for." He looked past her defiantly.

Clara sighed helplessly. Somehow, every conversation they had ended on this. *But I love you, too,* she was on the verge of saying, but something held her back. She wasn't ready. "Why don't we celebrate with Lilo, in the hotel?" she said, to change the subject. "She's planning a big party for her guests. I'm sure she'll hold a table for us."

"That's a good idea," he said, and his radiant smile returned. His lips drew close to hers, and his kiss was so heartfelt that it made Clara a little dizzy. Maybe she *should* have him stay?

But he was picking up his coat. "If you insist, I'll go ahead to the yacht club, all right? You come along whenever you want. But don't work too late, *mia cara.*" He turned around once more from the doorway. "By the way, don't be surprised if the next delivery of almond oil comes from a new supplier."

"What do you mean?"

Stefano waved one hand disdainfully. "If you ask me, it's time you tried out some other supplier and forgot your pharmacist, Mr. Weingarten. Someone cheaper, who can deliver faster."

"But you can't just . . ." Clara swallowed. "It was Mr. Weingarten who gave me my first job here! If you ask *me,* that counts for more than the fact that it sometimes takes a day or two longer for him to get what I need. You really should have asked me before making a decision like that."

"Clara, Mr. Weingarten will always be your friend. And he'll still be the one supplying you with beeswax and other products. This is just to try out, *va bene?* Sometimes it's just good to try something new. You know that better than anyone," said Stefano. "If you don't like the quality of the oil my new supplier delivers, you can always go back to Mr. Weingarten for it."

As Christmas approached, the work only increased, and with every passing day, there was more for Clara and her assistants to do. To meet the demand for beauty treatments, they had even stopped taking a lunch break. Face massages, foot baths, warm baths for relaxation—the women of Meersburg, suffering from all the travails that Christmas brought with it, could not get enough of the relief that Clara offered. For the first time since Clara had opened her shop, the men of Meersburg started coming in. The mayor bought face creams, soap, and rosewater, four of each, for his wife and three daughters. Mr. Weingarten came in to buy a nice soap for his Sabine. "When I see everything the Meersburg men are buying, there probably isn't a Christmas tree in Meersburg that doesn't have one of your soaps or creams beneath it," Stefano said, and laughed.

***

It was Christmas Eve, and Clara was massaging the face of her last customer of the day. She was doing the treatment at Bel Étage–Residenzia so that she could get to her room faster and get ready for the evening.

"Ow! You pulled my ear!"

"Sorry," said Clara. She hadn't even touched the woman's ear. *Why did I even agree to this?* she asked herself in annoyance. It was two in the afternoon, and a nap would do her a world of good. Or a stroll by the lake. Or attending the mayor's Christmas reception with Stefano. But the woman was one of her regular customers, so Clara didn't want to say no even though she didn't like the woman much: she was one of those people always looking for the hair in the soup—and finding it.

"Just make sure that none of that cream gets in my hair. I've just had it done," the woman said. "I want to look my very best this evening."

"Oh, you will," said Clara patiently. She looked longingly toward the door. The mayor's champagne reception for the town's most esteemed citizens was just down the hallway, in the hotel's ballroom. Clara had been proud to receive an invitation, but she had given the invitation to Stefano so that at least he could take part. She felt like nothing more than sitting and drinking a glass of wine with him, leaning against his shoulder, feeling his warmth . . .

"My children will be playing their recorders. We've been rehearsing three songs: 'Silent Night,' 'O Christmas Tree,' and 'From Heaven on High the Angels Sing.' Do you know them?"

Clara nodded. Of course she knew them. Just three years earlier, she'd practiced exactly the same melodies with Matthias. Although he had never much enjoyed playing the recorder, the prospect of nice Christmas presents had encouraged him to practice.

"You're not saying anything," the customer mumbled while Clara applied more cream. "Of course, as a young widow, you can't know how lovely Christmastime with children can be. When the little ones sing so beautifully, and when their eyes light up with so much joy . . ."

With every sentence the woman babbled, Clara felt her own hands growing colder. Every word felt like the stab of a knife. *Shut up!* she shouted silently at the woman. *Don't torture me so.* Dizziness overcame her, and she heard the woman's voice as if it were coming through a heavy wall of fog. A moment later—

***

Stefano was just walking down the hallway when he heard a loud scream. A robbery? An accident? He broke into a run.

Clara was lying on the floor. Beside her, wringing her hands, stood a woman with a thick layer of cream covering her face. "Oh, I'm so glad you're here! She just keeled over. And here I am with all this cream on my face. What am I supposed to do now?"

Stefano pushed the woman aside. "Leave, please! You can see that Mrs. Berg is not well." As he spoke, he dropped into a crouch. "Clara. Darling . . . Wake up, *mia cara.*" He shook her gently, then anxiously laid his right ear to her breast. Her heart was beating strongly. With a relieved sigh, he took a washcloth from a small table beside the treatment chair, dunked it into the basin of cold water, and held it to Clara's forehead and cheeks. She groaned, but did not wake fully. Had she fainted? Was it something else . . . her heart?

Should he call for a doctor? Or was it enough to carry Clara into her room where she could get the rest she so obviously needed? Stefano decided on the latter.

He loosened her dress where it was tied together at the back, then raised her legs on a pillow and fanned her face. After a little while, which seemed to him endless, she finally opened her eyes.

"What . . . Where . . . ?" Confused, Clara tried to sit up, but Stefano gently held her back.

"Clara, darling, it's me. Everything is good," he whispered in her ear, rocking her in his arms. "You fainted while you were working. It's lucky I got there when I did. The woman you were treating was very upset, so I sent her home. Then I brought you here."

Night had already settled over the lake. It was dark inside the room, too, the only light the golden glow of two candles. "You're safe. Everything is all right."

"Nothing is all right," Clara whimpered, exhausted. "I miss my children so much that my heart feels as if it's infected. I can't keep on like this. Oh, Stefano, everything is so terrible." She broke into tears. "I hate Christmas!"

"Clara, my heart, your children are well. And one day, a Christmas will come when you will be   with them again. In the meantime, I am here for you, *mia cara* . . ." As he rocked her in his arms, he showered feather-light kisses on her hair, her cheeks, her forehead. The children, the children! Always the same old song.

"If I didn't have you," she whispered, and she buried her face deeper his chest. "You smell so good. I don't know any man who smells as good as you." She pressed her breasts against him. "Kiss me!"

What's gotten into her now? Stefano wondered, and he felt himself becoming aroused. His arms closed around her tightly, and his lips trembled with desire, with lust. "Finally, *mia cara*," he said with a moan, and his mouth stretched into a smile. Finally.

***

They spent half the night making love, and it was the first time Clara had ever experienced such bliss. She had never felt as beautiful and feminine as she did in Stefano's arms. She sobbed, moaned, and laughed, all at the same time. So this was what love felt like!

At some point, Stefano got out of bed and began to get dressed. "Surely the Christmas party was over long ago," Clara said.

"As if I care about the Christmas party!" Stefano looked at her tenderly. "I'm just going to get us something to eat. I don't want you to faint again. They say you can live from love and air, but to be honest, my stomach is growling." With his hand on the doorknob, he blew Clara a kiss. When he opened the door, music and laughter found their way into the room.

"Ah, Lilo's party is still going. We've got a better chance of finding something to eat." Stefano's eyes shone with anticipation as he closed the door behind him.

He's so thoughtful! Clara thought as he left. Although it was cold in the room, she felt as if her entire body was on fire! She would never have believed that making love could be something so beautiful. With Gerhard, the act of love was usually over within a very few minutes, and it did not deserve its name, for there was no love in it. It was cold, coarse, and unfeeling. Stefano was tender and passionate, challenging and generous, all at the same time. Stefano Santo was a gift. He had drifted into her life suddenly, unhoped for, and on the very day that Josephine's letter reached her with the news of Gerhard's marriage. At their very first meeting, he had made her laugh, had made her think of other things . . . She remembered that clearly.

No man had ever done as much for her. And he had done all of it without ever asking for anything in return. And today, Christmas Eve, he had been there for her again. Stefano Santo. Her lifeline. What would she do without him? The very thought made her so anxious that she quickly buried it again.

A short time later, Stefano returned with a tray loaded with food.

"Canapés with smoked salmon, deviled eggs, ham in aspic—I even managed to grab a bottle of champagne." He set the tray down on Clara's bed.

"Stefano, I—" She wanted to tell him she loved him.

"Don't speak, *mia cara*," he said. "There is a time for everything. Now you have to eat. You have to get your strength back." Clara did as he said, and she washed down the salmon and ham with champagne. She had not realized that she was famished to the very core. Starved for love and life, for trust and togetherness. With every bite she ate, not only did her hunger fade, but also all the doubts she had been carrying about Stefano and herself.

The plates were empty, the bottle of champagne drained when she said, "Stefano, stay with me. Forever. Let's get married!"

He let out a confused laugh. "But, Clara . . . you . . . you're proposing to me? Isn't that what a man should be doing?"

Clara shrugged casually. "You're always telling me what a modern woman I am. I'm quite happy to do the proposing." Despite her courageous words, there was nothing she could do to hold down the nervous tremor rising inside her. What if he said no?

"You know I love you . . . ," he began slowly and let out a long sigh.

His unspoken "but" sounded loudly in Clara's ear. "I know you wanted to get a business up and running first," she said quickly. "But you don't have to prove anything to me. I've known for a long time that you are a good businessman, that we make a good team. And that won't change in the future, not in our private lives and not in business. If I open a third shop in Baden-Baden, there will be more work to do than ever."

"I will ease your burden wherever I can. You can rely on me. But there's something else," he said carefully. "Another reason I haven't proposed to you before now, although everything in me wanted to."

Clara frowned. Her heart beat anxiously. Was he about to make his big confession? Was there a wife waiting for him back in Elva?

"Somewhere, at some point in my travels, I must have lost my papers. Perhaps they were stolen; I don't know." He shrugged. "Whatever the cause, my passport is gone. And who knows what other documents I would need here to get married?"

"That's it?!" Clara laughed, and she was so relieved that her laugh came out a little shrill. "Papers can be replaced, can't they? Maybe you'll have to contact your parents back in Italy? Or you could go to the municipal office here, of course. I'm sure they could help."

"The last thing I wanted was to have you lose sleep about this. *Mia cara*, I will take care of everything, I promise you," he whispered, taking her in his arms again. "I love you . . ."

Chapter Twenty-Eight

"BRITISH KING EDWARD VII MAKES OFFICIAL VISIT TO KAISER WILHELM II IN BERLIN," announced all the newspapers in February 1909.

Dozens of articles were devoted to the details of the British monarch's schedule.

But as frantic as Berlin became in anticipation of their royal visitor, far less attention was paid in the rest of the German Empire to the British king's impending arrival. And in Meersburg, other matters were far more important . . .

Stefano looked at his reflection in the mirror in his room at the guesthouse. His black suit fit perfectly, and the dark-brown leather shoes he had had made by Meersburg's shoemaker were exceedingly elegant and very comfortable.

It was just before ten in the morning. The civil ceremony was set for eleven at the town hall, and before that Stefano had to pick up his bride and her friends, who had traveled to Meersburg with their husbands and were staying in Lilo's hotel. An automobile salesman and a winemaker—*probably arrogant snobs, both of them,* he thought. But who cared? He had learned how to deal with arrogant snobs. Perhaps he was one himself? No, he didn't look like a snob. He looked like a starry-eyed bridegroom.

Stefano laughed. For weeks—no, months—he had been trying to figure out how he could propose to Clara. He had never dreamed that *she* would ask *him*. In the end, it had been so easy.

Time was getting on, but Stefano remained in front of the mirror a moment longer. The fog-dulled daylight that filtered through the lace curtains did not exactly illuminate the room. But what he saw pleased him. Despite the sun-hungry winter, he still had the remnants of a tan, and his skin was smooth and unblemished. Since he'd started going to the Meersburg barber, his once straw-like mop had transformed into a glossy mane. Today he looked even better than he ever had. Stefano grinned.

The beard he had been growing since the beginning of the year made him look older than his twenty-nine years. Why hadn't he had an earlier birth date entered into his new and expensively obtained passport? It made no difference. His dignified appearance perfectly matched his thirty-five-year-old bride. No one today would see the few years between them. And tomorrow or in the days that followed, he would be getting new papers anyway. Stefano Santo would transform into Stefan Berg.

Both changes—the Germanizing of his first name and his adoption of Clara's surname—had been his idea.

"In business, things are easier if you have a German name," he explained to Clara. "If you were suddenly Clara Santo, it would only confuse your customers. They know Clara Berg as the woman who runs the Bel Étage, and that's the way it should stay. I've already made some inquiries at the registry office, and they will give us a special license." The "special license" had also cost him an exorbitant fee. The last of the money he had made from selling the hair had gone into the envelope that was to discreetly change hands before the ceremony. It didn't matter. From that day onward, he would be a well-heeled man. And from that day onward, he would be the one in charge, so he would only get richer.

Clara, apparently still feeling very modern and daring after proposing to him, had agreed to both suggestions regarding his name and had complimented him on the ideas. "Not that I don't like your name. I actually think it's much nicer than clunky old Berg. But from a business perspective, I would have trouble giving it up." She had been just as enthusiastic about his plans for their wedding reception to take place in the Hotel Residenz. Poached salmon, foie gras, black truffles—nothing but the best for them and their guests! he had told Lilo, who had been only too happy to oblige.

Stefano straightened his tailcoat and smoothed his hair one last time. He smiled. Clara would probably get a fright when she saw what it all cost . . .

Before going to the hotel, he stopped by the florist to pick up the bouquet of white lilies he had ordered. Fabienne Alber had recommended moss roses or delicate carnations, but he had insisted on the lilies.

"But lilies are funeral flowers!" Fabienne had said. "Why would you choose them for Clara's bouquet?"

"Because I can!"

Stefano was no longer sure if he had just thought the words or spoken them aloud.

***

Josephine sat through the wedding ceremony in the wood-paneled chamber at the town hall with an almost motherly pride. Stefan and Clara were seated side by side. Isabelle was next to Clara, and Josephine sat between Isabelle and Adrian. The women both served as witnesses for their dear friend. Josephine had never seen Clara so elegant, so beautiful, or so happy. She had always looked after her appearance, even after her divorce, when she had lived with Josephine in their house in the city and had been at the lowest point in her life. Josephine had often admired her for that, especially since she thought she herself always looked a little disheveled, despite expensive visits to the hairdresser and elegant clothes. "Like the devil you are!" said her husband, Adrian, stroking her unruly hair, which only made it more unruly.

"A pretty couple, don't you think?" she whispered to him then. Adrian nodded, but said nothing.

Isabelle whispered to Josephine, "What a pity Gerhard can't see this! Surely he thinks Clara is lost without him. It would drive him around the bend to see the successful and self-confident woman she's become." The two friends giggled with malicious glee. Their husbands gave them a reprimanding look, and the two women smiled apologetically and turned their attention to the front of the room.

Gerhard was such a disgusting specimen, Josephine thought. There was not a person on earth who revolted her more. She could not imagine what his new wife saw in him.

She and Marianne Gropius had become close acquaintances. At first, she had sought out Marianne's company so she could learn more about Sophie and Matthias to report to Clara. But something close to a real friendship had developed, a fact that she kept from Isabelle and Clara. The two would probably consider it high treason. But Marianne was well read, funny, and never at a loss for words. For Josephine, it was inexplicable that Gerhard had found a wife in a woman as modern as Marianne. She was not shy about expressing her opinions on politics, social ills, or cultural events. And to top it off, she loved sports! When the Olympic Games had taken place in London the previous year, she had practically breathed in every article about it. Marianne did not participate in any sport herself, but Josephine was impressed by her interest in the subject, and it made for some fascinating discussions between them. And how Gerhard had once railed against women riding bicycles!

He had even tried to forbid Clara from having anything to do with Isabelle and her—the cycling harpies! But at least in that, Clara had defied him. And now he had a wife who was a sports fan. *People were sometimes hard to understand!* Josephine dragged herself out of her thoughts as the registry official finished reviewing the bride's and groom's papers. Then he stood up and delivered a speech about fate and its often baffling but serendipitous turns.

Stefan took Clara's hand, placed it over his knee, and then covered her hand with his own, squeezing tightly. The gesture was meant to be loving, but Josephine found it strangely possessive. She hoped more than anything that Clara would truly find happiness now, but at the same time she had to acknowledge a vague sense of unease.

***

The fog lifted just as the champagne corks popped. The lake, which had been all but invisible for weeks, gleamed a kingfisher blue, and on the Swiss side the snow-covered peak of Säntis was in clear view. The sun bathed the elegant dining room in a warm yellow glow. *What a panorama and what a beautiful day,* thought Isabelle. When she thought about her own two weddings . . . Leon and she had gotten married on the way to visit his parents in the Rhineland-Palatinate region. The ceremony had taken place in a shabby registry office in Jena after they eloped. They had signed the necessary papers, marrying without a single witness present.

And she and Daniel Lambert had tied the knot in the small town hall in Hautvillers in June 1899. They had simply set aside the work in the vineyards for an afternoon, put on good clothes, and walked down to the village, pushing little Margie's carriage in front of them. Daniel's sister, Ghislaine, had cooked for the small wedding party, which included Isabelle's neighbors and a handful of friends. Of course, the champagne corks had popped for them, too, but her wedding had been far less grand, far less *imposing* than Clara and Stefan's reception.

Stefan. Isabelle screwed up her mouth. She found his change of name very strange indeed.

"What's the matter? You look like you ate a sour grape," Josephine said.

Isabelle forced a smile. "You know I wish Clara all the happiness in the world. And I can't say where this strange feeling in my stomach comes from, but . . ." She swept her arm wide, taking in the dining room and the bride and groom, surrounded by a throng of Meersburg citizens. "As lovely as all this is, it scares me a little. Not everything that glitters turns out to be gold. I can tell you that from grim experience."

"Oh, don't be such a sourpuss," said Josephine. "Be happy that Clara has so many new friends in her life. I think Fabienne from the flower shop is very nice, and Therese and Elisabeth, too. Besides, Clara has Lilo here. She can always go to her if she needs a sympathetic ear. With good friends like that, things work out, right?" But Isabelle heard the trace of concern in Josephine's voice, and noticed her friend's wrinkled forehead. Isabelle looked intently at Josephine. Did her friend simply not want to admit to a distrust of Stefano—Stefan—either?

"You're probably right. Good friends are there to help, wherever you are in life," she said. "Still, I'd be happier if we'd been able to talk Clara into arranging a marriage contract in advance. That would make her the sole owner of her company, regardless of what else happens in her life."

"What's going to happen? You don't seriously think that Clara will get divorced a second time?" Josephine replied. "Do you?"

Chapter Twenty-Nine

As it progressed, it was clear that 1909 would be no less strenuous than the year before. Both Bel Étage shops were completely booked every day from the start of the tourist season, and Clara could barely keep up with production of her products. And then there were the customers who would *only* have their treatments done by Clara. Even though these consultations cost Clara a lot of time, she enjoyed the contact very much. The women would tell her stories from their lives, things that made her heart ache. In the descriptions of everyday housewifery, so often with too few hours, too little appreciation, and even less love, she recognized her old life. "Sometimes, you just have to say enough! A business dinner can be very nice with only three courses, too," she advised one woman. "Hire someone to do the wash. You don't get paid to do that work," she told another. "Find the time to go for a walk. The fresh air will do your skin good, and it will do you good, too!"

Clara could see the spark of hope in the women's eyes when she made her suggestions, but she knew that few of them would put her advice to good use. In the upper class and among the nobility, it was normal to pay for one's freedom from drudgery by employing a maid, a cook, and a laundrywoman, and often other workers, too. But the mayor or the owner of Treiber's Emporium found it hard to accept that his wife might need some help. It was with these women that Clara put in special effort. In the time they spent having treatments at Bel Étage, at least, they should be able to relax.

"You should get paid for talking," Stefan teased her. "You'll soon be able to get more for that than the treatments." He believed that it was a waste of Clara's time to do so many treatments.

In contrast to how she treated her customers, Clara was anything but pampered. She still gave herself time for her morning swim in the lake, but that was the only luxury in her life. Gone were the days when she could read the newspaper over a relaxed breakfast and stay well informed about news, politics, and culture. Now all she had time for was a cup of coffee while she stood and scanned the headlines. If she heard anything at all about what was going on in the empire, then it came through Josephine, who wrote at length about happenings in Berlin and beyond. It was from Josephine that Clara also learned about cashless payments, which made it possible to pay an invoice with a bank transfer instead of cash. Clara was so taken with the idea that she wanted to open an account for her business, but Stefan—now officially responsible for all the finances as the general manager of the Bel Étage shops—was against it. He told Clara that he preferred plain old cash. Everything else, in his opinion, was too risky.

Clara was much better informed about the goings-on in Meersburg. Therese, Lilo, and her customers told her which personalities were currently staying in town, who was going to which parties with whom, and all the rest of the gossip. And then she heard even more first hand, when those same illustrious guests visited her shops. Countess Zuzanna of Poland was again spending the summer in Meersburg, and the vivacious woman was always happy to share stories. She invited Clara to her parties, too. But after a hard day in the shop, the work in the laboratory at night could not be ignored. So Clara sent Stefan instead, to mix and mingle with the upper-class guests. He usually returned from such dinners, dances, and parties when Clara was already sound asleep, a circumstance that did not please her at all.

"Would you help me prepare my creams and soaps now and then?" she asked him one day. "With two of us, we'd be finished much sooner and could even go for a nice walk in the evening." *Like we used to,* she added silently.

"You want me to stir the creams and go for a stroll afterward? *Mia cara,* how can you suggest that?" he replied in a horrified tone. "My presence at all these events is vitally important! I'm not going there for fun, you know. See and be seen, as they say. If both of us started turning down these influential hostesses, it would be very bad for the business. You don't seriously want that, do you?" He raised his chin, challenging her to answer.

Clara shook her head. Of course she didn't want that.

Some nights, standing in the laboratory, she heard music drifting softly through the streets of Meersburg. On nights like that, she felt truly lost.

In May, Heinrich Schmidt, Clara's landlord, moved out of the apartment above the shop in the Unterstadtstrasse to go and live with his daughter in Switzerland. Clara and Stefan, who had been sharing Clara's room in the hotel, were overjoyed. Finally, they would have a place to call home! When the old man offered to leave them his furniture, Clara was touched and delighted. What a generous offer! Especially because the furniture was solidly built from beautiful pearwood that would stand up to any children's games, though Clara knew she had nothing to worry about in that regard from either Matthias or Sophie. In her mind, she could already see them sitting on the sofa and drinking hot chocolate.

"If we get the chairs redone with dark-red velvet and some new curtains to match, it will look lovely," she said to Stefan.

Stefan screwed up his nose. "Can't you smell that? The sofa, the sideboard, the cupboards—everything reeks of age and rot. *Mia cara,* we don't want to spend our new life in an atmosphere as dead as this, do we? Countess Zuzanna had her drawing room redecorated by a furniture maker from Friedrichshafen who's really *en vogue.* That's what I want, too. This old junk can be used by the needy at the shelter."

"Refurnish the apartment? All of it? But that will cost a fortune!" Clara gasped. She didn't know what shocked her more: the cost or the idea of having to tell Mr. Schmidt where his furniture had gone.

"Money . . ." Stefan flicked one hand as if to shoo away the thought. "Don't go telling me that you're worried about *that.* The women are addicted to being beautiful. They buy whatever you offer them. Believe me, it's a spring that will never run dry. No, we're only going to get richer." He took Clara's hands in his and swung her around in a circle as if in a dance. "Can you hear it, bella Clara? It's the sound of our future." And he tilted his head as if he really were listening to beautiful music.

Clara laughed. The thought of living there with him in a few weeks made her dizzier than their dance.

"All right, then let's buy new furniture. As long as we have enough money for the business. You know I keep thinking about opening a shop in Baden-Baden."

"Ah, my dear, I have already set things in motion for Baden-Baden," said Stefan, in a tone one might use for a child who hasn't been paying attention. "On Countess Zuzanna's advice, I wrote to a gentleman at the regional bank in Baden-Baden two weeks ago. According to the countess, he has excellent contacts among the real estate people there. This morning, I had word from him that he wants to show us three possible locations there next week."

"But the season has just begun. How can we go off to Baden-Baden now? And then there's all the work in the apartment. Won't it all be too much?" she said, taken aback. "I thought we'd look closer at

Baden-Baden in autumn, when we can catch our breath a little. And now I find out that you've already made such concrete plans."

"*Mia cara*, now that I'm helping you run the business, the responsibility falls on two pairs of shoulders. Another shop will be child's play!"

"I don't know . . . ," Clara said with a pensive shrug. "Shouldn't we have talked it through together first?"

Stefan's expression darkened instantly. "Am I supposed to get your blessing for every little decision? Am I just your errand boy? If that's how it is, I might as well go!" He snatched his jacket so violently from Heinrich Schmidt's coatrack that one of the hooks fell off. Before Clara could say anything to calm him down, Stefan was gone.

***

Stefan's bad mood did not last long. Together with Countess Zuzanna's lover, Pawel, he went on a short boat trip. While they were out on the lake, Pawel talked in such glowing terms about Baden-Baden and its unofficial gaming rooms that Stefan could hardly wait to travel to the town on the banks of the Oos River. It would be best if he went there alone, he decided. Then he could spend as much time as he wanted playing cards. And Clara—who had oh-so-little time—could stay in Meersburg and do her consultations.

When he was back on dry land, Stefan went off in search of his wife, whom he finally found at the shop in the Hotel Residenz. Clara was sitting in one of the armchairs normally used by waiting customers. She was deep in conversation with a woman dressed in the latest fashion. On top of her close-cropped hair, she wore a tiny velvet hat with a wide veil and a single long feather. Stefan immediately recognized her as Beate Birgen, the Danish German film star. She was staying in the Hotel Residenz, and her presence was all the buzz in Meersburg. Although the town could not boast one of the new movie houses, Friedrichshafen had two. A week ago, Stefan had gone with a group of the men in town to see *Katzenjammer*, a twenty-minute film in which a woman, played by Beate Birgen, searches desperately for her lost Siamese cat and gets herself into all sorts of dramatic and uproarious situations along the way. None of the men had taken his eyes off the curvy and exceptionally exotic actress even for a moment. Throughout the film, Stefan could not stop asking himself how a woman as beautiful as Beate Birgen could voluntarily have all her hair cut off.

Excited at the prospect of meeting the woman herself, he wiped his sweaty hands on his pants. He was going to a party at the villa of Johann Martens that evening, and if he could tell everyone that such a famous figure had been in their shop, they would certainly prick up their ears! He cleared his throat, but neither Clara nor the film star noticed him.

"And the black paste I use to darken my eyelashes begins to run after just a short time. Look." The actress closed her eyes dramatically and fluttered her eyelids.

Clara nodded. "Of course that shouldn't happen. I'm certain that I could come up with a much better texture for this paste. It needs to be made with less oil, and perhaps with a little talcum." Stefan noticed that Clara was jotting down notes even as she spoke.

"Speaking of talcum, take a look at my face powder. It's an outrage!" Beate declared. "Some days, my skin itches so much, it feels like I've fallen into a patch of nettles." She produced a silvery metallic container from her purse, opened it, and let Clara sniff the contents.

Clara screwed up her nose. "Just the smell of it. I'm not surprised at all that it does your skin no favors. It's a shame, really, but as long as makeup like this is only used by a few actresses in the theaters and films, manufacturers aren't likely to develop something that's better for the skin."

Beate nodded. "A dash of rouge on the cheeks, darker lashes, and a little eyeliner will take the pallor off many a mouse. But most women look at makeup as something exotic, if not downright disreputable. Now that I think of it, why don't *you* develop a cosmetic line?"

Clara laughed softly. "Time. Time is the problem, you know? I could already be doing nothing but production day and night."

Still, neither had noticed Stefan standing in the doorway. He cleared his throat again, then put on his most charming smile and stepped inside. He had his hand out to greet their visitor when Clara finally realized he was there.

"Oh, Stefan," she said, her forehead momentarily creasing. "Excuse us, but we're in the middle of a discussion." She gave him a friendly nod in the direction of the door while Beate Birgen looked at him with open hostility, as if he were an interloper.

Stefan looked in confusion from Clara to the actress as if someone had slapped him across the face. Then, almost bursting with anger, he stalked off.

"What a wonderful woman! I can't remember the last time I had such a nice chat. I'd love to be better friends with her, but there's really no time to get to know each other. That's how it is with the vacationers—here today, gone tomorrow."

Stefan glared at her. Since entering the apartment, she'd been babbling away as if nothing were the matter. Not a word of apology at all!

"How dare you send me away like a schoolboy like that? And in front of Beate Birgen, no less!" he suddenly burst out, straightening his jacket. In a few minutes, he would be leaving for the party at the Martenses'. Mrs. Martens was also a customer at the Bel Étage and had handed Clara the invitation—on thick handmade paper—in person. But, as usual, he would be going alone.

He looked with distaste at the worn-out dress Clara was just pulling on. Over that, she tied an old apron. His wife looked like a Piedmontese farm girl!

"Oh, Stefan, it wasn't meant like that at all." Clara came over and kissed him, which he returned, but with reserve. "Some women simply want to talk to me privately about their beauty problems."

Stefan forced a smile. Why start a fight now? In a few minutes he'd be off to an evening of fun.

"In that case . . . ," he said. Maybe that young brown-haired noble-woman from Geneva would be there, the one he'd met the previous Sunday. Last time, he'd managed to withstand her charms . . .

Clara was still lost in the recollection of her conversation with the actress. She tilted her head to one side and said, "You know what surprises me?"

Stefan—already, in his mind, at the party—said nothing.

"So many women seem to avoid getting out into the fresh air! But it is so important, especially for an actress who spends so much time in stuffy rooms under artificial lights. Fresh air, a fresh breeze, sunlight—I told Mrs. Birgen that she absolutely has to take advantage of the outdoors as part of keeping herself beautiful. And I also told her that she should go swimming every day, like me."

"If you give this advice to your regular customers, too, pretty soon you won't be selling any more creams at all," said Stefan sarcastically. His resolution not to start a fight vanished like fresh snow in spring sunshine.

Clara only laughed softly. "Now don't be like that. I know you'd prefer it if beauty only came out of a jar. But if you ask me, true beauty takes much more, and that's exactly what I want to get across to these women. Or at least to try. And now, my darling, adieu!" And with her apron swinging like a flag, she went down to the laboratory.

Stefan watched her go. Was he imagining things, or had he lost some of his influence over Clara lately? He was the man of the house! And more than that, he was the manager of the Bel Étage. God knows, it would not be too much to expect that she would listen to him. Instead, she went off with her own ideas, again and again, as if she were still a single, independent woman. Should he have kept her more under the thumb from the start, as his father had with his mother, as long as Stefan could remember? Maria Totosano had never objected to anything her husband said. She was utterly dependent on his benevolence. The creases in Stefan's forehead deepened as he realized that he was taking his father—his father, of all people!—as a role model. It was all Clara's fault.

When, a short time later, as he walked through the May air, heavy with the scent of flowers, toward the vineyards where the Martenses' villa stood, Stefan came to a decision. He would teach Clara a lesson. Then she would quickly find out that it would be best to follow his advice.

***

Would five dresses be enough? And how many hats would she need? Clara stood in front of her wardrobe. Baden-Baden was a fashionable spot; she knew that much from her short visit to Countess Zuzanna the previous autumn.

She and Stefan would be there five days, and May weather was always changeable. Would it be cool and rainy or summer hot? Or both? Certainly, she would need a cardigan . . . A dark-blue cardigan went into her suitcase. And another light summer coat? She wanted to look as neat and fresh as she possibly could every day, and especially in the evenings! She would be meeting so many important people and would have to make so many decisions. Clara's heart beat faster at the mere thought.

First of all, she had to find the perfect Bel Étage location. Then she would have to track down reliable workers to set up the rooms just as she wanted them, and at a reasonable price. The new shop would, of course, have to be painted in lavender and light lime green. Shelves, treatment chairs, partitions, lamps, curtains . . . She hoped that the Baden-Badeners and her guests in Meersburg shared the same taste.

And it was just as important to find the right staff from the start. Young, good-looking, friendly women that she could trust to run her third shop properly. She would have to train them in her treatment methods, too, which would mean another trip to Baden-Baden. Best of all would be to entrust the new business to one of her experienced assistants from Meersburg. But which of them would volunteer to spend an entire summer in Baden-Baden?

I hope it all goes well, Clara fretted. There was a great deal at stake, a lot of money, especially. She pulled her hat boxes out of the wardrobe.

As nervous as she was, she was looking forward to the trip. It was certainly not easy to pry herself away from Meersburg once the season was underway, but now that Stefan had set everything in motion, it had to be done, one way or another. Making a lot of decisions together would ease the burden; that much was clear. And then there was the prospect of spending some romantic hours together—she was looking forward to that very much indeed. With a smile, she had just begun to pack her prettiest underwear into her traveling case when Stefan came into the room.

"Please don't tell me the car is already at the door. I need at least another hour to pack."

"I have to talk to you," he said curtly. "I'm going to Munich. Unfortunately, you will have to go to Baden-Baden alone."

Clara did not believe she had heard right. "But . . . why?" Munich? What business did he have in Munich? *Another woman!* The thought shot through her mind, although she didn't have the slightest grounds for it. But wasn't another woman always to blame? And women were certainly interested in Stefan; she witnessed that in her shop every day. "What are you doing in Munich?"

"Believe it or not, apart from your Bel Étage, there are other commercial enterprises in the world," he answered. "Mr. Martens has made me a very interesting offer."

For a moment, Clara felt relieved to know that her first suspicion was wrong. But then a new threat entered her mind. "I thought the Martenses left ages ago. Is he trying to steal you away?" She gave him a pained smile. Why was he telling her this so casually? And at the last minute?

"Keep in mind that his wife is a customer of yours, and it is never wrong to stay on the good side of such influential people," he said. "Besides, his latest enterprise sounds very interesting indeed."

"How can you leave me alone with so many decisions to make? And then there's everything that needs to be discussed with the carpenters and painters and . . . ," Clara said. Distraught, she sank back onto the bed.

Stefan shrugged. "You can put the trip off, of course, until I have the time to go with you."

Was it something in his voice? A small, almost imperceptible change in his eyes, as if they were no longer on the same level, as if he were looking down on her? *Don't be so sensitive. You're imagining things.* She tried to calm down. Cancel the trip—it was tempting. No more of this tightness in her belly, no more fear of the unknown. But would she really feel better? Or would she feel like a failure, forever a coward?

Abruptly, she stood up and smoothed her skirt. "That won't be necessary. I'll go to Baden-Baden by myself, and I'll handle the decisions that have to be made as best I can," she said with all the composure she could muster, listening to herself in disbelief.

Just as disbelieving was the look that Stefan gave her.

"Your room in the Villa Augusta is ready, of course. But perhaps madam would prefer to enjoy a glass of champagne on the terrace while the porter takes her baggage up to her room?" The concierge pointed out toward the inviting restaurant terrace.

Clara thought for a moment. Would she be comfortable sitting alone in an unknown town? She still had two hours until her appointment with the real estate agent, and she was planning to spend the time in her hotel room. But it was a lovely day . . .

"Please bring me a glass of champagne and a little something to eat, if you would," she said, easily overcoming her reluctance.

The concierge smiled at her. "You will enjoy the view over Lichtentaler Allee. The chestnut trees are still in bloom, and they are rather breathtaking. Henry Ford and his wife are doing the same, by the way." He nodded conspiratorially in the direction of an elegantly dressed couple drinking coffee at a white cast-iron table.

A bowl of strawberries, canapés with salmon and ham—the Brenners Hotel knew how to pamper its guests, Clara thought. The champagne cooled her throat. For a moment, she had to fight the urge to pinch herself. Was she really sitting a table away from one of the most famous men in America?

What a pity that Stefan isn't here to share this lovely view, she thought as the sunshine tickled her nose. If he'd been trying to show her that she was helpless and stuck without him, then he'd cut off his nose to spite his face. Clara laughed to herself. *Darling, I saw through you long ago,* she thought, and it was a pleasant thought. *And I have to disappoint you, I'm afraid, because I'm planning to be as successful in Baden-Baden as anywhere else!*

Astonishingly, the thought that Stefan might have engaged in a power struggle with her did not worry her very much. Maybe it was in every man's nature to want to establish his authority over women. In the past, she would have spent hours brooding over what she had done wrong and how she could placate Stefan. But those days were over. She'd spent enough years dancing to a man's tune. Either she and Stefan danced together or . . . or . . . No appropriate threat occurred to her.

Clara took one of the canapés and bit into it.

The day was too beautiful for such unnecessary thoughts.

Chapter Thirty

Meersburg, August 1909

Dear Josephine,

I am writing today with the blackest of consciences, because
I have not written to you in such a long time. And I must
say right now that I am therefore all the more thankful
for your regular letters and reports about my dear children.
Almost every evening, before I go to sleep, I take out your
letters from the drawer in my bedside table and read them
over and over. Sophie's pencil drawing is hanging on the
wall in my laboratory so that I can admire it every day. My
heart is so heavy when I think of my children! I miss them
so much that it hurts.

    Stefan believes it is best to wait a while longer before
I hire a lawyer to represent me against Gerhard. We've
only been married half a year, after all, and, as you've
also told me, it is important to demonstrate stability to the
judge who will make a decision about visitation rights.

One step at a time—I have to remind myself of that every time my impatience threatens to get the upper hand.

Clara looked up with a frown and out through the open window into the summer evening, then she started a new paragraph.

We have been living in the new apartment since June. Two of the rooms are still empty because I want to set them up for the children. The marriage suits me well, and Stefan and I feel very comfortable together in the apartment. If you could see our lovely furniture! Stefan chose it all himself, and he has a very good sense of style. Oh, Josephine, it is so nice not to wake up alone. Stefan is a late sleeper and not much use for anything in the morning, but I even enjoy watching him sleep. That has to be true love, doesn't it?

Apart from that, Stefan is a great help in the business. He works tirelessly to ensure we have excellent contacts among the high and mighty, and he's brought in so many new customers. He is—

Clara stopped. Should she tell Josephine that Stefan was out practically every evening at dinners or parties while she stayed in her laboratory working? Would Josephine understand such an unconventional division of their labors? She and Adrian were always putting their heads together, and so were Isabelle and Daniel. Maybe it was better not to mention it, she decided, and struck out the last two words.

Stefan does the accounts, too. And I am so happy not to have to think about all the numbers! Delivery notes, bills, contracts here, cancellations there—every day, there's more and more of it. And is that any surprise now that I have three shops to run? The new place in Baden-Baden was booked out for skin consultations and treatments for weeks within a few days of opening, can you believe it? The three women I hired and trained are turning out to be very skillful and capable. At least that's what my first assistant, Sophie, tells me. She volunteered to spend the rest of the summer in Baden-Baden to see that everything runs as it should. When I finished training the new assistants, I returned to Meersburg with the good feeling that I was leaving my new shop in the best of hands.

Content with what she'd written, Clara set her pen aside and drank some of the cool white wine Stefan had brought her before he had gone off to the summer festival.

How is the automobile business going? Here at the lake, we see more of them every week, and Stefan goes on and on about them. Speaking of automobiles, while I was in Baden-Baden, I met Henry Ford and his wife. They were staying in the same hotel, and we got into a conversation the very first evening. Of course, I had to show off a little by saying that I knew automobile importers, and we all had to laugh when Henry Ford told me that Adrian was his biggest importer in the entire empire! The world is very small sometimes. His wife promised that she would come to Bel Étage on her next visit to Baden-Baden. And I was able to meet with Countess Zuzanna there, as well. Her influence opened many doors for me in the town beside the Oos. She is such a good soul . . .

It had been a strange encounter, Clara recalled. An invitation to the countess's townhouse! She had wanted the chance to talk privately with the countess, but Pawel, the countess's young lover, circled around them. He whined about this and moaned about that, finding everything tedious and bleak—the town, the summer visitors, the parties, everything, simply everything! And he kept staring resentfully at Clara, as if she were disturbing his circling. Only when the countess pressed a few bills into his hand did he finally disappear.

Zuzanna had sighed as he left. "Isn't he a magnificent, wild young colt? You have to give him a lot of sugar to keep him tame," she had said with an apologetic shrug.

Clara had smiled but said nothing. She guessed that the young man was on his way to one of the private gaming rooms, of which there were many in Baden-Baden. Gamble away Zuzanna's money, well, he could certainly do that! The countess was such a warmhearted, generous woman. She deserved to find the great love of her life and not some freeloader who only had his eye on her money! Thinking these things, a strange sense of uneasiness had come over Clara, and she chose not to follow the feeling. Everyone was different. Everyone had their own ways of living life. End of story.

Not another word to Josephine about her meeting with Zuzanna, she decided, and turned to another topic.

> *When will you visit me again here at Lake Constance? The lake is becoming more and more popular as a vacation destination. The royal court of Württemberg moved into the castle in Friedrichshafen weeks ago, and there are nobles in from Italy and Baden and a lot of French visitors. I'm having terrible trouble trying to meet all the requests for appointments from the summer guests, but I will always find time for you and Isabelle!*

Clara smiled. Even though no plans had been made, the simple thought of a reunion with her friends was enough to lighten her mood.

As happy as my success makes me, I still haven't solved some of the problems. My biggest concern is that I simply cannot keep up with the production anymore! Sometimes I am up half the night making products in the laboratory, and the next day I still run out of a cream or a facial toner. You can imagine how my customers react to that . . . Stefan is pressuring me to stop giving treatments in the shop and dedicate myself completely to production. After all, I'm the only one who knows the recipes. It would give me more time, but I love the contact with my customers, and I simply can't bring myself to hide myself away in the lab. I'm sure you understand that, dearest Jo, don't you?

Clara yawned. She was so tired that she actually felt a little dizzy. She longed for her bed, but it wasn't even completely dark outside.

She ended the letter with best wishes to Berlin, then took a fresh sheet of notepaper. Would it be all right to simply copy Josephine's letter and send the copy off to Isabelle? As tired as she was, writing an entirely new letter was beyond her.

***

Berlin, September 1909

Dear Clara,
When so much time passes without hearing from a friend, it can mean that things are going either exceptionally well or quite poorly, so I was elated to read that you have become something like the "beauty queen" of Lake Constance! I've always known you were capable of a great deal, but I honestly did not count on your undertaking being such a runaway success.

A smile crept across Josephine's face. So all three of them had amounted to something.

As I write to you, I am in the office, waiting for a telephone to be installed. Admittedly, I don't know many people who already own a telephone, but Adrian says that is changing quickly and that they will soon be commonplace. Wouldn't that be something for you, too, dear Clara? A telephone? Or perhaps you already have one? Or maybe Lilo does at the hotel? Then we could actually talk to each other instead of just writing letters. And I could hear with my own ears all about what you are doing in your free time. Are you able to enjoy the lake, at least a little? Do you still go swimming with Lilo? Or is the business eating up all your time? Because that's what I read between the lines of your last missive.

Distracted by her thoughts, Josephine looked around the crowded office that had become her and Adrian's second home. And not just theirs—their ten-year-old daughter, Amelie, now preferred to come to the office than to go home, where only the maid and the cook would be waiting for her. She even had her own small desk set up in a quiet corner apart from the two large, solid oak desks that Josephine and Adrian used. And here Josephine was, casting a critical eye on Clara's workload, when she herself spent more time in the office than at home? Clara would know what was good for her.

Your children are doing splendidly. Matthias and Sophie came back just last week from their summer vacation by the Baltic Sea. Gerhard rented a house there. I heard about it from their stepmother when I happened to bump into her in the city.

Josephine swallowed. *Happened to bump into her in the city?* Why was she lying to Clara? Why didn't she simply tell her that Marianne Gropius and she had become friends? Or that they sometimes went out cycling together? Once, Matthias had even joined them, and he'd been in such high spirits that he rode so far ahead they lost sight of him. "How is it that Gerhard lets you go out riding?" she had asked Marianne. "He would never, ever have allowed his previous wife to do it. He used to be vehemently opposed to women riding bicycles."

Marianne only smirked. "I don't ask him for permission, that's all. I just do what I feel like doing. Gerhard knew from the start that I could think for myself."

Josephine, who could still clearly remember how Gerhard had tormented, humiliated, and demeaned Clara, could hardly believe how well his second wife was able to stand up to him. More than that, Marianne Gropius seemed happy with Gerhard. But she could not write that in a letter to Clara! Josephine was sure Clara would resent her friendship with her children's stepmother. The same applied to Marianne, to whom Josephine rarely mentioned her friendship with Clara. *Some things are probably better kept to oneself,* Josephine thought a little sadly.

***

Meersburg, September 1909

Dear Josephine,
It is a beautiful time of year here at the lake, with the September sun dousing everything in golden light. The smell of the ripening grapes wafts down from the hillsides and spreads a light sweetness all through the town.
Perhaps I really should consider getting a telephone. It would be very nice to be able to chat with you right now.

Instead, I find myself writing about a small incident that happened two weeks ago. You will like it, my dear, because it shows that there really is more to my life than work.

Stefan came to the shop and told me that he wanted to go on a little excursion with me. Just like that! He can be so spontaneous sometimes, my beautiful Italian! We drove up to the top of the lake—our first time together in an automobile!—to attend the private opening of an exhibition by a young painter. Don't ask me what kind of automobile it was. I was far too excited to take in details like that. Dearest Josephine, you can't imagine how much I enjoyed that drive. With the lake air whistling around my ears, the sun in my face, Stefan beside me, I could have driven to the end of the world. At the same time, I was acutely aware of how little time I had spent enjoying the lake this summer. And yes, I admit that all the work has meant that I haven't been swimming even once since returning from Baden-Baden. But in the weeks ahead I plan to change that, as long as the water is still warm enough.

Stefan met the painter, a young woman, not long ago at a reception in Meersburg. She creates wonderful paintings of flowers. I could have stood and gazed at them for hours, and I honestly believe I discovered my love of art that day. In the future, I want to go to more exhibitions. Then I bought five of the paintings, a treat for myself. They depict lush bouquets, all the flowers in full bloom. The paintings are now hanging in our living room and in the shop. Whenever I look at them, it seems to me that I can see the three of us in the pictures. You, Isabelle, and me. Because aren't we, too, in the bloom of our lives?

Clara suddenly thought how one of them was blooming more than the others. In her last letter to Clara, Isabelle had revealed, with the use of a great many exclamation points, that she was pregnant again: *My belly is so big that I'm starting to look like a wine barrel! What if it's twins again? Two more wild things like the two I've already got?! That would be the end of me!* Clara had immediately put together a package of rich skin cream and body oil and sent it off.

If you rub this into your skin around your belly regularly, you won't get the stretch marks like you did with the twins, she had written on the accompanying card. Would Isabelle take the time to look after her skin? Or would she use the time to trim a few more vines?

Clara put such distracting thoughts aside. In half an hour her next customer would walk through the door, and she wanted to have the letter to Josephine finished by then.

> *How times have changed, Josephine. Before, I couldn't so much as buy fresh flowers without asking Gerhard first. And today, I can go out and buy expensive flowers on canvas as if it were the most normal thing in the world—*

Clara jumped as the doorbell rang. Hadn't she locked it? But to her relief it was only Therese.

"What's the matter? You look like it's been raining for a week," said Clara with a frown.

"I got stood up! I sat and waited in the café at the market square for two hours. I've drunk so much coffee I feel sick," she said, obviously outraged. She threw her key onto the table, then pulled a chair over next to Clara.

Well, that's that with the letter, Clara thought, and she put the lid on her ink bottle. "Who stood you up? Thierry?" she asked, standing up to put fresh water on the stove. Therese might have had enough coffee, but *she* needed a pick-me-up. The previous night, she had crawled into bed at one thirty in the morning. Her first batch of rose cream curdled, so she had to throw it all away and start again.

"Thierry!" Therese sniffed dismissively. "I split with Thierry weeks ago. Don't tell me you didn't know that?"

Clara shrugged. "I thought—" She broke off. When it came to Therese's male friends, she hadn't thought much at all for a long time.

"Benno von Nordmannsleben!" Therese cried. "Oh, Clara, I don't think I've ever loved a man as much. All I have to do is look at him, and I get all warm and shivery." She leaned toward Clara confidingly. "Benno is in Queen Olga's dragoon regiment in Ludwigsburg, near Stuttgart, but he and three other officers are in Friedrichshafen now with the king."

Clara did her best to stifle a yawn while she brewed her coffee. An officer. Here today, back in Ludwigsburg tomorrow. Or worse, off to some war. *This can't end well,* she thought. *Poor Therese.*

"We had a date to meet at three. Benno was going to pick me up in his automobile, and we were going to drive to Friedrichshafen. He wanted to show me the castle there," said Therese, and she looked as if she would break into tears at any moment.

"Maybe the king had something important for Benno to do, and he simply couldn't get away."

"Do you think so?" Therese sighed, but then the next moment, she sounded again like her usual chirpy self. "You're probably right. Benno's such a wonderful man, you know. He . . ."

Clara sipped her coffee as she listened to Therese's seemingly never-ending tribute to the dashing officer.

"You're yawning!" Therese cried in horror. "Is what I'm saying so boring?"

"No!" Clara exclaimed, just as horrified. She had been trying to suppress her yawns.

Therese's expression grew serious. "You don't have to fake it for my sake, Clara. I can see how exhausted you are. But is it any wonder when you slog away from morning to night? Where's that husband of yours, by the way? Loafing around again at your expense, is he?"

"Therese, what are you talking about?" said Clara brusquely. "Stefan's social contacts mean so much for my business. And I'm glad I don't have to polish myself up for every party in town. Apart from that, he takes care of the bookkeeping and lots of other things."

"Other things. Uh-huh." Therese raised her eyebrows skeptically. "I'd love to hear about these other things."

Just then the doorbell rang. "My customer," Clara said with relief, and went to the front of the shop.

***

"I think I could get used to an automobile like that," said Stefan as casually as possible, but his heart was beating hard. What a beautiful machine! "Think about whether you might want to part with it after all. I'd be interested." With one hand, he caressed the highly polished bodywork of the Benz landaulet where it gleamed in the light of the setting sun.

"I've taken her up to thirty-five miles an hour, but the manufacturer claims she'll go seventy-five," said Martin Semmering, the owner, proudly.

Stefan nodded as if he heard such numbers every day. "And the horsepower? Forty?"

"Thirty-five. With a four-cylinder motor." Semmering, a good-looking man in his late forties, with dark hair and graying temples, opened the hood to give Stefan a look at the inner workings of the car.

"Impressive," Stefan murmured. But what interested him more than the technology was the question of how it would feel to drive alongside the lake in the beautiful machine.

As if he could read minds, Martin Semmering said, "Take my word for it, when you're driving along in this, everyone turns to look!"

"Then think about your price, and I'll think about whether it's the one for me or if I wouldn't rather buy a new automobile," Stefan replied.

"Can you even afford a machine like this?" Semmering asked directly.

They left the car behind and headed back into the Bar Coco, also Semmering's property. The bar, which offered a dozen kinds of champagne, was popular with the summer tourists. They closed in winter, however, and the Semmerings went down to a house they owned in the south of France. "Fog puts Viola in a bad mood," Semmering had once told Stefan, who had nodded but inwardly rolled his eyes. A bad mood because of fog?

"Do you think I'd be interested in it if I didn't have the money?" said Stefan with a trace of annoyance.

Semmering shrugged. "I mean to say . . . your darling wife would have to sell a lot of jars of cream."

The two men took their places at the round table where they had previously been part of a small group drinking champagne. The others had also heard Semmering's last remark, and they laughed.

"If she's really interested in actually selling anything at all," said Josef Meininger, a shoe manufacturer from Pirmasens sitting across the table from Stefan. "Your wife advised my Hilda to go for a swim in the lake once a day, and she said that that would make her skin stronger than any cream could. Hilda was very impressed when she told me about it. Now she goes down to the beach in front of our hotel and splashes about in the water every day." The man shook his head dourly, then leaned across the table toward Stefan. "If you want my opinion, my dear Stefan, your wife is not a particularly capable businesswoman. Though I doubt that any cream would do my Hilda much good. She'd have to bathe in pure gold!"

The two women at the table squealed in delight at that. One of them was Meininger's secret lover, but Stefan had no idea who the other was. They seemed to enjoy the fact that a man would talk about his wife with such disparagement.

"Then why not treat your little turtledove to her rejuvenating gold bath every day? If anyone here can afford it, then you can!" Semmering said.

"I'd rather treat myself to something younger," Meininger said, pinching his lover on her cheek.

Stefan joined in cheerfully with the general laughter, but he was boiling over on the inside. So Clara had been throwing around her "valuable" advice again. Walks in the fresh air. Enough sleep. Swimming in the lake. How many times had he asked her to keep that nonsense to herself? But when it came to her convictions, Clara was as stubborn as could be. He was waiting for the day when she started telling her customers to fill bottles with Lake Constance water and rub that into their skin instead of her expensive creams. But it wouldn't go that far. He could not simply forbid Clara to have contact with her customers, but he had a plan that would kill several birds with a single stone.

He looked around at the wealthy businessmen and smiled. *I'll show all of you,* he thought. *You—and Clara, too.*

"Champagne for everyone!" he called out, waving his wallet in the air.

Chapter Thirty-One

Clara was up early. The evening before, she had made a batch of lavender soap, and she wanted to get it ready for sale before she opened the shop. She looked lovingly at her sleeping husband and then went down to the laboratory, where she eased the soaps out of the molds and wrapped them in tissue paper. For some time, she had been pouring the viscous soap mixture into the flower-shape molds, instead of cutting the soap from a large block. She had had the molds made to order in a small factory that normally made forms for confectioners. "You can use my molds for cakes or soap or anything else you like," the factory owner, a gray-haired gentleman, had explained. "Would you like to draw the flower you have in mind, or do you already have a template?" he asked.

Clara, who had been prepared for a longer discussion, was surprised and happy to find the man to be so professional and willing to help her with her special request. A little shyly, she produced a page that she had torn out of a women's magazine. It showed pictures of various flowers. She had pointed at a dahlia and said, "I want it to look like this. What do you think? Would you be able get in all the petals?"

The man had laughed. "If I can work a rabbit's whiskers into an Easter mold, I think I can do a flower," he said, adding that the molds would be ready in four weeks.

The exchange had made Clara think back to her years in Berlin. She had always admired businessmen like Isabelle's father, Moritz Herrenhus, but when she had contact with such men, she could never get a word out and felt small and stupid. Now, though, she worked with men like that every day. Times changed, certainly.

Her flower soaps had become so successful Clara was considering having other molds made. A heart shape, perhaps? Or a four-leaf clover? Happy with herself and her world, she inhaled the scent of lavender.

She had just finished wrapping the first three dozen bars of soap when Stefan appeared.

"Surprised you, didn't I, *mia cara*? Well, I can get up early when it counts," he said with a laugh when he saw her astonished expression. "And today, it counts! I have a big surprise for you. Come, let's go." Even as he spoke, he stepped behind her and began to untie the knots on her apron.

"Stefan, what are you doing? As much as I love your surprises, I can't just leave. I have to get the soap stocked at both shops, and I must ship a package to Baden-Baden, too. My first customer arrives at nine. She's booked a pedicure and foot treatment, and I want to show her how she can massage her feet herself before going to bed so they don't swell up overnight."

"So you can sell one lotion less, right?" Stefan said with an undertone of mockery. "Don't worry, Evi Förster will take over with your customer. It's all taken care of."

"But Evi Förster has enough to do in the Residenzia—"

"No buts!" He took her hand, and it seemed to Clara he did so in the way he would that of a young and obstinate child. Clara was left with no choice but to follow. And she was, in fact, rather excited to find out what Stefan was planning.

It was a glorious day, no longer summer, but not yet autumn, either. The hectic tourist season was over, and Clara felt as if the world all around her had let out a long, deep sigh of relief. *If only I could do the same,* she thought, her mind still on the soap she had left behind half-finished.

"Where are we going?" she asked as they walked farther and farther out of town.

"Wait and see . . ."

The next moment, she saw from far off a heavyset woman coming toward them. Wasn't that Sabine Weingarten? Clara's eyes lit up. Did she have something to do with Stefan's surprise?

"Look at that blubbery creature," Stefan murmured. "We'll hear a loud bang any second and she'll explode."

"Stefan, that's mean," said Clara quietly. She waved to the pharmacist's wife and wanted to say hello and exchange a few words, but Stefan crossed the street and Clara could only give Sabine an apologetic look.

Arriving at the edge of Meersburg, Stefan stopped in front of a large, plain, and obviously empty building.

Clara frowned. She had never taken any notice of the building before, and she did not have the slightest idea of what they were doing there.

With exaggerated flamboyance, Stefan produced a key from the pocket of his pants and unlocked the massive door.

"May I welcome you to . . . our new cosmetics factory! Until a year ago, they made tin cans for preserving fish. Apparently, the owner sold his product all through the empire. But his process for sealing the cans—with lead, as it turned out—caused lead poisoning for those who ate the contents. His reputation was ruined, and he had to close." Stefan placed his hands on Clara's shoulders from behind and steered her into a large room. Inside, on long tables, all kinds of machines were still set up.

"Look around, Clara! He left everything behind. I'm sure we can use a lot of it, and if we can't, out it goes. We'll set up everything just like you want it."

Struck dumb, Clara looked from her high-spirited husband to the metal presses and punches and back again. She was seldom at a loss for words, but this was one of those moments. So she was supposed to make her beautifully scented, delicate creams in a former tin-can factory?

"Did I come up with the perfect surprise or not?" Stefan laughed. She didn't reply immediately, so he went on: "It might be enough at the beginning to mix your cream in a small pot like a housewife makes her soup, but the Bel Étage has taken on new dimensions, and you've been struggling to keep up with production for too long. Think about the future, Clara! We want to grow, don't we? So we take on some hard-working people to do the work for you, and you do the final quality check!" With unmistakable pride in his voice, he handed her the key. "*Prego!* The lease is already signed."

"You want me to hand over the production to strangers? To reveal my secret recipes? I've said I don't want to do that. And I'm supposed to pay the rent for this huge place, of which all I've seen is this single room? You signed me up for all this behind my back?" Clara's voice was decidedly shrill and louder than usual. "And it never occurred to you, even once, that you ought to discuss it with me?"

"All you want to do is discuss, discuss, discuss. But I want to roll up my sleeves and get to work!" Stefan said firmly, his Italian accent coming through strongly. "Why can't you just say you think my idea is good?"

Clara snorted. "You're acting like I am procrastination personified. Getting to work, as you put it, means more than signing a lease prematurely. I'm not sure at all if the recipes for my creams can even be scaled up to increase the production. The recipes for the tinctures and soaps shouldn't be a problem. But doing any of it means having a good chemist who knows how the different ingredients react with one another. And—"

Stefan raised his hand imperiously, stopping her short. "I've already found a chemist. Do you think I haven't thought this through? His name is Klaus Kohlwitz, and I met him through Martin Semmering. Kohlwitz's last position was in a factory that made boot polish and soft soap, and he was responsible for developing the various products. He told me he knows a great many manufacturers of glass containers, tubes, and other packaging materials. You will like the man, I'm sure. But more importantly, he will be a great help to you."

"A man who knows his way around soft soap and boot polish, aha. Do you really see that as a qualification for making the most delicate of face creams? And don't you dare tell me you've already hired him," Clara practically hissed, and she felt real anger rearing up inside her. How could Stefan overstep his authority like this?

"Of course not. Only you can make a decision as important as that," Stefan replied. "I simply asked him to come for an interview. Would it work for you to meet him this afternoon?" Clara realized that for the first time that morning Stefan sounded less than sure of himself.

She was silent for a long moment as her gaze swept across the production area. It looked well cared for, and she could detect no odor of fish at all. Heavy ceiling-high iron shelves lined the white-painted walls on all sides. One could certainly store a lot of products here, far more than in the cramped corners of her tiny laboratory. The ceiling lamps shone brightly, and they surely would provide enough light even on the darkest winter days. And the location, on the road that led to Friedrichshafen, was good . . .

Clara stalked past Stefan and out of the room without a word. Just as silently, she climbed the stairs to the second floor, where three doors opened from a square hallway. Clara opened the nearest door and found herself in a large room with two long windows, and spontaneously let out a little shriek of joy. "What a fantastic view!" she cried, and went over to look out the window.

Stefan, who had followed her, stood in the doorway.

Clara turned around to look at him and was met by his smile. "Don't you go grinning too soon, darling. I haven't said yes yet," she said as sternly as possible, as the most beautiful visions began to take shape in her mind. She could set up a laboratory there with absolutely every technical refinement she needed! With a decent Bunsen burner and gas bottle. Her desk would go under the window, and on the opposite wall she would have a huge bookshelf for her reference library.

"Think about it, *mia cara*," Stefan said quietly. "Once you've got the production off your hands, you can dedicate yourself to research. You could try new cosmetic products like rouge for the cheeks and eye shadow. It isn't only actresses like Beate Birgen painting their faces these days. I see it every time I go out in the evenings. More and more women are using makeup, although it must be said that the results are not always very successful. You could be the one to make all those women happy."

A dream come true. Clara pursed her lips, thinking. But what about the cost? She would need to take out a loan. She couldn't afford to set up this place from her own reserves. And could she really bring herself to entrust her recipes to a stranger?

Her own factory . . . that would certainly be a change from beauty shops. If she went to a lawyer as "Clara Berg, factory owner," he would have even better arguments in the battle for visiting rights for her children. Next spring! Next spring she would finally take up the battle with Gerhard anew.

The lake glittered bluer than it usually did and the sun shone a deep golden as Clara turned back to Stefan. With confidence she said, "You can tear up your lease. If I'm going to do this, then I'm going to buy this building, not rent it. If the owner is willing, if my bank comes to the party, and if the price is reasonable, this will become the Bel Étage Manufactory!"

The bank to which Clara applied for a loan was more than happy to oblige. It even provided the extra sum that Stefan needed to finance the purchase of his first automobile. "With a car, we can commute between Meersburg and Baden-Baden quickly, and I can use it to deliver the products from the manufactory," he explained to Clara.

Clara had no objections. Her first real estate investment was so monumental that buying an automobile paled by comparison.

And so, at the end of the 1909 season, Clara came to own her first piece of property, and Stefan his first car. And both were happy and content.

***

A period of new directions followed. Unlike most of the tourist businesses, which had to let people go in late autumn, Clara was interviewing for new staff. First in line was the chemist that Stefan had met through Martin Semmering.

Klaus Kohlwitz was in his midthirties. He had brown eyes and thin brown hair, but a mustache as black as if he'd painted it with the boot polish he made in his previous job. He wore checked pants and a flamboyant red sports jacket. His attire and his spectacular mustache reminded Clara of the caricatures of gigolos in the women's magazines. But the reference that he produced from his last employer praised him glowingly—the factory closing its doors in spring clearly had nothing to do with the chemist. He listened carefully, keeping focused on what Clara said. She could not tell what it was that finally convinced her to take him on as the manager of her new factory. Was it the deep seriousness with which he spoke of his old job? Or that he had gone to the trouble to find out in advance what kinds of products Clara manufactured and seemed to learn fast? Was it his friendly nature? Or the honesty she thought she saw in his eyes? She trusted her feeling that Klaus Kohlwitz was the right man. If in the end he absconded with her recipes, then she was out of luck. But she did not want to think about that.

Next, Clara went in search of women to work in the manufactory. She and Stefan agreed that it should only be women, although for different reasons. Stefan saw women as cheap labor to whom he only had to pay half of what a man would earn. But Clara wanted to give the women an opportunity to earn money of their own. It didn't matter to her if they were young or old, where they came from, or what they had done before. She wanted women who were willing to make something of their lives, here and now. Women who would be proud to work in Clara's "beauty plant," as one of the applicants called the manufactory. Everything else could be learned, and teaching them was the job of Klaus Kohlwitz and Justine Kaiser.

Justine Kaiser was forty years old, the widowed sister-in-law of Elisabeth Kaiser. "In the last twenty years, the woman has raised seven children and kept a grumpy husband happy. She's hardworking and unflappable. You won't find a better forewoman," Elisabeth had said when recommending her, as she once had praised her niece Sophie— Clara's very first assistant. As she was back then, Clara was happy to accept the advice of her experienced, loyal friend.

Stefan was not enthusiastic about Clara's choice. "You want to take on such an old woman? Reconsider it. She'll spend half the winter sick in bed. I doubt she's up to working a long day in a factory."

"May I remind you that I am only five years younger than she is? I don't see you worrying whether I'm up to working the long hours that I do," Clara snapped. Then she sighed; he probably didn't mean it like that.

***

Klaus assembled a list of equipment that he believed they would need for the larger-scale production of creams, tinctures, and soaps. Clara was relieved to see that it was less than she had expected. Scales, pots, test tubes, filters, beakers, and mortars and pestles. One of the more expensive items was a machine that filled containers with a cream. "It's cleaner and more effective than doing this step by hand," Klaus explained.

In addition, he insisted that every employee have two white sleeveless smocks. These would not leave the building and would be washed and ironed on the premises. It was the only way to ensure the necessary hygiene.

Klaus understood his profession, Clara realized, and he confirmed this every day.

In the weeks that followed, hardly a day went by without a vehicle pulling up at the manufactory to deliver equipment and supplies. Clara and Klaus conferred about the best location for each piece on the long work tables. Clara's heart leaped with joy so many times that she wondered whether it might be unhealthy in the long run.

"This manufacturer makes glass jars, tins, and tubes. And this one"— Klaus opened a catalog filled with illustrations—"supplies hand-cut decanters. You could use those for special tinctures. And this one"— Klaus pointed to another catalog—"produces porcelain and glass containers."

Fascinated, Clara leafed through the catalogs. Until now, she had always bought her containers through Frieder Weingarten, and his range had been limited. She hadn't known that there was such a variety available elsewhere. But when Klaus produced an order form, Clara shook her head.

"Many things look good on paper," she said. "I want to see the products with my own eyes and hold them in my hands first. Then I'll decide. Please ask the sales representatives of these companies to come by with samples this week."

"Do as my wife says," Stefan, who had just entered the manufactory, ordered Klaus.

"Do you have to take that tone?" Clara asked, when they were alone. "The man hasn't raised a single objection. Quite the opposite, in fact: Mr. Kohlwitz and I work together very well."

"It doesn't hurt to let your employees know their place from time to time," Stefan said, and he straightened his silk tie. Was it new? Clara had never seen him wearing it before. *I rarely find the time even to buy a new dress,* she thought with a sigh. How did Stefan manage it?

"What's all this?" said Stefan, pointing to the catalogs. "I thought we'd agreed that *I* would take care of all the orders."

"For the raw materials, yes," Clara replied. "But I would like to decide which containers I sell my creams in. For me, a cream jar has to be at least as high quality as what it contains. And it has to fit me and my . . . my aesthetic, too," she said.

"Not getting airs and graces, are you?" Stefan mocked. "The package is irrelevant. What counts is price. Your customers toss away the jars as soon as they're empty, anyway."

"That's where you're wrong. Many women have told me that they find the containers far too lovely to throw away. They use them to hold jewelry or buttons or—"

"All right, all right." Stefan raised his hands in surrender. "If your heart depends on it, then you choose them, but leave the rest of the orders to me. I can negotiate with the men much differently than you can."

Clara nodded. "According to Klaus, there's a shortage of lanolin. Last summer there was a virus that killed entire flocks of sheep. Do you think the shortage of wool wax could cause problems for us?" she asked.

But Stefan laughed it off. "If the Germans can't deliver, then I'll find it in Switzerland. The sheep there are still as hale and hearty as they come."

That made Clara feel better. What if all her great plans foundered because of a detail like that? "Oh, Stefan, everything is running along so well. Sometimes I can hardly believe it."

"For me, it was clear from the start, *mia cara*. All you have to do is follow my advice and everything will work out."

"Do you know what I'd like to do most of all?" she said abruptly.

Stefan look inquiringly at her.

"I'd love to drive to Grasse and look for a parfumier! Klaus is a good chemist, but he's never had anything to do with the creation of scents. When I talked to him about it, he suggested that a perfume specialist could put the final touch on my products."

"No problem at all! We can certainly spare the few marks it will cost for a good nose." Stefan laughed. "Didn't you once talk about doing that trip with Isabelle? Why don't you work out a plan with her now for next spring. I can look after things here." He stroked Clara's cheek. "But you'll have to excuse me now. I've got an important meeting. Business."

Chapter Thirty-Two

March 1910

"You want to pay twenty percent less than last time? Have you gone mad?" said Meinrad Kornbichler, owner of a large oil mill in Upper Swabia.

"Well," Stefan replied, "your competition is pushing hard to supply us, and at much lower prices."

"Supply *us*? The company still belongs to Clara Berg, doesn't it?" said the man. His eyes had narrowed to two unfriendly slits.

"Do you see Mrs. Berg anywhere here?" Stefan said calmly. "You're dealing with me, sir. And if you don't want to drive home with your oil casks, you would be well advised to accept my price."

Mr. Kornbichler furrowed his brow. He looked at his heavily laden wagon and back to Stefan, and the war he was waging with himself inside was clear to see.

"It's blackmail," the man growled. "And you're a crook."

"I've been called many things." Stefan laughed. He waved over Klaus Kohlwitz, who was just coming out of the manufactory. "Help Mr. Kornbichler unload, would you? And be careful with the containers.

I don't want the oil to suffer." He tipped his hat and was about to leave when the oil supplier took him by the arm.

"I might be dancing to your tune today, but that's only because I don't want to drive the oil home again. I won't let you treat me like this next time. You can count on that."

"As you wish," said Stefan. "Like I said, there are many oil mills that would be honored to supply us."

Klaus Kohlwitz, who had heard every word, looked in shock from one man to the other.

"The company still belongs to Clara Berg, doesn't it?" Stefan sniffed contemptuously. What impertinence! *Who did Kornbichler think he was talking to?* he thought as he made his way to the Bar Coco. Clara's errand boy? An accountant who needed his boss to sign off on every decision? Those times were over, and the sooner people got used to it, the better.

By opening the manufactory, he had taken care of several issues at once. Clara was now spending most of her time in her laboratory and had practically no contact with her customers, so she couldn't go handing out advice like "fresh air and lots of exercise." In her little laboratory, his wife was discovering one product after another, and each sold better than the one before it.

The best thing of all was that as long as Clara was busy with a test tube or was off traveling—as now, in Grasse with her friend Isabelle— he could do whatever he wanted, just as he had always wanted. And it had all been so simple.

The bar was already in sight as Stefan's mood soured. His thoughts turned to Kohlwitz, and the way the man had looked at him earlier, as if he expected Stefan to enlighten him about the dispute with the oil supplier. He would have to keep an eye on that chemist, he thought, as he kicked a stone off the road. Kohlwitz was important for the operations in the manufactory, admittedly, but that did not mean that he could do as he pleased.

He decided to reprimand Kohlwitz the next morning, before he drove to Baden-Baden. No—he would address the entire staff at the manufactory.

He nodded, pleased with himself.

The previous week, an entire crate of facial toner fell while one of the women was packing it, and the expensive bottles of toner were reduced to a pile of broken glass. They had been intended for the shop in Baden-Baden, and they were suddenly faced with a shortage. Stefan was not present when it happened, but had heard about the mishap from Clara. "It's annoying, of course, but things like that can happen" was all his wife had said. Stefan had held his tongue, but it was clear that he couldn't let the matter rest there.

He would cut everyone's salary for the month. That would teach the clumsy women a lesson. He wouldn't have to listen to their whining for long, though, because he would leave for Baden-Baden immediately afterward.

Thinking of the spa town improved his mood. A quick check of the Bel Étage–Baden-Baden . . . he'd promised Clara that. And after that he would go to one of the private gaming rooms. The back room at the Rouge & Blanc restaurant was currently *en vogue*. Champagne and cards, didn't that sound like the perfect plan?

He opened the door of the Bar Coco, where his friends were already waiting for him. After such a strenuous day, a bottle of champagne to set the mood for tomorrow couldn't hurt. He had enough money in his pocket. And what of it if he walked in without a penny? Stefan Berg was good for any tab he ran up.

Who would have guessed what the Italian with the scissors had become . . .

Because I can.

***

When Isabelle and Clara traveled together, they usually attracted a good deal of attention. The gorgeous redhead and the elegant brunette were always tastefully dressed and radiated a special aura.

In Grasse, though, no one gave them a second glance. In Grasse, people were used to beautiful women. Or it might be better said that they knew no other kind. But prettier than any woman was Grasse itself. The city was the prima donna among the towns of southern France. And it smelled better than all the world's women put together. When the first heralds of spring, like daffodils and irises, were breaking through the earth beside Lake Constance or in the Champagne region, entire forests of mimosa were already blooming in the south of France. Against silvery leaves, millions of golden floral pom-poms put themselves on display, and their scent wafted, full of promise, through the land. And Grasse, with its multilayered scent, was engulfed in another cloud of perfume.

"Can you smell the mimosa? And the lavender, roses, jasmine, verbena . . ." Clara tilted her head back and drank in the beguiling scent that drifted through the narrow streets of the medieval town. Parfumeries, distilleries, laboratories—from every building, every doorway, every window came a different combination of fragrances. The heady mixture made Clara dizzy. Of course, she knew before she arrived that Grasse was the capital city of perfume, and that the best parfumiers worked here to create the best fragrances in the world. But seeing it all with her own eyes, smelling it with her own nose . . . that was something else again.

Isabelle, too, was more than animated; she was exhilarated. "Look at that, the famous Maison Molinard. And here, Galimard. And there—Fleuron de Belle! So many famous makers so close together." Isabelle was jumping from one foot to the other like a little girl in a candy shop. "It's like Reims, with all the most famous champagne makers in one place. And I can hardly wait to spend some money! I want to take something back for Ghislaine and for my neighbors. And I should buy something very special for our nanny. If she hadn't been prepared to look after little Viola, I couldn't have come here at all."

"I'm grateful not only to your nanny, but to you, too," said Clara. "Without you, this trip would only be half as much fun!" Isabelle's daughter was only six months old, and Clara would never forget that her friend had left her baby behind to support Clara in Grasse with good advice and good French. But with feigned severity, she said, "But we're not buying souvenirs until we've taken care of business."

She jumped when a whip cracked behind her, then turned around to see a flatbed wagon fully loaded with dried purple flowers rolling up right behind them. Clara quickly grabbed Isabelle by the arm and pulled her out of the way. In the narrow streets, one could easily end up under the wheels.

"So do you think there's something like a school for parfumiers here?" Clara asked as she looked into a shop window where hundreds of glass bottles and jars were on display. Should she be keeping a lookout for new bottles as well?

Isabelle shook her head. "Unlikely. I think it's like things are for us in Champagne. A good nose and a sense for perfumes are essential to finding the perfect composition. And that only comes with practice and experience. No one can learn that in a few lessons in school." When she saw Clara's look of disappointment, she added, "But considering all the parfumeries here, it should be easy to find a talented young nose for your Bel Étage. Don't worry, you won't go home without your parfumier!"

"*What* do you want? You want to *poach* one of my men?" Small wrinkles formed around the eyes of Monsieur Gayet, chief parfumier of Escarbot, and he broke into roaring laughter.

Clara and Isabelle looked at each other in confusion, then Clara glanced around the large production hall. At every table, men were working away with all kinds of crucibles, kettles, and wooden frames thickly smeared with animal fat and flowers. She guessed there were two dozen men or more. The atmosphere reminded Clara of her own manufactory.

The Frenchman finally regained his composure and grew serious. "*Mesdames*, to work here, under my wing, is a great privilege. It may sound immodest, but"—he paused briefly to let the weight of his words sink in—"there are people out there who would cut off their right hand to work for me."

Clara nodded uncertainly. The men working there did not look especially happy; instead, they appeared rather grim and grumpy.

"Do you know someone who could work for Mrs. Berg or not?" Isabelle asked. Clara could hear her impatience.

The parfumier laughed again. Before Isabelle could react, he patted her arm condescendingly. "Young lady, my men are the elite! The best of the best! You can't seriously believe that even the boy who sweeps up would be willing to leave my employ of his own free will."

"But I would pay well. And the man would have a great challenge awaiting him."

Monsieur Gayet turned to Clara. Without changing his patronizing tone, he said, "My dear lady, mixing a little rose oil into a cream, as God is my witness, does not constitute a great challenge."

"Foot cream? Facial toner? I don't understand." The man who ran the laboratory at Fleuron de Belle shook his head in bewilderment. "And you would like me to create a fragrance for that?"

"No, I—" Clara began to explain, when the man interrupted her yet again.

"Then we agree! Madame, I am an artist," the man said theatrically. "And my canvas is the skin of a beautiful woman. I have nothing to do with jars of cream." The man bowed. "Please excuse me." And he was gone.

Clara and Isabelle were left standing like two schoolgirls who'd been rapped over the knuckles. The man did not seem to understand what they wanted from him at all. Or he didn't want to.

"Of course I can recommend someone!" Monsieur Bellimard's eyes sparkled. "I know just the man you need. Wait . . ." Monsieur Bellimard, the owner of the eponymously named parfumerie, shouted imperiously across the room. "Monsieur Epis! Where is Monsieur Epis? Tell him to come here immediately!"

Clara and Isabelle shared a look of relief. Finally.

They were standing in one of the smaller laboratories housed in a dingy building at the end of a street. From outside, everything looked shabby, and Clara had not even wanted to go in. But they had been to almost every other parfumerie and laboratory in Grasse without success, so Isabelle had all but pushed her through the door. What they found inside was no better: dirty floors, smeared windows that let through barely any daylight. The fragrance of roses and lavender rising from the huge copper kettle in the middle of the room mixed with the stink of the sewers, which drifted in through an open window.

A short, fat man, his balding head with an oily sheen, approached.

"May I introduce Monsieur Epis!" Monsieur Bellimard prompted the fat man to shake hands with Clara. His hand was sweaty and cold, and it took a lot for Clara not to immediately wipe her hand on her skirt.

"For a small fee, I would be prepared to let Monsieur Epis go. He is one of our best parfumiers!" Monsieur Epis, sweating from every pore, looked at his employer with a confused expression. It was clear that he was hearing such praise for the first time.

Clara swallowed. "That's very nice of you. But—"

"Thank you, we'll keep your offer in mind," Isabelle interrupted her. A moment later, they made their escape.

"My God, that man stank of sweat," said Isabelle once they were back outside. "I feel ill."

"I don't understand how a man who sweats so much can have anything to do with perfume at all." Clara took a last fretful look back at the rundown workshop. "If Monsieur Epis was the last parfumier on God's earth, I would live without him in my company."

"I think that Monsieur Bellimard saw his chance to get rid of an unpleasant or untalented employee. Like an old workhorse that eats more hay than it's worth."

The two friends giggled hysterically. "But what now?" Clara asked. They had been out looking all morning. Clara never would have believed that it would be so hard to find the person she was looking for.

"My feet hurt, I'm hungry, and I'm thirsty," said Isabelle. "Look, that sign points the way to the Jardin des Plantes, where there is certain to be a small café. And I'm sure we'll have a good view of the sea. We need to rest and work out a new plan."

Neither noticed the man who followed them.

Clara and Isabelle each ordered a cup of tea and a slice of *la fougasette*, an orange-flavored yeast cake, when a young man appeared beside their table.

"*Mesdames,*" he said slowly.

"We have everything, thank you," said Isabelle, without looking up.

"This cake of yours is just delicious," Clara added, being polite, then turned back to Isabelle. "I really don't know where to look next."

Isabelle snorted. "Those parfumiers were all so arrogant and rude. The man at Escarbot was the worst!"

Clara nodded. "Monsieur Gayet, yes. He was laughing at us from the moment we walked in."

It took a moment for them to realize that the young man was still standing beside their table.

Shielding her eyes from the sun, Clara looked up. She guessed he was in his late twenties, not particularly striking, with brown hair, a pale but even complexion, brown, animated eyes, and full lips.

"Yes?"

"I . . . well . . ." The young man scratched his head in embarrassment. "My name is Laszlo Kovac. Please excuse me for approaching you like this, but I work in the Escarbot Parfumerie, and I overheard your conversation with my boss. Not that I was eavesdropping, mind you!" His French was broken, and Clara thought she could hear a slight German accent. Strange. She exchanged a look with Isabelle. "You are looking for a parfumier, aren't you?" Laszlo Kovac crushed his hat unconsciously in his hands as he spoke.

"Yes. Do you know someone who would be willing to take on a new job?" asked Clara, her mouth suddenly dry with excitement.

The man gave an embarrassed shrug. "He's standing in front of you."

Laszlo Kovac came from Bohemia, or more precisely from its capital, Prague. His father, a German émigré, was an engineer with the railways, and his mother, Helena Kovac, sang at the Státní opera, Prague's opera house, where she was famous for her interpretations of Wagner. It was through her, the feted opera singer, that young Laszlo, from his earliest childhood, had contact with the world of the rich and beautiful. As a baby, he played in his mother's dressing room with his silver rattle, and later with his tin soldiers, while Helena Kovac warmed up her voice for the next act of *Der Ring des Nibelungen*. And it was through his mother that he grew to love—and understand—the best perfumes in the world.

"There wasn't a day that went by when my mother didn't wear perfume," Laszlo said. Isabelle and Clara had invited him to sit with them. "Mother would wear a mixture of ambergris, musk, and resin one day and a lemon perfume the next. The day after that, she'd be surrounded by the fragrance of damask roses. I don't know why, but even when I was a child, I could pick out the individual aromas, even though I didn't know all their names." Laszlo smiled. "For me, perfume is synonymous with love and warmth and beauty. As a little boy, Mother was, for me, a beautiful princess."

Clara's expression grew soft and wistful. Would her own son ever talk about her in such a loving way? She doubted it.

Then Laszlo grew earnest. His eyes took on a new intensity as he said to Clara, "Naturally, my father wanted me to follow in his footsteps as an engineer. But from the start, my greatest wish was to work in the world of fragrances. Or even better, to create my own."

"Then you've made your wish come true. Grasse is paradise for people who love perfume," said Isabelle, sweeping her arm to indicate the town that lay at their feet, bathed in golden spring sunshine.

Laszlo's expression changed. "A man can live in paradise and still feel like he's landed in hell." He looked thoughtfully at Clara, as if weighing how much of what lay deep inside him he should reveal. "Monsieur Gayet is a thief," he said softly. "He takes my creations to Monsieur Escarbot and tells him they are his own. Do you know *Zahara*?" He looked from Clara to Isabelle.

Clara shook her head, but her friend said, "You can buy that in Reims. It's very popular right now with society women."

"*Zahara* is my fragrance. So are *Fleur de Nuit* and *Grande Finale*. I developed those three in the last year. I even suggested names for them to him, all to do with my home city, Prague. *Loreto*, *Hradčany*, and

Vltava! The perfumes were meant to be an homage to my mother . . ." He laughed bitterly. "Gayet dismissed them all. 'Your creations are far too flat and empty! And those ridiculous names. You might be able to sell something like that in a Czech brothel, but not to the women of the world!' It was an insult. Then he ordered me to create new fragrances, but he kept my formulas for himself. 'You're wasting valuable raw materials and my time,' he said, and threatened to throw me out." Laszlo swallowed, close to tears.

Clara's frown deepened as she followed his story. Eyes down, she exchanged a glance with Isabelle. Her friend was just as enthralled as she was.

"Then Escarbot brought out a perfume that was my *Loreto*, down to the minutest detail. Gayet had not even taken the trouble to change a single note!" Laszlo laughed resentfully. "Try to imagine my disbelief the first time I smelled it. I took him to task, of course, but the great master just laughed at me, as he laughed at you today."

Isabelle shook her head in confusion. "Why didn't he simply admit that the perfumes came from you? You must be well paid for your work as a parfumier. Gayet and Escarbot could expect that you would develop good perfumes for them."

"Vanity," said Laszlo plainly. "No god will tolerate another god beside him." He sighed. "A word of thanks or praise would have been enough for me. But Gayet treated me and my colleagues like the last scum on earth, while he was celebrated publicly as the king of perfume."

"But that's just cruel," Clara burst out in German. "Why don't you defend yourself?"

"What can I do, madam?" said Laszlo, also in German. "It would be his word against mine. You can guess for yourself which of us would have the short straw."

Clara nodded. She knew that kind of situation all too well. "And now you're contemplating a new job?"

Laszlo nodded. "I want to finally prove to the world what I'm capable of."

Clara was going to ask another question, but she felt Isabelle's hand on her left arm: a warning. "What you've told us is all well and good. A genius whose ideas have been maliciously stolen," Isabelle said. "But how can we be sure you're telling the truth?"

Chapter Thirty-Three

The atmosphere in the back room of the Rouge & Blanc restaurant hummed with tension, excitement, fear, and joy, overlaid by a murmur of voices, pealing laughter, and the tinkling of glasses. Gambling chips slid across the green cloth at the roulette table, and women's diamond jewelry sparkled beneath the chandeliers.

Gianfranco de Lucca grinned to himself as the croupier pushed an impressive stack of chips across the felt. Winner! And not for the first time that evening. Feeling generous, he pushed some of the chips back to the croupier. "For you and your colleagues."

A business trip to Baden-Baden really had something to be said for it. In the last two days, his order book had practically filled up by itself. The local men's tailors couldn't get enough of his fine fabrics, and each one he visited ordered more than the one before. He had just sent a telegram back to Naples telling his only son to hire more people for their weaving mill. Silk-and-linen blends, wool-and-cashmere blends—his products were the highest quality available, and for that he needed the best weavers in the industry! Besides—

He was pulled out of his thoughts by the low, firm voice of the croupier: *"Faites vos jeux, mesdames et messieurs!"*

And why not? He'd place one more bet. One more spin, then he would head back to his hotel. The day had been long and successful, and it was best to finish at the top.

Content with himself and the world, Gianfranco slid a high-value chip onto red 32. His wife, Rosa, would turn that age next month, and he mustn't forget to buy her a birthday present on his trip home.

He held his breath and watched the silver ball. It landed in black 15, the pocket beside red 32. Gianfranco laughed.

"Damn it! Lost again," he heard from the opposite side of the table, not for the first time that evening. "Come on, a new spin! Can't this go any faster?" The man flailed one hand arrogantly toward the croupier, who was still distributing the winnings from the spin.

The croupier raised his eyebrows in disapproval. It was rare to meet impolite players in the discreet, secret gaming rooms, where the upper class met to play a genteel hand of cards or try their luck at roulette. It was an honor to be admitted—uncouth behavior could quickly lead to that honor being rescinded.

Gianfranco frowned when he saw how much money the man opposite placed on the table, another big bet. Did he really want to lose so much again? The guy had had a run of miserable luck for the last two hours, but he kept at it. *Stupido!* Gianfranco would never be so irresponsible, throwing away his money like that, even if he had sacks of it to spare!

But something about the man . . . he seemed familiar. *But from where?* the fabric merchant wondered. He'd been mulling it over the entire evening. One more spin, this time definitely his last . . . and a glass of red wine, he decided, then he really would leave. Would Alfonso be in the hotel bar? Or had the Genoan already retired for the night?

Alfonso was not only his traveling companion on many a business trip, but also his best friend. Unfortunately, he had been battling a cold and had no interest in gambling.

Pity. Alfonso had missed a nice evening, Gianfranco thought, and he placed three chips on red. No more experiments. Just for fun.

Where had he seen the man sitting opposite before? Here in Baden-Baden? It looked as if the man, a good-looking fellow with blond hair and a Kaiser Wilhelm mustache, was a regular guest. The waiter knew immediately that he drank only one kind of champagne: a Pommery *millésime*.

"Rien ne va plus!" Red. The blond man lost again. He muttered something that Gianfranco did not catch.

"Sometimes you win, sometimes you lose," said Gianfranco as he stood. He was halfway across the large, red-walled room when he pulled up short. A suspicion had crossed his mind, an inkling, perhaps, of where he had seen the man before.

But that was . . . Could it be? No. It was too absurd, wasn't it?

Gianfranco returned to the roulette table and edged in beside the unlucky man.

"Excuse me, my good man, but you look familiar to me. My name is Gianfranco de Lucca. Could it be that we have met before?" he asked with undisguised curiosity.

The blond man looked up sourly. "Not that I recall."

But Gianfranco was now certain. "But of course! I remember it clearly. It was in a small guesthouse in the Alps, in Piedmont. My friend Alfonso was there, too. And you, you were traveling with your brother. Wait . . ." He snapped his fingers. "I'll have your name in a moment. Santini? No, that was someone else. Totosano! The Totosano brothers, that was you and your brother. And you come from Elva, if I remember right. You're a hair trader, aren't you?" Ha! His memory had not let him down. Gianfranco let out a small relieved laugh while the other gamblers glanced with interest at him and Signor Totosano. Even the croupier, brushing the felt, paused to follow their exchange.

"You're mistaken, sir," the gambler replied curtly. "My name is Stefan Berg. I've never been to Italy in my life. Now please excuse me, I'm in the middle of a game." He picked up his last small pile of chips and placed his bet.

"But . . ." Confused, Gianfranco looked at the man again. Stefan Berg? He normally did not forget faces and names. Especially when the man with that face practiced a profession as extraordinary as that practiced by the Totosano brothers. He'd cut the hair from young women, then sold it on to wigmakers. Gianfranco could still clearly remember the others at the table having a good laugh at the expense of the brothers.

The croupier looked at him inquisitively. Gianfranco raised his hands. No, no more for me. He walked away, pensive. Strange. He could not be mistaken . . .

***

That night was the longest of Stefan's life. He did not close his eyes at all. In his mind, he saw the roulette wheel spinning and spinning, heard the clattering ball rolling over the frets and pockets. He'd lost three hundred marks. More than he'd ever lost before, and no trifling amount. But still insignificant, utterly insignificant, compared to the second phantom haunting him, robbing him of sleep, putting the fear back into his body.

"Could it be that we have met before?" Stefan's heart had nearly stopped on the spot. Fear, his old companion, had latched onto him in that moment.

He had learned all about fear as a child, back then, when he heard his father outside the room. The fear had always crept into little Roberto's head on those nights, too. Was it one of those nights when their father would come into the room and beat them? Would he attack Michele? Or would it be his own hide turning bloody and bruised beneath Giacomo Totosano's fists?

The fear had always crept in quietly, and even when he was an adult, it had never left him. Only when he married Clara did he finally feel as if he had left it behind, he hoped forever. But he'd learned a lesson tonight. The fear was back. Stefan had recognized *it* instantly. And he knew *it* wouldn't be satisfied to make his heart beat faster. *It* wanted more: *it* wanted space, wanted to steal away his breath, to suffocate him . . .

He jumped out of bed, prowling the room like a tiger. He could not shake off the fear. His chest grew tighter and tighter, his breathing more labored. He threw open the window, stared out into the blackness of Lichtentaler Allee at night, and sucked in the air deeply to try to expand his lungs.

"Could it be that we have we met before?"

Stefan laughed bitterly. He had immediately recognized the man across the roulette table from the guesthouse in the Piedmont. He was the fabric merchant, and he had been with friends the night that Roberto and Michele had stopped there. The two mountain climbers had been at the guesthouse, too. *"Because I can."*

Looking back, that encounter had been fateful for him, Stefan thought, lying on his bed again. The businessmen throwing money around, the young mountaineer's arrogance . . . It was then that he had begun to believe that dreams didn't always have to remain dreams. One could bring a dream to life. And that was exactly what he had done.

"I've never been to Italy in my life." Had he convinced the fabric merchant? Outside, the sky was finally starting to lighten. Bone tired, Stefan heaved himself out of bed again. He went into the bathroom and glared at his reflection in the mirror. What if the *famiglia* found out about his life here? Through the grapevine? Then . . . He did not want to imagine the *then*.

Don't drive yourself insane, he tried to calm himself. Be happy that you didn't meet that man in Meersburg. Then things might have gotten tricky. But like this, the Italian, who no doubt had to travel on quickly, could draw no more conclusions.

Baden-Baden was not good for him. It was high time to turn his back on the town. He would pay one more visit to the Bel Étage, just to check that everything was in order, and then he would leave immediately. The idea of departure brought a little confidence with it. He was Stefan Berg. No one else.

The moment Stefan walked through the door to the shop, he smelled fresh-brewed coffee and something else, something sweet and warm. He looked around the empty shop and frowned, then heard laughter coming from the back room. What in the world?

Just then, Senta Schmauder came out from the back. After Clara's first assistant, Sophie, returned to Meersburg a month earlier, Senta had taken over the day-to-day running of the Baden-Baden shop.

"Mr. Berg! How nice to see you again." She reached out from behind the counter to shake hands with him. "Welcome to the Bel Étage–Baden-Baden. Luise turns twenty today, so we're using our break to give her a little party, with coffee and fresh *hefezopf.* May we invite you to join us?"

Hefezopf! That's what he had smelled when he entered. It was like walking into a bakery. The shop should smell of lavender and lemons. Stefan shook his head. He looked around at the shelves that occupied the entire right-hand wall. The jars of cream and other products for sale stood in orderly rows. No cause for complaint there, he realized, with a touch of disappointment. He turned back to Senta Schmauder.

"Coffee? I must say I'm surprised. You invite me to your little break-room party while the shop is empty." He crossed to the other side of the room, where three treatment stations were separated from one another by heavy curtains, which he quickly pulled back. None of the three gilded armchairs was occupied.

"Shouldn't there be women sitting here with cream covering their faces? Shouldn't the Baden-Baden ballerinas be having their ravaged feet tended to? Isn't that the fundamental concept of this shop? Or have you turned it into Clara's Coffee Shop in the meantime? Because that's what it smells like!" He stepped over to the nearest shelf, grabbed a spray bottle, and frenetically sprayed its contents into the air. A lavender fragrance immediately filled the room. Then he went behind the counter and looked into the back room, where the two younger beauty experts were hurriedly clearing coffee cups and cake plates into the sink. At the sight of Stefan, they froze like paper cutouts. After a moment, Luise curtsied.

Stefan looked at them with contempt. "When the cat's away, the mice will play. Isn't that the saying? If Clara Berg knew how you're abusing the trust she put in you . . ."

"But, Mr. Berg, I feel obliged to point out that it was your wife herself who told us to take a coffee break from ten thirty to eleven. Look at the clock. It is still five to eleven," said Senta. Unlike her two younger colleagues, who looked close to tears, she was not so easily intimidated. "We work through the midday hours to offer treatments to the women whose husband go to lunch then. If we're not supposed to fall down from exhaustion, we have to eat sometime."

Stefan eyed Senta's well-rounded figure and said, "You're not going to waste away so fast, my dear. And I am certain that when my wife talked about breaks, she did not intend for the shop to look so deserted from the outside that anyone passing would think it was closed." He turned the handle on the register, and the cash drawer sprang open. Inside lay a few bills and coins. He didn't bother counting it, but simply stuffed it all into his pants pocket. He'd gambled away the previous day's income yesterday evening.

"Pity I can't report very good earnings here. But given your slipshod approach to your work, should it surprise me that it's nearly empty?" he said, closing the register again forcefully. Then he looked at the three women.

"Your breaks are canceled from now on. You can drink water or eat a slice of bread between treatments, just like my wife does. Or do you think Clara Berg has time for coffee and gossip?"

"But—" Senta began to object.

"No buts," Stefan cut her off. "And something else: your base salary is also canceled. From now on, you will be paid according to your individual receipts. The more treatments you provide, the more money you will have in your envelope at the end of the month." He touched the brim of his hat. "I'll be back again next week, and I expect to see a full shop."

***

The three women looked at each other in dismay. "No salary? He can't mean that, can he?" said Luise.

Her colleague, Emma—whom many customers reported to have golden hands—merely shrugged.

"But I need my salary, especially in winter when there aren't any tourists in town. We won't do nearly as many treatments then!" Luise said in horror. "We want to buy a piano."

"You take care of your piano, and I'll take care of the cash register," said Senta. "Do either of you know how much money Mr. Berg took with him? How can I keep good accounts if I don't know what was in the register? And how am I even supposed to record the money he took?" She looked helplessly at her two younger colleagues.

"He'll say *we* took the money," said Emma dispiritedly.

"Clara Berg knows that she can trust us. I need the work, I really do! If she came back herself just once, we could tell her everything," said Luise, almost crying.

"What would you tell her? That her husband helps himself to the register whenever he wants? I'm sure she would love to hear that," Senta shot back sarcastically. Normally, she took no part in chit-chat about their employer. She shook her head. "Clara Berg is a wonderful woman, and I've learned a great deal from her. But these days she has better things to do than look after her shops. Well, I have better things to do than to listen to a lout like that scold me! If Mr. Berg thinks we're dependent on him, he's got another thing coming."

"You're not going to quit, are you?" Emma asked Senta in a panicky voice. She and Luise only did the treatments, no more. Senta coordinated all the appointments and organized everything else around the shop.

"I'm not ready to decide yet," said Senta, lowering her voice. "But I can promise you this: if I go, I'm taking you with me!"

***

"Guess who I ran into yesterday evening?" said Gianfranco de Lucca the next morning, sitting at breakfast with Alfonso. With an unwavering frown, he told his friend about the strange encounter in the gaming room of the hotel. "I'm one hundred percent sure I was looking at the hair trader from Elva. I don't care how vehemently he claimed to be someone else!" he said. He waved over the waiter and asked for more coffee.

"I remember that evening well," said Alfonso. "And the two brothers. I had reason to think of them last summer, too, although through a sad connection." Alfonso sneezed, whipped out a handkerchief, and blew his nose loudly.

Gianfranco looked at his friend impatiently. He hoped he wouldn't be sneezing and sniffing in the coach the whole way home.

"Our nanny, Silvia comes from Lombardy, from a town called Morbegno, to be exact. Her family is very poor, and the girl sends money home every month, although she doesn't earn very much with us."

Gianfranco sniffed. He could certainly believe that. Alfonso was not the most generous man in the world. "And? What did your nanny have to do with the hair trader?" He reached into the bread basket again, wishing that the Germans would learn to make bread that wasn't so dark and heavy!

"A lot. Last summer, we had to give her some time off in the middle of the children's vacation so that she could go to her sister's funeral. The young woman—I think her name was Eva—had killed herself after her fiancé walked out on her. It seems he told her that he could not stand her ugliness any longer, and demanded that she give back the engagement ring. Just before it happened, Eva had allowed two hair traders from Elva to cut off her hair. They duped the young woman with their sweet words. The money they offered her for her hair was tempting, of course. Well, before she knew it, her beautiful black braid was gone and her scalp all but shaved."

"You mean to say that the hair traders were to blame for the young woman's death?" Gianfranco swallowed hard. He could not understand how any woman could voluntarily give up her hair. If his Rosa cut off all her blond hair . . . unimaginable! "No doubt she wasn't the only young woman whose life was destroyed by the Totosano brothers and their *profession*," he said, and the word "profession" sounded like a curse.

Alfonso nodded grimly. "Now that I think about, I remember something else. Last summer, at about the same time Silvia left for her sister's funeral, posters suddenly appeared on the walls of every guesthouse in northern Italy saying that the Totosano and Sorri families urgently wanted information about a certain Roberto Totosano. And that they were offering a large reward for his whereabouts. Didn't you see them?"

Gianfranco screwed up his nose. "I didn't get out of stinking Naples once last summer. Did the posters say why they were looking for him?"

"No. Though rumor had it that he stole a lot of money from his family and headed for the hills. At first, they searched for him themselves, but when they didn't have any success, they went public."

"Headed for the hills . . . I think he may have headed for Baden-Baden instead," Gianfranco said, and laughed.

"If you've unearthed Roberto Totosano, that would really be something. I haven't heard anything about the man being found, which means you'd be in line for the reward. It was a considerable sum, though I don't remember the exact amount anymore, I'm afraid. How about this: you accept the money, then you donate it to the poor women who fell victim to the nasty hair traders? A generous gesture . . ."

Generous enough when it's not your money, Gianfranco thought as he chewed his bread. "Do you still remember where the posters were hanging?" he asked with his mouth full.

Alfonso nodded. "The guesthouses. We'll pass a lot of them on the way home."

"Good. Because before we leave Baden-Baden, I'm going to do a little more research into Stefan Berg. And if he really turns out to be Roberto Totosano?" Gianfranco shook his head. "If the guy hadn't lied to my face like that, I might have forgotten meeting him again. But now it would be my great pleasure to be able to tell his family that I've found their prodigal son." He laughed, and Alfonso joined him.

Chapter Thirty-Four

"This is beautiful!" Isabelle leaned back in her chair and sighed deeply. A small sparrow pecking at breadcrumbs beside her chair stopped what it was doing and looked up at her. When it saw she presented no threat, it turned back to the crumbs.

"It's gorgeous. Like everything in Grasse," said Clara.

It was their last day in the town, and like every morning they were sitting on the terrace of their small pension for breakfast. The waitress had put out a basket of fresh croissants and white bread on every table, and there was raspberry jelly, lavender honey, coffee, and steamed milk. The roses climbing up the building's stone walls were not yet flowering, but there were already butterflies fluttering around them. Clara imagined how lovely it must be when the roses were in bloom.

"It's so good to sit at a real table, with cutlery and a tablecloth and everything," said Isabelle as she took her second croissant. "At home, I'm so busy the whole day preparing all kinds of meals, and I rarely know how many people I'm actually cooking for. The children bring friends home, and we often have Claude and Micheline at the table, too. And Ghislaine comes on Mondays because her restaurant is closed. And just the other day, she brought *Alphonse* along!"

The two friends laughed, enjoying the intimacy between them. They found a fiendish pleasure in the knowledge that Isabelle's sister-in-law, Ghislaine, was now officially living with her lover, because the man was previously married to Isabelle's archenemy, Henriette Trubert. And the way that Henriette hounded Isabelle was despicable. In Clara's and Isabelle's eyes, it served the old witch right that her husband left her for beautiful, merry Ghislaine.

"Don't start acting as if it's all too much for you!" Clara teased. "You wouldn't have it any other way, would you?" She remembered back to when Isabelle couldn't even peel potatoes decently. But now the champagne queen fed a large household and the grape pickers who came by the dozen to her farm every autumn.

Isabelle's eyes were radiant. "You're right. I miss everyone at home so much that my heart aches. Not that I haven't enjoyed these days here with you," she hurried to add. "For me, Grasse has been a big adventure, and a fragrant one. And I'm going to feel the hole that all my purchases burned in my purse for a long time to come." She grimaced. "But I can hardly wait to throw my arms around Daniel and the little ones again."

Clara gave her a melancholy smile. Her friend could truly count herself lucky.

Isabelle leaned across and laid one hand on Clara's arm. "And you? What about you?" she asked quietly.

"What about me?" said Clara breezily. "I'm looking forward to being with Stefan again, naturally. And to the work. Our life is just a little"—she waved casually—"different."

"Different. Aha."

"Stefan and I . . . we don't see very much of one another, not like you'd expect of a married couple. In the morning, for example, if I have breakfast at all, it's in a café by the lake, while he sleeps until nine. Why should I make coffee and butter bread if I'm the only one there to enjoy it? So you can see that the luxury we have here is something I get to enjoy every day," said Clara with a smile. "During the day, Stefan takes care of the bookkeeping, or he checks to see that everything is all right in the manufactory. He deals with incoming orders and makes sure the shops always have enough stock. I spend most of my time in the laboratory, trying out new recipes and refining my old ones. A great luxury, but also a lonely job . . ." A yearning tone had crept into her voice. As much as she loved her work in the laboratory, she missed the contact with her customers terribly.

"But that leaves the evenings for the two of you," said Isabelle consolingly.

"Don't speak too soon!" Clara said with an affected laugh. "When I finally emerge from the laboratory, I'm so tired that all I want to do is put my feet up. Stefan is a night owl, and a popular guest at parties. The contact that he maintains with our customers at those events is very important for the business."

"He should maintain a little contact with his wife," Isabelle growled. "If you ask me, you work much too much!"

"You're a good one to talk," Clara teased her friend. "But don't worry, I'm well," she added, before Isabelle could vent any more about Stefan. Neither Josephine nor Isabelle had actually said anything, but Clara could sense that both women harbored some resentment toward Stefan. Clara had not managed to puzzle out exactly *what* they had against him.

"When I get back, I'm going to start looking for a suitable lawyer. I've become a respectable, married businesswoman, and the chances can't be too bad that I can at least see my children occasionally. Stefan says he'll support me in whatever I do, and I'm very grateful to him for that."

Isabelle looked as if she were about to say something else, but she fell silent for a while before saying, "So, are you satisfied with the outcome of this trip?"

This time, Clara's laugh was less artificial. "Oh, definitely. Grasse itself is more impressive than I ever would have thought, and I've bought better ingredients than I've ever had to work with before. But even more important: I've found the right parfumier. Unlike all the arrogant gentlemen we've met here, Laszlo Kovac is not above using his art for creams and tinctures. And who knows, maybe we'll create our own perfume one day. I can hardly wait to start work with him!" Clara sighed.

"You're really sure about him?" Isabelle asked. It was a question she had asked before. Since Clara and the man had shaken hands on his employment, Isabelle had been expressing her concern: "*Why do you take everything the man says as the gospel truth?*" "*What if he's a conman and was no more than the errand boy in Escarbot's factory?*" "*How can you be sure he really knows his craft?*"

"Do you really want to take him with you to Germany and give him a job? Do you really think he's the right one?" asked Isabelle again.

"I do," said Clara plainly, and she smiled.

***

"At the same time, the scent of lemon flowers is completely different from the essential oil you get from the skin of a lemon."

"Absolutely. But for most people, lemon is just lemon."

Clara and Laszlo laughed.

What's so funny? Isabelle wondered. Since boarding the train in Avignon, Clara and the parfumier had been talking about fragrances. Which scent created which mood. If one should perfume a face cream with lavender or if it would just make the user tired. When one should use plant extracts and when one would do better with an essential oil.

"... a cream as light as whipped cream, with just a hint of verbena ..."

"... or a combination with some vanilla and ..."

Isabelle yawned conspicuously. She had been looking forward so much to being able to spend the time in the train talking with her friend, but instead Clara and Laszlo were carrying on endless technical discussions. She hoped it wouldn't last all the way to Lyon. Clara and she would go their separate ways there, and Isabelle had no idea when or where she would see Clara again, which made it all the more important that they make the most of every minute.

Clara, her cheeks flushed, leaned across to Laszlo on the seat opposite. "Do you know what I've been dreaming about for a long time?"

Isabelle instinctively pricked up her ears. She had seldom seen her friend as animated as she was then.

"A complete product line with soap, facial toner, face cream, and bathing lotion. And all of them with the identical perfume so that the women can cover themselves from head to foot in their favorite fragrance."

"Then you should add a shampoo," said Laszlo.

"Right!" Clara clapped her hands, as excited as a small child.

"But a fragrance that runs through an entire line can't be too idiosyncratic. It ought to . . ."

Isabelle, bored, opened the newspaper she had bought at the station in Avignon. In two weeks, the Brussels World's Fair would open. The previous year, the Champagne Makers Association had asked Daniel and her if they would be interested in participating, but she had turned down the offer with regret. In April, there was so much work to be done in the vineyards that Daniel couldn't be dragged away from his beloved vines. It would have meant traveling to Brussels alone and leaving the children with the nanny. She had done just that to spend this time with Clara, but a world's fair was not worth the sacrifice.

"And do you know what else I dream about?" Clara's voice had taken on such a delicate tone that Isabelle looked up from her reading in surprise. What now?

"A simple line for women with little money to spare. I want to give them the chance to look after themselves, too."

"And from what I know of you, even your simple line should be a very good quality. A real challenge. But one that it would be worth pursuing," said Laszlo. "When I think of the longing in the eyes of the chambermaids whenever they looked at my mother's perfume bottles and jars of cream . . . and how grateful they would be when my mother gave them a nearly empty jar."

"Oh, I know from experience exactly how they felt," said Clara softly. "There was a time in my life when I didn't dare spend even fifty pfennigs on myself."

Isabelle's brow creased. Clara and this Laszlo were speaking on very familiar terms, as if they had known each other for years.

"Doesn't matter if it's a perfume or a cream, do you know what the most important ingredient of a good product is?" Laszlo suddenly said.

Clara tilted her head to one side and waited for him to answer his question.

Now he's going to babble about orange petals or something, Isabelle thought scornfully. So she was all the more taken aback when Laszlo said, "Love. When my grandmother would cook—she lived with us— she would always say, 'Love is the most crucial ingredient.' Indeed even the simplest dishes tasted special when she made them." He smiled, but quickly grew serious again. "And today, when I work with my jars and test tubes and scents, I always think of my grandmother."

"Love, yes." Clara nodded. "But there's another ingredient that's part of every good recipe." She paused, then said, "Hope."

"Hope. How right you are, dear Mrs. Berg." Laszlo grinned. "It looks like we have our work cut out for us, doesn't it?"

The two of them exchanged a knowing look.

Isabelle frowned again. She was still puzzling about the unusually familiar relationship between them when Clara turned to her and said softly, "When I get home, I have something else to take care of. And that is far more important than all my beauty products put together."

Isabelle, who knew immediately what Clara was referring to, took her friend's hands and held them tightly.

"Everything will work out. The judge will have no choice but to give you visiting rights to your children. And if he doesn't, I'll drive to Berlin and personally slap his face."

Chapter Thirty-Five

Meersburg was wearing its prettiest spring dress when Clara and Laszlo arrived. The sun shone, the lake glittered, a light breeze blew, and foam-capped wavelets danced across the water. In the front gardens of houses, forsythias bloomed, tulips opened their fleshy flowers, and daffodils dipped their heads elegantly, swaying in the wind. Café terraces were open for business after the winter closings. The people smiled, and Clara met with many a friendly greeting on her way home. When she saw how Laszlo's gaze swept admiringly across the beautiful Lake Constance town, a warm wave of happiness washed over her. She was so grateful to be able to live there. And she was sure that Laszlo would soon feel as at home as she did.

Her feeling of happiness lasted an hour before collapsing into the deepest desperation. Wherever she looked, all she saw was chaos and strife. The manufactory, where she went with Laszlo first, was empty. Klaus Kohlwitz met them in the production hall, and told them that not a single employee had come to work for three days. They were on strike. First, it was the cut in wages because of the broken bottles, and then the new rubber gloves that Clara had told them they had to wear. They were damaging their skin, the women claimed. One was suffering from a rash, another from blisters, and three of the women had open sores. Almost all the women were afflicted by an uncomfortable itching and scratched themselves in their sleep. They would not put the gloves on again! And until their hands healed, they would not come back to work.

Clara could not believe what she was hearing. Her manufactory was a place that produced creams that made the skin healthy, but her employees were suffering from a painful rash? And what was this about cutting their wages?

"Can rubber gloves be toxic?" she asked her chemist in horror. She glanced at Laszlo as she said it. *What must he be thinking?*

Klaus shrugged. "The gloves from our old supplier were fine. They were made of natural rubber, and that isn't damaging to the skin at all. Unfortunately, I can't work out what the new gloves your husband ordered are made of. They smell strange, though, I can tell you that much."

"Then order the old gloves again, and fast," Clara told him.

"It isn't as easy as that," the chemist said carefully. "Our previous supplier is no longer prepared to sell his gloves to us. Mr. Berg wants to pay him less than before, and he has withdrawn from our contract. I'm sad to say that he isn't the only one. Several of our regular suppliers have left us. Just yesterday, we had a letter from Meinrad Kornbichler, our oil supplier—" He stopped talking when the mailman entered the room and handed Clara an envelope.

"Sign, please!" he said grimly, and held out a form and pen.

What was this? Clara opened the envelope with trepidation, while Klaus and Laszlo looked on.

We hereby advise that we are resigning, with immediate effect. I have enclosed the key for the Bel Étage—Baden-Baden with this letter. In the future, we will be working in the Belle de Jour Beauty Shop in Maria-Victoria-Strasse.

Signed: Senta Schmauder, Emma Maier, Luise Wagenström

Thunderstruck, Clara lowered the letter. All three had resigned at once?

"There has to be some misunderstanding," she said, breaking into a hysterical laugh. She looked around helplessly.

"Where is Stefan?" He'd gone to Baden-Baden to check on things there. *If there had been any problems, he would surely have sorted them out,* she thought.

Klaus shrugged.

Clara was suddenly so dizzy that everything began to spin before her eyes. The two men were at her side in an instant and helped her to one of the chairs otherwise used by the workers. Klaus hurried away, reappearing almost immediately with a glass of water that Clara drank greedily.

"I'm afraid I have more bad news," he said, when Clara was back on her feet again. "Because of the stop in production, we are running out of products in the Bel Étage–Residenzia as well as in your first shop. In the Residenzia, the face-cleansing lotion ran out the day before yesterday, and the foot cream today. And both places have been out of dry-skin facial cream since yesterday, too. I don't know how the Baden-Baden shop is doing, but your women here are complaining that they can't carry out a proper treatment anymore."

Clara stared at the chemist in disbelief.

"This is a nightmare," she murmured. "I don't understand." She shook her head. "When I left, everything was running perfectly!"

"Sometimes—" Klaus began, but he stopped when the door was thrown open so forcefully that the windows vibrated in their frames.

"Clara! Finally!" Therese literally ran to her and, before Clara knew what was happening, threw herself on Clara's breast, sobbing.

"You would not believe what I've been through in the last few days. I—"

"Therese," Clara whispered. "Therese! We're not alone." She freed herself, rather roughly, from Therese's grasp.

"Oh." Therese blinked when she realized Klaus and Laszlo were standing there. "You're in a meeting, I see. I'm sorry, I didn't mean to disturb you. But I—"

Gently but firmly, Clara guided her friend toward the exit. "We'll talk soon, all right?"

The last thing Clara needed now was one of Therese's boyfriend stories!

When she returned to the two men, she said, "Excuse me, but in the midst of all this, I completely neglected to introduce you. Klaus, this is Laszlo Kovac, our new parfumier from Grasse. Laszlo, this is Klaus Kohlwitz, our chemist. He runs the manufactory. The three of us will be working together very closely.

The men shook hands and exchanged a few words. For the first time since her arrival, Clara exhaled properly. At least here the chemistry seemed to work. She turned to Laszlo and said, "I'm sorry that such chaos is the first thing you see. I can't begin to imagine what is going through your head right now. Everything *was* running like clockwork, which is why I'm utterly stupefied to find it like this." She sighed. "I had planned to take you to the Star guesthouse. You'll feel at home with the Bauer family until we've found an apartment for you. And then I wanted to introduce you to your new job. But I fear I have some fires to put out first."

"It's very nice of you to want to get me settled, but it isn't necessary. I'd much rather help *you* extinguish at least one of the fires," Laszlo said. "If you and Mr. Kohlwitz have no objection, I can speak with the women. I will have to work side by side with them in any case, so it will be an opportunity to get to know them. And perhaps it isn't a bad thing if someone from outside mediates. I imagine you won't ask the women to use the damaging gloves?"

Clara looked at him in consternation. "Lord, no! I don't want to hurt the women! The gloves were only there for the hygiene."

Klaus cleared his throat. "I assumed you would approve and went ahead and ordered two dozen pairs of rubber gloves through Weingarten Pharmacy. They should be delivered today. The price is certainly higher than those your husband bought, but—"

"As if the price is of any interest," Clara scoffed. "Thank you, Mr. Kohlwitz, you've done well. And yes, I would be happy to have you talk to the women," she said to Laszlo. "The sooner we can start production again, the better. Mr. Kohlwitz can give you the address of Justine Kaiser. She's the forewoman. If you can get her to return to work, the others will follow her example, I'm sure. I'll go to both of the Meersburg shops today and deal with Baden-Baden tomorrow." She smiled apologetically at Laszlo. "I fear it will be a few days before we can start working together properly."

Laszlo smiled back. "There's something to be said for putting out fires together."

And Clara, for the first time since her arrival, laughed.

They agreed to meet the following morning in the manufactory to see where things stood, then Laszlo and Klaus left. Clara stayed behind, pensive. Wasn't someone missing from this firefighting team? Where was Stefan?

"How could you let things get so far?" was the first question Clara threw at her husband when he finally appeared in their apartment late that afternoon.

"Can't I at least welcome you home properly? Such trifles aren't worth all this uproar, are they?" he said, going to Clara. He leaned to kiss her, but she turned her face away.

Then she planted her hands on her hips and said, "Stefan! What's going on here? The women are striking, suppliers have deserted us, the day-to-day work in the shops is falling apart. And then this!" She held the letter with the calamitous news from Baden-Baden under his nose.

"What of it? That's good!" he cried, when he had scanned the few lines. He looked at Clara seriously. "I wanted to toss Senta Schmauder and her colleagues out on their ear when I was there. Drinking coffee and lazing around at our expense—that was their idea of hard work! Empty chairs mean no income, but that made no difference to them, oh no! And I fear their accounting has been, let's say, less than accurate. When I dropped in unannounced, I found the register all but empty. Be happy that you're rid of them, drive to Baden-Baden tomorrow, and hire new ones. Simple."

"*Simple!*" Clara almost choked. "It's anything but *simple*. I trained all three of them with care, and after that I left Sophie in Baden-Baden for a long time to make sure that everything was running smoothly. It will be *weeks* before I have any new women up to that level. And besides, a trip to Baden-Baden right now does not fit well at all, not now that I've hired a new parfumier." Her thoughts turned longingly to the crate of essences, herbs, and other fragrant ingredients she had bought in Grasse. She found it hard to believe what Stefan was telling her. She had come to know Senta Schmauder as an exceptionally reliable person. Could she really have been so mistaken about someone? She would probably only find the real answer to that question in Baden-Baden. Clara decided not to pursue the point for the time being.

"What's going on at the manufactory? And why are the suppliers deserting us? Klaus Kohlwitz says you've been trying to pay them unfair prices."

"Kohlwitz! As a chemist, I'm sure he knows all about business matters! He should stick to making sure the women do as they're told," Stefan spat back. "And what is this inquisition about?" A deep, indignant crease appeared on his forehead, and his eyes flashed angrily. "I was slaving away while you were off having a wonderful time in France, and all

I hear when you get back are unfounded accusations. The old suppliers didn't desert us. *I* exchanged them for wholesalers who can supply the same products for a lower price. There is no reason for you to get upset about that. And as far as the women in the manufactory are concerned, if they were my responsibility, this strike would not be happening, I can tell you that! Today they whine about the gloves, tomorrow it will be some ingredient that's making their eyes water, and the day after that it'll be something else. All of it is because they want more money, but they're not having their way with me!"

"I'm hearing all this for the first time," said Clara, suddenly a little unsure of herself. "If they want more money, they can just say so, can't they?"

Stefan laughed. "Clara, Clara . . . When it comes to others, you are a picture of benevolence. But with me, all you do is look for mistakes. You disparage what I do! Am I supposed to cringe around like a beaten dog? I did enough of that when I was a child. Are you trying to take over my father's role?" He looked at her intently, and for a moment Clara was afraid that he would burst into tears.

"Stefan, please, I didn't mean it like that," she began. "I'm just amazed that you—"

"Ah, you're *amazed*. How would it be if, for once, you *admired* me, as a man might expect from his loving wife!" He laughed bitterly. "It's really sad. You have all the time in the world for your business, you're constantly applauding Klaus Kohlwitz, and I guess you'll soon be singing the praises of the man from Grasse. But have you ever stopped to think how much your behavior hurts me?" He snatched his hat and stepped past her to the door. "I have an appointment. If I'd known you were coming back today, I would have postponed it. But you don't fill me in on your plans. All that counts around here is your word, and everyone else has to toe the line."

Dismayed and hurt, Clara watched him leave. His last words cut like a whip. Had she really turned into such a domineering person?

357

Did she have to have the final word in everything? Then she wouldn't be one bit better than Gerhard, under whose despotic rule she had once suffered so long. And that would be terrible.

The next morning, when Clara packed her bag again, this time for the journey to Baden-Baden, Stefan was still asleep. She was almost glad of that. She had had trouble getting to sleep herself, thinking about his accusations and the whole mess. What could she say to him? She had no idea even how to begin. No, she would let him sleep and leave a note for him. *Forgive me. I love you. We'll talk when I get back.*

She already had the pen in her hand, but the words wouldn't come. Slowly, she set her pen down again.

The next cut of the whip came in Baden-Baden. A new beauty shop had opened, not even a hundred yards from her Bel Étage, which looked gloomy and abandoned. Belle de Jour was operated by a Baden-Baden hotelier, and it was there that her three beauty experts now worked.

Clara had never given any thought to competition, but to have it appear now that she was in such a difficult position unsettled her so much that she felt like fleeing. *No backing down!* she said sternly to herself. Then, gritting her teeth, she opened the door of the new shop.

The bell rang melodically as she entered. The treatment room was spacious, well lit, and painted pale yellow. The space was brightened by women's laughter, and there was a penetrating smell of violets in the air. Clara immediately saw three treatment stations, but before she could look around any more, Emma appeared, smiling and wearing a pale-yellow apron.

"Good afternoon, what—" Emma's smile froze when she recognized Clara. Startled, she took a step back, then looked around to her colleagues for support.

"Is Senta here?" Clara asked quietly.

The young woman dashed away to get Senta.

"I'm really so terribly sorry," said Senta, and Clara could hear the true regret in her voice. "I would gladly have continued, but your husband . . ."

When Clara stepped outside again ten minutes later, she felt so angry and so let down that she was blind and deaf to all around her. She did not even react when someone called her name. She walked to Lichtentaler Allee, where she sank as if numb onto the first bench she reached.

Could it be true that Stefan had behaved so unfairly? Had he really helped himself to the contents of the register as Senta had claimed? He had accused the women of taking money, and whenever she spoke to him, others were always at fault, never he. His overbearing father. The ill-willed suppliers. The insolent employees . . .

Clara bit her bottom lip so hard that it hurt. She had accepted every word he said as unvarnished truth and never probed deeper. But in recent weeks, the picture she had of him had transformed, had become overlaid with scratches, cracks, and dark shadows.

Was he the man she thought him to be at all?

The question was there before Clara could hide from it. And as if it had been waiting in ambush all along came another frightening thought: Had she chosen the wrong man a second time? And if she had, what would that mean for her? She suddenly felt very hot. Fragments of images appeared in her mind's eye. The court in Berlin. The judge in his black robes. The patchwork of voices . . . *"There! The tramp!"* *"A divorced woman. Disgusting!"* Fingers pointing at her . . .

Clara began to breathe faster, and her heart was pounding. She would not go through something like that again.

"Mrs. Berg! Hello! Can you hear me, Mrs. Berg?"

She looked up. It was like peering through fog. Her heart was still racing as she made out the well-to-do couple standing in front of her, looking at her expectantly.

It took a moment for Clara to realize who it was. "Mr. and Mrs. Loblein!" she exclaimed with relief. She stood up and shook hands with the industrialist from Stuttgart and his wife, who was a customer at the Bel Étage–Baden-Baden. "Excuse me, I'm afraid I was lost in thought. The business, you know. We're going through some changes . . ." Clara was certain Mrs. Loblein was going to complain about a missed appointment.

"Didn't I tell you that Mrs. Berg was probably spying out something new? That's why the shop is closed. A businesswoman like her always has new plans," said Mrs. Loblein gleefully to her husband. Without waiting for him to reply, she turned back to Clara.

"But perhaps you'd still like to hear an idea I've had. It's like this: above our emporium, which is right by the market square in Stuttgart, the first floor has suddenly become free. The seamstress who used to rent the rooms has moved out to the edge of the city. And then I thought . . . well . . ." She cleared her throat, then said in a rush of words, "I wanted to ask you if you wouldn't perhaps be interested in opening a Bel Étage in Stuttgart. All my friends would come to visit you, and of course I would, too."

"The rooms my wife is talking about are very nice indeed," her husband went on. "And it's not as if we don't have enough potential lessees in Stuttgart. But my wife wanted to give you the chance to look at everything first."

"Stuttgart?" Clara repeated.

"We're traveling back tomorrow. We could take you with us, if you like," Mrs. Loblein said, looking expectantly at Clara.

She would certainly have enough time to think everything through during the drive to Stuttgart, maybe even work out what to do about the Baden-Baden shop. She had to avoid jumping to conclusions.

Perhaps everything wasn't as bad as it looked. Work had always got her through her troubles in the past.

Clara took a deep breath, then gave the couple the best smile she could muster. "I have, in fact, been thinking about where to open my next shop. Maybe I should include Stuttgart in my plans?"

Chapter Thirty-Six

Laszlo had inherited his passion from his mother. And from his father, the engineer, he had learned self-control. And that was good, because otherwise anyone looking at him would have seen in an instant that he was hopelessly in love. And worse, that it had been love at first sight. Clara Berg had stolen his heart, and she didn't even know it. It hit him the very first moment that he had seen her talking with Monsieur Gayet. Was it her beauty? Her radiance, so warm and brilliant? Was it that she came from his father's homeland and that the German language flowed like music from her lips? Or maybe it was her charming smile, and that she seemed so strong, so sure of herself, but vulnerable at the same time. Laszlo knew that Clara Berg was the woman that he had been waiting for all his life. He felt bound to her as he did to no other person on earth. But she was his employer, and she was married. And because of that she could never discover the depth of his true feelings. How he was supposed to manage that, Laszlo did not know. But manage it he *must*.

***

It was a dejected Laszlo who left Justine Kaiser's house. He looked up at the restless sky and turned up the collar of his jacket. The weather had turned. The sunshine of recent days had given way to heavy, black clouds gathering over the lake. A gusty wind whistled through the streets, and the air smelled of seaweed and rain.

Thunderclouds. How appropriate. Laszlo's steps were heavy as he walked toward the manufactory.

At first, Justine Kaiser had not been willing to talk to him at all. But when he finally persuaded her that he was there in Clara's name—more, that he was Clara's trusted colleague—Justine began to talk.

"The gloves were just the final straw," she said miserably. "The new cleaning chemicals that Mr. Berg bought to clean the filling machine are so caustic that they practically eat the skin off your hands. And the fumes from the vinegar essence we use to rub down the stirring spoons, ladles, and other tools burns our eyes so much that they still tear up at night. I never knew vinegar to be as aggressive as that stuff. Clara Berg's creams might make other women beautiful, but they're going to be the end of us! And it's been this way for weeks."

Frowning, helpless, Laszlo couldn't do much more than listen and try to reassure the forewoman. "I promise you that you will not have to handle a single damaging chemical again," he had said. "Mr. Kohlwitz and I will go through our entire inventory this afternoon and check everything thoroughly. If you had spoken with Mrs. Berg about these problems, I'm sure she would have listened to you."

Justine had looked at him with skepticism and simply answered, "Mrs. Berg never sees us anymore."

What did that last sentence mean? Laszlo wondered as he walked by the Bel Étage in the Unterstadtstrasse. Clara's laboratory was just one floor above the production rooms of the manufactory. Didn't they see each other all the time?

As he paused to admire the elegant window display, everything painted in shades of lavender, the door opened, and the young woman Clara had gently but firmly sent away the day before stepped out.

"You're Clara's new parfumier, aren't you?" the woman asked and held out her hand. "I'm Therese Himmelsreich. I'm the hairdresser. I share the shop here with Clara." She was wearing a heavy perfume, and Laszlo could smell peonies, oak, and vanilla. The scent matched well with Therese's red hair.

"And you're a good friend of Mrs. Berg's," said Laszlo with a smile. "Clara told me about you on the train on the way here." Clara . . . It felt so good just to say her name. Good and a little dangerous.

"A friend . . ." Therese sighed sadly. "Whenever I need Clara the most, she's either in her laboratory and can't be disturbed, or she's off traveling, like right now." She held a piece of paper out to Laszlo. "This telegram just came. I'm lucky you've come by. I can spare myself the walk out to the manufactory to let you know."

Laszlo hurriedly read the spare message. A business matter required Clara to travel to Stuttgart, and until she returned a few days hence, he should work as best he could with Klaus Kohlwitz. The chemist could show him everything. She had instructions for her staff in the shops, too, but said nothing about the strike.

"See? Clara has no time for our friendship anymore." The hairdresser covertly wiped her eyes with the back of her hand.

Laszlo frowned. Was she crying? "Perhaps I can help you?" he said cautiously.

Therese burst out sobbing and ran back into the shop.

More confused than ever, Laszlo headed to the manufactory. Clara had no time for friendship? But she had spoken so warmly, so lovingly, about her friends.

***

He found Klaus at one of the production tables. The chemist was staring at a beaker that he had apparently been heating over the flame of a Bunsen burner. There was a thick notebook and several pencils on the table, as well as an accumulation of open bottles and jars. In the containers, Laszlo recognized pastes, oils, and various powders—were those the ingredients that went into Clara's products?

"Strange, very strange . . ." Klaus murmured to himself. Laszlo noticed the chemist's raven-black mustache was at an angle across one cheek as if, lost in thought, he had tugged at it too many times.

"May I ask what is so strange?"

Klaus Kohlwitz jumped in fright. He clearly had not heard Laszlo come in. But his expression changed to relief as soon as he saw the parfumier. "Oh, it's you," he said.

Laszlo handed him Clara's telegram. "I've just been to see Justine Kaiser. She and her workmates are ready to start work again, but on one condition," he said, when Klaus had finished reading the telegram, and he told him about his meeting with the forewoman. "I had to promise her that she and her colleagues would not be exposed to any more hazards. That . . . was what you wanted?" he added, suddenly feeling very presumptuous.

Klaus frowned and said, "I hope you haven't promised too much. I started analyzing the various ingredients early this morning. But I can't say I've learned very much. It's more the opposite: if this keeps up, pretty soon I won't know what to think!" He gestured toward a large dented metal container with a label that read "Liebnacht-Soda. Manufactured with the modern Solvay process."

"This soda ash, for example, comes from a very reputable maker with whom we have so far had only good experiences."

"But?" Laszlo glanced at the innocuous-looking white powder.

"Instead of the anhydrous Na_2CO_3, what they call calcined soda, that should be in this box, there's something completely different. Normally, to a hundred parts of salt, you would have eighty parts of sulfuric acid. But this soda has less than seventy parts sulfuric acid, and very impure at that. Can someone please explain *that* to me!" The chemist threw both hands in the air helplessly. "And that's not the only box where the label and the contents don't match." He pointed to another container. "*Rouge fraise*—it's a coloring agent that gives Mrs. Berg's soaps a pale-pink shade. It comes from a company called Guckelsberger, which is well known for quality and for using cochineal as the dyestuff. Cochineal is an organic red dye of the highest quality, and until today it has proven its worth. The problem with this container, however . . ." The chemist fell silent for a moment and shook his head. ". . . is that I can't find any cochineal in it, and find picric acid instead! Picric acid gives a slightly yellow coloring, which I am quite sure Mrs. Berg does not want in her soaps. But the much more serious problem is picric acid triggers very strong skin irritation. And—even worse—if you don't work with it properly, it can be explosive." Klaus looked around the room. "This entire place could be blasted to smithereens in a moment."

Laszlo furrowed his brow. The "Meersburg Affair," as he had begun thinking of the situation, was getting stranger and stranger.

"Containers with labels that wrongly declare the contents . . . Excuse me for asking so directly, but are you certain?"

The chemist laughed bitterly. "I've double-checked everything."

"Then we're talking about fraud. The companies have not been delivering what the packaging promises, but have sent lower quality and even dangerous substances instead. How is that possible?" Laszlo looked inquiringly at his new colleague.

"A better question is whether these producers know what is being perpetrated in their good names. Perhaps a counterfeiter copying their labels? For some time now, Mr. Berg hasn't been ordering the ingredients for our beauty products directly from the manufacturers, but through wholesalers. It was a puzzle to me from the start, how they could offer him better prices than buying directly from the producers. But a few things are now clear to me." He screwed up his mouth. "It's easy these days to copy packaging. And if you know how to do it, the contents can be easily swapped. Selling cheap product for a lot of money—and making customers believe they're getting the same quality as before. It's criminal, and a case for the Department of Health! I should be reporting what's going on here immediately. But . . ."

"What would that mean for Clara Berg? She'd probably get into all kinds of trouble," Laszlo said.

The men exchanged a look, and each saw the same thing: loyalty and devotion to Clara.

"I don't know how to tell Mrs. Berg about this," Klaus said in hushed tones. "It will break her heart, for a number of reasons."

Both fell silent for a long, helpless moment.

Then Klaus took the open jars and containers and began throwing them into a large steel trash can. "It's no wonder the women who work here developed rashes. This terrible stuff belongs in the trash, not in our production. And certainly not on any woman's face."

Working together, it only took them a few minutes to throw it all away.

"What now? Until we restock with good quality raw materials, production can't start again, can it? And that means no treatments in the shops," said Laszlo as they wiped down the tables.

"And *that* means no money coming in, that our own salaries are in danger, that everything that Clara Berg has put so much into setting up is at risk." The chemist snorted and his expression was grim. "I'm as sure as I can be that Mrs. Berg knows nothing about all this. Her husband is responsible for everything that comes in. He scared off our old, reliable partners, and I don't know what he's arranged with the new ones, these so-called wholesalers." The disdain in his voice was obvious.

"You think Mr. Berg knows that his suppliers don't deliver what they're supposed to? Then he's abetting their fraud."

"At the very least, he doesn't seem to care much that his wife ends up with low-quality materials. As long as he can save a few marks or line his own pockets."

"He's jeopardizing his wife's entire livelihood!" Although he hadn't even met Stefan Berg, Laszlo already felt anger toward him that was strong and growing stronger. How could he cheat his wife like that? How could he knowingly risk the health of the workers and the women who used Clara's creams and lotions? What kind of person would do that? He wanted to ask Klaus all these questions. But they had known each other less than two days, and it took time to build that kind of trust.

"Problem found, problem solved, as my old professor always said. This junk won't hurt anyone anymore." Klaus nodded with satisfaction toward the trash can. "What matters now is to get a new supply of good raw materials. If only Mrs. Berg were here." The chemist began toying with his mustache again. "Talking to her husband makes no sense. All I can do is take it on myself to go to Weingarten Pharmacy this afternoon and order the most important materials there. From good suppliers for a fair price! With a little luck, most of it will still be delivered this week, and we can start production again."

"If you like, I'll come along," said Laszlo.

The chemist looked at him in surprise. "Your offer does you credit, but are you aware that we'd be putting *both* our jobs on the line? What if Mrs. Berg throws us both out for exceeding our authority? Of if her husband does? I wouldn't put anything past him."

Laszlo returned the chemist's look steadily and said, "Clara Berg will make the right decision."

"I will tell you this now—for the time you've been on strike, you will not get a pfennig of your wages. I'd like nothing more than to throw out all of you. And that's exactly what I'll do if even one of you starts to complain!"

Stefan looked out over the assembled workforce. "Now get to work! For the next two weeks, I expect three hours overtime every day to make up for the backlog." The women, who had stood there in their white aprons and listened half-afraid, half-angry, began to dissipate, but they heard a different man's voice, and they stopped still.

"Stay just another moment, please." Laszlo lifted his right hand in the air.

"What—" Stefan, irritated, started to say, but Laszlo did not react.

"For those who don't know me, my name is Laszlo Kovac. I am the new parfumier, and together with Mr. Kohlwitz, I will ensure that the beauty products you make here in the Bel Étage Manufactory don't just make women look good, but that the products also smell good." He smiled engagingly at the gathered women. Tentatively, they smiled back.

"First of all, I want to thank all of you for returning to work. As for your wages, I can't say anything about that, though I am sure that as soon as Mrs. Berg returns, she will find a good solution. I also think that Mrs. Berg will have something to say about overtime." He glanced sideways at Stefan, but before he could say anything, Laszlo continued. "There is one more thing I would like to add before we all get back to work, and I speak for Mr. Kohlwitz as well." He looked from one woman to the next, his expression earnest but not unfriendly. "You can come to us at any time—*any* time—if something in the production process is not in order. It makes no difference: defective gloves or bad raw materials. Your observations are critically important to us, because only when we all pull in one direction can we manufacture products of the highest quality. *You* are the experts, and *you* are the first to notice if something is not as it ought to be."

The women looked at each other in surprise. They relaxed their tense shoulders and faces, and they lifted their chins. No one had ever spoken to them in this way.

"You . . . you think you can come here and—" Stefan began, puffing himself up, but his voice was lost in the applause and excited voices of the women.

Until that moment, Clara had observed everything in silence from just outside the doorway. Like a stranger, an outsider, she had witnessed the meeting, overheard the men. If she were working at one of the tables here, whom would she trust? The good-looking Italian in his elegant, tailor-made suit, flailing his hand in the air like a furious general? Or the pale stranger in work pants, his gold-brown eyes shining like polished amber? Her thoughts were interrupted by the women's appreciative applause, and she smiled to see her employees return to their work tables.

The next moment, Stefan rushed toward her. "You're back, finally," he said. "Things can't work like this, Clara. Your new perfume-*meister*—"

She raised her hand authoritatively. "Not here, not now. Please get out the ledgers for the past year. I'll be in my office in a few minutes and would like to go through all the books. *Then* we can talk." She walked away from him and went to Klaus and Laszlo and, unlike with her husband, greeted them warmly and shook both men's hands.

"You've done well, gentlemen. It looks as if the worst of the crisis is over." Laszlo's hand felt warm and comfortable in hers. "I have good news, too. I will very soon be opening a fourth shop, this time in Stuttgart. I've already signed the lease, and am looking forward to getting started there as soon as possible." She exhaled deeply with relief; things seemed to be moving forward again.

The two men exchanged a glance. Klaus cleared his throat, then said, "I fear your good mood will be short-lived. I have to tell you some rather bad news."

Clara listened expressionlessly to what Klaus had to say. It was not as if she were frozen, or as if she were hearing the chemist's words through a veil of fog. It was the opposite—Clara had never heard or understood something as clearly as she did Klaus's words. She was discomfited, embarrassed. In her heart of hearts, Clara knew that what he was telling her amounted to one thing: her husband was a liar and a cheat. His wheeling and dealing had endangered the health of their employees and their customers, and he had risked permanent damage to her reputation.

But something—a kind of unyielding shell, like a cocoon—protected Clara from falling apart with pain and disappointment. Maybe she had grown this protective shell during her journey to Stuttgart. Then again, she may have grown the same impenetrable armor if she had returned home directly from Baden-Baden. Clara did not know. But what she did know was that she was prepared to face the bitter truth that for the second time in her life she had been wrong about a man. She would think about the consequences of that truth later. When she found the courage.

"Thank you for your frankness. Nothing like this will happen again. I will make sure of that," she told Klaus and Laszlo. "I can only hope that my ignorance does not mean that I have lost your trust." Both men immediately assured her that that was not the case, and that they were on her side.

It was with a heavy heart that Clara left them and went to her office, where she wanted to examine the books that Stefan, to her astonishment, had in fact laid out neatly for her on the desk they shared. Clara had expected him to be present and to have a matching fairy tale at the ready for every dubious document. But the office was empty. Did he sense that she was no longer prepared to believe his lies?

She began with the file marked "Miscellaneous Business Expenses" and found invoices for bars, restaurants, and tailors. Invoices for the rental of expensive yachts and visits to the racetrack in Munich, hotel bills and Baden-Baden bistros.

"Miscellaneous Business Expenses"—Stefan might as well have written "Stefan Berg's Entertainment" on the file.

Next came the "Suppliers" folder. Orders placed, invoices. She was shocked to find that apart from the mold-casting company that made her soap forms, she did not know even one of these suppliers personally. What had happened to Meinrad Kornbichler? Or to Valentin Gross, who specialized in cocoa butter? When had Stefan abandoned them? And why? It could not have been for cheaper prices, because the invoices from the new wholesalers who supplied them now were no cheaper at all! Prices like that for low quality goods—was there other money changing hands? Clara felt more and more anger gathering inside her.

What an idiot she'd been. She had handed over the ordering process and all the accounts. She had been convinced that Stefan would take care of everything. After all, didn't he love the Bel Étage just as she had set it up? That mistaken belief had been enough to lull her into a passivity bordering on neglect.

Clara sniffed contemptuously when she found a bill for three bottles of perfume. *Fleur Exotique*—she could not stand the stuff! It was pungent and smelled cheap. She would never use it in her production. *How careless of Stefan,* she thought bitterly. He should have filed that under "Miscellaneous Business Expenses" . . . She swept the file off the desk in anger. How stupid Klaus must think she was. And what an impression Laszlo must have gotten of her! Surely he was regretting ever deciding to follow her to Meersburg.

She had begun to think she could stand on a pedestal with businesswomen like Lilo, Isabelle, and Josephine. But all along, she'd been an ignorant, blind fool. Clara's shame was bitter and painful. With her head in her hands, she stared down at her desk.

"Oh, thank God! I thought I'd never see you again! It's a catastrophe . . ."

Clara looked up. Therese was standing in front of her desk. She had not even heard her come in.

"What is it?" she asked tiredly.

The hairdresser pulled up a chair and sat across the desk from Clara. "You know that Benno von Nordmannsleben and I have been a couple since last September. At least, that's what I *thought*. But now that I—"

"Therese," Clara interrupted her. "Can't you see what's going on here?" She pointed to the mountain of documents on her desk. "I feel like the ground has fallen out from under my feet. If we're talking about *catastrophes*, I'm quite sure I can keep up." She stood up and walked around the desk.

"But you don't even know what the matter is!" Therese looked at Clara with hurt in her eyes.

Clara sighed loudly. "Don't think badly of me, but I really don't have time right now for another story about one of your men. Let's have coffee in a few days, then you can tell me all about it in peace and quiet."

Therese had been holding her handbag on her lap, and she now pulled it up to her chest and pushed back her chair. "Drink your coffee with someone else. You've shown just how interested you really are in me," said Therese, then stormed out of the office.

Chapter Thirty-Seven

It took three attempts for Stefan to get the key into the lock. Vodka cocktails! They might not get him drunk, but they certainly made him unsteady. He stumbled into the apartment. Everything was dark and quiet. He was relieved that he did not have to deal with Clara. Surely she would interrogate him about every little detail in the books, and he was not up for that right now. It was well past midnight, but he wasn't tired in the slightest. Maybe a nightcap would remedy that.

He went into the living room and was feeling around for the light switch when the chandelier suddenly lit up. Stefan startled.

Clara was sitting in the gold-upholstered armchair by the window. No, she was *enthroned* in it. With her back as stiff as if she'd swallowed a broomstick, his wife stared straight at him.

"Why aren't you asleep? You must be worn out after such a strenuous day," he said.

"After everything I've had to go through today, I can't sleep," said Clara in a voice as cold as ice. "Sit!" She pointed to the second armchair.

Stefan glanced despairingly toward the silver tray with its glass carafes on the sideboard. If he poured himself a cognac now, he would be giving Clara more ammunition. And it looked like her rifles were already loaded. As obediently as a hound, he sat down. "What is it?"

As expected, a litany of complaints followed. Excessive spending. Questionable invoices for perfume and flowers. Falsely labeled deliveries . . . Stefan's head was throbbing, and he had trouble following all of Clara's allegations. Gripe, gripe, gripe. But even if he was not listening to every detail, he could hear clearly enough how serious it all was to his wife. This time, he would not get away with a flimsy excuse.

"Have you ever stopped to consider what it feels like for a man to get no more than pocket money, like a schoolboy?" he asked when she finally stopped. "Can you imagine how miserable I feel?"

Clara sniffed and shook her head. "If I drank as much alcohol as you do every evening, I'd feel miserable, too. And don't talk to me about pocket money. You get a generous salary as manager. But I'm wondering if you come close to earning it, considering your proclivity for amusing yourself. Tomorrow morning, I will be writing a new contract for you; your authority will be substantially reduced. I'm sorry, but you brought this on yourself."

Although she was working hard to maintain her composure, Stefan could see how upset she was. "I brought this on myself?" he repeated with exaggerated horror. "Isn't it more that, in your eyes, I'm a hopeless failure? It doesn't matter what I do; I can never do things well enough for you. I admit that not all my decisions in recent months have been smart or correct. But whose fault is it that I'm a bundle of nerves? Thanks to your perpetual complaints, my self-confidence is gone, utterly gone. Before we met, I was a successful hair trader. No, I was the *best*. And I gave that up for *you*. Because I believed that we could do great things together, and because I thought you would trust me as I trust you. I even took your name—could there be any greater proof of my trust? And what thanks do I get? None. Just never-ending suspicion."

"Stefan, that isn't true. I—"

"No! Now it's my turn," he interrupted her. He leaned forward and looked Clara straight in the eyes. "Did it ever occur to you that *I* might also have been taken in by the fraudulent wholesalers? How can you assume I'd collude with criminals like that? And how can you assume that I see other women behind your back, let alone give them gifts? If you found receipts for flowers and perfumes, it is because I bring gifts for the hostesses at parties I attend, where I do my very best to promote Bel Étage! That you would assume anything else cuts me to the quick . . ." He rubbed his eyes until they first burned, then teared up. He let out a sob. "All I wanted was to do things right for you. I wanted you to look up to me the way I look up to you. I wanted you to be proud of me. Proud of *us*. You and me—we make such a wonderful team."

Vodka doesn't just make the Russians sentimental, he thought grimly. Abruptly, he buried his face in his hands. His shoulders heaved.

"Stefan, please." Clara stroked his back gently. He sobbed louder. "Don't cry, don't. That's so terrible, I . . ." She trailed off helplessly.

He took his hands from his face and looked at Clara through teary eyes. "Bella Clara, I love you more than anything in the world. I gave up my family for you, left everything I had behind. How can you kick me like a stray dog?" Because he had only drunk vodka, he hoped his breath didn't smell of alcohol. He touched his lips to her cheek. A kiss as light as a feather. She let him. Then the other cheek, which Clara turned to him. Delicate kisses on her forehead, her eyelids, fluttering kisses, like a butterfly's wings.

"Clara, *mi amore* . . ." His arms slipped around her; his kisses grew more urgent.

He heard her choking sigh, felt her resistance fall away. *"Mi amore,"* he breathed again. "Come, let me show you, let me prove how much I love you."

***

It was ten in the morning when Stefan, freshly shaved and feeling confident, set off for the manufactory. The previous day's thunderstorm had blown off toward Switzerland, and a bright sun shone from a polished sky; its rays lit a path for him to a brilliant future.

They had made love not once but twice the night before, and Clara, as expected, had melted into his arms along with all her hostility. That was the last he'd hear about a contract with reduced authority! After a night of lovemaking and with the coup he was planning that day, Clara would be eating out of his hand again.

Stefan took a deep, satisfied breath. He could count himself lucky that he had such a way with women.

He had learned one lesson from the whole affair: in the future, he would need to be more careful. Clara was not dumb, and she now had two watchdogs as allies, Klaus Kohlwitz and that man from Bohemia. The disdain with which Laszlo had looked at him—sheer impertinence! He would have to make sure that Clara's two lackeys fell out of favor with her, and the sooner the better. Stefan rubbed his hands together. The manufactory came into sight, and he walked faster. There was a lot to do.

"Have you considered using the same name for your low-cost range as for your luxury line?"

Clara laughed. "Can you read minds, Mr. Kovac? In fact, I've been thinking about just that for quite some time, and I've concluded that a new name would allow the two to be clearly differentiated." She smiled at the parfumier, then slowly said, "What do you think of the name . . . Belle Époque?"

"Belle Époque." He spoke the two words, testing them aloud. "A beautiful era—it fits. Times have really changed for the better for women, haven't they?"

How long is she just going to ignore me? Stefan thought angrily. He'd been standing in the doorway for what felt like five minutes. He cleared his throat loudly.

Clara and Laszlo moved apart like lovers caught in the act.

Stefan felt like nothing more than hounding the man out of the building and down the road. But Clara seemed to be crazy for the man, so he had to move cautiously. He forced himself to smile.

"Clara, my love, what's this I hear about a 'low-cost' line? I thought you'd given up on that harebrained idea long ago." A low-cost line! They were there to earn as much money as possible, not to make products cleaning women and waitresses could afford to smear on their faces.

"Oh, far from it," said Clara gaily.

Was he mistaken, or was the smile she gave him less friendly than the one she had given her parfumier? And was that a trace of derision he heard in her voice?

"I think it's wonderful that women of simpler means will soon be able to afford my products," Clara went on.

Wonderful?! Stefan was growing more irritated, but he clenched his teeth and waved off the idea as casually as he could.

"Whatever you think is best. I'm here about something more important." He looked intently at the parfumier, a clear signal that he was intruding on a conversation between husband and wife. But either the man was utterly insensitive or simply didn't care that Stefan was disturbed by his presence.

"Have you heard that your friend Countess Zuzanna is selling her Villa Carese? The house would be ideal for us. Very impressive and with an excellent view over the lake. Many rooms, plenty of space for the chil . . . you know," he corrected himself at the last moment. *Very nice,* he silently praised himself. Clara could do with a little reminder that he knew her secrets. "To get to the point—it is a dream house. But I don't need to tell you that. You know your way around there far better than I do."

"Zuzanna is selling her house?"

Ha! That little snippet not only took her by surprise, but has thrown her train of thought completely, Stefan thought, sure of his ground. He straightened up. "I've already arranged a time for us to look at it. Of course, she's asking an absolutely exorbitant price, and I have no plans to—"

"It's good that you have no plans." Clara interrupted him so suddenly that he was taken aback. Gently but firmly, she placed one hand on his shoulder and steered him toward the door. When they were out of the parfumier's hearing, she whispered, "We have both made mistakes in recent months. I put too much burden on you. After all that has happened, it is best that I make all the important decisions alone for now. Your new contract is waiting in my office. I had it drafted early this morning. Take as much time as you need to read it and sign it."

He looked at her in bewilderment. Had he heard her correctly? "What are you talking about? I thought we sorted out everything last night?"

"Please don't worry. Contracts can always be changed again. For now, I think we should let some water pass under the bridge," said Clara in her most conciliatory tone. She stroked his arm softly. "As for Zuzanna's villa, I'll think about it."

***

So this was what true love felt like. Despairing, lost. Therese plucked one of the stalks of grass grown beside the park bench on which she sat. The sharp edge of the grass cut into the flesh of her finger, but she barely noticed. She looked far out across the lake, where the water dissolved into nothingness.

In the past, she had only toyed with men. She loved all of it: the flirtatious glances, the exuberant dancing, the erotic nights. Other, deeper feelings like love and trust were extras, like an embroidered handkerchief given as a bonus if you bought an elegant robe. Something she could easily have lived without. Something that was easily lost.

Then Benno von Nordmannsleben came into her life. And from the first time they met, she knew: with him, everything was different. She wanted him without hesitation, and she had believed that he would return the deep love she felt for him.

But now here she was. More lost than she had ever been in her life. Filled with feelings she could not even name.

"A child?" Benno had looked at her with utter disbelief. "It isn't mine!" he immediately said, claiming that he had been careful every time. "If you think you can saddle me with your brat, then think again. You're not the first to try that." All his gallantry and elegance vanished in a second. Suddenly, she was facing an angry man with a contorted, beet-red face.

"I thought we were in love," she had said helplessly. "I thought we had a future together." She had held one hand protectively over her belly.

When her monthly bleeding did not come for the third month, she had been overjoyed. A child! A child from her beloved Benno. The most beautiful jewel in the crown of their love.

"You really have a vivid imagination!" he had said contemptuously. "I am an officer. My first love is and always will be the Queen Olga regiment. And if you ever thought anything else, you were deluding yourself." Without another word, he had stormed off. He had left her there without even *trying* to make the situation more bearable for her.

Therese sobbed. The little foaming caps of the waves on the lake blurred before her eyes. The story was repeating itself! Once again, she was pregnant and abandoned.

Wasn't she worth it? To be loved? And the words that the men whispered in her ear . . . all lies? What had she done wrong?

She heard laughter as a group of tourists strolled past her along the lakeshore esplanade. Young women carried lacy parasols. Men swung their walking sticks as if drawing delirious patterns in the air. One woman led a small dog on a silver-studded leash.

Therese was reminded of Countess Zuzanna. Was the dog that Clara had once saved from drowning still alive?

What had happened to her would never happen to a woman like the countess. Women like Zuzanna, Clara, and Lilo were smart, and not only when it came to business, but in every respect. And she herself was nothing but a dumb, trusting little girl.

That realization made Therese cry again. Then she gulped for air and felt as if she could not breathe. How was she supposed to go on? Alone, with a child . . . the very thought of it made her dizzy with fear. She didn't have her own life under control. How could she ever look after a child?

***

Mr. Stefan Berg's position as manager is hereby discontinued, effective immediately.

Mr. Berg shall continue to act in his role as public representative of the company Bel Étage, and shall promote the company positively. For this, he will have at his disposal an allowance of 80 marks per month. All expenses over and above that amount are to be approved in advance by Clara Berg as the sole manager.

Signed: Clara Berg, Meersburg, 5 May 1910

Countersigned: Stäuble, attorney-at-law, Meersburg, 5 May 1910

Stefan stared in disbelief at his new contract. Never in his life had he felt as debased as he did in that moment.

"We have both made mistakes . . ." He heard Clara's saccharine words in the back of his mind. Really? If they both had made mistakes, why was *he* the only one to pay for it?

For a moment, he was tempted to storm right into the laboratory and take the arrogant, miserly witch to task on the spot. But he composed himself. With the anger he felt just then, there was no telling what he would do.

And in her effort to demean him, she had even gone to a lawyer! He tore the contract into a thousand tiny pieces and let them fall on Clara's desk like petals. She could not treat him like that!

In his fury, he ran from the building, then stopped and looked around. Where would he go? The Bar Coco? The yacht club? He walked aimlessly in the direction of the shore, and his thoughts were as aimless as his feet.

Clara, with her angelic face but more ruthless and arrogant than anyone he'd ever known. What did his wife think she was doing? An "allowance" of eighty marks! Wasn't he even worth a salary anymore? It was an affront.

He kicked the gravel so hard that the stones flew in the air. A second later, close by, he heard a squeal of pain and saw that he had hit a woman sitting on one of the lakeshore benches with the gravel. It was Therese, of all people, sitting there with slumped shoulders.

"You've got a lot of energy this morning," she said, rubbing her leg.

"Unlike you," he growled back, not wanting to stop. Therese was the last thing he needed.

"So stop and sit for a while. Or we could go and have a glass of champagne somewhere. I could use a little diversion," said Therese, holding on to his sleeve as he walked past. "Oh, come on. Your wife doesn't have any time for me as it is."

"Does it surprise you that Clara has no time for you?" He sniffed and looked at her with distaste. "In case you didn't know it, for Clara you're no more than a useless, wanton little trollop. My wife laughs about people like you. You're unreliable, and you let yourself be kept like a common whore," he said.

Therese looked at him, her eyes wide.

Stefan took a deep breath, then continued in a gleeful tone: "Worst of all, in Clara's eyes, you are utterly incapable as a businesswoman. In short, you are nothing, a zero, a nobody. The world would not be a poorer place if you were not in it."

He gave her a final disparaging grunt, then turned so abruptly that the gravel crunched beneath the sole of his shoe.

***

Therese continued to sit, feeling nothing, numb. *"You are nothing, a zero, a nobody."* Stephan's words droned in her head, pressed against her forehead, wanting to get out, away, to escape across the water.

As if guided by an unseen hand, Therese stood up. *A nothing. A zero. A nobody.* Slow as an old lady, she tottered down to the water.

She was a nothing. Clara laughed about her, looked down on her. And probably everybody else did, too.

The water was cold. It penetrated her thin leather shoes at the first step.

Stefan . . . he had sounded so full of hate. And how he had looked down at her. At her, the nothing.

The water was up to her thighs. Therese exhaled, and the air came out like a sigh. Her dress rose around her, floating atop the water like a carpet.

You are nothing, a zero, a nobody. The world would not be a poorer place if you were not in it.

The water had reached her throat. The little waves washed over her face, and she had to puff and blow to breathe. But she didn't want to puff and blow—she wanted to go out farther. Out where the great emptiness was. The nothing, which she would receive with open arms.

She could not swim. She had never tried to learn. Why bother? The big party always took place on dry land. Clara could swim. So could Lilo. Just from that, you could see how clever they were. They knew how light one felt immersed in water. Like you were weightless. They knew how one's cares grew smaller, became weaker . . . exactly like her . . .

***

"Let's go and get some something to eat. I'm hungry," said Clara to Laszlo, shortly before midday.

They had spent the entire morning talking about the new product line. A face cream, a facial toner, and a general skin cream—that would be enough to start. Laszlo had suggested using a lavender scent for the new line. It was not expensive, yet it was very popular with almost all women. Clara, who was very fond of lavender, had agreed. Clara chose a simple restaurant situated directly by the shore of Lake Constance. The proprietor was a fisherman, and his wife prepared his catch for diners. Fried in butter, spiced with herbs, potatoes and vegetables on the side—that was all the restaurant offered.

"I've always wanted to eat here," said Clara, piercing a delicate piece of fish with her fork. The gentle sloshing of the water along the shore was the loveliest background music she could imagine. The fight with Stefan, their reconciliation—she had not slept a wink the previous night. But to her own amazement, she felt fresh and cheerful.

"Why haven't you?" Laszlo asked.

"It just never happened," she said with a shrug. Stefan would never have been satisfied with the plain tables, hungry enough for the simple food, or thirsty enough to drink out of the heavy glass beer steins. When it came to being picky, he was worse than her most spoiled customers.

The waitress came to their table with a steaming bowl. "More potatoes?"

They looked at each other, nodded, and laughed. Work had made them hungry!

"You're the woman who sells all those lovely creams, aren't you? You can see it," the woman said. Suddenly, she reached out and stroked Clara's cheek. "I wish my skin was as soft as yours. But I can't afford what you sell."

Clara and Laszlo shared a conspiratorial look.

"That will soon change," said Clara, glancing at the woman's hands. They were rubbed raw and so dry that the skin was practically clinging to her bones. Clara spontaneously reached into her bag. Because she suffered from dry hands herself, she always kept a hand cream with her. "If you don't mind one that's already been opened, I'd like to give you this one," she said, and pressed the cream into the woman's hand.

"Thank you, madam. Thank you so much!"

When the waitress left the table, Clara turned back to Laszlo and said, "See? Less expensive products really are needed." And they went back to talking about the new line.

The early May sunshine felt comfortably warm against her back as she enjoyed the conversation and the food. *Why can't life always be this simple?* Clara thought a little wistfully. Why were there so many disruptions that made her despair about herself and everything she did? Why couldn't life just flow along easily and evenly? Was that kind of thinking naive?

"We should be getting back, shouldn't we?" said Laszlo, and nodded in the direction of the manufactory. His eyes were shining as if he could hardly wait to get back to work.

Clara smiled. As insecure as she was about many things, there was one that she knew beyond doubt: she could not have found a better man for her business than Laszlo Kovac.

She was still caught in that thought when Laszlo abruptly leaped to his feet. He ran down to the lakeshore and held his right hand to his forehead, shading his eyes from the sun.

"That's—"

Before Clara could grasp the situation, he had jumped into the water and was swimming out into the lake.

What . . . Clara's heart began to pound. At first glance, she saw no more than a dark figure in the water. It went under, then came up again. Zuzanna's little dog that she had once saved from drowning popped into her mind. Panic came over her as she realized that this time it was no animal out there in the water. She let out a loud scream, then ran to the woman who ran the restaurant and took her by the arm. "Go and find the lifeguards, quickly! There's a woman drowning out there!" As she spoke, she pulled off her cardigan, kicked off her shoes, and jumped into water.

They saved Therese at the last minute and hauled her to the shore. While Laszlo ran into the restaurant to find a blanket, Clara held her friend tightly.

"Therese, you get some crazy ideas sometimes," Clara murmured, weak but relieved.

"I'm so sorry," said Therese. Her entire body was trembling. "I could not see another way for me and the baby . . ."

Clara struggled with the bleakest conscience she had ever had. *"I really don't have time right now for another story about one of your men,"* she heard herself say. *"If we're talking about catastrophes, I'm quite sure I can keep up."*

Since her return from Grasse, she had shooed her friend away like a bothersome fly. The business, Stefan, her new ideas—everything else had been more important to her. She had not had any idea how deeply hurt Therese had been. What a terrible friend she was.

"I was so selfish and mean to you. It's unforgiveable," she whispered in Therese's ear as she choked back tears. "But from now on things will be different. I'll be there for you whenever you need me. And we'll take care of your child, too!"

Chapter Thirty-Eight

"My wife is not only a successful businesswoman; she has a soft spot for the weak and the poor of the world, as well," said Stefan, leaning over the table toward the lawyer as if he were revealing a secret. "Clara Berg is too modest to talk about herself in such terms, so allow me to mention one example: just recently, my wife spontaneously offered her support and financial assistance to a friend of hers—a woman who is unmarried and expecting a child, and who, given her desperate straits, tried to take her own life. When the child is born, I know that Mrs. Berg, as the child's godmother, will assume a role as benefactress for the child, as well."

With an effort, Clara smiled at her husband. "I'm not sure the attorney wants to hear all that," she said a little self-consciously.

"That stupid creature tried to kill herself? Why did you stop her?" Stefan had sneered at Clara, the evening after Therese's rescue. Clara had been struck dumb by the malice in his voice.

The lawyer conscientiously scribbled notes as Stefan spoke, then looked up and said, "In a case such as yours, every little piece of information is vital, in particular anything as positive as this. After what you have told me about the father of your children, we must assume that he will do everything to show you in the worst possible light."

He looked grimly at Clara. "Mr. Gropius will probably engage one of my colleagues from Friedrichshafen or Konstanz. In the coming weeks and months, if it happens that affable strangers appear and start asking unusual questions, be on your guard. Don't give away too much, weigh every word you say before you say it, because your statements may easily be twisted against you."

"You talk about my former husband as if you already know him very well indeed," Clara said, trying to lighten the conversation a little.

Stefan laughed, too. "Unfamiliar faces are the order of the day in vacation towns like Meersburg. If we were to meet every stranger with mistrust, my wife might as well shut up shop entirely next week. Isn't that right, darling?"

Clara looked at him from the corner of her eye. Why was Stefan's voice suddenly so shaky?

"I have nothing to hide," she said with conviction. "Gerhard can set his spies on me whenever he likes."

"If I were in your shoes, I would not treat the matter so lightly," the lawyer warned. "You want to win visitation rights for your children, rights that have already been taken away by a court. You are contesting a legally valid judgment, and that will require a great deal of determination. The other side will leave no stone unturned in trying to discredit you. Wasn't there a strike in your factory not long ago?"

Clara answered affirmatively, but added that the matter had been settled quickly and to the satisfaction of everyone involved.

The lawyer shook his head. "That's not the point, Mrs. Berg. The mere fact that your employees refused to work gives your adversaries enough ammunition to paint you in an extremely unflattering light. For that reason alone, it would perhaps be advisable to wait with the application and to let the proverbial dust settle on the matter a little longer." He looked from Clara to Stefan and back. "Please excuse my indiscretion, but is your marriage . . . sound?"

"Completely sound," said Stefan, and patted Clara's hand. "I will do everything I can to support my wife in her wish to see her children again."

The lawyer nodded, obviously relieved. "Very good. Because a marriage scandal is about the last thing we would want to rear its head." He withdrew a sheet of paper from his desk drawer and said, "Well, let's begin to sketch out a strategy. The question of whether I send your application to Berlin now or in a few weeks is something we can settle later."

"'A marriage scandal is about the last thing we would want to rear its head . . .'"

The door to the lawyer's office was barely closed when Stefan mocked the lawyer's words. He placed one arm around Clara's shoulders. "You and me and a scandal! There will never be anything like that for us, will there, my dear?" His voice practically dripped with derision.

Clara said nothing. She wanted his arm off her shoulders.

"I see we understand one another," Stefan said and pressed a kiss to her cheek. "Would you like me to accompany you back to the manufactory? I *do* have an appointment, but . . ." He shrugged, a sign of his willingness to compromise.

"Thank you, I'll manage by myself," said Clara tightly.

"I know that, my dear. By the way, I might be back a little later than usual today. I'm going for a drive with Estelle Morgan in her new Ford Model T. I like the car very much, maybe so much that I'll buy it." Stefan lifted his hat with exaggerated gallantry and walked away.

Clara's heart was heavy as she watched him go.

A new car. Countless visits to the best tailor in Friedrichshafen. More champagne tabs than ever before from the Bar Coco—and she signed for all of it and held her tongue. Instead of helping himself in underhand ways to company money, he simply took it.

390

Everything has its price, she thought dejectedly. The artificial facade. The marriage that only continued to exist on paper. Silence. Life itself. But she was prepared to pay anything to see her children again.

"You were right, dear Clara. Work really is the best medicine. Every day, I think of Benno a little less. And if my thoughts do turn to him, then I tell myself: what a bastard!"

Clara and Sophie laughed. "Exactly right," Clara said as she stood alongside Therese and Sophie, helping to fold a huge pile of freshly laundered towels. When was the last time she had done something like that? she wondered. The towels smelled of lavender, like the Bel Étage itself. She looked around her shop in the Unterstadtstrasse with pleasure. Everything was so lovely, so harmonious. She would have loved to work with her customers every day! The fragrances, the creams, the treatments . . . coming up with the right beauty regime for every customer and feeling how the skin relaxed beneath her hands, then the whole woman, too. Suddenly, her work in the laboratory and office seemed staid and bleak.

"For now I can still work, but what do I do when the child is here?" Therese said, pointing to her hairdresser's chair. "I can't really set a permanent wave with one hand and give the child a bottle with the other. But if I don't work, what am I supposed to live on? And the rent! My landlord looks at my belly every day, and I can see the question marks in his eyes! He and his wife are decent, church-going people, and then they have a single mother like me living in their house. What if he throws me out on the street? Where am I supposed to go? Into the poorhouse?" She sounded close to panic.

"As if I would stand around and watch you go to the poorhouse! I'm not going to leave you in the lurch a second time," Clara said vehemently. "There's a solution for everything. There always is. You will only work as long as you are able. And for the weeks before and after the birth, we'll think of something. Won't we, Sophie?"

"I've already had one idea." Sophie looked from Clara to Therese and back. "We could convert the hairdressing side into another treatment station for a few months. That way, half of the shop would not be empty, and we could help more customers."

Clara loved it. "What a clever idea!" She grabbed hold of Therese's hands excitedly. "I'd take over the rent for your half of the store, of course, and you'd get a percentage for every treatment, as well. And we would make sure your customers got special prices, too, to keep them happy until you come back."

"And as soon as you're able to start again, we'll find a good nanny," Sophie added. "I could ask my sister-in-law. She has two children of her own, and I'm sure she could add a third without too much trouble. Times have changed. There lots of mothers nowadays who also work. Isn't that so, Mrs. Berg?"

Clara flinched inside at Sophie's innocent remark. "That's true," she said. "And if your landlord really does evict you, then you can stay at Lilo's hotel. I've already talked to her about that possibility, and she said that, at least through the winter, there will certainly be a room for you." She swung a large pile of folded towels up onto their shelf.

Therese burst into tears. "You're so kind to me," she cried and threw her arms around Clara. "Oh, Clara, I admire you so much. Your shops. The manufactory. You can truly be proud of yourself."

A hard knot suddenly formed in Clara's throat. Wasn't she the biggest fraud of all? Two failed marriages, two children she wasn't allowed to see—how could she be proud of that? She was relieved when the doorbell rang. Clara freed herself from Therese's embrace.

"Do my eyes deceive me? It's Clara Berg! In the flesh," cried Elena Viska, one of Clara's first customers.

"How nice to see you again," said Clara warmly. Elena Viska was a young Polish noblewoman, a member of Countess Zuzanna's entourage.

She had no husband, and she devoted herself to looking after her disabled younger sister. During every vacation that she spent at Lake Constance, she booked several treatments per week at the Bel Étage. Clara recalled with pleasure their past conversations.

"Are *you* doing my treatment today? Like you used to? That would make me so happy," Elena said.

Clara looked at Sophie, who was scheduled to do the treatment. Klaus Kohlwitz was waiting for Clara in the manufactory. The chemist wanted to show her a discovery he had made. But that could wait, couldn't it?

"I most certainly am!" Clara said before she could think about it too long. "Just like the old days."

***

The summer of 1910 came dressed to the nines, putting the many vacationers in the best of moods with plenty of sunshine, a fresh breeze, and a radiant lake so blue that it competed with the sky.

Clara's days were fuller than ever before. But instead of working all the time, as she had in the previous two years, she now found the time for other things, as well.

She met Lilo early every morning to go swimming. When the sun was just rising and ribbons of fog drifted across the surface of the water, they had the lake to themselves. Clara often thought of Isabelle and Josephine, who had gone out cycling in the same early hours of the morning. "While the world is still asleep, the streets are ours," they had said. Only now did Clara understand the gift of those early morning hours.

She was not able to stop for lunch every day, but whenever it was possible, she went out with Klaus or Laszlo or one of her friends. Sometimes, Clara preferred to keep her own company, and on those days, she took a book to the lakeshore and read. Perhaps a few pages of *Cleopatra's*

Beauty Secrets or *Oriental Bathing Rituals,* and more technical treatises as well, like *The Chemistry of Cosmetics* or the recently published *Brush Massages for a Healthy Body.* Upon reading the book about brush massages, Clara bought a suitable brush from Treiber's Emporium and used it on her own body until her skin had turned a rosy pink and she was in seventh heaven. She thought about offering the massages to her customers, but decided against it on practical grounds. She could hardly ask a woman to strip in a narrow treatment station and sit naked on a chair for a brush massage. Her shops were simply not suitable for something like that.

It was only when she started reading again that she realized how much she had missed it in the months when she had done nothing but work. Now, her reading hours became precious again, not only for increasing her knowledge, but also for restoring her strength, both spiritual and physical.

Clara began using her renewed strength to give treatments on a regular basis. It was a source of pleasure to take care of her customers, and whenever she saw dull or damaged skin become radiant—and with it, the woman to whom the skin belonged, as well—then she was reminded that her work was worth doing.

Sometimes, Clara met with her customers outside her work, among them Countess Zuzanna, who had decided against selling her Villa Carese after all. "The mood of a moment," she said, excusing herself, when Clara mentioned Stefan's suggestion. But if she were ever serious about the idea in the future, she would offer the property to Clara first. Clara had nodded politely, but the idea of moving into a new house with Stefan had lost its charm for her.

She swore to herself that she would never again let herself be pushed into isolation as she had, neither by Stefan nor by her own obsession with her work in the laboratory.

What surprised Clara most of all was that she was making better progress with all her experiments and research than ever before, even though she was spending far less time in her laboratory. It was as if all the newfound variety of her active life inspired her work in the laboratory.

Thanks to her close collaboration with Klaus and Laszlo, her less-expensive cosmetic range was coming more and more to fruition every day. In Clara's view, it was high time that it did, especially since many women were still firmly convinced that beauty and skin care were only for the rich.

The shop in Stuttgart was flourishing after just a few weeks thanks to her carefully selected and trained personnel. And the Baden-Baden Bel Étage was back on its feet, too. Because of the competition, of course, she did not have as many customers as before, but there were still enough to keep her three new beauty specialists on their toes.

All the traveling among her shops took up a great deal of Clara's time, but she did not regret a minute of it, because then she was able to talk to her staff. Whether it was about which laundry could return their towels smelling fresher, or how often the front windows should be cleaned, Clara kept an open ear to everything her women had to say. And her employees, who were not used to working in such a trusting atmosphere, responded with their dependability, punctuality, and hard work.

***

Berlin, October 1910

Dear Clara, dear Isabelle,
Please don't be alarmed to receive this letter a little stained and blotchy. Because I wanted to write to both of you, I thought I would try out our carbon paper system, which we use in the office to duplicate our written records. If I had known that carbon paper would smear

and spot like this, I think I would have taken the time
to write everything twice. But you will forgive me, won't
you, my dears?

Clara smiled. Duplicating written documents? She could use something like that herself. Then every time she had to send new or revised instructions to all her shops, she would only have to write them once. At the same time, the duplicate that she had received from Josephine did not look very good at all. Was Isabelle's letter just as messy? It didn't matter. She was so happy to hear from Josephine that she would ignore the blue smears.

Don't be surprised if I don't write about too many
personal things today. I have so many thoughts going
through my mind that I would like to share with you.
But I will say this: we are all well. And your children,
dear Clara, are also in the best of health. I see Sophie once
or twice a week. She and my Amelie are still best friends.

History is repeating itself, Clara thought. And in this case, that's good.

Clara scanned the next few lines quickly, but found nothing about Gerhard's reaction to the letter from her lawyer, which he had sent in the middle of July. She wasn't sure Josephine would know anything about it anyway, but she could not completely get rid of her disappointment. So far, there had been no reaction from Berlin at all, not from Gerhard, not from his lawyer, and not from the court. This particular case, her lawyer had told her the last time they met, was special, and it would take time. Maybe she would visit him later that day and ask if he had heard anything new in the meantime. Clara sighed and went back to reading Josephine's letter.

Please excuse me if I sound a little sentimental. I don't know if it has to do with the autumn or with getting older, but I have been thinking back more and more to our younger years. We were the best of friends when we discovered cycling for ourselves. And weren't we scorned for it at the time! These days, when I walk or cycle or drive through Berlin, seeing a woman on a bicycle is perfectly normal.

Clara looked up from the letter and out the window of her laboratory toward the lake. Every day, she saw men and women riding along the lakeshore, and she never gave it a second thought. She read on.

So much has changed in the last twenty years! Women are so much more willing to try new things these days. Do you recall how we wished for what we called a "turn-of-the-century wind"? A wind that would come and sweep away all the dusty opinions about us as the "weaker sex." One that would blow fresh thinking into people's heads. We wished that women could have their own bank accounts, study at university, run their own businesses. When I look back at it now, I find it strange that it was always about what we were allowed to do and what not. But the men never needed to ask permission for anything!

Clara frowned. Was Josephine going to become a suffragist? And, in fact, the next thing her friend wrote was:

It may be these thoughts about how hard it was for us back then have moved me to join the General Association of German Women. Have you heard of this organization? We are fighting for a woman's right to earn the same pay as men for the same work. We are working on education and income protection for mothers who have to stop work to care for their children, and on the conditions for working women. I've already given two talks about that, and there were over a hundred women in the audience! Very few of them work in conditions anywhere near as good as the women Adrian and I employ. At first, Adrian was a little skeptical about my involvement with the association, but now he understands the necessity for it and supports me wherever he can.

My Adrian, your Daniel, dear Isabelle, and your Stefan, dear Clara—these are the kinds of men that society needs! Do you think so, too? When a man and a woman work shoulder to shoulder and not against one another, then it is a sheer joy to see what we can get done. Of course, there are so many things in a sorry state. I am not foolhardy enough to believe that we will soon achieve everything possible for women—we are still not allowed to choose who decides on the political direction of the German empire. But when I look around, my conviction grows that our turn-of-the-century wind, the wind of change for which we yearned so wholeheartedly back then, is already whistling through every lane and alleyway in the land.

Clara let Josephine's letter sink. For a moment, she heard a loud droning in her ears; then she grew calm again.

Their turn-of-the-century wind might well be whistling through society, but in her own life, all she could hear was the death knell of her marriage. In short: it had failed.

As painful as it was for Clara to admit it to herself, it was also a relief. It was enough to feign a stable marriage to the rest of the world, but at least she no longer had to pretend it to herself. And while it was nice of Josephine to mention Stefan in the same breath as Adrian and Daniel, the truth was that Stefan had nothing in common with her friends' husbands. And she herself was different from Isabelle and Josephine in a crucial way: when it came to men, she simply had no luck at all.

She had brooded over what had gone wrong. Who had made mistakes? When? Had she expected too much of Stefan? Or had she entrusted him with too *little*? The questions never ceased. Would such questions even be asked in a trusting marriage? Shouldn't a couple be able to find common ground, whatever problems might appear?

In the end Clara had come to a simple conclusion: she had been wrong about Stefan. He had bewitched her with his charms, and she was only too happy to let herself be enchanted. In times in which she was all but drowning under her workload, he had relieved her burden. And she had been so happy about that she had not realized until it was far too late about his vanity, his superficiality, the way he was always looking to turn things to his own advantage. What she found hardest of all to swallow was how much he enjoyed riding roughshod over those weaker than him. For that, she might as well have stayed with Gerhard! Had she really been stupid and blind enough to fall for the same kind of man twice?

It made no difference how much she pondered and agonized; one thing was clear: any love she had once had for Stefan was gone, though their marriage, on paper, was still intact. But she could not bring herself to write that to either Isabelle or Josephine. Maybe she wanted to spare herself an "I told you so!" Maybe she was ashamed of her own stupidity. Whatever it was, she now had other things to think about.

Lilo—and maybe Therese, too—probably suspected the truth about her marriage, but they were discreet enough not to mention it. And Clara was grateful to them for that. A second divorce or even a separation was out of the question if she ever wanted to see her children again, so she had no choice but to put on her facade for the rest of the world and to hope that Stefan was prepared to do the same. As long as she continued to pay him enough for it, she probably didn't need to worry. In fact, whenever they appeared somewhere together, he played the perfect husband. "Bella Clara," he always called her, and held her as if she were the most precious thing on earth. *"Mia cara,"* he said in her ear so that everyone could see and hear it. Women looked enviously at Clara—for some of them, so much loving attention from their husband existed only in their dreams.

What surprised Clara was how easy it was for *her* to maintain the farce. When she had still been married to Gerhard, she had carefully covered bruises with locks of hair, and cried into her pillow at night, only to bravely smile at every insult and disparaging comment the next day. Compared to that, her life these days was good. She consoled herself with this whenever the melancholy threatened to overwhelm her. She had her own life, her own money; she had dear friends and valuable employees. She could think whatever she wanted and do whatever came into her head.

Clara slipped Josephine's letter back into its envelope. She would write back that evening, but for now, she needed to get to the Hotel Residenz, where she had agreed to meet Laszlo and Therese for lunch. Lilo had invited them; there was something to be celebrated, her friend had confided mysteriously the night before. She decided to be on the safe side and to buy a small bouquet for Lilo at Fabienne's flower shop.

When Clara stepped outside, the wind off the lake tousled the strands of hair that had worked loose from her chignon. She smiled. It seemed the turn-of-the-century wind was blowing for her after all. And if it hadn't brought with it the love of her life, so be it.

Chapter Thirty-Nine

"He's such a sweet little boy!" said Clara, and she tickled Therese's two-month-old baby Christopher's tummy.

With a blissful smile, Therese took her son from Clara, and she sat in a comfortable armchair by the window and unbuttoned her blouse.

The sight of the feeding mother awakened a familiar yearning in Clara. She had sat like that herself once, very long ago. Matthias was now fifteen, Sophie ten. The childhood years vanished so quickly. She had missed so many . . .

"Oh, did I tell you? I've received a letter. It's from Gerhard's new wife, Marianne. She sent a thick envelope," Clara suddenly said.

Therese's eyes at first widened in surprise, then narrowed suspiciously. "What does *she* want from you?"

Clara laughed. "That was my first reaction, too. I was trembling all over when I opened it. But then I found two letters inside from my children and a brief message from Marianne herself. She said she hoped it would make me happy to receive the letters from my children for Christmas. Admittedly, Matthias's letter consisted of a few lines in which he wished me a merry Christmas and happy New Year. But

Sophie's was overflowing! She wrote five full pages and put in two pictures that she drew herself. I'm going to have them framed, of course," said Clara.

"That's very nice of their stepmother. Do you think Gerhard knows about it?"

"Unless Matthias said something, I doubt Gerhard knows anything about it at all. I expect he's spitting bile about my application." Clara sniffed. "All things considered, I think Marianne Gropius has really shown some courage, sending the letters. Josephine has written several times about what an attractive and smart woman Marianne is. I find that hard to believe, somehow. I mean, what kind of attractive and smart woman would fall for a man like Gerhard?"

"You," said Therese.

The two women laughed. At the same moment, someone laughed out in the hotel hallway, which only made Clara and Therese laugh louder.

Therese had been right. When her pregnancy was beyond doubt, her landlord had thrown her out. At first she had stayed at the Hotel Residenz, but shortly afterward Therese had moved into Lilo's small apartment in the left wing of the building. Lilo had sailed off to America in October. Love—or, more precisely, Jonathan Winter, widower and one of Lilo's summer guests—had spirited her away to his ranch in the Rocky Mountains of Colorado. When she had told Clara about her plan to live with Jonathan for three months at the ranch—as a kind of test—Lilo's eyes had sparkled, full of adventure.

Clara's first question was "What about the hotel?"

"I will be leaving it in the capable hands of my staff. And if there is an emergency, they can reach me quickly by telegram. I'll be back in the new year, regardless." And that was the end of that subject. Her new life on the ranch, with the horses and surrounded by the wilds of the Rocky Mountains, had filled the rest of their conversation. And

Jonathan, too, of course, a giant of a man with a full beard, a man like no other.

Clara looked out of the window and watched a pair of seagulls gliding in slow circles above the lake, and wondered if Lilo was already snowed in in the Rocky Mountains. And would she really come back? Her letters so far had practically dripped with love and bliss.

"Has your attorney been able to get anywhere yet?" Therese asked, drawing Clara out of her thoughts.

"Not yet, I'm afraid. But he has had a message from the court in Berlin to say that my case is being reviewed. Apparently, my situation has no legal precedents."

Therese shook her head and scowled. "At least I don't have to go through a divorce from Benno." She buttoned her blouse and lifted the baby to her shoulder; a little burp, then the boy smacked his lips and gurgled.

Clara smiled. "Well, now that Christopher's satisfied, I have to be going. If I don't get my packages into the mail today, my Christmas presents won't get there on time at all."

"Clara, wait. There's something else I'd like to talk to you about," said Therese, one hand on Clara's sleeve.

Despite the late hour, Clara had no choice but to sit again.

"It's like this . . . ," Therese began haltingly. "I wanted to open my hairdressing shop again at the start of the year, but now I dread the idea. To be honest, I'm not sure I ever enjoyed hairdressing very much."

That possibility had occurred to Clara, especially when Therese didn't come in to work or left early.

"I can take over your half of the shop. I'd like to, in fact. But how will you live?" she replied.

Therese pursed her lips. "This is where you come in. See, I've had an idea . . ."

***

The package to send to Josephine was ready: a large selection of beauty products for Josephine, letters and sweets for Matthias and Sophie, and for Amelie, too. At the last moment, Clara had included an extra hand cream for Marianne Gropius.

If you think it's all right, please give the cream to Marianne, and let her know I was very happy to receive the letters. But if you think it will cause problems with Gerhard, then don't, she had written to Josephine on a separate card.

Next came Isabelle's. She loved all of the Bel Étage's products.

"Oh my goodness, that looks like a lot of work," said Laszlo, who came in carrying a load of loose papers and jars of cream. He looked around for somewhere to set it all down, but space was a rare commodity in Clara's office.

"I'm packing Christmas presents for my friends," Clara explained. "But Isabelle's neighbors have started using my products, so now Isabelle's wish list is so long I have to send it as two or three separate packages. And I want to send something to Lilo, too. They must get frightfully cold winds so high up in the mountains, so a protective oil-rich hand cream can't hurt, can it?"

The parfumier pulled a chair over with the tip of his right shoe, then heaved the things he was carrying onto it. "Send her a jar of our newest hand cream as well." He handed her a frosted-glass jar.

"It's finished?" Thrilled, Clara took the cream from Laszlo. It was the last of the products for the Belle Époque line.

"Sent with best wishes from Klaus," said Laszlo with a smile. "And he wants you to know that if you're still not satisfied, then he's at his wit's end."

"I know I've been on your backs about it, and I apologize for that. But if I weren't satisfied now . . ." Clara opened the jar. The contents were a pale pink, like buttercream on a strawberry tart. It looked wonderful, and Clara had to suppress a squeal of delight. *No singing anyone's praises prematurely,* she warned herself. She dipped her right index finger into the cream and smeared it onto the back of her hand. It spread easily and had a slight shine, but left no oily film on the skin, as the last attempt had done. It gave off a fresh, delicate scent. "Outstanding! Now I'm satisfied. Women who work hard with their hands every day deserve the best. Our new advertising specialist can get started with the Belle Époque line in the new year."

"Our new advertising specialist?" Laszlo's eyebrows rose.

Clara laughed. "Yes. Therese, would you believe, convinced me that we desperately need someone like that, and that she would be just the one for the job. And now I've taken her on, just like that, though I can hardly believe it myself." She hoped silently that she would not regret her rash decision one day.

Stefan's voice interrupted them. "What's going on here?" he grumbled. "Has there been an earthquake and I missed it?" He waved a hand at the chaos on Clara's desk.

"I'm in the middle of packing presents," Clara said. Stefan rarely came to the manufactory, especially this early in the day. What was he doing here?

Laszlo cleared his throat. "I'll be going—"

"No, wait," Clara said hurriedly. "There's another matter I want to talk to you about." She hoped that the look in her eyes was not too obviously pleading.

"Generous as ever when it comes to others, I see," said Stefan, looking at the packages and ignoring the parfumier.

"My friends are at least as generous as I am. Remember the three crates of champagne that Isabelle sent us just last week?" said Clara, angry that she should have to justify herself to Stefan. "How can I help you?" she said then, as nicely as she could, hoping he would not ask her for money in front of Laszlo.

"Champagne!" said Stefan, as if he were talking about well water. "Don't you see how much time you're wasting with all your charity? Visiting Therese, checking on Lilo's hotel, and now here you are packing dozens of Christmas gifts! What's next? A visit to the orphanage or the soup kitchen? Didn't you say something about problems at the Stuttgart shop? Shouldn't you be taking care of that? If you're going to shut me out of the business, then at least do the work yourself instead of frittering away the day."

Stefan turned on his heel and went out, leaving Clara thunderstruck. What did he think he was doing, making a scene like that? And for nothing!

It had been happening more and more often lately. Stefan had adopted an inappropriate tone—irritated, arrogant, erratic. Several times now, he had gone off to an event in the evening only to return an hour later. If Clara asked him about it, she got sullen silence in response.

Stefan and she were oil and water. They simply did not belong together, Clara thought sadly, yet again.

Laszlo cleared his throat a second time.

Clara looked up, unable to hide her hurt. "Forgive me," she said with a helpless shrug. Oh, marvelous! Now Laszlo knew about the friction in their marriage, too.

Laszlo picked up a length of wrapping paper. "I'll help you. We'll get it done much faster together."

For a time they worked in silence. Laszlo held the paper while Clara cut it to length. Then he wrapped the packages, and she bound them with heavy twine.

We work so well together, Clara thought, not for the first time. From turned-down eyes, she watched her parfumier. He was a modest man who worked well in silence, but who radiated a strong natural charisma. She had observed that she was not the only person who felt very good when he was close by. Laszlo was always friendly and uncomplicated. He wasn't moody, didn't seem to have a darker side. At least, that was the man Clara had come to know. Why hadn't she met someone like him earlier in her life?

Useless thoughts! She rapped herself mentally over the knuckles. She put the twine aside and said, "That other thing I wanted to talk to you about . . ."

Without a word, he moved the pile of documents and jars of cream from the chair onto the floor, then he sat down. Elbows on knees, supporting his chin on his thumbs, he looked at her earnestly.

"I've been thinking about this for a while," Clara began cautiously. "I've been asked many times by my customers if I would open a Bel Étage in their hometown. Then they could buy my products and use them the whole year. I tell them that I would love to do that, but more shops right now would simply be too much work. I only have to think about Stuttgart . . ." Clara sighed and raised her eyebrows.

So far, she had lost her entire staff twice over—to pregnancy, marriage, loss of interest, a broken leg. At the moment, the shop was closed, but Clara was planning a trip to the city in the new year to look for new personnel and train them. Or she might close the shop there permanently.

"In short, what do you think of starting a mail-order branch? A catalog with the main products from the Bel Étage line and the complete Belle Époque line. Then my customers in other towns could order whatever they wanted the whole year. In fact, *any* woman could order my products, even if she's never been to a Bel Étage or can't afford a holiday to Baden-Baden or Meersburg."

Clara waited excitedly for Laszlo's reaction.

"It's a good idea," he said after thinking it over for a moment. "You would have to talk to Klaus to find out if the manufactory can increase its production, but with the hardworking women there, I don't think that will be a problem."

Clara nodded. "I could always take on more women and introduce a second shift. People are always asking me about a job."

"And you would need storage space and women to take care of the shipping and invoices. There probably isn't enough space here. But I'm sure we could find a suitable warehouse and reliable personnel. Maybe you should consider hiring a secretary, too? Someone to give you a little support every day. An assistant like that could save you the trip to the post office, for example," Laszlo said, pointing to the stack of parcels.

"You're reading my mind again, aren't you? I've been wishing more and more lately that I had an assistant. I might have been smarter to get an assistant before I hired Therese for the advertising. But somehow I've been relying on the right person to just . . . cross my path one day. Sometimes things just sort themselves out." As she said it, she knew it didn't sound very professional.

But Laszlo nodded. "Sometimes you can do worse than to sit back and let things come to you! Maybe Therese could take over a task or two. She won't be drafting advertisements the entire day, after all, though I could imagine that advertising is very important if the mail-order trade is to be a success."

"I never thought about it like that."

"But there's still one thing we haven't considered: Will the women who order your creams and lotions be able to use them correctly? In your shops, you show the women exactly how to cleanse their skin, how a face massage works, and everything else that's important for their beauty. It isn't nearly enough to just smear on a cream as if you're rubbing lard into a Sunday roast."

Clara frowned. "That's true. I hadn't thought about that. That means I need to add a kind of instruction manual where I describe the benefits of each product and how to use them properly. Maybe even with a few illustrations?" Clara's heart beat faster, as it always did when something kindled her enthusiasm. An instructional brochure!

She wanted to drop everything and start on it there and then! But dozens of questions were popping into her head. How were the women supposed to find out at all that they could order her products by mail? Advertising in a newspaper? Wasn't that terribly expensive? Just then, there was a knock at the door, and Sabine Weingarten appeared.

"Klaus Kohlwitz said I'd find you up here, but I can see that you're busy."

Clara gave the pharmacist's wife a friendly smile and said, "We're in the middle of discussing something, but I can spare a few minutes. What is it about?"

Laszlo stood up again to go. And, again, Clara asked him to stay. She didn't want Sabine to settle in for too long.

"Unless it's something you'd rather talk about privately," Clara said to her.

Sabine shook her head. "I really don't know where to begin." She let out a small, embarrassed laugh. "At home, I've been finding the walls closing in more and more. My two little boys are darlings, but spending the whole day building towers out of blocks with them . . ." She groaned. "Every morning, I see your workers coming here to your manufactory, and they all seem to be in such a good mood that I . . . I envy them. They meet other people, they earn their own money, they get to see something outside their own four walls." Sabine let out a profound sigh. "I've offered to help Frieder in the pharmacy so many times, but he rejects it out of hand!" Sabine's shoulders sagged, her head, too, but then she looked up again. "But I'm very good with numbers! And I can hold my own when it comes to organizing things. I know it! If only Frieder would see it the same way."

Clara frowned. It was not news to her that Frieder Weingarten preferred Sabine to be the good housewife and mother and nothing more.

In recent years, she and Sabine had gotten to know each other a little better. Their lives were quite different, and while they were not close friends, they were always friendly with one another. "How can I help?" Clara asked cautiously.

Sabine took a deep breath and blew all the air out again before saying in a rush, "I wanted to ask if you perhaps have a job for me! Don't worry, I don't mean as one of your beauty specialists, but as something in the background, so to speak. I can take the children to the new kindergarten for a few hours every day. I know it won't be easy to convince Frieder about it, but I have a right to a bit of happiness and satisfaction, too, don't I?" Clara was flabbergasted. In the years she had known Sabine, she had never seen her so courageous. She seemed very serious about it indeed.

"Well, that's . . ." Laszlo began to speak, but then held his tongue, as if unsure whether his opinion was wanted. He looked inquiringly at Clara.

Clara grinned. "Are you thinking what I'm thinking?"

When she saw him nod, they both burst out laughing. "Well, isn't that a coincidence."

"What is it? Why are you laughing? Did I say something wrong?" Sabine looked shocked at their reaction.

"Absolutely not," Clara hurriedly reassured her. "Quite the opposite, in fact. You are in exactly the right place at the right time."

When Sabine left—with the promise of a contract as Clara's future assistant—Laszlo said, "'Sometimes things just sort themselves out'—who said that just now?"

And they burst into laughter again.

Clara leaned back in her chair, content with the world for now. Everything was so much fun and was going so well! She could not remember the last time she had felt so lighthearted.

"Now that you have your first staff member for the mail-order business, I've got another suggestion that I've been mulling over for a while," said Laszlo.

"I'm all ears!"

"It's about the labels on your products. They're lovely, don't get me wrong. But perhaps now is the right time—looking ahead to the possible mail orders—to take a fresh look at them."

"Yes," said Clara slowly. She was starting to feel almost intoxicated by the day's sudden turns and all the new ideas.

"You are the founder of the Bel Étage, the figurehead," Laszlo said. "Without you, this company would not exist at all. Without you, women would still be using creams that smell as antiseptic as a hospital and do more harm than good to the delicate skin of the face. But you are also the very best example of just how effective and beneficial your creams are. You look so . . . young and beautiful!" he exclaimed.

Clara's heart fluttered a little, as if it had sprouted wings. "I didn't know you were such a flatterer," she said, sounding sterner than she felt.

His cheeks reddened, and he turned away in embarrassment. "I'm sorry. I didn't mean to overstep. What I'm trying to say is this: Could you imagine having labels printed with your own likeness on them? That would be the best advertisement of all."

"My face on a label?" Clara couldn't help herself. She burst into laughter again, and she laughed so hard that she soon had tears rolling down her cheeks. She explained to her confused parfumier how she had suggested to Isabelle to try something new instead of using the same old plain labels for her champagne. "Back then, I suggested she put her likeness on her champagne labels. She had her portrait painted by Renoir, and this portrait was reproduced for the labels on her bottles. It was a huge success, and these days everyone calls Isabelle the Champagne Queen." She shook her head to regain a little composure. "I still can't believe I ever came up with the idea in the first place. But to do the same for Bel Étage never even crossed my mind."

Laszlo had listened with interest, and said, "Do you want to have Renoir paint your portrait, too?"

"Good heavens no!" Clara laughed. "The photographer around the corner will do just fine."

Therese had pinned Clara's hair up into a perfect chignon, highlighted her eyes with kohl, and skillfully applied a little rouge to her cheeks. Clara could not understand why so many women still thought of makeup as somehow disreputable. What was wrong with making the best of oneself? She had the same thought when she chose her dress: the cream-colored fabric and round neckline showed off her flawless skin to best advantage.

Clara placed great store in a good appearance. She would never allow herself to be seen wearing a stained laboratory coat or with her hair unwashed; also, for her, beauty was something internal, an attitude. When a woman was beautiful, she was beautiful every hour of every day. A woman who made herself beautiful for an hour did so only to please others, not to please herself.

Today, however, Clara had to appeal to herself and others as well.

"Lift your head a little higher."

Clara raised her head slightly.

"Too far. Down a little. Now turn to the left."

Clara lowered her head again and looked to her left. Her nose actually touched a wave-shaped element that was part of a huge stucco mural on the wall, depicting a near-naked woman in a flowing dress.

"People are apt to associate beauty with a Greek goddess. I attempt to reproduce this same association in my work," the photographer had said when Clara had explained what she was looking for. He could also offer her a backdrop of a distant mountain range or a wintery background, if she preferred. He had shown her one large canvas backdrop after another. When Clara dared ask if it might be possible for her to be photographed in front of a plain white wall, the photographer had looked at her with horror! Now she was standing in front of the stucco bas-relief with the Greek goddess. She worried that the background would be too much for her cosmetic labels. The plaster tickled Clara's nose, and she stifled a sneeze while the photographer's young assistant arranged various lamps around her.

It felt like half an eternity passed before the photographer was satisfied, but finally he barked, "Do *not* move!"

She had not realized that having her photograph taken was such a serious undertaking. How must it have been for Isabelle when she sat for Renoir?

"Almost ready," the photographer muttered.

Clara's nose touched the plaster again. At the same moment, motion outside the photographer's window caught her eye. She blinked. But that was . . .

"Young lady, you moved!" the photographer cried out, outraged, as Clara turned to face the window.

"Someone is looking in," she said.

"What of it?" The photographer rushed up to Clara and adjusted her head back to its previous position. "It is perfectly normal for someone to watch an artist at work."

"But I saw the same man this morning, twice already. First in Unterstadtstrasse and then beside the Hotel Residenz. What if he's following me?" she said, and felt a touch of panic come over her. Is this what her lawyer had warned her about? Was someone spying on her for Gerhard?

"Nonsense," said the photographer, although he didn't sound very sure of himself. He, too, looked out of his front window where the dark-haired man was still standing.

Who was it? Clara's brow furrowed as she tried to think. No doubt the photographer thought she was crazy, but she was extremely uncomfortable.

One look at Clara's pinched face and the photographer said, "This won't do at all, young lady. I'm going to go and chase the man off." And he was gone.

Clara's relief was short-lived, however, because the photographer returned a moment later with the stranger in tow.

"My apologies, madam. The man just will not leave. He says he has a question he wants to ask you."

"My name is Lombardini, Carl Lombardini, and I come from Italy," said the man, and he raised his hat. "I'm searching for an old acquaintance of mine to give him some important news."

"How can I help you with that?" said Clara suspiciously. Why would Gerhard send an Italian to spy on her?

"I heard, madam, that you are married to an Italian. Would your husband's name be Roberto Totosano, by any chance?"

"My husband's name is Stefan Berg. Before we married, he was Stefano Santo," Clara said, relieved. A mix-up. This had nothing to do with her.

"Stefano . . . I see." The man nodded. "Then it seems I've been on the wrong track."

"Can we get back to this portrait?" the photographer asked, and he shooed the stranger toward the door with both hands.

The man already had his hand on the doorknob when he turned back.

"Still, it would be very nice to exchange a few words of Italian here in this foreign land. Perhaps your husband might be interested in drinking a glass of wine with me? Where did you say I could find him?"

She hadn't said anything about that, and was about to reply as much, but then it occurred to her that Stefan might enjoy chatting with someone from his homeland. "My husband often lunches at the yacht club. Maybe you will be lucky and find him there?"

The stranger smiled, nodded, and exited the studio.

"We have work to do!" said the photographer. "Closer to the relief, please. Head up."

Chapter Forty

"Sailing!" Stefan said the word with disdain. "Every man and his dog has a sailboat these days. And I know perfectly well why I haven't bought one. Oh, I have the money. But do I want to spend it on that? Has sailing perhaps fallen a little out of fashion?" He looked at the group around him; they were listening as attentively as usual.

That morning in January 1911, the regular group of sailors—tourists and locals alike—had gathered in the harbor restaurant, as they did almost every morning, although every boat had either been pulled out of the water or was tied up tightly and under cover in the harbor. No one wanted to venture out on the raw, windy lake, but spinning a few yarns while the winter wind whistled outside was a popular way to pass the time.

The men narrowed their eyes and grumbled into their beards. What was Stefan trying to tell them? That they were all just old-fashioned journeymen? They certainly wouldn't put a suggestion like that past him, brash as he was.

Still, in their eyes, Stefan Berg was someone to be admired. He was generous and eloquent, and he often had a story or two to tell about the rich and the famous who passed through the doors of his wife's shops. He laughed at himself as much as at others, and enjoyed gossiping, too. "Come on, out with it!" said one of the men at the table, grinning. "If it isn't a sailboat, then what new toy did your wife give you for Christmas?"

The group burst out laughing.

Stefan laughed along. It didn't matter to him that everyone there knew *where* his money came from. On the contrary—who else there could claim that because his wife worked he didn't have to?

"None of you have any imagination at all. Hasn't it ever occurred to you that not everything in the world revolves around money . . ." His last words trailed off as two men sitting by the window caught his eye. He had never seen them before. Why were they scrutinizing him like that? Did they want something from him? And why was one of them constantly taking notes?

Stefan excused himself from the table. On the way to the restroom, he walked past the table by the window. His heart almost stopped when he heard the two men speaking Italian. And weren't there a few words of Occitan, as well, the old language of the *caviè* from Piedmont?

By the time he reached the restroom, his knees were trembling so much that he had to hold on to the washbasin to stay on his feet. A chalk-white face stared back at him from the mirror. *They've got you!* screamed a hysterical voice inside him. *They've got you!*

Pull yourself together, pleaded another voice. *Goddamn it, pull yourself together!*

He felt the old fear of discovery tighten around him.

For a long time, he was certain that he had wiped away all trace of his past life. He was Stefan Berg—a German businessman with a German wife. He'd been clever. He'd covered his tracks. And the reward was a carefree life.

Because I can.

In truth, ever since the incident in Baden-Baden, he had felt many times that he was being observed. Had he convinced Gianfranco de

Lucca that he wasn't who the merchant thought he was? Since that fateful encounter, every unfamiliar face made him nervous. He only had to think about that Lombardini fellow who appeared from nowhere ten days earlier! He was passing through, the Italian maintained, and Clara had told him where he could find Stefan. He had invited Stefan to drink a glass of wine, but Stefan had turned him down. The man had then started asking Stefan questions. About how long he had lived at Lake Constance. If he liked it there. If he knew other Italians who lived in the area. What his profession was, how old he was.

Stefan had done his best to answer every question with a question of his own, but it was like talking to a stone wall. The stranger had given away nothing about himself. That, in turn, had only reinforced Stefan's conviction that the man was a spy working for his family. Had his family been watching him for a long time? He had stolen from his father and made him the laughingstock of the village, and Giacomo Totosano would not shoulder that burden easily. And his brother, Michele, was probably still furious at him for leaving him there.

Maybe it wasn't his family at all, but the Sorris who had set a dog on him. From Lorenzo Sorri, he had stolen the equivalent of thousands of marks, a packhorse, and a huge load of women's hair and finished wigs. And he had left Lorenzo's daughter, Gaia, behind with an unfulfilled promise of marriage. The longer Stefan thought about it, the more people he thought of who had a bone to pick with him. A bone to pick—it sounded so harmless! If he fell into the hands of the *famiglia*, then may God have mercy on him.

If Lombardini had been a spy, then who were the two men in the tavern? Grim Reapers?

Should he return to the table at all? Or would it be smarter to climb out the small window and run? A hard choice . . . Shamefully, he squeezed out through the window, just eighteen inches square. Outside, as he wiped away the white marks the window putty had left on his dark suit, he looked around fearfully.

He saw nobody. But the feeling of being pursued would not leave him, even when the harbor was far behind him.

***

"The labels are beautiful!" Therese squealed. "*You* are beautiful, dear Clara. And photogenic, too."

"You really are the best advertising for your products," said Sabine Weingarten. "But is this particular photograph also what you want for your advertising campaign? Wouldn't the one where you have your hand on the plaster balustrade look better printed in a newspaper?"

The three women were bent over Clara's desk, which was covered with various photographs. On the first day of the new year, the photographer had come by and, his chest swelling with pride, presented the portfolio of pictures.

"We could use this one for the advertising *and* for the instructional brochure," said Clara, picking up one of the photographs.

Stefan stood in the doorway and listened. Photographs of Clara? New labels? An advertising campaign? An instructional brochure? What were they talking about? He felt a small, sharp pain in his heart. There had been a time when Clara had talked about everything with him. His advice had counted for something. Now he was no better than Estelle Morgan's lapdogs. Or Pawel, who lived a nice life at Countess Zuzanna's expense.

"Then this one has to go on the shipping cartons," said Therese, tapping a finger on another image.

How the former hairdresser liked to show off! It wasn't so long ago that she had tried to kill herself. And today, she was the one taking care of Clara's advertising. Such a rise was only possible in the Bel Étage, he thought, annoyed.

His mouth turned down even more at the sight of Sabine Weingarten. Stefan did not like it at all that Clara had hired the pharmacist's fat wife. Her own husband did not want her in his pharmacy, yet Clara welcomed her.

"Listen, I've had an idea for the heading for the newspaper advertisement," Clara said. "'Belle Époque—because every woman can be beautiful today.' What do you think?" Her eyes turned to the door for a moment, and her smile vanished. "Stefan. We're in the middle of a meeting. Is there something important?"

He had an acrid remark on his tongue, but he surprised himself when he instead said, "I just wanted to ask if you ladies might like some cake and coffee. I could organize that for you." How pathetic he sounded! Almost pleading. As if Clara would be doing him a favor if he were allowed to bring them cake and coffee.

Clara, Therese, and Sabine looked at him unenthusiastically.

"Thank you, but we've just come back from eating lunch. We are trying to finish with the shipping boxes today." With a nod, Clara dismissed him.

Bile rose in his throat. He swallowed hard. He wasn't even good enough to run an errand.

A little while later he was pacing around their apartment like a caged animal. Things couldn't continue like this. What had become of his life? Lightheartedness had turned to fear. It scuttled through his head like a cockroach. His once-important position with Clara had evaporated into insignificance. He was heading for oblivion; he could feel it.

He poured himself a glass of cognac, carried it from the living room into the drawing room, and looked out the window, where the winter-bare trees offered no protection.

He saw nobody. And he heard nobody.

But did that mean that there was nobody there?

The ticking of the clock on the wall, the beating of his heart—suddenly, the silence in the apartment was unbearable to him. He looked around. All the pictures of flowers . . . had they always been there? The colorful glass ornaments on the windowsill . . . were they new? Clara loved everything beautiful, everything that had to do with beauty. *"My beautiful Italian,"* she used to call him, back when she still loved him. Back when he still had a say in things.

Because I can.

He felt himself sway a little, and he set down the glass of cognac. It made no difference where he looked—all his hopes were slipping away, and he could not hold on to them.

He had to toss out his anchor again, find a new hold. Even if it meant hiding out beneath Clara's skirts for a while.

***

Although the day had been long and strenuous, Clara could not sleep. She tossed and turned, crushed her pillow, fluffed it again, then pushed it aside completely. Stefan was sitting out in the living room, drinking a glass of red wine and leafing through old newspapers, and she found it so unsettling that she could not sleep. Angry at herself, she got out of bed, pulled on her robe, and went out to him.

"Why aren't you out at some party or at the bar? Why are you home so early?" she asked without preamble, taking a seat on the chaise longue.

He looked up from his newspaper. "Isn't this still my home?"

"What kind of question is that?" Clara replied, ignoring the sad undertone in his words. "You're the one who loves going off to parties."

"Maybe that was the mistake." Stefan shrugged. The next moment, he jumped up so abruptly that the individual pages of the newspaper slipped off his lap and sailed to the floor. "Clara!" he said, kneeling before her. "Don't you wonder sometimes what became of us and the love we shared? What we had was so infinitely valuable! And we were dumb enough to let it slip away."

Clara frowned. She had been prepared for almost anything but this.

Before she could say a word, Stefan went on. "I know the start of the year is already behind us, but don't we want the new year to perhaps be a good start for *both* of us?" His eyes were pleading, his voice even more. He took her hands in his and held them softly.

"Stefan," she said. Carefully, she extricated her hands from his, ignoring the agony in his eyes.

"I know you don't love me anymore," Stefan continued, and his eyes were moist. Clara almost contradicted him automatically, but he did not give her the time. "But that doesn't have to mean that we hate each other, does it? Why can't we at least be friends?"

"We are," said Clara, very gently.

Stefan sniffed softly. "Friends spend at least a little time with each other. They talk. They share their thoughts. But you treat me like a stranger. I . . . feel lonely."

Clara looked away, feeling guilty.

"Clara. I know the business matters most to you. And I know that your friends mean the world to you. But is it asking too much to spend a little time with me now and then?"

"If that's what you want, gladly. But until now, that's not the impression I had at all. I take it you already have something in mind?" she said with reserve. No doubt his suggestion had a catch. Did he have his eye on a boat, a new car, or something else and was trying to get her approval? Or had he been up to something? Fresh gambling debts?

So she was all the more surprised when Stefan suggested going for a walk with her the following morning.

"Why do you look at me like that? What did you expect? That I had some dubious ulterior motive?" he said, shaking his head. "Is it so hard to imagine that I might just want to spend some time with you?"

***

The next morning, they left the apartment just after sunrise, both wrapped in thick winter coats, scarves, and warm hats. For Clara, this was quite normal. She had grown accustomed to starting winter days with a brisk walk. It always cleared her mind and readied her for the day ahead. If that would still be the case today remained to be seen. She glanced at her husband, who walked beside her narrow-eyed and pale. It was still a mystery why he would drag himself out of bed so early. Spontaneously, she took him by the hand and said, "Isn't it wonderful by the lake so early? While the world is still asleep, the day belongs to us, only to us." Small clouds rose with every word.

"You put that very beautifully," Stefan replied with a smile. "When I was a boy, I loved getting up before everyone else. I went out to the stable and milked the cow so that my mother didn't have to. And, of course, I drank a few cups of milk on the spot." He laughed. "I was always so hungry as a child."

"Well, they practically had to talk me into eating anything," said Clara. "My mother always said I couldn't keep pace with a sparrow. She must have tried everything to get me to . . ."

While they exchanged childhood stories, the atmosphere between them was far better than it had been in a very long time. Suddenly, Clara stopped.

"This is the spot where Lilo and I always met to go swimming, but it looks like I'm going to be swimming by myself this year." She looked out over the lake. Clara had just received a letter in which Lilo had written that she would be staying in Colorado a little longer. Clara did not know what to make of that. Was Lilo still unsure about whether she was in love? Or was it the first step in saying good-bye to Germany?

"I can't swim, to be certain, but I would gladly walk here with you, *mia cara*. Every morning," Stefan said beside her, his voice very low. His mouth was suddenly dangerously close to her own, and before Clara knew what was happening, he kissed her.

With an embarrassed laugh, she tried to take a step to the side, but she stumbled on the loose gravel along the shore. Stefan's hands were immediately at her elbows, supporting her. "I would never let you fall, *mia cara.*"

It was supposed to sound affectionate, she knew, but in Clara's ears his words carried a strange undertone, something she could not put her finger on.

"Don't worry. In the last few years, I've learned to pick myself up when I fall. I dust off my skirt, and I simply go on." She had wanted the words to convey some humor, but a strange undertone had entered her own voice.

Walking back along the road, they had reached the outskirts of Meersburg again when they stopped outside a large house surrounded by a high wall.

"For Sale" read a large wooden sign that had been rammed at an odd angle into the earth.

"But this is the Palazzo Margherita, the villa where Margherita of Savoy-Genoa spent two summers. And now it's being sold? Do you know anything about this?" Clara asked.

Stefan nodded. "They say the Italian king does not look favorably on his mother's excursions to German waters, and that Margherita of Savoy-Genoa will be spending next summer at Lago di Garda instead. The owner of the villa lives in Munich, and he doesn't come to Lake Constance often. The Italians renovated and redecorated the entire villa at their own cost—a lot of money, apparently—to meet Margherita's demands. By my estimate, the owner now stands to make quite a profit from the sale."

Clara chewed on her bottom lip. The house was painted in a pale yellow, but the ornate shutters were white, giving the building a cheerful Mediterranean character. There were two floors, and Clara counted eight windows along the facade on each floor. If there was a room behind each one, that meant quite a lot of rooms indeed. Because of the high wall, she could not see very much, but she knew from what Stefan had told her about it previously that a generous garden surrounded the house on all sides and extended all the way down to the lake.

"Owning a house like this . . . that would be something! I could jump into the lake and go swimming from my own garden every morning," Clara said, dreaming out loud.

"And you'd have plenty of room for all your paintings of flowers. The rooms on the lake side are perfect for the sun. That large still life of the sunflowers would really shine there."

Clara sighed. "I can see just how it would be . . ."

"Behind the house, there's also a large conservatory, completely glassed in. The palms they brought in especially for Margherita must still be housed in there."

"A conservatory! How opulent. That was something my mother always dreamed of having. Sitting behind the glass in the cold months, drinking tea and enjoying the winter sunshine. Unfortunately, my parents had to make do with a small bay window on the second floor." Clara did not miss her parents often anymore, and she had never forgiven her mother for constantly taking Gerhard's side in all the years they were married. Still, sometimes she wished that her parents could see what had become of her.

"Your children would also love it here, I'm sure," said Stefan. "And if we were to be blessed with a bambino of our own, we could put the cradle right by the lake."

"Stefan, what are you talking about?" A bambino? What had come over her husband? They still shared the same bed, that much was true, but they had not slept together for more than six months. "All this with the house, it's all daydreams, no more," she said, avoiding the question of another child.

"Maybe the house isn't so expensive after all? And maybe a child would bring us closer together again. Oh, Clara, let's start a new life together. It would be possible here, in this house, I'm sure of it. And maybe I will even be able to show you that I'm still good for something."

"If you're trying to make me feel bad, then hear this: it isn't working. But I do like the house, very much! The more I look at it, the more ideas I have."

The house would be very useful for business purposes, too, she thought. A Bel Étage right on the lake. With rooms where her customers could spend the night as they would in a hotel. A beauty hotel, so to speak. She would be able to pamper the woman all day, starting with a champagne breakfast on the terrace to a nice cup of herbal tea at night to help them sleep. They could do calisthenics and other sports in the garden, out of sight of passersby. There would also be enough space to give the brush massages that she so enjoyed herself, and to do so in privacy. At the Villa Bel Étage, the women would finally have a place where they could be completely at ease, and simply be themselves.

"You look very happy all of a sudden. What are you thinking about?" Stefan looked at her expectantly.

"Counting chickens before they hatch. Maybe I should get in touch with the agent, though I expect the place will be horrendously expensive. But if business keeps up as it has been, then I can at least dream a little."

When they met again that evening in their apartment, Clara was feeling better than she had in a long time.

Stefan had good news, too. The agent selling the Palazzo Margherita wanted to show them the house the following morning.

"Then it's even better that we finished with our shipping boxes today, so I can take the time for a house visit tomorrow," said Clara. She pulled off her boots, then sat beside Stefan on the sofa. He had opened a bottle of wine and set out two glasses and a plate of canapés.

"Here's to you, Clara! And your new mail-order business," Stefan said, and they clinked their glasses together.

While they had been out walking, she had told him about her plans. At first, he had seemed quite stunned, but he quickly became enthusiastic. Mail order? This would be her greatest success yet. He was sure of it and had said as much. Near to the customs house there were two empty warehouses. Perhaps one of those would be suitable storage for Clara's products? Clara had liked the idea and promised to look at them as soon as she could.

"If you like, I can show you a finished sample of one of our shipping boxes. I've brought one home with me," she said, looking at him over the rim of her wine glass. Her eyes were sparkling with anticipation.

He jumped to his feet. "Tell me where it is and I'll get it!"

Stefan inspected the cream-colored box with Clara's photograph on the lid. He looked up. "Very chic! Which printer are you using for them?"

Clara told him the name.

"I hope you negotiated a good price?"

"Yes, I did," she said with a laugh. She watched excitedly as he opened the carton. Inside, it was padded with cream-colored tissue paper in which Clara's products were bedded. The sample box held a face cream, a hand cream, and a bar of rose-scented soap. Since Laszlo had taken over her fragrances, everything smelled finer, fuller, more expressive. She inhaled deeply.

"'Wash your face thoroughly, then stimulate your skin with a light massage. Only then should you gently massage in your Belle Époque cream.'" Stefan read the instructions aloud.

Clara smiled proudly.

"What this, then? You'll soon turn every woman into a skin-care expert like this! Are you aware of that, Clara?" Stefan looked at her in disbelief.

"Of course I am," she said, smiling. "That is exactly my intent. Now don't you dare say that the women soon won't need me at all. We are talking about a mail-order business and about women who, for whatever reason, will probably never find their way into one of my shops. Whether it's because they don't have the money or because they can't get away from the house or because they're not allowed to."

"But with your instructions, the women can look after themselves with any old cream they choose. Why should any of them order from you a second time?"

Clara could not believe what she was hearing. "Because my products are *good*! Because most of the other creams smell like zinc and leave white marks on your skin. Because—" Angry now, she stopped. "If you don't know by now why my customers remain loyal to me, then I am truly sorry."

"I didn't mean it like that, Clara. Of course your products are the best. But the most important goal of selling is to make customers dependent on you, to turn them into regular customers. If your customers only order once from your catalog, what have you gained?"

"I am firmly convinced that any woman who has once tried one of my creams will want to buy them again. And if not, then that is fine," Clara said, louder than she wanted. "The days in which we women allow others to tell us what to do are over, Stefan. We can choose for ourselves. And if that doesn't always work out like you men would like it to, then that's just how it is."

"Oh, I understood long ago that you won't let anyone tell you what to do, Clara dear. But please allow me to express my opinion. I fear that, by handing out instructions like these, you are dooming your mail-order business before it even gets started."

"Maybe you're right. Maybe I'll end up looking stupid. But I am happy to make an attempt," Clara said, surprising herself with her firm belief that she was going in the right direction.

"Then let us drink to *you* being right," said Stefan, and he raised his glass.

Clara, looking at Stefan, was puzzled. This was new. No angry outburst? No dramatic, door-slamming exit? It seemed as if Stefan was actually intent on them getting along better.

Chapter Forty-One

If Clara had harbored any doubts the previous year about whether the winds of change were blowing for her, too, they were swept away decisively at the start of 1911. No wind blew gently through her life; rather, it roared, it thundered, and it howled. And every day brought new adventures with it. Clara welcomed every one with a happy heart.

The mail-order business boomed from the very start, and revenues grew month by month. As wonderful as that was, Clara and her employees faced new challenges: the manufactory was bursting at the seams, workers to staff a second shift had to be hired and trained, and the raw-materials storage had to be rethought. Luck was on Clara's side when, in March, the building beside the manufactory went up for sale. Clara knew immediately that she had to buy it. The purchase solved all her space and storage headaches in a single blow. Nervously, she approached her local bank again. Would they give her another loan so soon after she had bought the Palazzo Margherita?

The bank did not let her down. Clara's real estate portfolio was growing.

***

While Clara and Klaus Kohlwitz transferred part of the production to the new building and reorganized the warehouse, the season began at the lake. Tourists streamed through Meersburg's cobblestoned streets and filled every table at the cafés along the esplanade. The lake was almost as busy as the town. Anyone who could call a sailboat, dinghy, or even a small rowboat their own was out on the water.

Clara's beauty experts often worked overtime into the evenings to meet the demand for appointments. After the first month Clara gave each one a large bouquet of flowers and a generous raise.

In the middle of May, something Clara had been dreaming about for a long time finally happened. She could already count nobles from many states and countries among her clientele, and now a lady from the royal family of Stuttgart came to her shop: Princess Pauline, the only daughter of King Wilhelm II. The wife of Friedrich, Prince of Wied, was a mature woman with a resonant voice. "I don't know whether all this about beauty is really anything for me," she said in a Swabian accent so heavy that for a moment Clara thought she was speaking a foreign language. Evi Förster—one of Clara's oldest employees and fluent in the Swabian dialect—replied: "Then we shall just have to surprise you!"

Pauline enjoyed the most comprehensive treatment the Bel Étage had to offer. After three hours, the princess's formerly pallid face shone with a new radiance, and the princess herself was beaming, too. "Such a wonderful feeling. Every woman should experience this," Pauline said to Clara when she came to inquire whether everything had been to Pauline's satisfaction. Then the princess told her about her involvement in the German Red Cross, where she trained young women to look after others.

Clara was very impressed. "I will have my women put together a box of hand creams for you. Your Highness is welcome to distribute these as you like among your volunteers—such dedication should be appreciated," she said, earning Pauline's everlasting favor for the gesture.

In the midst of the busy season, Clara had no time to take care of her new house at the lake. Early in the morning, when she went swimming, the sight of the empty villa made her heart ache. She would have liked to wander around the overgrown garden and make plans for the future. There was some work to be done: some walls to demolish, others to be built, new wiring and plumbing to be installed. But she would have to postpone any talks with builders until the season was over. Stefan had offered his assistance more than once, but Clara was afraid that he would resume his domineering ways and scare off Meersburg's experienced tradesmen. Aside from that concern, she had a deep need to take care of everything to do with the villa herself.

As much fun as her diverse life was, Clara did not want to neglect her work in the laboratory. Creating new products was still what she most wanted to do, so when Laszlo asked her one day if they shouldn't perhaps develop a perfume together, she agreed enthusiastically. "It would be the high point of your products," he said plainly. "We could even name it after you."

Clara was tempted to agree to that, as well, but then she looked at him and said, "If we do this, my perfume can have only one name— *Winds of Change*."

As she did every morning, Clara flipped through the morning's mail, hoping for some news from the court in Berlin. Months had passed since she filed her application. Her attorney had told her the week before that the magistrates were close to reaching a decision in her case. She could receive a judgment any day. Finally, finally . . .

It surprised both Clara and her lawyer that there had been no interference at all from Gerhard in the previous months. She had long discarded the idea that the Italian who had spoken to her in the photographer's studio might be a spy, and nothing else untoward had caught her attention.

"Well? Has it arrived?" Stefan asked, joining her at the breakfast table.

"No word at all from Berlin, I'm afraid." She still was in the dark about why the former late sleeper now joined her for breakfast every morning. It puzzled her just as much that he preferred to eat breakfast at home rather than out in the café where Clara still often went.

Stefan also had begun spending most evenings at home instead of going to parties. "Always the same faces, the same stories," he had told her with a wave of his hand when she had asked him about it. "I'd rather spend the time with you."

Clara did not find his company unpleasant. Sometimes, they even laughed together. But Clara was not about to give up her time with her friends. Lilo was back, and occasionally, Clara met her friend for a glass of champagne. After more than six months away, Lilo had reappeared in Meersburg without warning. "Mountains, mountains, mountains . . . that's not for me. I missed our lake," she said nonchalantly, though Clara was astonished. Lilo did not say a word about Jonathan Winter. Clara had embraced her old friend and said, "Welcome home." Neither said a word about the tears Lilo shed on her shoulder.

Because Lilo had returned to Meersburg and her apartment, Therese was back to living in a room at the hotel. Therese and her son could not live in a hotel room for very long, but they hadn't yet figured out the next move. Clara tried to spend one evening a week with Therese, and when they were together, they talked about this, and many other things, while Clara rocked little Christopher on her lap.

"I've had an inquiry from Munich," said Clara, pouring more coffee for Stefan. "A large department store is interested in adding my products to their range. I think it's fundamentally a good idea, but do you think I should take a look at the store before I sign a contract?"

"I could drive to Munich and let you know what I think about the location, the customers, the other products they sell," Stefan offered. "I'd enjoy a drive to Munich. I've been closed up in the house too long."

For a moment, Clara hesitated. If she gave Stefan an inch, would he take a mile? On the other hand, he was making such an effort to create a good feeling between them again that she was glad to have the opportunity to offer something in return. She would give him this one small task, but no more.

"That's a good idea," she said. "At midday today we should be getting the laboratory tests back for the Lake Constance water. If they turn out to be as good as I suspect, Klaus and I will probably have our hands full for the next few days. So I'd be grateful if you could take that on."

"Products with Lake Constance water—it's such a zany idea that I don't know if I should be tapping my forehead about it or clapping my hands," Stefan teased. "The things you come up with."

Clara shrugged and smiled. When it came to their views on business, they would probably never see eye to eye, not like they once had. But since Stefan had stopped making a scene and yelling at her whenever his opinion differed from hers, their life together was bearable.

"Calcium, magnesium, potassium, iron—outstanding! Practically no trace of arsenic, no mercury, no cyanides—excellent!" Klaus Kohlwitz leaned over the laboratory report and studied it carefully. It had cost Clara a lot of money to have it done. To get the water samples she needed, she and Laszlo had gone out the week before in a rented sailboat. Too close to the shore was no good because of the danger of contamination, but farther out the lake water was crystal clear, as Clara well knew from her morning swims.

"The composition is flawless. It can stand up to any mineral water I've heard of, even from the most expensive springs." Triumphantly, as if he were personally responsible for the quality of the water, Klaus turned and smiled broadly at Clara.

"That's fantastic," said Therese, who had come in just then. "If you help me with the wording a little, I'll see if I can't finish an article that sings the praises of our Lake Constance water today. Baden-Baden and Bad Kissingen might have their mineral springs, but it sounds like we don't have to play second fiddle to either of them. Clara, this is going to send even more customers your way!"

Clara smiled as she looked into the eager eyes of Klaus and Therese. Who would have expected to find such an advertising professional hidden inside the former hairdresser?

Klaus rubbed his hands together theatrically and stood up. "I'm off, too. I'm going to go and work out exactly how to introduce the lake water into our products in place of distilled water."

"And I'm off to an appointment of my own," said Therese. "The *German Women's Fashion Magazine* wants to do a half-page report on 'the latest thing: the beauty shop,' if I can give them enough information. Their circulation is eighty-five thousand copies! I can add your photo to the article, can't I?"

Clara nodded, and her friend left, obviously eager to get to work. Clara wondered when the last time was that Therese had felt such euphoria. Alone in the deserted laboratory, she looked around, suddenly feeling a little lost.

A knock at the door drew her out of her thoughts. It was Laszlo.

"Congratulations, Clara. Klaus just gave me the good news. So in the future we'll be producing the Bel Étage products using pure Lake Constance water!"

"Isn't it marvelous?" Clara said, forcing a smile. "We'll not only be saving the cost of distilled water and the expensive mineral water we import from France, but we'll be using the treasure at our doorstep."

"Brilliant," he replied. "But why do you seem less excited than I'd imagine you would be? What's the matter?"

That took Clara by surprise. She had tried very hard not to let her slightly downcast mood show, but Laszlo recognized that something wasn't right. "To be honest, I don't really know."

He sat down opposite her and looked at her expectantly. "Everything's running like clockwork, but . . ."

Clara had to smile. Not for the first time, he had spoken exactly the thought that was running through her mind. "But, for some reason, I'm . . . not satisfied," she said, finishing his sentence. "Every day, I get the feeling that what I do to help women be more beautiful is only the beginning, and that I'm still far, far away from true beauty! I *know* my products are a boon to many women. But do the products really help them, even a little, in their day-to-day lives? The good housewife wears her fingers to the bone trying to do everything right for everyone around her. A woman in a factory spends all day on her feet, running a machine in a noisy, filthy workshop. Fresh air? Or a chance to rest? All she can do is dream about those things. And whether they are at home or in a factory, women are always working into the evenings. They darn socks, iron clothes, and let out hems. They don't see that all the work is damaging them! As they get older, fear becomes their constant companion, fear that their husbands will leave them for a younger woman. Women hate getting older! They don't know how grateful they should be for every year they're given." Clara's voice was trembling. These thoughts had been blurry and indistinct for a long time. Only now, talking to Laszlo, did she manage to give them form. She was surprised at the outrage she felt as she spoke. "A woman is supposed to be the perfect lover. The devoted wife. The caring mother. The good daughter-in-law. And all of it takes so much strength, and takes so much out of her. I don't think that an hour in one of my shops is nearly enough. It can't replace more than a fraction of the energy they have lost."

"But think about how happy the women are when they visit one of your beauty shops. That time belongs to them and no one else."

"Visiting a beauty shop is a start, yes. But women have to think about themselves far more than they do." There was distress in Clara's voice. "Isn't true beauty linked to inner harmony? To having your own inner house in order? And doesn't true beauty also mean recognizing and appreciating the beauty of nature? Getting out in the fresh air, exercising. And then there's food! Women don't eat nearly enough fresh fruit and vegetables. Everything gets cooked for hours and drowned in thick brown gravy because that's how their husbands prefer it. But it is not good for the body. It causes pimply, pasty skin and curves where a woman doesn't want them." Clara threw her hands in the air. "Oh, Laszlo, I can't claim to be particularly bright or clever. I've made every mistake a woman can make, and not just once. So maybe I'd be better off keeping my mouth closed. But still I feel a deep need to bolster the courage that too few women have. I know how they feel, and I know that there is always a chance to break free of a life that is too constricted. Maybe it isn't as easy or comfortable to take a new path as it is to follow the well-worn one, but it's a lot more fun!" And she laughed out loud as she said it. If Josephine had heard her, she would have been proud of Clara.

Laszlo smiled at Clara. "Then why don't you tell the women what you've just told me?"

"When I give a treatment, I do. But I can't spend all day standing in one of my shops, delivering my ideas on health and self-care and beauty! My assistants would probably see it as an intrusion. And besides, I do have a thousand other things to take care of." Clara sighed.

"But if it means so much to you? Didn't you just say that it's always fun to try something new? Maybe you should just follow the call of your own heart." The parfumier touched her arm gently, then left.

Clara watched him walk away. Follow the call of her heart? If she were really to do that, she would go after Laszlo now just to spend more time in his company. Laszlo . . . why hadn't she met him sooner?

Back in her office, Clara sat at her desk. When it came down to it, did she really have anything to say that women would want to hear?

Clara opened the bottom drawer of her desk, where she kept a stack of notebooks. Whenever she had a new idea, she would take out a fresh one and make notes. She did that now, opening the notebook in front of her, breathing in the smell of fresh paper. She stared at the blank white pages, then—hesitantly—picked up a pencil.

Think that you can do something / take care of yourself / don't spend every minute looking after other people / get out in the fresh air, move, do sport / brush massages / clean the whole body, head to foot, with water / drink plenty of water . . .

Ideas, words. At first, that was all, but then Clara began to fill in the details, and it wasn't long before she had the first page full. Then the second, the third . . .

Clara wrote and wrote.

The grape diet in autumn. Beauty sleep! Staying beautiful with age. Brush massages for good circulation. Cold baths for better resilience . . .

Laszlo and Sabine came by to see if she wanted to go for lunch, but Clara turned them down. She had so much swirling in her head that she wanted to get down on paper.

And then it was evening, and downstairs, in the manufactory, the lights had gone out long ago, but still Clara sat and wrote.

At around eleven at night, she took out a second notebook.

How to correct minor blemishes and flaws . . .

The church bell in town had just struck midnight when the light went on in the corridor outside her office.

"Clara! My God, you're still here!"

For a moment, Clara did not know where she was or how late it had become. "Laszlo . . ."

"I was walking and saw the light on in your office. What in the world are you still doing here?" He looked around the room with real concern.

Clara blinked at him from overtired eyes. When she put the pencil aside, her right hand trembled from the strain she had put it through. At the same time, her stomach growled loudly. She had not eaten a thing since breakfast with Stefan, and now she was so hungry she was dizzy.

"What I'm doing is following my heart, as you suggested." She smiled at him. "I'm writing a beauty guide!"

Although Clara had only slept a few hours, she woke at daybreak the following morning. She felt more invigorated than she had for a long time. She put her swimsuit in her bag, then went out. Dark clouds were looming over the lake, and Clara guessed that it was raining already in Switzerland. No doubt the rain would reach them before midday, Clara thought as she walked along the shore. But she did not care about the weather. As soon as she got to her office, she had a letter to compose to Stuttgart. A customer at her Bel Étage there was married to Robert Kröner, the manager at Cotta Publishing. Clara had met him briefly when he had come to collect his wife, and they had exchanged a few words. She wanted to ask the publisher if she could show him her beauty guide.

She laughed to think about it. She had written a book. A beauty guide for any woman. Who would have imagined that? She could hardly wait to tell Lilo about it! Considering the rain clouds over the lake, she hoped her friend would not forego her swim that morning.

A fresh breeze was blowing as Clara changed into her suit. She had just begun to do a few stretches when there was a rustling in the reeds beside her. Two men jumped out, and before she could even react, one of them had pulled both her arms behind her back. The other planted himself in front of her. He had a black cloth tied around his nose and mouth, so Clara could only see his eyes, which were dangerously narrowed.

"Where is Roberto? Tell us, or God help you!" he growled through the cloth.

"I don't know any Roberto! Who are you? What do you want?" Clara tried frantically to free herself from the grip of the man behind her.

"Liar! We know that you're his wife," the man screamed at her. "Where is the bastard?"

The second man twisted her right arm so painfully that she cried out.

"You've got me mixed up with someone! My husband's name is Stefan." Tears were welling in her eyes from the pain. *Don't start howling now,* she told herself. "Let me go. You're hurting me!"

"*Putta!* Tell us where he is, or there'll be an accident right here!"

"But—" Clara began.

She was interrupted by a dull thump. The man behind Clara released her and staggered forward, groaning and holding his head. The other man took a step back. Both of them stared at Lilo, who was swinging a long, pointed piece of driftwood through the air like a lance.

"Clear out! Go!" Like a fury, Lilo stepped between Clara and the men. "The police will lock both of you up!"

The men exchanged a glance. "Tell Roberto that there is no escape. We'll be back," the masked man muttered to Clara, then they turned and scuttled off through the reeds.

Shaking all over, Clara sank to the ground. "Thank God you came."

"Are you all right? Are you hurt?" Lilo crouched and looked at her with concern. "Did they want money? What were they after?"

"No money." Clara shook her head. "They kept asking me about someone called Roberto. But I don't know any Roberto! They . . . must have mistaken me for someone else."

"Mistaken or not, two men can't threaten a woman like that! They probably would have done something to you if I hadn't come along. I think we should go straight to the police and make a report," said Lilo resolutely, helping Clara back onto her feet.

"No. No police, please. Nothing happened to me," Clara said, her knees trembling.

Lilo protested, but Clara wasn't listening. She looked in the direction in which the two men had disappeared. Who were they? And what was this about Roberto?

She thought of the stranger who had appeared in front of the photographer's studio in January. Hadn't he also asked her about a Roberto? A suspicion rose in her, unsettling and lunatic: Did all of it perhaps have something to do with her husband? Was it possible that Stefan and Roberto were one and the same?

What secret was he hiding from her? *When he gets back from Munich, he has some explaining to do,* Clara thought grimly as she slowly made her way home with Lilo at her side.

***

The May wind stroked Stefan's face gently. The briny scent of seaweed blew off the lake and up to the street, where it mixed with the smell of boiled meat as he drove past a restaurant. Then he drove by a brewery, and his nose filled with a combination of malt mash and heady ale.

Stefan briefly considered stopping to enjoy a beer, but he was making such good time that he was happy to do without a stop. He zoomed along in the car, which took every curve in stylish stride, its motor purring like a kitten. He smiled, feeling pleased with himself. Clara would be very happy to hear that his research in Munich had turned up only good news. The department store on Marienplatz in Munich that wanted to sell Clara's products was not only the premier store on the plaza, but also a supplier to the royal house. Only the finest goods in Europe were on sale, and Stefan had not passed up the opportunity to refresh his wardrobe.

To his own surprise, Stefan found himself humming an old Italian melody as he drove. It was called "The Happy Wanderer," and he and Michele had often sung it as they walked from village to village. *How fitting*, Stefan thought. Oh, it was so good to be on the road again! He laughed to think how many months he had locked himself away like a coward for no reason. No one was after him. All his supposed observations, his fears—all just a false alarm! Fantasy, all of it. But it was over, as of now. He would live the sweet life once again.

"Ciao, paura!" Stefan shouted, and laughed even more when he realized he had used the Italian word for fear. *Paura . . .*

He was as free as a bird. He could do what he wanted, when he wanted, even speak Italian if he felt like it.

The first buildings of Meersburg came into view. The streets were wet and shining, and the dark clouds of a departing thunderstorm towered against the sky. The cobblestones were covered in small branches and young, new leaves, suggesting it was a big storm, but the sun was already appearing again between the clouds, transforming the town on the lake into a fascinating play of light and shadow.

He had planned on driving straight to the manufactory to tell Clara the good news, but as he passed by the harbor, he changed his mind. The idea of a beer was appealing, and he wanted to see his old friends again. No doubt they would be wondering where he had been keeping himself, and he knew they would like to hear about Munich.

Clara could wait.

He slammed the door of the car. The paintwork gleamed in the sunlight like the finest silk. He, the hair trader from Elva, had really made it.

"Speak of the devil!" Martin Semmering, the owner of the Bar Coco, laughed and banged his fist on the table. "We were just talking about you." He clapped Stefan on the shoulder.

"Nothing but good, I hope," Stefan grinned back. Then he pulled up a chair and ordered a beer. It was good to be back again.

"So where have you been all this time?" Josef Meininger asked. "Hiding out under your wife's skirts?"

Stefan joined the others in their good-natured laughter. "I've just got back from Munich," he said between mouthfuls of beer. "Meersburg is a lovely town, but now and then I have to breathe a little big-city air. I think I'll get myself an apartment there. Maybe even a business address. We'll see."

The offhand manner in which he said it garnered appreciative looks from the others.

"Munich, is it?" Semmering and Meininger exchanged a look. "Then what we have to tell you probably won't interest you at all."

"What is it?" Stefan leaned forward curiously.

"Just before the storm came through, two men tied up with a sail-boat. Swiss businessmen. The owner and his brother want to sell it here, and the price would be hard to beat. The boat is in tip-top shape, and if I didn't already own a very nice yacht, I would have bought it in a heartbeat. Strange fellows, if you ask me, but obviously wealthy enough to own a beautiful boat. They even asked after you. Seems they had heard somewhere that you might be interested in buying a boat. But if your head is full of Munich . . ." Josef shrugged.

"One doesn't necessarily preclude the other, you know," said Stefan. Someone wanted to sell him a yacht? Then had his reputation as a well-to-do businessman already preceded him? Well, he could not have been in a better mood to spend some money. "Where are they now? Why didn't you stop them?"

"We had no idea when you'd be coming in here again! But it was half an hour ago, if that. If you're lucky, you'll catch up with them." The bar owner nodded toward the exit. "Out the back, pier seven."

***

The two men had their backs to him as he walked out on the pier and approached them. They seemed to be doing something to the boat, perhaps a repair or touching up the paint. *Trying to hide a blemish?* Stefan grinned. Forewarned was forearmed. They wouldn't put anything over on him.

"Good day, gentlemen," he said loudly when he had almost reached them. Stefan assumed the men would jump in fright because they had not heard him coming. Instead, they turned around slowly, taking their time, as if they had been expecting him.

"*Ciao*, Roberto," said one of the men, a powerful fellow with greasy hair and a thick goatee.

Stefan's heart skipped a beat. "What. . . Who are you? What do you want?" he choked out. His mind struggled to comprehend the situation. These weren't Swiss businessmen. The boat was a trick, and the pier—a trap.

Stefan turned, looking for help. But the pier was empty. Even the lake was abandoned, so soon after the storm. Stefan opened his mouth to shout for Meininger or Semmering or anybody, but he could not get out more than a croak.

The bearded man laughed. "Cat got your tongue, *amico*?" he said, putting himself between Stefan and dry land.

"If you search long enough, you will find what you are looking for—that's what they say in the German countries, isn't it? Believe me, your father searched for you for a long time," said the second man, who was lean and pale, as if he normally spent his days underground.

His father . . . Stefan gulped. So this was the end. Panic ran through him. He tried to stay calm, to keep his nerve. It was not the first time that he had to talk his way out of a predicament.

"I don't like your tone. And I think you're confusing me with someone else," he said, with as much arrogance as he could muster. He flicked one hand toward the yacht. "And your tub isn't to my taste, either, so if you'll excuse me." He tried to push past the men. But the second man grasped him by the collar.

"Not so fast, *amico*! Don't you want to hear the message your father sends?"

A fist hit him hard in the belly. The blow knocked the wind out of him. He doubled over.

"Gentlemen," he rasped. "We can talk about this. I have money."

The bearded man laughed. "You have an unpaid account with your father, not something you can settle with money. Only like this . . ." The man flicked open a knife. The cold blade flashed dangerously in the May sunlight, every turn of the man's wrist sending out glittering Morse code signals.

"How did you find me?" Stefan whispered. He forced his eyes away from the blade and along the pier. Damn it, why didn't anyone come to help him?

The two men were practically drinking in his fear, thriving on it. The bearded man flipped the blade open and closed, and Stefan found the clicking sound it made maddening. The next moment, he felt the point of the blade an inch above his navel. It dug through his shirt and into the skin of his belly. He took a step back, away from the sharp pain, and found himself standing on the plank at the edge of the pier. A jump into the water . . . would that save him?

"Don't even think about it," the pale man muttered, holding him tightly.

The bearded man spoke again, casually, as if he were talking about the weather. "Your father sent out every man with eyes in his head to look for you, every year. And of all people, it was one of those arrogant Neapolitans who gave us the first clue about where you were. Gianfranco de Lucca. Your father rewarded him well. Then he hired us. Finding you was child's play. Do you recall the elegant gentleman from Italy who appeared in Meersburg just before Christmas?"

Stefan was dizzy with fear. He remembered. Only too well. The man had questioned Clara about him. Then he had invited Stefan for a glass of wine at the yacht club. Stefan had turned down the invitation. His instinct had warned him not to trust the man.

"Friend of ours." The pale man grinned.

"Enough talk!" the bearded man shouted, taking a step toward Stefan. Bloodlust shone in his eyes. He rolled his shoulders as if he were warming up for gymnastics. His right arm shot forward. Stefan saw the movement, but he had nowhere to go.

The blade glided into him. He was engulfed in immeasurable pain, and a flood of images raced through his mind. He gaped in disbelief at the blood that poured from the wound.

"*Ciao, amico!*" The man gave him a small push. That was all it took.

And Stefan felt the pain suddenly cool, becoming colder, colder . . .

Chapter Forty-Two

"I still can't believe it! A false name and everything else, all lies and deceit. And I fell for it. I fell for him." Clara pounded her fist into one of the cushions on her sofa.

Josephine and Isabelle looked at each other. Each had set off for Meersburg immediately after receiving the news of Stefan's death to be with Clara in her hour of need. But instead of a grieving widow, they had found their friend in a fury.

Clara had kept her composure throughout the funeral. She had shaken hands and accepted condolences. And she had gotten through the meal afterward, which Lilo had hosted at her hotel, with poise and dignity.

But the moment they were alone in Clara's apartment, the mask of self-control vanished. Josephine had never imagined that Clara could fly into such a rage.

"He was so smooth, so convincing! And there was always a grain of truth to his lies. Yes, he *was* a hair trader from Elva. Yes, his family *had* sent him to open a shop." Clara looked at her friends from half-mad eyes. "But what my dear husband unfortunately forgot to mention was that when he sold the wigs, he *did not* send the money back to Italy.

He used it to act the rich playboy with big plans. And silly little me . . . How could I have fallen for it? Why didn't I look deeper?"

"Stefan had a very endearing nature. He could charm most people off their feet," said Isabelle consolingly.

Clara glared angrily at her. "But not you, apparently! You and Josephine, you saw through him from the start, or else you wouldn't have *insisted* on a marriage contract."

Isabelle looked away guiltily.

"It was no more than a suspicion, a strange feeling," said Josephine.

"I am so mad at him! But when I think about how they stabbed him and threw him in the water . . ." Clara sank back onto the sofa, holding the cushion in front of her as if it offered protection.

Josephine swallowed. Even though she hadn't particularly liked Clara's husband, his violent death had affected her. At least they had caught the men responsible the same day. Hired killers. Unmoved, they had told the police about what they had been paid to do, and why. The police in Italy had been informed immediately and had already arrested Roberto's father for ordering his son's death.

"I hardly dare to say it, but somehow, I miss him." Clara's voice was no more than a whisper.

"Of course you do," said Josephine. "You were married, you shared your life with him, and from one day to the next, so much is gone." She swallowed. Poor Clara. "But you're a strong woman. You've already gotten through so much, and you will get through this, too."

"I'm not so sure about that." A second bout of tears shook Clara, but this time they were tears of despair and desperation. "Earlier, at the funeral, my lawyer took me aside. He said that now that I was a widow and my husband died violently, everything had changed. In those circumstances, I would probably have to brace myself for the court to reject my application."

"But . . . ," Josephine began. She and Isabelle looked at Clara in dismay. "You couldn't help what happened in the slightest! The judges can't hold that against you."

Clara sniffled. "I'm sure the high and mighty old men in their old robes will see that differently. After my divorce, I was the evil adulteress, someone that no one would entrust with children. Today, I'm . . ." She gave a helpless little shrug. "I have no idea what I am today, not in the court's eyes. The widow of a criminal. Maybe even his accomplice? In either case, my dream of seeing my children again anytime soon is over." Clara sobbed again.

With one arm around her despairing friend's shoulders, Josephine thought about Clara's situation. She could not bear the thought of being separated from Amelie for years because of a court judgment. Why was everything so complicated? Wasn't it the most normal thing in the world for a mother to see her children? To accompany them as they grew up, even if only from afar?

Things could not go on like this. If the judges proved obstinate, then there had to be another way to help Clara get her happiness back. She decided that she would talk to Isabelle about it as soon as she had the chance. A deep crease appeared between her eyebrows, as always when she was working out a plan . . .

***

Several weeks had passed since Stefan's death, and Clara was trying to get back to a normal routine. Though she still hadn't resumed having breakfast at a café, she was sitting at her dining table, sipping coffee and reading the newspaper.

> Major Concert Series: In honor of recently deceased composer Gustav Mahler, the Vienna Opera is planning a series of concerts . . .

Opera visits did not interest her much. Soprano voices hurt her ears. Clara turned the page.

Hottest Summer Since 1874! Berlin Struck by Heat Wave! The effects of the continued spell of hot weather are becoming more serious. Yesterday, the Parliament building had to be closed because of the unbearable heat. Many schools have closed their doors a week in advance of the scheduled summer vacation due to the increased danger of heatstroke among the children.

Clara frowned and looked up from the newspaper. She hoped that Sophie and Matthias were all right. Early vacation . . . They could already be having a lovely time there at Lake Constance. A fresh breeze was blowing, and if one got too hot, it was easy to cool off in the lake. She would teach both of them to swim! Or perhaps they had already learned how long ago. There was so much she did not know and probably would not find out in the near future. As feared, the Berlin court had informed that, in the current circumstances, they saw no possibility to grant Clara's application for visiting rights for her children. She would have to file another application in due course.

With a sigh, she turned the page. Advertising for Glauber's salt. Advertising for a new laundry powder that claimed to take the gray out and brighten whites. Next to that, in a large, framed box: *Belle Époque. Because today, every woman can be beautiful. Ask for our mail-order catalog today.* And beside that she saw her own image, smiling back at her. *Good work, Therese,* she thought. The ad was perfectly placed. Then she turned to the next page.

Scandalous fashion! Several French designers have followed the lead set by Paul Poiret and in-

cluded culottes in their new collections. Now the
Vatican has decided to speak up, condemning the
new fashion in the severest of tones.

If Stefan were still alive, she would have said to him, "Josephine and
Isabelle were wearing long trousers twenty years ago!" Now, she needed
to be sure to tell Lilo. At least she still had people to whom she could tell
things, she realized, and she was grateful for that. Without her friends,
she would have fallen into despair long ago.

She cleared away the coffee cup, packed her swimming bag, and
went out.

Just after Stefan's death, she had refused to go swimming again. Thinking about the two men who had attacked her sent a chill through her.
Stefan's murderers! If only she had taken Lilo's advice at the time and
gone to the police. Maybe Stefan would still be alive today.

"Nonsense," Lilo had shot back when Clara had told her that the-
ory one day. "You heard what the police said. Stefan's family had spent
years looking for him, and they would never have let up." Then she had
said that a rider who has fallen from a horse has to get back in the saddle
immediately or live with fear the rest of his life. And for that reason, she
insisted that Clara go swimming with her.

It was good that she had a friend as smart and stubborn as Lilo,
Clara thought as they swam out into the lake together. The swimming
was good for her. She had the feeling that the lake would help her heal
on the inside, too. Sometimes, when she lay on her back in the water
and felt the warming sun on her nose, she managed to think of the good
times with Stefan. Not all of it had been bad. She had been left with a
scar, and not the first one she had suffered in her life. Gradually, though,
she was learning to wear her scars with dignity.

"Would you like to come to the hotel for coffee?" Lilo asked on their walk back as they were passing by the Palazzo Margherita.

Instead of replying, Clara stopped. She stood on tiptoe and tried to look over the wall. Just then, she could not even remember where she had put the key to the villa.

One of the white roller shutters had sprung from its anchor and was rattling in the breeze. A dog-rose was growing wildly from inside the garden up and over the wall. The path was covered with its dried petals. The windows were dusted with the yellow pollen that had blown around in May.

She turned to Lilo and said, "The house is looking more and more desolate and lonely every day, isn't it?" A pang of guilt came over her. She should have turned her attention to the building long ago.

Lilo shrugged. "It's not good for a house to be empty. Why don't you do something with it? Move in, or turn it into that beauty hotel you were talking about, or sell it. As it is, it's just dead capital. I'm surprised the bank hasn't already talked to you about it."

"They did," Clara said. "But I played for time." They started walking again. "Everything has changed since Stefan's death. I didn't want to use the house only as a beauty hotel. It was supposed to be a second home for my children."

"Just because something is one way doesn't mean it can't change," Lilo replied. "Your lawyer has advised you to start a new application next year, hasn't he?"

"Next year! That's an eternity from now," Clara said dispiritedly.

"Pull yourself together, Clara. Dejection doesn't suit you." Lilo gave Clara a playful punch on the arm. "I'd much rather hear about your charming parfumier and if anything is finally developing on that front."

"Lilo!" Clara cried, but her dismay was partly feigned. "Stefan hasn't even been dead for three months, I'm in my year of mourning—"

"I know the circumstances and the etiquette, thank you," Lilo interrupted her. "But a blind man could see he's in love with you. And I think that *you* quite fancy him, too."

Clara laughed out loud. "The things you get into your head! Therese said something similar just the other day. But Laszlo Kovac is the epitome of kindness, and not just toward me. Everybody likes him. People just feel good to be around him, and it's the same for me. But wasn't it the same with Stefan?" As she said it, Clara realized how much the thought frightened her. As much as she might deny it, she knew well before Stefan's death that she had feelings for Laszlo. With his circumspect, unassuming manner, he was always there for her. She felt safe with him, and sometimes she truly believed that he could read her mind. But hadn't she believed the same about Stefan? What if she was doomed to fall for the same kind of man every time?

Lilo swung her bathing suit and towel over her shoulder. "Really, Clara, you can't possibly compare them! Forgive me if I put this so bluntly, but your late husband used his charm to con his way into everyone's hearts. Laszlo Kovac, on the other hand, is a naturally likeable man. There's nothing artificial about him; he isn't putting on an act for anybody!"

Lilo's words had grown increasingly vehement, and her face was so red when she finished that Clara had to laugh. "All right. Maybe your suspicions are not so far off. I do like Laszlo. I like him perhaps more than I should. But for me, the whole subject of men is settled once and for all. The last thing I need in my life is another letdown. As far as love is concerned, I'm just unlucky. And now I have to get to my office." She finished her sentence just as they reached the junction where, every morning, she and Lilo went their separate ways. She had had enough of difficult conversations for one day.

Clara was walking off toward the manufactory when she heard Lilo call out after her.

She turned around. "What now?"

"You're an old chicken, you know that?"
Laughing, Clara continued on her way.

We are happy to inform you that we like your manuscript very much indeed. It would be our pleasure to publish your beauty guide . . .

Clara looked up happily from the letter from Stuttgart. "This is truly wonderful news!" she said to Laszlo and Therese, who had both joined her in her office. She read on quickly. "Robert Kröner, the manager at Cotta Publishing, is requesting that I go to Stuttgart to work out all the details with him. My advice in a book—who would have thought?" She laughed.

It took a moment for Clara to realize that both Laszlo and Therese only halfheartedly shared her enthusiasm. "What's the matter? Aren't you happy about it?"

"Oh, of course," Therese said. "It's just that . . . actually, *we* wanted to be the ones to deliver fantastic news."

"Oh, yes?" She looked curiously from one to the other as she pushed the letter aside. "What is it?"

"One of our customers—Hella, the daughter of Count Zeppelin—has invited you to Friedrichshafen. A zeppelin is supposed to be landing there on the weekend. Then there will be zeppelin tours over the lake for people in the town. It is the count's way of showing his appreciation for the solidarity and support of the town."

Clara nodded. When a zeppelin had had an accident close to Stuttgart three years earlier, a campaign had been started to solicit donations from the public, and it was those donations that allowed the count to continue his work.

"Now for the best part," said Therese. "A few selected people have been invited to take part in a special flight with a program of events!"

The royal couple of Württemberg will be there, the carmaker Karl Benz, Mr. Kienzle from the clock company—and you."

"Me?" Clara could not believe it. She looked at her two friends. "What business do I have in such illustrious company?"

Therese and Laszlo were grinning from ear to ear.

***

Laszlo accompanied Clara to Friedrichshafen. Although he had been living at Lake Constance for more than a year, he had not yet seen much of the area outside Meersburg. While Clara took advantage of her invitation, he wanted to see Friedrichshafen.

He didn't drive, so they went by ferry. Clara was so excited that she could hardly even make a sound, let alone carry on a conversation with him. It was rare for him to be alone with Clara, and he enjoyed being so close to her as much as their mutual silence.

The previous months had been a long rollercoaster ride for him. Some days he'd been on top of the world, others close to despair. The love he felt for Clara at the start had long ago developed into something more. But he did not know if he could call it love. Didn't love mean reciprocation? Sometimes, for an instant, he felt that Clara returned his affection, at least a little. Those moments gave him hope and strength. But most of the time, he feared that Clara did not see him as a man at all but only as a creator of beautiful scents.

There was no question that they worked well together. Since his arrival, he had refined the fragrance of every one of Clara's products. Her famous lavender scent now smelled even more intensely of lavender, and her rose-perfumed line was more elegant than ever. He had even succeeded in retaining fragrance in the volatile extracts! He had become well known throughout the industry as the one who had created the inimitable fragrances for the Bel Étage and Belle Époque products. Just after Easter, a letter had come from Grasse in which his old employer Escarbot had practically begged him to return. Laszlo could not suppress a smirk as he read it. And just two weeks ago, he had received an inquiry from a well-known perfume house in Paris that wanted to make him their head parfumier. He had torn up the letter from Escarbot on the spot, but he had put the second letter away carefully in his night table.

Paris . . . promise or perdition? This question, too, was behind Laszlo's fluctuating feelings. Whenever he felt that his love for her would destroy him, all he wanted to do was go away. Away from Meersburg, away from the manufactory, and most of all away from Clara. Somewhere on this earth there had to be a woman who would return his love, didn't there? If he did not see Clara again, perhaps his heart could open up to others. But whenever he reached this point, everything in him screamed, "Stay!" The idea of never seeing Clara again was more than he could bear.

Wasn't the idea of being close to her when he couldn't really be close to her even worse?

He longed so much to reach out and touch her! With his spirit and his heart, but also with his hands, his entire body. He wanted to kiss her awake in the morning and massage the tiredness from her shoulders in the evening. He wanted to make her rose-petal tea and an omelet because she often forgot to eat.

But he knew that all his pretty pictures of togetherness had nothing to do with reality. First, Clara was a married woman. Now she was a grieving widow. He could twist and turn it how he liked—for him, there was simply no place in Clara's life. Knowing that did not stop him from loving her.

But how much longer could he endure the situation? It made no difference how long he pondered the question; it took him nowhere.

***

"It was amazing. That's all. Amazing," Clara breathed. "Seeing the lake from above . . . It looked huge and tiny at the same time. And as blue as a forget-me-not."

Laszlo smiled and pointed to a small restaurant directly beside the water. "There's still over an hour till our ferry arrives. Something to eat?"

"Oh, yes, I'm starved. They had all kinds of hors d'oeuvres and champagne during the flight, but I was too excited to eat anything. The view, the interesting conversations—all together it was really too much. I can still hardly believe that I got to fly like a bird." Clara laughed like a high-spirited child.

The waitress had just brought two glasses of white wine to the table when Clara's face took on a wistfulness. "Me, in a zeppelin, flying over Lake Constance—I would so love to tell my children about it."

Laszlo found the pain in her voice intolerable. He wanted to shout, "Which street do they live in? I'll go and get them for you!" Or "Let's go and visit them right now." Anything to alleviate her yearning. But instead, as so often, he said nothing. That Clara had even told him about her divorce and her children had been strong proof of her trust. Until that time, he, like everyone else, had assumed that her first husband had also died and that she had been left childless.

Proof of trust? Or just a moment of weakness?

Clara swirled the wine in her glass absently. "The business doing so well, the social recognition, my beauty advice appearing as a book—in the end, it's all a poor substitute for what I can't have. The love—"

For a moment, Laszlo was not sure if he had heard her correctly. Was this the sign he had been waiting for? *But I love you!* he almost said, but she suddenly went on: "—of my children."

A weight like solid lead sank onto Laszlo's chest. He drank a sip of wine, but all its sunny sweetness was gone.

"Don't doubt the love of your children. Just because someone isn't around you every day does not mean they don't love you." He saw how his words brought a little hope back to Clara. She was looking at him so hungrily, and for a moment he thought he saw in her eyes the same loneliness that he felt in himself. "There are many kinds of love. Everyone talks about passionate, romantic love. But what of the quiet, heartfelt kind? The kind that does not trust itself enough to show its face? Is it worth less just because it is not returned? Or is it even more important to be open to that kind of love? To give it the room it needs to grow . . ." What had gotten into him, going on like this? What inner voice had moved him? What would Clara say? Was it all over? Or could he at least be allowed to hope?

To Laszlo's dismay, the waitress came just then and served them two plates of fish and vegetables. He wanted to push it aside, take Clara's hands in his, and look deep into her eyes.

His dismay only increased, however, when he saw Clara pick up her knife and fork. How could she think about eating now?

"You want to talk about love with me, Laszlo? Of all the people in the world, with me?" Her eyes flashed roguishly, and her tone was ironic and without the slightest trace of romance. "I fear that's like trying to teach a fish"—she pointed with her fork at her plate—"to fly! When it comes to love, I'm sad to say, I have no talent at all," she said with conviction. Then she stabbed her fork vigorously into the fish.

Laszlo's cutlery lay untouched beside his plate. He had wanted a sign from Clara. And he got one.

Chapter Forty-Three

It had been a long, tiring day. A conversation here, an explanation there, everybody wanted her opinion, her knowledge, her approval—for Clara, the expression "to talk until she was blue in the face" had taken on a new dimension. She was actually supposed to attend a small function in Lilo's hotel; an important client had invited her. But Clara was exhausted. She wanted peace and quiet and to be alone.

Barefoot, she went for a walk along the water's edge. It had been a hot day, and even at the lake, where a breeze blew constantly, the thermometer had climbed high into the eighties. Clara enjoyed the quiet and solitude by the lake, and the water splashing around her ankles was soothing. On the Swiss side, an orange-red sun was slowly sinking. In the dwindling light, seagulls soared. Two swans sat on the shore, not even bothering to stretch their necks as Clara walked by. Still, she kept her distance from them. *How nice it would be if Laszlo were here now.* The thought was in her head before she could fend it off. They didn't have to talk when they were together. When they took breaks, they would sometimes sit silently on a bench by the lake, she in her thoughts, he in his, and yet connected with one another. Other times, there was so much to say that they had not stopped talking.

In recent weeks, she had the feeling that Laszlo had less time for her. Of course, they talked every day, made decisions together, discussed their impressions and perceptions of different fragrances. Often, Therese or Klaus was present at these meetings, too. Clara enjoyed this time with her employees, all of whom she could also count as her friends. But when was the last time she and Laszlo had lunch together? When had they last gone for a walk? When the working day came to an end, he went his way and she went hers.

"You want to talk about love with me, Laszlo? Of all the people in the world, with me? I fear that's like trying to teach a fish to fly! When it comes to love, I have no talent at all." Clara had more than once regretted her flippancy that evening in Friedrichshafen. Laszlo was not a man of compliments and flattery. If someone like him opened up his heart like he had that day, it meant very much indeed. Perhaps it was exactly that circumstance that caused Clara to react as tactlessly as she had. Why hadn't she been able to respond with "Why don't we wait and see what life still has in store for us?" or "Perhaps a silent love can stay silent a little longer"? Instead, she had replied with all the sensitivity of an axe in a flower bed, so horrid that she had hurt even herself with her words. Was it any wonder that Laszlo had withdrawn?

Oh, Clara, you have no talent for love, she thought when she arrived at her usual swimming place. But instead of her swimsuit, she had packed other things today. She kept going along the shore.

Her right hand felt down along her skirt until it reached the sewn-in side pocket. The small notebook and pencil there, so close to her body, felt warm, as did the bundle of keys that she had been carrying around for a week.

When the Palazzo Margherita came into view, Clara left the shore and went around to the entrance gate at the front. She took out the keys, and after several attempts she found the right one for the massive lock on the gate set into the stone wall. It opened with a light creak. Hesitantly, she stepped inside and was immediately struck by a fragrance of roses. She knew with certainty that Laszlo would have found the scent as beguiling as she did.

It was so quiet. Dragonflies shimmered through the air in all the colors of the rainbow, and the hum of their wings mixed with the soft splashing of the lake beyond the house.

Clara stood for a moment and enjoyed the warm feeling that spread through her. But only for a moment, then she went into the house.

She had been planning to do an inventory of the place for some time. What was in good repair, what needed to be fixed, and so on. Since visiting with Stefan, she had not been back. And at the time of the viewing she had been too excited to pay any more than scant attention to the details. But now she had to decide what to do with the property, and for that she needed to know more about it.

With the notebook in one hand and the pencil in the other, she went from room to room. On the first floor was a kitchen and a pantry, and directly beside the kitchen was a very large dining room. Clara smiled to see it. The Italian king's mother's court must have had a banquet or two in there. For a family, too, it would be the ideal place to eat, laugh, and talk. But for her, alone, it was out of the question.

Beside the dining room was a large drawing room with an enormous double door that led directly out onto the terrace. Beside the terrace was the conservatory, or "orangery," as the agent had called the glass room.

All the rooms were in good condition, with floors of either parquetry or a multicolored stone that Clara had not seen before. The walls were covered with wine-red wallpaper with a pattern of gold crowns. Clara thought it was ugly. A simple, light coat of paint would be so much lovelier! In lime green and lavender, for example, the color scheme of her Bel Étage shops.

The rooms on the second floor were also in good condition. One bedroom after another, with three bathrooms! Luxury! It was clear that the house had belonged to a demanding woman. *But for your customers, it won't be nearly luxurious enough.* Suddenly, she heard Stefan's words in her ear. He had talked about gold faucets and Carrara marble.

Clara stopped in the rear-most bedroom, on the corner. One window opened out toward Meersburg, but the view was blocked by a large apple tree with branches all but growing into the room.

Sophie will love being able to pick an apple right outside her window!

Back in the hallway, Clara opened another door that led up to the space beneath the roof. It was a large space, the agent had said, and it should not be any problem to have a small apartment built up there.

Clara rattled at another doorknob, but found only a small, empty space behind it.

Perhaps a toilet could be built in here? Then the children and I would not need to go to the toilet downstairs at night.

Clara paused. What was she doing here? She was not even sure that she would keep the place, and it was far from certain if her children would ever be able to visit her here. And there she stood, already arranging their rooms for them?

Annoyed at herself, she went downstairs again. *Best to stick to the plain facts,* she thought. And that meant taking stock of the garden next.

She threw open the double door in the drawing room and stepped out onto the terrace. The view out over the lake was breathtaking. Not a neighboring house in sight. Just water, space, and sky.

Clara sat down on the tiles of the terrace in a state of reverence. Her notebook was forgotten, along with all the questions and daydreams. She closed her eyes, enjoyed the warmth that the terrace, after a long, sunny day, had soaked up. Her mind was suddenly very still.

What a magical spot this was! Why hadn't she noticed it earlier? How good it felt just to *be* there. She closed her eyes and saw, in her mind, how Elena Viska would sit here, worn out from looking after her disabled sister, restoring her energy in this tranquil place. She saw Countess Zuzanna, deeply saddened to see her young lover, Pawel, leave her for a twenty-year-old, but finding new hope. There in the Villa Bel

Étage, Zuzanna would be able to drop her mask, let herself be spoiled, and find her way back to the cheerful creature she was inside. And to hell with all the Pawels of the world!

And as for her children and herself—she would never give up the fight. It might take years before she was allowed to see Sophie and Matthias again, but nobody could tell her that she couldn't set up a room for them now. Hope was powerful.

Clara felt a light tickle. She opened her eyes and saw that a dragonfly had settled on her hand, the beat of its wings imparting only the lightest touch.

Beauty. Fragility. Tenderness.

The Villa Bel Étage—beauty hotel and family home. It was time to try a new dream.

She started the very next day. The first thing she did was reserve a large table at Lilo's hotel. She assembled her team of beauty specialists. Laszlo, Klaus and, of course, Therese joined them as well, as did Sabine Weingarten—she was now in charge of the finances, after all. And she invited Lilo. Over a glass of sparkling wine, Clara told them of her plans for the villa, and wanted to hear from each of them what they thought would need to be included in her renovations. Clara noted everything, relying on the experience of her specialists as well as Lilo's knowledgeable advice as a hotelier. Clara looked around the assembled group happily—with these wonderful people behind her, her new project would be wonderful, too.

Then she found the tradesmen she needed, and the renovations were quickly underway. Walls were torn down and new ones erected. Clara stopped by the villa several times a day to check on the progress. Were the new shutters easy to open and close? Had the electrician remembered to add a ceiling fitting and one that could be used for a reading lamp beside the bed? Surely her female visitors would enjoy that, as would Matthias. Her son had always been an avid reader.

Clara's abundant enthusiasm and energy seemed to infect her tradesmen, too. Stucco workers, plasterers, the carpenter and his apprentices, the electrician, the painters, and the wallpaper hangers—all were in full swing. Clara wanted the villa ready to open for the start of the 1912 season.

Only over Christmas did the work cease. Clara used that time to visit her shops in Baden-Baden and Stuttgart, and to review the annual accounts. When Therese and Lilo admonished her and said that she, too, was in urgent need of a rest, Clara waved it off. She had never felt better! Just before Christmas, Josephine had sent along mail from her children, along with a note from Marianne Gropius, sending her best wishes for the holiday season. Since then, Clara had been happier than she had for a long time.

***

While Therese, as their advertising woman, was deeply involved in many parts of Clara's new project, Laszlo watched everything from a distance. Sometimes he wondered whether Clara, by throwing herself with so much verve and vigor into the villa, was consciously putting more distance between them. For his part, he would most have liked to continue work with her on her first perfume, the *Winds of Change* fragrance. But she did not have a head for pretty scents just then.

The love he felt for Clara remained undimmed, but he had come to realize that he could not compel her to do anything. In matters of the heart, she was like a shy horse—if she came to him at all, it would have to be of her own accord.

***

Meersburg, April 1912

Dear Isabelle,
Thank you for your lovely letter. Once again, you have
written about the Champagne region so sensuously that
I felt like jumping on the next train and paying you a
visit! But I can't think about a journey at all just at the
moment, and we'll see each other again soon anyway,
because the way things look, there's nothing to stand in
the way of opening the Villa Bel Étage in mid-May. The
last few renovations are coming along nicely, the garden
is looking beautiful . . .

Shaking her head, Isabelle read through the list of all the different jobs that Clara was apparently supervising simultaneously. All that work would kill the strongest horse! Wasn't her friend taking on too much? Or was she again using work to distract herself from her troubles?

I feel very close to you right now, dear Isabelle. I have
good but melancholy memories of our many intimate con-
versations, and that's when I miss you the most. In a few
weeks it will be the anniversary of Stefan's death. And
your Leon, too, passed away in May, all those years ago.

Isabelle felt a heavy weight descend on her chest. Leon's death was thirteen years earlier, but the horror of that day was still present. She read on quickly, not wanting to let sad memories take hold. She had enough of that whenever she visited Leon's grave.

Do you still remember Josephine's and my visit to you after Leon's death?
Isabelle snorted softly at that line. How could she ever forget? She had buried herself so deeply in her grief that, without her friends, she might

never have clawed her way back to life again. She owed Jo and Clara so much for so many things.

> *Back then, we sat down and thought about how things could go on with the winery after Leon's death. And I suggested that you could open a small pension, a place where rich city people could rest and recuperate. I remember talking about lavender baths, Kneipp cures, and sunbathing, and I was so passionate about it all, remember?*

Isabelle smirked. Her house certainly had had the potential for something like that, but Isabelle had wanted to focus on leading the crumbling winery back to success.

Isabelle turned and looked out the window, where Daniel and the children were tying up vines. Her decision back then had been the right one.

> *And now I'm on the cusp of making my dream of a beauty hotel come true myself. Oh, Isabelle, isn't life crazy? And aren't we blessed to be able to live through times of so much change?*

Isabelle let Clara's letter sink to her lap. There had been some changes in her life that she could really have done without. But whenever she started to brood about those things, she realized that one thing did, indeed, lead to another. After the bad times came the good. A loss could contain the germ of something new, and something good could grow from a catastrophe. Taking life as it comes—for Isabelle, that was the hardest lesson of all. But she was able to do it more and more.

*Though I have every reason to be happy, I wonder
what all my triumphs are worth if I cannot share them
with my children.*

Poor Clara! Isabelle sighed and folded the letter and replaced it carefully in its envelope. She would read it again later.

Then she reached for the telephone. Taking life as it came was all well and good. But sometimes you had to give fate a good kick. And this was one of those moments.

While she waited for the operator to connect her with Berlin, she thought about Clara's letter. The ability to talk to your best friend hundreds of miles away, at least, was one change she was very glad about.

"Your party is connected, madam. You can talk now," said the operator. There was a grating sound, then a series of clicks, and then she heard Josephine's voice on the other end of the line.

"Isabelle, how are you? Has anything happened?"

"Not here, no. But I'm far more interested on what is going on along *your* front," Isabelle replied.

"Not much, I'm afraid." Josephine's voice sounded muffled. "I asked about it again yesterday, but all I got was a lecture about how one can't have a conversation like that in passing. It looks like the opportunity hasn't presented itself yet."

Isabelle had the feeling that she could see Josephine's face turning grim through the telephone line.

"No opportunity. Ha! What's lacking is the backbone it takes to do it. We're running out of time," she said, upset and angry. "I've just had a letter from Clara, and she writes that her renovations have all gone smoothly and that the opening of the beauty hotel is actually going to take place in the middle of May. That's less than a month from now. Look, our surprise has to work. Clara has always been there for us when we needed her, and now we can finally do something for her in return. Just for that, we have to try everything to get . . . you know." They had been through this same conversation many times since Christmas, but to no end. No time, illness, not the right moment . . . "If I have to, I'll come to Berlin and deal with it myself! And I'll cover whatever it costs; feel free to pass that on!" Isabelle said, her tone almost threatening.

"It has nothing to do with the cost; you know that as well as I do. Now calm down. I'm still confident that it will all turn out for the best."

Isabelle nodded halfheartedly. Then it occurred to her that Josephine could not see her.

***

Lost in thought, Josephine replaced the heavy telephone receiver on its hook. Isabelle was right. Time was running out. But she had done what she could, and her hands were tied. Now it came down to the courage of another.

"Do you really think it's fair that Sophie and Matthias's mother is still not allowed to see her children?" she had asked Marianne Gropius some weeks before. It had been a warm day, heralding spring, and they had ridden their bicycles out to Wannsee lake.

"Of course I do!" Marianne replied. "You can't entrust children to an adulteress like her."

Josephine had sighed at her words, disappointed and sad. How could she have expected anything different?

"The official reason that led to their divorce back then was that Clara committed adultery. But have you ever wondered whether the truth might have been very different?" she had asked as they sat beside the lake.

"Gerhard never talks about that time. And whenever *I* dared to raise the subject, he got angry, so I let it drop. But that's all old hat now," Marianne said, gesturing dismissively.

Old hat? If she only knew! Josephine had thought angrily. "Clara is suffering severely from being separated from her children," she said quietly. "If she could just see Sophie and Matthias now and then. And Sophie talks about her mother all the time, as you know. But Gerhard . . ." She pressed her lips together to stop herself from saying the wrong thing.

"Are you trying to turn me against my husband?" Marianne said, her tone sharp. "You won't do it, because I happen to love Gerhard. For me, he is the best man in the world."

"With you, Gerhard has really turned into a different person. Your love is good for him," Josephine said. "But his marriage to Clara was not born under such a lucky star." She felt like slapping herself in the face for uttering that kind of saccharine nonsense. But when it came down to it, she wanted something from Marianne, and she knew that Marianne's defenses would go up if she said a word about Gerhard's abuse, his spitefulness, or his domineering manner. So she talked instead about two people who were simply not suited to each other. About parents who pushed Clara into marrying the good doctor. And about Gerhard Gropius himself, who was apparently such a man of honor that he complied with the expectations of Clara's parents and married Clara, although he felt no love for her."

Marianne had hung on each of Josephine's words. Two hearts that did not beat in harmony. Gerhard and Clara, the two of them trapped in a loveless marriage. A misunderstanding, of a sort.

"Clara fabricated the entire story about the adultery. Do you understand that? If she had not gone through that farce, there never would have been a divorce. Clara Berg has been shunned for something she never did. When all is said and done, you can be grateful to her that she had the courage to free herself from that unhappy marriage. And Gerhard, too, because it meant that he found you, his true love."

"I've never thought about it like that before. Clara accepted a great sacrifice." Marianne frowned. "But you can't count on the judges sharing that view. Those men probably know as little about true love as they do about the yearning of a mother's heart."

Josephine nodded in agreement. Her mouth had gone dry with excitement, and, her voice high-pitched and cracking a little, she said, "A matter like this can also be handled another way. Privately, so to speak. Would you have anything against Clara seeing her children occasionally?"

Marianne shrugged. "If it's only occasionally. And as long as she doesn't try to get involved in their upbringing. But Gerhard would never agree to have her come to the house. And I wouldn't feel comfortable with it, either."

"That goes without saying." Josephine had to suppress a squeal of glee. "It isn't even necessary for Clara to come to Berlin. There's another possibility . . ." Then she had taken Marianne's hand in hers and painted her a picture of that possibility in all the colors of the rainbow.

"That really does sound very tempting," Marianne had finally said. "The only question is whether I can make the idea palatable to Gerhard."

With a heavy heart, Josephine finally stood up from her telephone table. She had tried to sound as confident as she could with Isabelle, but she was far from certain that Marianne would succeed.

Chapter Forty-Four

It had been a mild winter, and the trees had started blooming earlier than usual. Now, at the end of April, the mosaic tiles of the terrace, the beautiful new rattan furniture, and the Villa Bel Étage itself were covered in countless millions of white petals. When Laszlo went to Clara's house, a single falling petal landed on his nose, making him smile. But his mission was far from cheerful.

The house was teeming with people, but Laszlo found Clara easily. She was standing in the garden like a military commander, surrounded by a crowd. Therese was standing beside her, holding out a thin sheaf of paperwork to Clara. At the same time, two tradesmen were talking to her, and a third man stood beside them, shifting his weight impatiently.

And now there he was, too. Downcast, he approached the group. He had put off this talk for too long. Now it simply had to be done. The perfume maker in Paris had written to him again. He needed a good man, and as soon as possible! Laszlo had played for time, but he knew full well that he could not stall indefinitely.

"The reconstruction work inside is almost complete, and the extension for the cosmetic treatments is finished. Almost all the outside work has been completed, too. All except the Kneipp pool, which is still just a hole in the ground." Clara looked down in annoyance at the shallow excavation beside her, provisionally covered with a few planks.

"It all looks very good," Laszlo said, turning back to the house. "But with the lake at your doorstep, I still don't really understand what you need with a Kneipp pool."

"According to my specialists, there are many women who are terrified of the lake and won't go near it, let alone actually bathe in it. They're afraid of the depth, the fish, the swans. These women should also be able to enjoy the benefits of water treatments, thus the pool. I know that some people will think me mad for putting in all this effort . . ." She shrugged apologetically. "But the villa has become very dear to me, and everything has to be perfect!" As she spoke, she began to leaf through the paperwork that Therese had given her. "The first drafts for the hotel brochure. I have to look at them right away."

Laszlo cleared his throat. "Clara, there's something I have to tell you." His heart was beating in his throat and his mouth was parched. "Something very important."

"I'm glad you have the time," she replied. "Because I would love to show you my concept for the perfect beauty day. I've been shaping it and reshaping it for so long that I can't see the forest for the trees anymore. But you could look at it with fresh eyes and an open mind, and you could perhaps tell me if you see any problems with it."

Had she heard him? Laszlo wondered. Just then, Sabine's voice came from inside the house.

"The first housekeeper is here. Can you come, Clara?"

"Oh, yes, the interviews." For a moment, she seemed to Laszlo to stagger a little.

"A thousand things at once—it's too much for you," he said, exasperated. "Won't you let Klaus deal with the new staff? He's good at that kind of thing." Among the women working in the manufactory—all diligent, reliable, and with good morale—there were few resignations.

"I appreciate Klaus's depth of experience very much," Clara said. "But for the villa, I want to be the one to decide. I know what a mistake it can be to let someone else make too many important decisions. That time, it ended in chaos. I don't want that to happen again."

But she can't possible compare her no-good husband with decent, upright Klaus, Laszlo thought, irritated. He said, "Either way, everyone has to take a rest now and then, even you. Why don't we go and have a cup of coffee together. My treat." He could see clearly that in that madhouse he would not be able to turn their discussion to his resignation. It made him queasy to think that he had to tell Clara that he was going to Paris.

"No time, no time!" she laughed. "It's really nice of you to worry about me, but not necessary. I can relax once we've opened, when my friends are here. Josephine and Isabelle are coming, and Therese and Lilo will join us whenever they can find the time. And I've invited Beate Birgen, the actress, too. And Countess Zuzanna, of course. I'm friends with both of them now, I'm happy to say." Clara laughed again. "Because my very first guests have to test for themselves what I'll be offering here. Not everything will work from the start, I'm sure of that, but everyone gets to stay here for free! It's going to be a lovely week." Clara sighed with pleasure at the thought, but a moment later, she almost lost her balance again.

Laszlo reached out to catch her, but she had already caught herself. "If you last that long," he said with a mix of concern and anger. She was so pigheaded!

"I'm just a little dizzy, that's all. I haven't had any lunch yet."

He would have loved to take her off to the nearest restaurant and feed her tasty tidbits, but Clara did not want his help. She had shown that clearly more than once.

He took a deep breath. Now or never! Or else he would stay in Meersburg and wither away from unrequited love, like a field of lavender waiting too long for rain.

"Clara, I have to go," he said abruptly. "To Paris." Every word was the stab of a knife, but he went on. "My resignation is already on your desk."

Clara looked at him with wide eyes. "You want to . . . but, Laszlo! That . . . I . . ." She flapped at the air helplessly with her arms, as if trying to catch the right words out of the air. At the same time, she took a step back and trod on one of the planks covering the Kneipp pool-to-be.

Laszlo saw the accident coming. His arm shot forward, but the plank slipped, and Clara fell two feet down into the shallow pit.

Chapter Forty-Five

Clara had been lucky, all things considered. "Someone told you to break a leg, but you only broke an ankle," said the doctor who had treated Clara in the hospital in Friedrichshafen, and laughed alone at his joke. Her leg would be immobilized in a cast for six weeks. And to observe her for any signs of thrombosis, they wanted to keep Clara in the hospital for a week or two.

Clara had burst into tears when the doctor gave her this "good" news. Now, when the villa still needed a thousand decisions and Laszlo was probably already . . . She could not bear to think that thought to its end.

She had begun to bargain desperately with the doctor. Couldn't she go home? She would keep her foot raised, the whole day if need be, and at night, too, of course. And she would take it easy. Easy, easy, easy!

But the doctor was not the negotiating kind.

So Clara found herself lying in a stiflingly hot hospital, with a stack of magazines that Therese had brought her beside her bed. But instead of losing herself in the pages of the *Gardener's Weekly* or *Berlin Illustrated*

News, Clara was frantically going through a pile of documents that Therese had handed her with Sabine's compliments: paychecks that she had to sign, invoices requiring approval, calculations for the expected running costs for the first year, something the bank had asked her to supply when the reconstruction of the villa had become more expensive than originally planned. Pieces of paper were constantly sliding off the bed, and Clara had to struggle to retrieve them. The skin beneath her cast itched terribly, and she had to poke a long hairpin beneath the bandage to get any relief at all.

In her irritation, Clara looked up from the paperwork to the gray walls around her. God, it was ugly in there. And the air was so stale that she perpetually had to fight a vague nausea. For the thousandth time, she looked at the watch on her wrist, only to find the hands moving much slower than usual.

Everything was chugging along just fine, Therese had informed her the day before. Klaus had shouldered the responsibility for the personnel, and Lilo had taken over supervising the various workers. With a grin, Therese had said that the workers had at least as much respect for her as they did for Clara. Which meant that everything was going as it should. Clara, by rights, should have been able to lean back and let her convalescence take its course. But a loud voice inside her was screaming: *I have to get out of here!*

The urgency and persistence of that voice had nothing to do with the villa.

A long time ago—she had still been quite young—she had spent some time in a hospital because of a broken leg. She had practically torn her hair out with boredom. Out of sheer desperation, she hobbled down to the hospital library on her crutches to find something to read. Fascinated, almost reverently so, she had peered into tomes about the internal organs, the structure of human skin, and other specialized subjects.

With a stack of medical textbooks pinned beneath her arm, she bumped into Gerhard on her way out, and the books fell to the floor. Gerhard gallantly bent down to pick them up for her. "That's not what a young lady should be reading!" he reprimanded her and put the books back on their shelves. And she had been so intimidated by his good looks that she simply accepted the way he imposed his will on her . . . and worse, she had fallen in love with him. One could say that her broken leg was to blame for the disaster of her first marriage.

And now her ankle was broken.

Clara let out a stifled, despairing scream that was immediately swallowed up by the gray walls. Then she closed her eyes and began to compose the most important words she felt she would ever speak.

"Lavender water!" Clara smiled with relief. "I wanted to ask Therese to bring me a bottle." She immediately began sprinkling a few drops of the fragrant liquid on her pillow and blanket, and it soon became easier for her to breathe. "Thank you," she said softly, and looked into his eyes for the first time. She saw a jumble of emotions there, and felt as if she were looking into a mirror.

She knew it was him as soon as she heard the knock on the door. Laszlo radiated such a presence that she could sense him there. Her heart had started to thump, and Clara could not have said whether it was caused by fear that he was bringing her his resignation, or by the joy she felt seeing him again. Or was it the inner turmoil she felt about what lay ahead? *Probably all of it at the same time,* she thought.

And now he was there. And it was time. She cleared her throat. "Laszlo, we have to talk."

"In a moment," he said. "I have something else for you." Carefully, as if he were handling a fine porcelain ornament, he withdrew a book from his bag and placed it on her lap.

The book was small and delicate. The cover was an elegant beige-colored linen bordered in pale rose-pink. The title was printed on the front in large, sweeping letters in the same pink tone: *"Beauty for Every Woman*. By Clara Berg."

Clara blinked back the tears that rose to her eyes. Her book. Her work. Another dream come true. Almost fearfully, as if she might find only blank pages inside, she turned back the cover, and just below the subtitle, "A Guide for Modern Women," there was a faithful reproduction of a rose. On the following page was a table of contents, each entry also separated by a rose. How lovely.

"Congratulations. That's something to be really proud of," said Laszlo, and there was pride in his own voice.

Without thinking about it, Clara took his left hand in her right. "Without you, I would never have dared to write it. I want to thank you for everything you have done for me. You are a wonderful man." She bit her lip. Forgotten was her carefully arranged speech about how love could grow if one allowed it the time to do so. Instead, the words came tumbling out. "Laszlo, I love you!"

His face was suddenly incredulous, almost fearful, as if he thought she might be playing a trick on him. Clara felt herself on the verge of tears.

"I have no right to expect any love in return, especially given how impossible I've been to you all along. What I said in Friedrichshafen . . . I've regretted those words a thousand times. But I didn't have the courage to ask you to forgive me, because that would not have been possible without admitting how much I loved you." She picked up the book and tapped on the subtitle. "'A guide for modern women'—that sounds so presumptuous," she said self-mockingly. "I would love to be one of those modern women. If I were, I might have tried to tell you earlier how much you mean to me. And if I were the least bit brave, I would have admitted even in my year of mourning that I feel more for you than just affection. But when it comes to love, I'm a coward."

Why doesn't he say anything? Clara wondered. *Serves you right, letting you stew. But why does he look so strange? Is he smiling?*

She picked up her thread uncertainly. "I'm better with things like willfulness and stubbornness and impatience." She laughed softly. "At least, that's what my mother always used to accuse me of. She said, the way I acted, it was no wonder I made my husband angry. What I'm trying to say . . ." She looked at Laszlo almost pleadingly, felt the words pouring now not from her rational mind but from her heart. ". . . is that, really, I'm am the wrong woman for you, unequivocally. But still, I am gathering up my courage now and—" Clara tried to sit up straighter, pushing against the lumpy mattress. Blast it, she could not finish this conversation if she was half lying down! But her cast had gotten tangled in the blanket, and she gave up and sank back again. Jumping around in bed like that, she was probably just embarrassing herself. Laszlo probably thought her entire declaration of love was embarrassing.

"You were just gathering up your courage . . ."

Clara looked up and saw that Laszlo was trying hard to hold in a laugh. If he made fun of her, well, she deserved that.

"I said this wasn't easy for me," she said, flaring up. "Anyway, what I wanted to say . . ." She swallowed her fears and doubt a final time. Then she took his hands in hers and pressed them firmly. "Please don't go, dear Laszlo. It breaks my heart to think that I could lose you."

Finally, finally, Laszlo's face softened. "Now? With your ankle already broken? I really can't allow that."

He leaned down to her, and their lips met as if they had always been destined to.

Two weeks later, at ten o'clock on a Friday morning, the doorbell at the Villa Bel Étage sounded melodically. The guests! Clara hobbled to the door on her crutches, excited to see who would be arriving first. As she passed the coatrack, she glanced quickly at herself in the mirror hanging there.

Her new peony-pink ensemble fit like a glove, and the chignon that she had fastened in place with a diamond comb complemented it perfectly. She looked good and, more importantly, she felt good!

"Countess Zuzanna! How lovely to see you." Clara leaned her crutches against the wall and held out her hand to the countess, but the noblewoman threw her arms around Clara and crushed her to her ample bosom.

"Thank you for inviting me! I've been looking forward to this day for weeks. I can hardly wait to have a good look at your house. But, my dear, you don't have to call me Countess. Zuzanna will do nicely."

Clara smiled. Would she dare speak so informally to the countess? The doorbell rang again.

"Excuse me, Coun . . . Zuzanna?" With a laugh she freed herself from the countess's embrace.

"Isabelle!" With a cry of joy, the two friends fell into each other's arms.

"My suitcases are still outside—all three of them! I fear I've over-packed again," said Isabelle when they finally let go of each other. Her copper locks were tousled, her eyes shining like two emeralds.

"You could have saved yourself the packing completely. As long as you're here, all you'll need is a few day dresses, a nightgown, and a dressing gown," Clara laughed. She surreptitiously signaled to one of the chambermaids Klaus had hired in her absence to get Isabelle's luggage.

"And I've brought you a few crates of champagne, too. A gift for the hostess," said Isabelle, but she was already turning in the direction of the drawing room, sun washed and looking as if it had been dipped in pale gold. "Oh, how beautiful . . ." She left Clara standing at the door and, as if hypnotized, moved toward the large windows of the drawing room.

Clara, who was already well aware of the allure of the stunning view, stayed behind, smiling.

"Speaking of gifts: wait until you've seen mine!" Zuzanna cried enthusiastically, but the doorbell was already ringing again, and Clara opened the door to the next guest.

"Where could Josephine be?" Clara asked Isabelle when, a little later, they were sitting and drinking champagne with Beate Birgen and Zuzanna.

"Her train has probably been delayed. If something serious had come up, she would have sent a telegram or called." Isabelle frowned. "Your telephone is working now, isn't it?"

Clara nodded. "I got that ugly black thing for your sake, you know. But it's not here in the villa. I have it at the manufactory." She thought for a moment, then clapped her hands together. "Why don't I show you all the house now? Then you can get settled in your rooms and take a rest, if you like. We still have a lot ahead of us today, after all." Clara's eyes were shining with anticipation.

"Here on the second floor, we have six guest rooms. My dear Zuzanna, I've chosen this one for you." Isabelle had helped Clara up the stairs, and Clara now swept her hand wide, displaying the first room on the right of the long corridor.

"How gorgeous!" the countess exclaimed as she stepped inside. Clara proudly stepped aside to let Beate Birgen and Isabelle enter, too.

In Zuzanna's room, as throughout the villa, the walls were painted a pale lime green and the high stucco ceiling in cream. A magnificent chandelier hung from the center of the ceiling, and on the all the walls, small twin lamps radiated their warm light. Instead of heavy carpets, Clara had chosen several smaller, narrow woolen carpets, handwoven and undyed, to spread across the walnut-parquet floors. They managed to look both airy and cozy, and the wool would feel good beneath her guests' bare feet. On the walls, Clara had hung several pictures of flowers chosen from her own collection. Against the lime-green walls, the painted roses and violets looked almost freshly picked.

"Everything looks so breezy and light. This is just the place to put aside all the headaches of home," Isabelle breathed.

Isabelle and headaches? Clara asked herself, but this was not the right moment to ask.

Zuzanna plopped down on an ottoman that Clara had had arranged beneath the window. "I'll be able to watch the sun go down every evening," she said.

"Sunsets from the terrace are also very beautiful," said Clara with a smile. "But sometimes one simply enjoys being alone, so the guest rooms have to be as comfortable and welcoming as possible. For me, that also means having time to read, so I've made sure that every room has a bookshelf, too. I've taken the liberty of adding my own book to the others," said Clara, a little abashed.

"*Your* book?" Isabelle's brow creased. "Have I missed something?" She was already at the bookshelf and running her fingers over the spines of the books. Her finger stopped at the second-last volume. "'*Beauty for Every Woman.* By Clara Berg.' Now you've turned into a writer, too. I can't believe it."

"What, really? I'd like to see that!" Zuzanna cried, and even Beate peeped curiously at the book that Isabelle already seemed to have become absorbed in.

Clara smiled. Then she cleared her throat. "Each of you will get a copy of your own. You can read it later—let's continue with the tour of the house." When Isabelle had put the book away again, Clara went on: "The nights here at Lake Constance can be rather chilly in May, so you will find extra blankets in the top of the wardrobe." As she spoke, she took out a cream-colored woolen blanket and held it out to the others. "Sniff this."

"Lavender!" The women breathed in the calming fragrance appreciatively.

Clara picked up her crutches again and grinned proudly. "Laszlo created a lavender scent especially for the villa. It's in the atomizer you each have on your nightstand." She pointed to an elegant glass bottle. "If you spray a little on your pillow, I guarantee a good night's sleep."

Isabelle shook her head. "Clara, you amaze me more and more."

"It's so beautiful here. I will never want to leave," Beate sighed.

"I think I'll stay here forever, too," said Zuzanna, who had returned to the ottoman and her view of the lake.

"By the way, if you feel like a glass of champagne or fruit juice, all you need to do is ring. One of our girls will bring you whatever you need immediately." Clara showed them a bell pull of lime-green silk that hung beside the bed. "And if you are overcome by a different need, every room has its own private ladies' room. I simply don't want any bedpans under the beds in this beautiful house."

The women liked this very much. Clara went on cheerfully. "As nice as it is here, there is still a lot to see in my Villa Bel Étage. The extension with the cosmetic and bathing section, the Kneipp pool, the garden . . . Would you be so kind as to follow me?"

"Well? What did your first guests say about the house?" Laszlo asked her when they sat together over coffee on the terrace an hour later.

"I think they are very pleased with it," said Clara modestly, but she could not hide a mischievous grin. Her friends had loved it! She had not imagined in her wildest dreams that it would go as well as it had. The feeling of having done everything absolutely right spread inside her like the warmth of good cognac.

Laszlo leaned over to her and gently lifted free a ladybug that had gotten caught in Clara's hair. "For you, for luck and happiness," he said with a smile and held it up for her to see.

"It should fly off to wherever it wants to go. I am more than happy enough," she whispered and blew gently on the beetle. It opened its wings, rose into the air, and flew away.

Clara watched it go until it was out of sight. As a young girl, Sophie had loved ladybugs more than anything else in the world. In every picture, she smuggled in at least one of the little spotted creatures, whether she was painting a horse, a house, or a field of flowers.

Why, why couldn't her children be with her? Sophie would most likely calmly examine everything in her room, while Matthias would probably go straight down to the lake and jump in for a swim. How lovely that would be . . .

Clara sighed. Over the years, her yearning for her children had not lessened. It had gotten worse.

"Don't be sad on such a beautiful day," Laszlo said quietly.

Clara had been gazing off in the distance after the ladybug, but now she turned her eyes to the man she loved like no other before. "It scares me how well you know me," she whispered. Laszlo . . . His love helped make the burden of the old, yearning pain a little lighter. She took his hand, kissed it, and nestled her cheek against his palm. She closed her eyes and for a moment enjoyed his nearness, his scent, his warmth.

There was so much still unclear between them. Her year of mourning was only just over—would she risk marrying a third time? Or would they live together without the formality of a certificate? Then where would they live? In the small apartment under the roof of the villa? In the apartment in Unterstadtstrasse, where every piece of furniture carried Stefan's signature? Clara could not really imagine either.

So many questions, so many uncertainties. But she knew one thing. Laszlo was the man she had waited all her life to meet.

The next moment, the loud horn of a pleasure steamer sounded from the lake, interrupting her silent moment.

"What else is still on your program today, before the reception with the mayor?" Laszlo asked, refilling Clara's coffee.

A shadow passed over Clara's face. The reception with the mayor! She had not planned anything of the sort for her opening weekend. It was supposed to be a treat reserved only for herself and her friends. But the town council had shown such an interest in the first "beauty hotel on Lake Constance" that Clara, on Lilo's advice, had extended an invitation to the council as well. A dozen guests, a short speech—according to Lilo, the mayor also wanted to say a few words—a glass of champagne, and that was that. The rest of the evening would then just be for Clara and her friends.

"We are meeting here on the terrace at three for a little something to eat. Then I'll give Isabelle and the others a copy of the brochure describing the daily routine—Therese really outdid herself with that. No doubt there'll be some questions, and I'll do my best to answer whatever comes up."

Laszlo laughed. "Gymnastics, brush massages, facials—watch out that your guests don't need a vacation to recover from this one."

"How dare you?" Clara laughed, slapping his arm playfully. Then she went on earnestly. "My program is pure relaxation, start to finish. For most women coming here, just doing something for themselves and not for others for a change will be a completely new experience. It will do them nothing but good. But to answer your question—the reception will follow at five. And once the councilmen have left, it will be time for dinner. I'm sure we will have earned it by then." She looked toward the kitchen with concern. This evening would be a baptism by fire for the Swiss cook that Klaus had taken on. She was short and round and spoke a thick dialect that Clara could barely understand. Until now, they had managed to communicate more with their hands than with actual words. And suddenly, Clara was a little worried. She hoped against hope that it would all go well.

"And you will definitely be back here at five?" she asked anxiously.

Laszlo, who had something to take care of in the manufactory, nodded. "Klaus, Therese, Lilo, me—we will *all* be on time and we will *all* be there to stand by you."

"We will all be there . . ." Those words were so comforting to hear. She was no longer a lone warrior, but could rely on her comrades-in-arms in times of need.

"But where is Josephine? I don't know if I should be worried or annoyed. It would be such a shame if she misses much more of our opening weekend."

Chapter Forty-Six

"A week just for me. Oh, Clara, this is like heaven on earth," Isabelle sighed. They were waiting on the terrace for Zuzanna and Beate. When Isabelle had come downstairs, she had caught Clara and Laszlo in each other's arms, kissing good-bye, and Isabelle had discreetly withdrawn back into the house.

"But you have your heaven on earth in the Champagne region," Clara replied.

Isabelle's smile turned soft and warm, as it always did when she thought of her home. "I do. But sometimes I feel as if all the responsibility is weighing too heavily on me. Don't worry, nothing bad has happened," she said when she saw the concern on Clara's face. "But there's always *something*. Two of our north-facing vineyards froze during the Ice Saints, and Daniel has been in a state ever since. We will certainly feel the lost harvest. And I'm worried about Micheline. She's been getting more confused and forgetful lately. And don't get me started on my own little troupe of children." Isabelle grimaced. "Unless Daniel takes care of it while I'm here, I will have to face the mayor as soon as I get back and hear a lecture about the twins." The two little devils had really gone too far this time. All the benevolence in the world could not change the fact that breaking through a church window and stealing the money from the collection bag crossed the line between a childish prank and a crime. Where had she gone wrong with those two? "Let's talk about something besides my day-to-day lunatic asylum. I am so happy to be here! Tell me about you and Laszlo. He's the one, isn't he?"

Clara nodded. "I would never have expected God to send me such happiness. Me, of all people, the—"

"The most untalented woman in the world in matters of the heart, I know," Isabelle finished Clara's sentence mockingly. Impulsively, she took Clara's hand in hers and squeezed it. "Sometimes you have to take a more roundabout path to reach a goal. But isn't it the most important thing of all, to keep giving love a chance? If you cease to love, you cease to live, *n'est-ce pas?*" She thought as highly of Laszlo as she did poorly of Stefan. Clara would be happy with him, of that she was certain.

"You and your French pearls of wisdom," Clara laughed. "But you're right."

Isabelle folded her hands behind her head and stretched her tense neck a little. With a contented sigh, she looked out over the lake, glittering in the sunshine. "You, Josephine, and I—we did not always have it easy, but we each found our happiness in the end, didn't we?" She placed one hand on Clara's arm and said, "Thank you for your friendship. Without Jo and you—I don't know where I would have ended up after Leon died." Her voice suddenly sounded husky, and she struggled against a lump forming in her throat.

"I feel just the same," said Clara, her voice just as raw. "Without you and Jo to stand by me, I never would have got through the divorce. Then losing my children, and after Stefan was killed . . ." She inhaled pensively. "We have been through quite a bit, all three of us. And we've still got a long way to go," she added with a laugh, with a nod toward the crutches lying beside the table.

"If life weren't a challenge, it would be as dull as dishwater," said Isabelle sardonically. "And speaking of challenges, I'm beginning to wonder if Josephine is going to make it today at all." Isabelle raised her eyebrows doubtfully. The last time she and Josephine had spoken by telephone, Josephine had assured her that everything was going according to plan. Had something come up after all?

Clara bit her bottom lip. "Up to now, I've been more annoyed than worried. But I know what you mean. I hope nothing's happened."

***

Josephine could not remember the last time she had felt so worn out. Not at the motor show in Geneva, where she and Adrian had been run ragged the whole day. Not on the cycling tour to Vienna that the two of them had completed the previous autumn. And not even after Amelie's appendix operation, when she had sat awake in the hospital for two days and two nights. The inner tension of the past few weeks, the knowledge that she couldn't do anything more herself, and the nightly brooding on all the things that could go wrong—it had all been incredibly trying. She was a woman who liked to get things done; relying on others had never been her forte.

She looked at her two traveling companions. After all the drama in Berlin, the delayed train, and the missed connection, they seemed positively chipper. They were chatting brightly, looking out the window of the coach that was finally going to get them to their destination, although quite a bit later than planned, while the sun was sinking slowly toward the water.

They should have arrived hours earlier. It was already late afternoon, and Clara must have been wondering where they were. If only she'd been able to telephone her and let her know about the delay! But at the train station in Mannheim, where her train had been stranded with a broken axle, the operator had been unable to establish a connection to Clara's telephone. Why then?

"Look, you can see the lake shining. It's tremendulous and boaty-ful!" said the girl.

Josephine could not help herself, and laughed a little. Her Amelie could have said just that.

"Why are you laughing? Don't you think the lake is pretty?"

"I do, I do. Tremendulous and boatyful," Josephine replied, and she felt all the strain of recent weeks and days falling away. Everything would work out.

She reached out spontaneously and grasped the hand of the woman opposite. "Thank you! For your courage, your energy, and . . . well, for everything."

Her companion screwed up her nose. "I don't have the slightest idea what to expect when I get home again. We never had a fight like that before. And I have never known Gerhard to be so inflexible, although, until now, *I've* always been the one to back down if we could not agree. Sometimes it was easier, sometimes harder, but even if I knew I was right I was always the one to step back. But this time I simply could not. It is new for both of us that I did not give in," she said quietly, leaning forward so that only Josephine could hear. "But after everything you told me, I could not do anything else."

"You are a wonderful, strong woman. And I am sure your husband will recognize that in the time you're away," said Josephine with emotion, hoping fervently that she was right.

"Look at all the lovely houses!" the girl said. "That little one there looks like a pink cupcake and the big one over the road like a light-green peppermint. And that one makes me think of chocolate milk. Is this a town of confectioners?"

Josephine laughed out loud. "No, my darling, this is Meersburg." She looked ahead happily. They had made it!

***

With trembling hands, Clara pinned the last strand of hair in place. She could hear the murmur of voices beyond the half-open window. The good weather had held, so they had decided to hold the mayor's reception out on the terrace. Clara's looked over at Laszlo, who was straightening his tie in front of a mirror. It was almost time to go down.

Clara felt her knees grow weak. A speech in front of so many people—would she even be able to get through it? Therese had told her that a few newspaper reporters had joined the crowd; everyone wanted to write about the beauty hotel beside Lake Constance.

"You look lovely," said Laszlo, behind her, and he kissed the curve of her neck.

"I'm so excited I think I'm going to pass out," Clara croaked, her mouth bone dry. "I don't think I'll get a word out."

"I've got a cure for that." Laszlo smiled as he produced a small golden bottle from his trouser pocket. "May I?" He pointed the bottle at Clara's neckline.

She nodded, frowning a little. "I've completely forgotten perfume, I'm so on edge. What is that?" She felt the delicate spray against her bare skin, and an unfamiliar scent rose to her nose. But although she had never smelled it before, it seemed strangely familiar.

"Lavender, vanilla, peony . . ." She fanned the perfume, which was warming on her skin, toward her face, savoring the combination. "And a trace of ambergris? Mmm, it smells so good." She looked at Laszlo in confusion. "This is not one of my products, and I have never smelled it on a woman. Laszlo, what in the world is it?"

"Clara."

"I mean, what's the name of the perfume?" she asked again. "It's like something you just can't get enough of."

"Clara," he repeated, and his eyes locked with hers. "That's the name. I formulated this fragrance for you. Only one bottle of it exists anywhere on earth. It is meant to accompany you wherever you go, and wrap around you like a silken cloth. And who knows—maybe the

scent will give you a magical power or two?" The folds around his eyes deepened as he grinned.

Clara accepted the golden bottle with a reverence befitting a precious gem. The five letters of her name had been hand-engraved artfully into the glass, which itself was permeated with gold. Such a treasure could only have been made by a highly skilled glass smith. Laszlo had put so much effort and love just into the container for his fragrance!

She was so moved by the gesture that she felt tears coming to her eyes, but she managed to keep her composure and said, "This is the loveliest gift I've ever received in my life."

Laszlo held out his hand to her. "Let's go down. Your guests are waiting for you to beguile them with your speech."

"If *I* don't manage to do it, then this perfume certainly will," she laughed, and she sprayed it once more into her hair.

"I want to thank the craftsmen, my employees, and my very dear friends, all of whom have worked absolute wonders while I lay in the hospital with a broken ankle. Thank you especially to Sabine Weingarten for keeping a close eye on the finances all the way through this project, and now, as well. After all this work, I would probably be a poor woman now if it weren't for you!"

Clara turned from Sabine to Lilo and Therese. "And thank you to my dear Lilo, for overseeing everything while I lazed around in my hospital bed. Without you, the annex would probably still be roofless. And a thousand thanks to you, dear Therese, for your beautiful brochures and advertisements—if the customers don't come now, then I am the only one to blame!" Clara smiled broadly at the two women.

"And I would like to thank my chemist, Klaus Kohlwitz, and also . . ." While Clara continued with her thank-yous, she swept her eyes over the crowd yet again. Still no sign of Josephine.

After she had delivered her heartfelt appreciation, Clara looked out over her audience, and her tone grew more serious.

"To stand here today in front of all of you means a great deal to me, and not only from the point of view of my business. Recent years taught me that it was best to do everything myself. For a long time, I did not trust anyone, and I felt best when I answered every question and made every decision on my own." She looked from person to person and saw only understanding on their faces. Almost everybody there knew the unfortunate history of her second marriage. But instead of denigrating her for falling for the deceptions of a man like Roberto Totosano, the people of Meersburg and her customers—locals and tourists alike—had stood by her.

"The Villa Bel Étage means so much to me not least because, without the help of many, many people, it would never have existed at all. And I have to thank one man in particular for the circumstance that I was prepared to accept that help at all." She waved to Laszlo to come to her. When he was standing beside her on the small podium, she felt the warmth he radiated, and the calmness that surrounded him like an aura. She squeezed his hand covertly, then picked up her thread again. "Laszlo Kovac has more than a nose for the finest fragrances in the world. He showed me how important it is to trust people again, and—" From the corner of her eye, she saw movement at the terrace door. But that was . . . She blinked. Then she blinked a second time and screamed, "Josephine!"

Joy and relief flooded through her, and she wanted to do nothing more than run to her friend and hug her, but she could not simply stop in the middle of her speech—and she could not run, in any case. A little abashed, she looked out at the audience, begging their forgiveness, and was about to go on when she realized that her friend from Berlin had not come alone. With her were a woman Clara vaguely recalled having seen before and a tall, young girl looking all around with wide eyes.

"Sophie . . ." A choked cry escaped Clara's throat. Her legs gave way beneath her, but then she felt Laszlo's arms supporting her and saw Therese running to her. Therese was grinning from ear to ear, and stroked her cheek for a moment.

"Did we manage to surprise you?" she whispered in Clara's ear, then she turned to the gathered guests and said, "Ladies and gentlemen, honored guests—Mrs. Berg would like to invite you all to join her in a glass of champagne. If you have any questions, I know she will be happy to answer them for you later."

With Laszlo's help, and with her legs trembling, Clara stepped down from the podium. Therese picked up her crutches, but Clara hobbled forward without them. As if on cue, the crowd moved back to give her room. Most of the audience, indeed, had no idea who the new arrivals were, but they sensed the powerful emotions swirling through the air, like the wind rising off the lake. Anxiously, joyfully, Clara approached her new guests. She hardly dared take her eyes off her daughter, afraid she might be some sort of mirage. But a glance over her shoulder showed that Isabelle, Laszlo, and Lilo were behind her. Were they also afraid that it could be no more than a bad joke?

When Clara reached Josephine, Sophie was still standing there. She was wearing a flowery summer dress, and she had long pigtails tied in red ribbons, like the ones that Clara had always tied in her daughter's hair. With her head tilted down a little, she looked at Clara a little hesitantly, but also with curiosity.

"I brought someone else along, too. I hope that was all right," said Josephine with a smile.

Clara could not hear her words. She only had eyes for Sophie. Laughing and crying at the same time, she took her daughter in her arms, pressed her to breast. She did not ever want to let her go again. "My child, my angel, my Sophie . . . finally. I missed you so much," she sobbed in Sophie's ear. She realized that her behavior might scare the twelve-year-old, but she could not do anything else.

Uncertainly, Sophie looked up to the woman that had come with her and Josephine.

Clara heard Josephine clear her throat. "May I introduce someone, Clara?"

Reluctantly, she let go of Sophie. But instead of turning to Josephine, she bent down to her daughter and said, "I'm sorry to have such an emotional outburst. I am just so endlessly happy." And she was fighting back tears again. "I've got a lovely room already prepared for you. If you like, I can show it to you in a little while?"

Again, Sophie looked up to the unfamiliar woman, but before she could say anything, Sophie asked, "Can I see Lake Constance from my window?"

Clara nodded. "The lake, the boats, the beach . . ."

A smile spread slowly across Sophie's face. "But how did you know I was coming? I thought our visit was going to be a surprise."

"I didn't know you were coming today. But it was what I wished for more than anything else in the world. And because of that, I prepared a room for you."

Josephine cleared her throat again. "Clara . . . can I introduce Marianne Gropius? Without her, this reunion would not have been possible."

Clara straightened up and looked at the young blond woman. So this was Gerhard's second wife. Sophie's stepmother. She had a pretty face and a friendly smile, and seemed very nice. But even if she were a hunchback with a permanent scowl, Clara would have been forever grateful to her.

"Welcome. And thank you for bring Sophie here," she said, her voice breaking with emotion as she reached out her hand.

Marianne clasped Clara's hand. "I would have liked to have brought Matthias, too, but he . . ." She lowered her eyes, and she left her sentence unfinished.

Clara swallowed. Her son probably had not wanted to see her. Or Gerhard had forbidden it. But now was not the time to be sad about her son; the joy of seeing her daughter again was too overwhelming for that.

"Matthias is well," said Marianne reassuringly. "If time allows, I would be glad to tell you about him."

"That would be—" Clara had been about to say wonderful, but just then she felt a gust of wind at her back that was so strong that she could not help rocking forward a little. The others were caught in the gust as well, and here and there she heard a shocked squeal or an embarrassed giggle as a woman's skirt flapped up in the wind. The afternoon wind had picked up considerably in recent days. Unusual for this time of year, people said.

"What kind of wind was that?" Sophie asked curiously.

Clara, Isabelle, and Josephine looked at one another. Each could see in the eyes of the other what she herself felt: gratitude for the great gift of a friendship that was not carried away on the first gust of wind, but which had withstood its share of storms over the decades. They had been through so much together, and there was so much yet to come. Whatever came, though, their friendship would help them stand up to any storm.

"One that comes just once every hundred years: a turn-of-the-century wind," said Clara, and laughed.

And Isabelle, Josephine, and Lilo—and Marianne and Sophie, too—laughed with her.

Afterword

This novel is an homage to those queens of beauty like Elizabeth Arden, who opened her first beauty shop in 1910, and Estée Lauder, who began with just four products in 1946 and created a global company. It is also a tribute to German beauty experts like cosmetician Margarethe Sendler and Dr. Bertha Roeber, who together founded the Marbert brand. And then there was Gertraud Gruber, who in 1955 established the first destination spa in Germany at Tegernsee Lake. So Clara was actually ahead of her time!

Until the rise of these beauty pioneers, nobody had dared believe that women could do something purely for their own well-being. Instead, a woman always had to be there for her husband, her family, and the society around her. She had to function, no more, and with the minimum possible input. The cows in the stall were looked after, but not the woman. The idea of finding "some time for herself" had not yet been born. But in this, too, a different wind began to blow after 1900—a turn-of-the-century wind.

In the novel, Stefano manages to trick his way into using Clara's name. At the time, legally speaking, that would not have been possible. For a man to take his wife's name has only been permitted since

Germany's matrimonial laws were reformed in 1976. Before that, the husband's name was invariably used as the married name. Having said that, it has been possible since 1957 for a woman to attach her own surname to the married name.

A few words about the setting of this novel—Meersburg, the town I love so much. Around 1900, the Lake Constance region was already very popular with tourists, although there were probably not quite as many strolling through the streets of Meersburg as I have described in this book.

One piece of advice for those who, having finished this book, are inspired to visit Meersburg: please don't waste your time going in search of Lilo's hotel. You will also hunt for the yacht club in vain. As I always do, I have taken a few small creative liberties with real-life locations whenever required by the story.

However, if you walk along Unterstadtstrasse, you can certainly consider which building I used to house Clara's Bel Étage. If you are close to the old castle, you might also notice a building that matches the description of Weingarten Pharmacy.

And you should certainly treat yourself to a glass of Meersburg secco and enjoy, like Clara, the fantastic views over the vineyards and the Swabian Sea.

About the Author

Photo © Privat

Petra Durst-Benning is one of Germany's most successful and prominent authors. For more than twenty years, her historical novels have been inviting readers to go adventuring with courageous female characters and experience their emotions for themselves. *The Queen of Beauty* is the third book in the Century Trilogy, following *While the World Is Still Asleep* and *The Champagne Queen*. Her books and their television adaptations have enjoyed great international success. Petra Durst-Benning lives with her husband in Stuttgart.

About the Translator

Photo © 2012 Ronald Biallas

Australian-born and widely traveled, Edwin Miles has been working as a translator for fifteen years.

After studying in his hometown of Perth, Western Australia, Edwin completed an MFA in fiction writing at the University of Oregon in 1995. While there, he spent a year working as a fiction editor on the literary magazine *Northwest Review*. In 1996, he was shortlisted for the prestigious Australian/Vogel Award for young writers for a collection of short stories.

After many years living and working in Australia, Japan, and the United States, he currently resides in his "second home" in Cologne, Germany, with his wife, Dagmar, and two very clever children.